THE
LAST
MIGRATION

THE
LAST
MIGRATION

Roger Frison-Roche

TRANSLATED BY DOUGLAS GARMAN

Harper & Row, Publishers
NEW YORK AND EVANSTON

CONTENTS

PART ONE

THE OLD MAN

CHAPTER ONE

BACK at Suojaurre, Kristina found everything as it had always been. Once again she slept in her pinewood bunk, piled with skins, into which she could slip fully dressed, her head resting on a pillow stuffed with soft reindeer fur. No longer was there a set time for sleeping, getting up, eating, as there had been in the school at Viddakaïno, nor was Fru Ingrid, the social worker, there to insist upon special periods for resting and working. How good it was to feel free again! Here you slept when you felt sleepy and got up when there was work to be done! For Kristina had resumed all the duties of a Lapp girl. When the bucket was empty she would fill it from the river, dipping it through the hole in the ice, then return, heavy laden but happy, churning her way through the waist-high snow. When she had first got home the dogs had made a great fuss over her. Now, once a day, while she was preparing their food, they would swarm round her, yapping, barking, howling; and though she made free use of her stick, famished and savage they would cheerfully return to the charge again and again, until it was all she could do to maintain her authority.

Day by day her strength was returning. It had not been the long, lonely journey over the snow-bound tundra that had exhausted the young girl, but the headlong fall down the face of the Agjiet which had left her battered and weak from her injuries for a long time afterwards. Then everything had returned to normal, and now that she had once more taken her place in the cita[1], and was satisfied that the man who saved her, Paavi the Finn, had been accepted as a member of it, her experience at Viddakaïno seemed to her no more than a bad dream. How simple everything had become! The Finn had started trapping

[1] A group of related families, forming a Lapp clan.

again, in a hurry to make up for lost time. He had spent a good many days searching for Kristina, and now that he had brought her back to the great herd, comforted and well-cared for, he had to make up for all those days' hunting he had missed. Easter would soon be here, the time for selling snow-fowl and for getting the best price for the most valuable furs from the kvaens² in the town. He would be out at all hours of the long day or the very short night; and his catch was piling up in the ice-room attached to the hut. All of them went about their own business, only returning to the cita for short periods of rest : the lads took turns watching over the great herd, as it ceaselessly roamed over the immense vidda³ in search of lichen; and when it was not their turn, they busied themselves with odd jobs, looking to their harness or breaking in a stag that happened to have strayed into the small herd of sleigh-deer which was always kept near the encampment. As soon as she had fed the dogs, Kristina would be off setting traps, at which she was as skilful as her friend, the Finn. Meanwhile Ellena prepared food for them all, and saw to it that there was always plenty of meat and marrow bones in the huge cauldron.

Soon Easter would be here, and already Kristina was secretly looking forward to the revenge she would take on the Viddakaïno folk! They thought she was just a kid, but just wait till she confronted them with her Finn! She felt sure she would be able to stand up to the stern Pastor Brombdal, as well as to Fru Tideman! But there were also those who had helped her, like the good doctor Olafsen and Sara the Kvaen. She would take Fru Olafsen a pretty pair of skallers,⁴ made of white reindeer fur!

Yes, everything was just as it used to be, thought Kristina; or rather, it would have been if it were not that since she had got back a new cloud had begun to hover over the cita of Suojaurre, threatening its future. Fru Tideman would

² Lapps who have settled in the Norway-Finland border country.
³ The high desert plateau in the interior.
⁴ Moccasins made of reindeer fur, stuffed with dried grass.

not be at Viddakaïno. By the time Kristina got there at Easter, she would already be far away in the Tröndelag, with Kristina's father and other cita headmen . . . They had all let themselves fall into the trap, she thought to herself, making an angry, scornful face. She was the only one who had resisted, by escaping from the gilded cage where the Pastor and Fru Tideman had tried to keep her prisoner. But the others? Would they be able to stand out against the cunning intrigues of the Norwegians?

From Simon Sokki, who had set off with his companions and the district officials to inspect the land that was being offered them in the Tröndelag, there had so far been not a word. Now and then a brief item of news would reach the hut : all letters and information were sent to Pastor Brombdal, who would then dispatch a hurried message, giving the gist of what he had heard from Per Oskal, the Lappefogden,[5] or from Fru Tideman, who was in charge of assistance to the Lapps. And they always displayed the same enthusiasm : Everything was going well . . . important decisions would soon be taken . . . they had visited every part of the Tröndelag, and it was a marvellous district, just outside the Polar circle, with high mountains sloping down to the fjords, which ran far inland, and narrow, fertile valleys where the soil was alluvial, and where it would be possible to make a decent living by growing crops and raising stock. There winter lasted two months less than in Finnmark, and the coast was more accessible. Everywhere there were farms, villages, parishes, and, in the high mountains, abundant pasture not yet exploited, which would be excellent for reindeer since there were still herds of musk-ox living there, which had elsewhere disappeared from the face of the earth.

This enchanting description gave little satisfaction to the people of Suojaurre, for the Pastor never said a word about the decisions that had to be, or perhaps already had been, taken. One letter had announced that the mission was to

[5] A Norwegian official, responsible for settling legal disputes between the Lapps and Scandinavians.

11

stop at Tromsö on its way back, in order to take part in a great congress of all the Norwegian Lapps. This congress was a regular event, and at it were discussed all the important problems confronting the Lapps: the route to be taken by the different herds during the migration, the sale of skins and meat; and it was here, too, that the Norwegian advisers sowed the seed of the new ideas that were scaring the old folk. What was going to happen there this time?

Simon Sokki and his companions would certainly not be back at Viddakaïno by Easter. Every time a letter arrived, Ellena, Simon Sokki's wife, would heave a sigh . . . what good could it bring? 'Read it! Kristina, read it!' she would say impatiently, afraid of what Simon might have been up to. This brutal man was as impulsive as he was weak: with him, it was always the last person he had been talking to who was right, especially when there had been any alcohol about. Ellena should have gone with him! The Finn had explained to her that it was the Lennsmann[6] who hadn't wanted her to: the government were all too well aware that women have more influence than they allow to be seen.

One day Mikael had brought a note from the Pastor, carefully folded up in the pocket of his koufte.[7] Kristina was out visiting her traps and Ellena was impatient at the long hours she would have to wait to hear the news. Of course, she could have asked Martha Risak, but was such a frivolous creature to be trusted with secrets? Or Karin? Ellena didn't like to admit her ignorance before such a young girl. Like Martha Bongo, the mother of Mikael and Karin, Ellena belonged to an older generation, for whom there had been no school! Kristina's short stay at school in Viddakaïno had had at least one positive result, for now she could read and write fluently, both in Samisk and Norwegian.

The two people who could have satisfied Ellena's curiosity were away. Kristina was out hunting, and the Finn had gone

[6] Government representative.
[7] A kind of cloth jacket with a wide collar.

with Andis and Pier to get some sleigh-deer from the small herd. He was the first to get back, and Ellena, unable to await her daughter's return, handed the note to him; and when he read it straight through, everybody was amazed at his knowledge. Ellena had described the scene to Kristina, who was delighted. Yes, her mother was quite right! The Finn was no ordinary man, he would achieve great things!

A few days later, a gale started blowing from the river Elv, sweeping the snow from the rocks so that the bald, rounded hills seemed to be covered with smoke, then forcing its way into the river gorges, through which it flew at a crazy speed whistling and shrieking, scattering the short notes of its song so that they hung, suspended singly, from the slender, quivering branches of the birch trees. Coming from the east, it promised a very cold night, yet the sky was almost completely clear, and the sun, nearing the end of its journey, moved slowly through the maddened clouds that sometimes closed in upon it, then broke apart, fleeing in long streamers to the west.

Andis, with the help of the Finn, had brought back a dozen sleigh-deer from the small herd; castrated veterans, broken to collar and shafts, who were peacefully chewing the cud with lowered heads. But there were also two powerful males picked from the great herd, two superb stags, which he and Pier intended to break in for the races during the Easter festivities; magnificent deep-chested animals, still in their thick white winter coats, whose superb antlers were still intact, uninjured by the lasso.

'If they can get them to draw a sleigh,' Kristina said to herself, looking at them in admiration, 'there won't be a finer turn-out in all Viddakaïno . . . if they can!' But this was by no means certain; the two stags had been firmly secured and were closely hobbled with short leather thongs. At the slightest sound they reared violently, their protruding eyes flashing with fear, their muzzles quivering, and a long shudder swept over their coats as though some hidden current flowed between flesh and skin.

13

'You needn't think you've finished with them yet!'
Kristina called to them mockingly.

'We know that! They're not like that great white calf
of yours!'

Kristina drew herself up furiously. She was proud of
her big white reindeer, one of the best in the cita. Though
her brothers were only joking, for anyone to attack your
reindeer was a personal insult!

But, at that very moment, cutting short any further discussion, the wind flung an enormous flurry of powdery
snow over them, nearly suffocating them. Then, almost
before they had time to regain their breath, a fresh blast
of wind drove the snow away, clearing the atmosphere.

All of a sudden the cold had become acute.

These days before Easter were the most carefree in the
whole year, quite different from the great annual migration.
The migration was a grave and solemn occasion, when
everyone had a feeling that they might be setting out for
the last time, that perhaps they would never again see
their winter encampment! But the preparations for the
Easter journey are made joyfully and impatiently. It is the
great gathering of the Lapps, the best time in the year,
which, from time immemorial, empties the tents and huts
where they have spent the winter. Then only the herdsmen
and the old people who are incapable of making the journey
stay behind. The gaily cavorting sleighs converge upon
the great central valley of the Elv, for it is a time of feasting
at Viddakaïno. And all the citas assemble there, all the
tribes and clans of the Samisks[8] from the West and from
the East, and sometimes even from Finland and Sweden
in the South, those semi-settled Lapps, who are subject
to the law and recognizable by their red caps with leather
peaks, surmounted by enormous woollen pom-poms.

The people of Suojaurre gathered at sunset in front of
Simon Sokki's hut, a scene of gaiety and noise. Martha,
the widow, and her nephew Anders were there, and Thor

* The word the Lapps use when speaking of themselves.

14

Risak and Karin Bongo; but Martha Risak drove her sleigh alone, determined to remain independent throughout the festivities. As for Kristina, she was driving her white reindeer, which had been harnessed for her with the greatest care by the Finn, who had done the same for Ellena's placid old beast; an attention she had appreciated. As it was all that Pier and Andis could do to manage their unbroken stags, it had been decided that Mikael Bongo would lead the caravan. He would go ahead, hauling two long sleighs heavily loaded with pelts and frozen snow-fowl, the result of the Finn's hunting. He had asked Mikael to sell them for him since, by agreement with Ellena, it had been decided that he should stay behind to look after the herd.

The day before, when this decision was made, Kristina had been taken by surprise and at first she had joined in the general chorus: 'Why wasn't he going to the Easter festival with them?'

'Since you're the cita's hunter,' Pier Sokki had declared wryly, 'it's your job to take your own skins and game and sell them.' And with a shifty glance in his mother's direction, he had added: 'I'm not too keen about leaving him with the great herd.'

The others had hesitated: it was true that while they were away the reindeer would be at the mercy of the Finn, a stranger to the cita. But though they were haunted by ancestral fears, the desire to take part in the festivities at Viddakaïno was so strong that they were almost prepared to accept this easy way out. At first they had thought of Thor: but would it be wise to entrust the great herd to a man who had failed to prevent the raid by the Isaksens? What would Simon Sokki have to say when he got back, if he discovered that the feckless Thor had been left to look after the cita's reindeer, while all the others were eating and drinking and playing around with the girls at Viddakaïno? It was Ellena who had come out in support of the Finn: in Simon Sokki's absence she was the mistress of the cita, and what she decided was not to be disputed.

'That's enough chatter,' she said roughly. 'Is the Finn one of us now? Yes or no? And who's prepared to take his place? What's the point of quarrelling about it? You'd be better employed checking up on your harness.'

And everyone had obeyed, only too pleased by a display of authority that freed them from any responsibility. Kristina, torn between conflicting feelings, had been present during this scene without taking part in it. She was serious and thoughtful, and did not even notice the tenderness with which Paavi was looking at her. He went over to her, and said : 'Goodbye, Kristina, have a good time.'

But she shrugged her shoulders :

'You'd rather stay behind with the great herd and play at being boss?'

It was unfair and she knew it, but her wild blood got the better of her. She felt humiliated that he should let her go without any apparent regret, and she wanted to hurt him. He had taken her by the shoulders and forced her to look him in the face, and staring into the limpid pools of his eyes she had felt confused.

'Come with us, Paavi!'

'It's all been settled,' said he. 'Go with your brothers. It's no good quarrelling with fate. I'm not going back to Viddakaïno with you until the day we're married. People are gossiping about us enough already. My place is with the great herd, and I shall start preparing for the migration. Go in peace.'

And, hiding her disappointment, Kristina had joined the others, while he set off in the other direction with long sweeps of his skis.

At last everything was ready. Only Pier and Andis were still struggling to harness their restless stags. One of them, rearing and plunging, had already broken two shafts, so that they had had to cut new ones from branches of birch, boring a hole with the point of a knife to take the thongs made of reindeer sinews. When the animals quietened down for a moment, they swiftly put on the breast-collars and belly-straps, fastened the traces, muzzled the animals with

16

a slip-knot, and then, holding one end of the long lead attached to the base of the antlers, they prepared to set off. But, pawing the ground and jibbing, the stags again got caught up in the traces and seemed to be quite out of control. The others looked on enjoying the struggle between men and reindeer; especially the girls who adored such trials of strength.

'You've taken on more than you can handle, Pier,' said Martha Risak. 'That stag of yours is worse than a wild one.'

But it was too late now: if they were to change their steeds at the last moment they would lose face.

'We'll see about that,' Pier retorted angrily, and flinging himself at the reindeer's head he bore down with all his weight, waiting for the signal.

Ellena was the last to leave the hut; she was wearing her best pesk,[9] and her white skallers were carefully attached to the supple belingers[10] with thongs of plaited red wool. Stout and imposing as she was, she still remained remarkably agile.

Night had fallen. The moon, in its first quarter, had risen behind the hill, and its brilliance, combined with the glitter of the scintillating stars, was enough to light up the tundra. It promised to be a fine night for the journey.

The men, who on the sly had already started swigging from the bottles of spirits they carried in the pockets of their kouftes, were singing yoks[11] at the top of their voices while they waited for Ellena to give the signal to start. The procession had gradually become organized, stretched out in line of battle on the frozen surface of the river, each man at the head of his reindeer. Mikael was in the lead, then came Ellena, then Thor, with Kristina behind him. The others were herded together, bumping into one another, struggling to get into line; and the red caps, the white and fawn-coloured pesks and the sea-blue cloth of the women's skirts made a cheerful sight. They gave vent to their

[9] A fur jacket, with a hood.
[10] Long leggings, made from reindeer skin.
[11] Extemporaneous folk-songs, chanted or sung in gutteral tones.

happiness in raucous yoks, plaintive songs, wild improvisations—a vast chaos of dissonant sounds, as if each of them were tuning up his own instrument.

At last Mikael uttered a short cry and his reindeer broke into a gallop, followed by all the others. Kristina managed to throw herself on her sleigh flat on her stomach, but Ellena, taken by surprise, had turned hers over, and her reindeer was dragging her along face downwards. Well protected by her furs, the stout woman let the reindeer exhaust itself, running in circles until it came to a halt and she was able to install herself properly. Pier and Andis were still having considerable difficulty in mastering their stags : plunging wildly, they overturned their sleighs, trapped themselves between the shafts, fell down, got up again, ran in circles, all to a wild accompaniment of cries and shouts. But gradually order was restored, and then the exhausted animals fell in behind the placid steeds of Mikael, Karin, Thor and Kristina, who were descending the steep slope at a steady trot, escorted by the panting dogs.

The moon lit up the tundra, the stars shone down, and now nothing could be heard save the tinkling of the bell on the leading reindeer, accompanied by the plain-song of the wind, sweeping across the solitude.

This marvellous night was brought to an end by a dawn halt at Galanito, at Maria Siri's inn. Then, further on, they picked up the Einontekio trail and, after a final turn through a narrow gorge, the river widened out into the broad valley of Viddakaïno. There the caravan dispersed, and everyone went off in search of relatives. Ellena and her sons went to an uncle's; Kristina preferred to seek hospitality from her old friend, Sara Joanna, the kvaen who had been in favour of her running away from school. But they all arranged to meet again for the races, and at the Easter mass which would be followed by weddings and baptisms. Meanwhile they would have plenty to do, completing the purchases that were essential before every migration at the shops that remained open for them night and day.

When the rest of her cita had gone, Kristina found herself alone among a noisy, joyful crowd of Lapps. She felt a momentary sadness, the result perhaps of seeing Viddakaïno again, the place where she had experienced so much unhappiness. Now she was returning from the tundra, a free woman, and wearing her native costume as a challenge : belingers, and the short, heavily pleated skirt gathered in at the waist, which Fru Tideman had insisted upon her giving up. She should have been very happy, for now she could show off, gallop her great white reindeer, challenge others to race; yet an infinite sadness had fallen upon her as during the worst days at school. She was oblivious of the happy crowd coming and going outside the post office, of the carefree shouts of the other girls strolling about on their young men's arms, ablaze with all their jewels; and she paid no heed to the daring banter of the young men. She had been looking forward to it all these weeks, and now it gave her no pleasure.

She felt more alone in the midst of this friendly crowd than ever she had during her flight. Two months had gone by since she had fled from the Lapp school into the fjell.[12] It had been during the cold of the long night of winter, with a storm blowing up and no means of protection, that she had braved the dangers of the Arctic, but she had succeeded in overcoming them, and had outwitted all those who had set out to look for her, the soldiers, the wolf-hunter and the doctor. Through hostile country, in the malevolent darkness, wolves all around her and men worse than wolves, she had fled like a hunted animal, and yet she had felt strong and confident, strong enough to defy the whole world!

Why then, now, should she suddenly feel sad? Why had she lost all desire to show herself off to the crowd, so that her white pure-bred reindeer, left to itself, was wandering around, hanging its head like any common sleigh-deer?

Then suddenly she realized the cause of her melancholy : the Finn was not with her! From now on, unless he was

[12] A mountainous area between the high plains and the sea.

19

there to share it with her there could be no joy or happiness! Why hadn't he come with her? Resentment restored her pride, and anger overcame her disappointment. Gathering up the reins, she set off at a gallop, colliding with other sleighs, crossing the old wooden bridge over the Elv like an arrow, heedless of the people who barely had time to get out of her way. Then, she left the crowded main road and turned down a little frequented track that ran alongside the river, making straight for the house of Sara the kvaen.

Not until she got there did she pull up, breathless, her hair blown across her face, her cheeks tingling from the biting cold. Other reindeer were already tied up to the rail, but she found a space for her own and put down a bundle of reindeer-moss for it to eat. Then, proud and upright, she entered the ancient hut.

'Bazza derivan!' she announced in a solemn voice.

Sara came to greet her, hands outstretched:

'Mana derivan, Kristina. God be praised, you've come back to us!'

CHAPTER TWO

THE hut was packed with men and women squatting on the floor, and their fur clothing gave off a strong smell of grease. They were all talking at the top of their voices, laughing, yokking, most of them half drunk. But as soon as Kristina appeared, pausing on the threshold to see who was there, the silence could be felt. The heat was stifling, the atmosphere sickening. Recognizing her, one of them exclaimed: 'Bouriz! Bouriz! It's Kristina Sokki.' Then, having returned the greeting, she embraced Sara, who asked no questions: Kristina was making herself at home as she used to do, and the kvaen, flattered by this mark of confidence, would gladly have driven anyone out if that would have given the young girl the slightest pleasure.

Kristina sat down on Sara's bed, out of range of the men's sallies, content to let the hours flow by in a state of peaceful somnolence. She felt reassured, everything was still the same. People kept coming in and going out, slamming the door, and each time a gust of icy air revived the foul, smoky atmosphere in the hut.

No one asked her any questions. They were too busy drinking, eating, or making love. Besides, since she had escaped from the Lapp school and made her way back to the cita without showing fear of men or wolves, or even of the stallos[1] of the Agjiet, they looked upon Kristina as Simon Sokki's emancipated daughter; a real woman of the Lapps, utterly aloof, independent and free.

Later on, when everyone was snoring, huddled up pell-mell on the floor, Sara came and lay down beside Kristina:
'Now tell me all about it!'

And Kristina had described to her her flight into the mountains. It was at Sara's that she had found the Finn,

[1] Malevolent spirits.

21

who told her the news of the reindeer, stolen by the Isaksens, and of her father's hurried departure for the Tröndelag. That was when she had made up her mind to escape and flee across the tundra to rejoin the great herd. She had been afraid that Simon, her father, tired of thieving and murdering, of organized feuding, might persuade the others to go away and leave the reindeer behind. And on the threshold of her crazy venture it had been this fear that had proved stronger than all others . . .

'There were two occasions when I was really frightened,' she admitted. 'Once, quite near here, when I got caught up in the soldiers' barbed wire! All those claws tearing at my pesk and the alarm being given . . . I was afraid I might be caught! But that was nothing compared with crossing the Agjiet!'

'You dared to do that?' Sara asked quietly.

'I had to. It was the only place where they wouldn't look for me. Oh, Sara, I wouldn't go through such an experience again for a chestful of gold pieces! Why, I could see the stone men standing there, motionless as ever, and the altar of the reindeer!'

'You actually saw them?' Sara murmured, marvelling at such courage.

'And then, suddenly a huge bird flew over the mountain, like some gigantic eagle that was going to carry me off. I just turned my skis downhill, and headed straight down the slope. It felt as though I was flying; and then suddenly nothing. I had gone right over the cliff . . . Long afterwards they told me it was the wolf-hunter's aeroplane, but at the time I was sure that it was the stallo of the Agjiet swooping down on me.'

As she described her adventure she had begun trembling again; and Sara watched her, petrified.

'You aren't like the rest of us, Kristina. You are so much stronger than most people. There are very few men who could have done what you did . . . But who found you?'

Sara knew very well who it was, but she wanted to make Kristina talk to her about him.

'After he had seen me on the Agjiet, the wolf-hunter came down at Suojaurre, and suggested going out to look for me. But the Finn was too quick for them. When I came to again, I was in his arms, and we had a long, long way to go before we reached the great herd. It was like a wonderful dream.'

'But have you forgotten all the trouble you caused us? Why, the whole countryside was looking for you!'

Kristina shrugged her shoulders. Whatever they might think of her, whatever the Norwegians might say or do, mattered little to her now!

'Fru Tideman was terribly angry,' Sara went on. 'It was lucky for you she'd already gone off to the Tröndelag. For days the telephone never stopped ringing, and for a moment everyone thought she'd return to Viddakaïno! Oh yes, there was great excitement, and Fru Tideman kept insisting that you should be sent back immediately to the Lapp school, as an example. But all the others'—Sara pulled a disdainful face—'were just weaklings and idlers. Fru Ingrid got a terrible letter from her superiors, and since then she's never stopped crying. It's pretty certain she won't come back in the autumn. People will miss her. She was a good woman,' Sara concluded.

But Kristina did not agree: 'She was too weak. There's no room for weaklings in the North.'

'It sounds as though you prefer Fru Tideman, from the way you talk,' commented Sara with astonishment.

'I detest her, but I admire her. She's a real woman!'

'You've changed a lot in the last few weeks. The experience has matured you!'

Then, in a confidential tone of voice, Sara asked: 'And the Finn?'

'He's in charge of the herd,' Kristina said firmly.

'Well, well!'

'Does that surprise you?'

'You and he will make a fine couple. He's come a long way in a short time. And now you say, he's in charge of the herd!' And she whistled admiringly.

Then Kristina began worrying about Dr Olafsen.

'You ought to go and see him, Kristina. He's stuck up for you more than anyone else.'

'I am going to. And I shall also see Fru Ingrid, and, if he's there, the wolf-hunter, Sven Haraldsen.'

'He's working over at Karasjok. But there's also the Pastor.'

Kristina looked up defiantly : she held Pastor Brombdal responsible for everything, and if things now went wrong for them it would be his doing. It was he who had fixed up Simon Sokki's visit to the Tröndelag, and if her father sold the herd so that he could emigrate, she would blame the Pastor for it.

'So you're not very fond of him, then,' said Sara laughingly.

'I'm afraid of him, and you don't love people you fear !'

Next day, her head still heavy with smoke and lack of sleep, she put on her reindeer again and galloped off through the town. There was great excitement amongst the big crowd of Lapps that had gathered beneath the wooden bridge where the races were to start. The whole cita would be taking part : Andis and Pier, Thor Risak and, amongst the women, Martha Risak and Karin Bongo.

'Aren't you entering, then, Kristina?' Martha asked in surprise.

'I'm not going to race.'

'So that's how it is,' chuckled Martha. 'You have to have Paavi with you if you want to win !'

'Of course,' Kristina retorted. 'You yourself aren't short of admirers who'd be ready to harness your reindeer for you—that's the least they could do !'

'There's no need to get annoyed, Kristina,' said Martha.

The Finn had been right; it was better for him to stay with the herd.

Then Karin Bongo tried to persuade her :

'Mikael will help you. Your reindeer's in good shape, and you might win. Just think how fine that would be : Kristina, the little rebel, winning a race! It would be enough to give Fru Tideman a bilious attack when she gets back from the Tröndelag!'

The two girls laughed, for it was notorious that when she was angry Fru Tideman often used to turn yellow. But Kristina refused Karin's offer, and, tired of arguing, her companions left her to sulk, and she found herself alone. She spent the evening wandering amongst the crowd, going from Sara's to the 'Café' which was run by another kvaen.

Every room in the place was full of smoke and people, drunk and happy. The young men caught hold of the girls by their belts and pulled them outside, and they made no attempt to resist. It was all part of the game, a revival of the ancient custom, the abduction that preceded love-making. Several men put their arms round Kristina, and the boldest of them, Per Bira, son of one of the biggest reindeer owners in the Oestfjellet, had finally picked her up, to an accompaniment of shouts and laughter, and carried her off to his sleigh. Out of bravado, she got in beside him and he galloped away with her; and for a short while she forgot everything, her loneliness, the absence of the Finn and her fears about the future.

Having succeeded in carrying her off, Per Bira decided to try his luck with her. He whipped up his reindeer and, as they left the town behind them, he warmly invited her to come to his sister's wedding on Easter Tuesday. But as she was already committed to two other marriages and four baptisms, that would go on until the middle of the week, she refused. Yet she felt sorely tempted, for the wedding of Eileen Bira, whose father owned ten thousand reindeer, twice as many as the cita of the Sokki's, would be the high spot of the holiday. They drove on, far beyond the town, until they found themselves far away from the noise and lights of the houses in the silence of the forest. Per kept snatching a drink from the flask of spirits he carried in his pocket, and not wishing to seem stand-offish Kristina pretended to drink with him, though every now and then, thanks to the bumping of the sleigh, she swallowed a mouthful in spite of herself. Though afraid of getting a taste for it, she nevertheless enjoyed the delicious warmth that suddenly ran through her limbs. But everything was spoilt for her when Per attempted to take liberties. She sat up furiously and, like an angry cat, savagely scratched his face. But though this at once sobered him up, it also revealed him in his true colours, coarse and artful. Did she think she could insult the richest match in the whole of Finnmark!

'I was forgetting,' he sneered, 'you prefer tramps.' And he added ironically: 'How many reindeer will your Finn bring you? Two or three of those that damned uncle of his, Mikkel Mikkelsen Sara, stole from us?'

The eternal clan rivalry had flared up between them: henceforward they saw themselves simply as hereditary enemies.

'Take me back to Viddakaïno immediately,' she said, white with anger. 'If you don't, you'll be sorry.'

She seized the handle of her knife and, if he had refused to obey, she would have had no hesitation in unsheathing it. Realizing that she was not joking, he became scared, and drove her back at a gallop. As soon as they reached Johan Haetta's, she leapt out of the sleigh, and Per drove away, disappearing into the darkness.

She was still so pale with anger that the shopkeeper asked her whether she was ill, and to put him off the scent she hastily made a useless purchase and left the shop. She felt in need of a refuge, and knew she would find it at Dr Olafsen's. He was at home, entertaining friends who had turned up for the festivities. A gramophone was playing, and the guests were dancing in the living-room. The doctor took her to his consulting room.

'I imagine you'd prefer us to be alone.'

He stood before her, with his handsome features and bushy hair, greying at the temples, and smiled at her. She strove to find words to express her gratitude to him, but he stopped her with a gesture.

26

'I know . . . Or, at least, I can guess what it is you're trying to say, Kristina. But there, don't let's talk about it. It's all over and done with . . . But what about you? Are you happy? For I must say, you scarcely look it.'

She remained silent, at a loss for words.

'Are you upset because Paavi didn't come with you?'

He pondered for a moment, then smiled and, taking her by the shoulders as though to make his words more convincing:

'He's got his reasons, little one. You know, I'm getting to like your Finn more and more!'

What? So the doctor also approved?

'Don't you realize? If he had come with you it would simply have made people talk—the poor rupes-hunter, strutting about Viddakaïno with the rich heiress! He's behaving very sensibly, and showing real delicacy of feeling . . . Yes, definitely, I like your Finn!'

Then she recalled Paavi's last words before she came away:

'I shall never go to Viddakaïno with you again until we go there to get married.'

Now that the doctor had explained it, she understood his attitude better.

Then Olafsen asked her how her wounds were getting on, and sounded her heart, but no trace of her fall remained.

'Why, you're stronger than ever,' he said. 'But you gave us all a terrible fright, Kristina. People are very fond of you, you know . . . in their own way. Even the Pastor.'

He laughed, seeing from the expression on her face that his words had gone home. Then he continued in a serious tone of voice:

'You know, Kristina, if you really want to show your gratitude to me, you'll go and see the Pastor, and Major Thorp and poor Fru Ingrid . . . and all the other people you got into such hot water. Though maybe for Fru Ingrid it was a good thing; she wasn't cut out for living in the North. So that's a promise, then,' he concluded. 'You'll go and see them? And I can return to my guests?'

She hesitated a long time before putting the question that was burning her lips :

'Have you any news of Simon Sokki?'

He frowned :

'They are having a conference at Tromsö, and their plan is taking shape. But I'm afraid there won't be any news for you before autumn.'

'They must never do it, never.'

'Good for you!' he exclaimed. 'Now you're talking like yourself! Now you can go, for you're just as you used to be. When you arrived, you were pale and upset, and I thought you had lost your nerve. Be off with you, Kristina. In the Finn you have found the man you needed! You are right to put up a fight. May the Lapps never leave the Finnmark!'

She handed him the beautiful pair of white fur skallers she had brought with her :

'These are for your wife.'

'Wait a minute,' said the doctor, as she opened the door to leave, 'my wife would like to thank you herself.'

Fru Olafsen came in almost immediately, expressed her delight at the beauty of the moccasins, and kissed her affectionately. But Kristina, embarrassed, ran out of the room, though not before she had heard the doctor's laugh and his wife's comment: 'Still as wild as ever, our little Kristina!'

Her visit to Fru Ingrid was very short. She remembered her as a kindly, timid young woman, rather withdrawn, and had decided to make all sorts of excuses for her escapade. But Fru Ingrid's attitude was enough to discourage her good intentions : the young assistant received her coldly, then quickly started to speak, overwhelming Kristina with reproaches and giving her no chance to get a word in. Throughout this flood of words, she kept coming back to the fact that she had lost her job, and that thanks to Fru Tideman's severity she would have to leave the country, all because of a little Lapp girl she had once been so fond of and had done so much to help! Kristina realized that she had lost all self-control, for suddenly she pushed her towards the door, and concluded their conversation by saying :

'There's nothing more to be said between us. Goodbye.'

Taken aback and upset, Kristina left her and returned to Viddakaïno. She still had two further tasks to carry out: to thank Major Thorp, and to submit to the Pastor's scolding. Having given her word, she would go through with it. Actually, she was curious to find out how it would all end.

Major Thorp, jovial and good-hearted, pinched her ear in a friendly way.

'You cost the government a tidy packet, Kristina, making them send a squad of polar police and an aeroplane to search for you. I hope you're not going to do it too often.'

He found it impossible to treat her severely, and added :

'You caused us a lot of worry, you know. We're very fond of you, and the thought of you out there all by yourself in the winter darkness . . .'

They all liked her . . . but in their own way. For Kristina realized that, if the Major had happened to find her before the Finn, he would have taken her back to school, however much she might have protested.

To fulfill her promise she still had to confront Pastor Brombdal, but she hesitated. Talking things over with Sara, she repeated that she held him responsible for everything! True, there was also Fru Tideman, but the two of them were hand in glove: for the last two or three years they had both been trying to persuade Ellena Sokki to entrust her daughter to them, and she had ended by agreeing to send her to the Lapp school for the winter. But Sara agreed with Dr Olafsen :

'He's quite right! You ought to go and see the Pastor. After all, you won't be risking anything. You've won. There's no going back now.'

It was Easter day and the church was crowded. From all sides the Lapps had come to attend the service, and their reindeer were tied up outside to the palings and barbed wire surrounding the church. This was simply a wooden hut, temporarily replacing the building burnt down by the Germans during the war. It was not nearly big enough to hold the crowd of worshippers, and those inside were mainly women, dressed in their best clothes, with their silk scarves pinned across their bosoms and copper brooches gleaming in the light. It was as hot inside the church as it was cold outside, but the door had been left open so that the cold air tempered the stifling heat within. The bright red caps of hundreds of women formed a brilliant carpet covering the whole nave, and their magnificent costumes contrasted sharply with the sober dress of the Scandinavian tourists and officials who were also attending the service. The former were there simply to take photographs, and the light of their flash bulbs distracted the Lapps from their prayers, which irritated Pastor Brombdal. He was wearing the traditional white collar, like a rennaissance ruff, and it seemed to accentuate the smooth pallor of his face and his fine, austere features, so like a profile embossed on a medal.

Kristina timidly slipped into the church, and joined in the prayers and singing. She was relieved to see that her return aroused no special curiosity amongst the Finns. She had run away from school, completely alone; and she had crossed the Vidda by the mountain route—there was nothing so wonderful about that! So what could be more normal than that she should go to church at Easter? Only the Norwegians would see anything extraordinary in her behaviour. She could hear them whispering to one another, 'Look, there's Kristina. Kristina's back!' Then she became absorbed in her prayers, for she was genuinely devout. From the Pastor's sermon she remembered many things concerning herself, and this scarcely helped to reassure her about their forthcoming interview. The Pastor had certainly recognized her, for borne along by the crowd of worshippers, she had found herself in the front row, near the fire and in full sight of the officiating priest.

Never had Pastor Brombdal seemed to her to look so

stern, and, as the last prayer came to an end, she was seized with panic and hurriedly joined the crowd of people leaving the church. Outside, despite the acute cold, the people gathered in groups and stood about in the snow exchanging news. All round the church, along the palings and beneath the sleighs, the ground was strewn with empty bottles, and Kristina noticed that some of the men were already drunk. Nothing distressed her so much as a drunken man; alcohol was the Lapp's greatest enemy, and she blamed it for all the misfortunes that were happening to them. It turned men into weaklings, ever more ready to desert their herds, seizing every opportunity to go into town to procure their poison. Some men, indeed, had sold their whole herd, reindeer by reindeer, and instead of being well-to-do, free proprietors had become the servants, even the serfs, of the big citas. Kristina could never forget that it was the Scandinavians who had first introduced this alcohol that was slowly killing her people! A miserable gift! It confirmed the ideas that the Finn had been the first to implant in her mind. Only a return to their past way of life could save the Samisks from decadence. Nevertheless, she thought to herself, both the Pastor and Fru Tideman are sincere, convinced that they are acting in our interest when they try to get us to settle down.

This reminded her that she had still one more visit to pay, but she could not make up her mind to face it. During the service her courage had melted away. She should have taken advantage of the crush, and quickly shaken the Pastor's hand like all the others, wishing him the compliments of the season. Then her visit would have passed unnoticed, and he would have had no time to question her. But would it not be better to face him? She admired both his strength of character and his authority, for she detested weak people. She was much more afraid of being convinced by his arguments than of being scolded for her escapade. She would wait until the end of the day before going to see him, by which time he was sure to be at home.

He lived in a pretty one-storied house made of wood and

31

painted white, not far from the church on the right bank of the Elv. A maid took her into the icy room which he used as his office, in the centre of which was a large pinewood table, covered with papers. The bookshelves were filled with books and files, and through the window, half-covered by white muslin curtains, shone the harsh light from the snow-covered fjell.

He came in so quietly that he surprised her as she stood dreaming in front of the window.

'Good evening, Kristina,' he said. 'So you've come. This morning I thought that you were trying to avoid me. Why did you hurry away so quickly?'

She blushed, without answering.

'You must have thought that I was not very pleased by the way you behaved.'

He spoke gently, without anger; and she would have preferred him to speak sharply, for his gentleness disarmed her.

'You set a shocking example to the other pupils. Just fancy . . . starting a rebellion in the dormitory, deceiving those in charge of you, running away! It was nothing short of insubordination! But that's not all! You upset the whole district for a week . . . a search had to be organized over a vast area, and some of the people caught in the blizzard ran considerable risks on your behalf. Do you think that was right, Kristina? Because of what you did, Fru Ingrid has had to resign. That may have been a good thing, because she has not proved altogether satisfactory, and she will be of more use in the South. All the same, she deserved to complete her school year with us without suffering this reproach which will follow her throughout her career. And all through your fault, Kristina!'

He was speaking to her as though she was grown up, and this increased her confusion, for she had no excuse to offer. He continued to enumerate his complaints:

'You have ill repaid the solicitude of those concerned for your future. For example, Fru Tideman . . .'

She sharply interrupted him:

32

'Fru Tideman doesn't love me, and I detest her!'

At this he began to scold her severely:

'Fru Tideman is concerned with your good, and not only with yours, but with that of your cita, that of all Lapps. If she was anxious to teach you it was precisely because we consider you to be one of the most intelligent, one of the most gifted of the Lapp girls. For us you represent the future, the future of the Samisks, which we do not want to be so hard and precarious. Don't you realize the truth? You ought to be completely integrated in the Norwegian community, in our Western civilization, in a Christianity freed from the last survivals of paganism.' (Obviously he was alluding to the Agjiet, and she blushed once more). 'And to ensure this we have to provide you with a way of life comparable to our own, we have to help you to settle down!'

'Never!' she exclaimed, almost despairingly.

'You're as stubborn and proud as ever!'

His voice rose. He was on the point of bursting into one of the formidable fits of anger that he found almost impossible to master, but he made a violent effort to control himself, and little by little his features relaxed. His face lit up, his eyes became gentler, and in the brief moment when he made a feeble attempt to smile she realized that he'd been touched by grace; and she dared to speak. She did so vehemently, with a youthful violence devoid of expediency or subterfuge.

'I ask you to forgive me for betraying your trust in me, for causing all the authorities of the Finnmark to be called out, for being the indirect cause of harming Fru Ingrid, and for disappointing those who, in their own way, were trying to help me. I beg your forgiveness for everything, except for what I actually did. If I ran away it was because I had to. I did it for the good of all the others: our herds are threatened, the life of our clans, our migrations, our race, its whole way of life! Is it wrong to defend our traditions? Look at my father, Simon Sokki! It will be your fault if he decides to sell the herd and emigrate, and then

what will he do? Why do you want to destroy us? Shall we
be any happier if we become a part of the poverty-stricken
tillers of the soil? With our reindeer, we are rich, and we
are free!'

'Who has been stuffing your head with such notions, little
one?' he asked calmly.

'I'm no longer a child. I know how to kill and skin a
reindeer, feed the dogs, light a fire with wet wood, make
garments and shoes of reindeer skin, and thread from their
sinews. I can harness and drive a reindeer, and put up a tent
in the strongest wind. Is that child's work?'

She raised her head, and from the look in the Pastor's
eyes she could see that he admired her reply.

'No, indeed. But in the twentieth century nor is it work
for a girl, or for a woman, or even for a man. Why go back
to the Stone Age? I didn't mean to offend you, Kristina.
I know you are strong, but I'm afraid your pride may prove
even stronger than you, and lead you to do stupid things . . .
But there, today I'm not going to reproach you any more.
You came to see me, and that must have cost you a great
deal. Look, I forgive you. And I hope we shall no longer
be enemies.'

She was beginning to feel exhausted; the struggle had
been an unequal one.

'Our roads lead different ways, but we're not enemies.
In a year's time I shall probably be married . . .'

'To the Finn, I suppose?'

'Yes, why not? What do you make of him?'

'There, there! Calm yourself! I think the Finn is a strong,
serious man, and he doesn't drink. If it wasn't that his ideas
belong to a different age it would be perfect. All right,
then, I will marry you.'

'And later on, you'll baptize our children? They'll come
to church, and I'll send my daughters to school.'

She had spoken spontaneously and was astounded by her
own words.

'You will always surprise me, Kristina. You're fourteen
years old, yet I discuss things with you as though you were

grown up. What's more, I don't believe any other Lapp has ever talked to me so seriously. If you weigh your deeds as you do your words, Kristina, everything will be all right. And later on you will educate your children! Bravo! But is that going to be compatible with living a nomad's life? Do you believe that once they understand how things are they will be content to trudge along in the traditional way?'

'And why not? The time I spent at school has done me good: I learnt to read and write and do sums, and now it's I who give everyone at Suojaurre news of everyone else. You can know how to read and still remain a Lapp.'

She drew herself up with an air of such youthful pride that the Pastor laughed aloud, whereupon she broke off abruptly, completely taken aback. So the Pastor could really laugh like any ordinary person, like a Lapp. In a flash, half the fear he inspired in her had disappeared.

What followed was quite unpremeditated. Her fingertips happened to touch the packet in the deep pocket of her pesk. It was the pair of red leg bands, skilfully woven and embroidered, which she had intended to give to Fru Ingrid but had decided not to because of their quarrel. She held them out to the Pastor:

'For your daughter.'

For a moment he did not move. Then, without saying a word, he stooped down, and in a fatherly way kissed her on the forehead. She turned and fled, furious with herself, ashamed of her weakness. She, who had dreamt of being revenged, who had spent days and nights thinking up all the cutting things she was going to say to the Pastor when she saw him again, had allowed herself to be carried away by this encounter. He had begun to sow doubts in her mind: and she had taken fright and escaped from his influence. What would the Finn say? He, at least, remained faithful to their traditions, making no attempt to reconcile the past and the present.

Thousands upon thousands of reindeer were streaming through her head, journeying from the marshes to the mountains by the sea, the great herd churning up the snow of the vidda. And behind them followed men, women, children, dogs, and wherever they went they were free and happy, knowing neither want or poverty! For her this was the truth: the Finn was right! She must flee from Viddakaïno for the second time!

She was seized with panic. Perhaps the Pastor's kindly words were only a trap. In a week the school would be starting again. Maybe they were trying to coax her back. It did not take her long to make up her mind. She had a capacity for completely changing her thoughts, her actions, her whole outlook, in a few seconds. She had made up her mind: she would leave at once. Nobody was going to get her back to school.

'I'm going back to Suojaurre!'

'Surely you're not going to travel at night,' Sara objected.

'My reindeer knows the way.'

And that same evening she bade Sara farewell.

CHAPTER THREE

A L L night she had urged her white reindeer along the Galanito trail, without even stopping on the way at Maria Siri's inn. She did not want to meet anybody. A girl who could leave Viddakaïno when the festivities had scarcely begun, and when everyone knew that she had been invited to several weddings and baptisms, could scarcely be normal. She wanted to avoid indiscreet questions.

Alternately trotting and walking, she reached Suojaurre in the early morning. The long sleigh trip through the freezing night air had soothed her nerves. The further she penetrated into the solitude of the vidda, the more the dangers she had dreaded seemed to disappear. Then, in the ice-cold, temporarily deserted hut, she found herself alone with her thoughts, and already she had to resume the daily struggle to protect herself from the enveloping cold. With the point of her broad knife she stripped the bark from some dry birch logs. The flame leapt up the chimney, and the branches she threw into the stove caught alight in turn, and blazed merrily. And, in truth, the smell of the wood fire, the light and warmth that glowed from the red-hot stove, brought her more happiness than all the festivities in the world.

She was glad to be alone, to be able to give herself up to her thoughts and dreams. Before long the others would be returning to the hut, and then the interminable discussions would start all over again, the endless palaver in the smoke-ridden, communal room; and she would have to put up with the belching of drunken men, Ellena's snoring, her brothers' indifference and the jealousy of the women, accusing her of trying to make the Finn one of their leaders. She felt a sudden burst of pride. Although she was the youngest, because they were afraid of her she was also the strongest! Yet the knowledge that the others distrusted the Finn wove around her a web of solitude that neither love nor friendship could fill; and this sense of emptiness weighing on her soul was sometimes more than her youthfulness could bear. The Finn had given warning of the raid, he had tried to put them on their guard against the men of Isaksen's cita. But the others had refused to listen to him. And now he was warning them against the promises of the Norwegians and against Simon Sokki's unreliability and weakness. Had he not, right from the beginning, at their very first encounter, stood up to the irascible head of the cita? Yet the others remained distrustful: he did not fully belong to their people, although his mother had been one of them. And Andis had asked: 'Why should he be so concerned about what might happen to the reindeer, about the future of the cita? That's Simon Sokki's business. He's the only master here.' So, for all of them, Paavi the Finn still remained a foreigner. And what of herself, Kristina thought; was not she betraying the Lapp tradition by resisting her father, by refusing to accept her lot? She had become a rebel, a doubter, and it was the Finn who had planted these ideas in her mind!

And as Kristina sat there, crushing her thoughts like a sprig of bitter-sweet sorrel, mixing her fears and hopes, a succession of disconnected images inscribed themselves one after the other upon her brain, recalling haphazardly the people she had met at the Easter feast, the Pastor, the doctor, Sara. Suddenly, she found herself thinking of that time many weeks earlier when the Finn's big, grey reindeer carried her at the gallop towards the secret place of the great herd.

It was on that day that they had won. Only a short time before she had almost died, hurling herself mad with terror from the top of the cliffs of the Agjiet. But the Finn had saved her and brought her back to her brothers who were guarding the great herd. And now it was he who was watching the reindeer, alone, while all the others were at Viddakaïno. Too late, he would become the future chief, but would he be able to change anything, save everything? She felt elated. Yes, together they would change the world. Life would be born again on the fjell and the tundra, even if all the others forsook it; and thanks to them there would always be reindeers and Lapps. In her joy she had ceased to feel either fatigue or anguish; she was happy. She told herself that the next day she would go to the slopes where the great herd was grazing. She had to see the Finn, in order to explain to him what she had done. For the moment she needed to rest after her long night's journey, and she threw herself on her bed, falling asleep immediately, lulled by the eternal song of the wind.

Out there, Paavi, alone in the vast solitude, a reindeer amongst the reindeer, one with the snow beneath his whitened pesk that scarcely showed above the hole which sheltered and concealed him, Paavi the Finn, the invisible and vigilant guardian, interrupted his dreaming. It seemed to him that he could hear a noise, far away but disquieting. He cocked his ear and listened. It was the barking of a dog, muted by distance, a joyful barking like that of a friendly animal leaping around his master's sleigh, not the cry of a dog chasing a wolf. But since it announced the arrival of a human being somewhere in the infinity of the vidda, it aroused misgivings in the Finn's mind.

For several days now, in the course of his lonely vigil, such sudden misgivings had alternated with the endless succession of dreams that filled his mind during the long hours of watching. Now and then, yielding to the warmth and comfort of his reindeer skin, he sank into a doze, haunted by the faces of friends or enemies, of dogs, of reindeer, of wolves. And his dreams invaded the present, so that the effort he had to make to sort out the confused threads of his ideas was so great that he forgot the rigorous duties of the watch; and, at such times, it took nothing less than the barking of the well-trained dogs, rounding up a straying reindeer, to shake him from his lethargy, to arouse his fear. Then, suddenly, the dramatic memory of the raid passed through his mind. He seemed to see thousands of stolen reindeer being driven away by the raiders, separated from the great herd like a silken scarf drawn from a cardboard box, drawn up in a long line that stretched away into the distance, grew smaller, and finally disappeared into the darkness. Isaksen's shaman[1] sneered, and a long burst of laughter from the raiders from the Vestfjellet echoed from every hill, bringing home to the whole of Lapland the shame that had befallen the cita of the Sokkis. Such nightmares were so violent that they awoke him, shouting aloud.

Then he would get up, stirred by a feeling of uneasiness, attentively examine the herd, the fjell, the sky filled with scurrying clouds. But everything was at peace, there was no cause for alarm. Besides, who could be threatening the great herd? The raid had been consummated and vengeance achieved. And the Finn, reassured, would bury himself once more in his memories, wandering in that indeterminate region where thoughts and dreams become confused. And, for the thousandth time, he would recall the events of the past few weeks . . .

One thing was certain, that he, Paavi the Finn, nephew of Mikkel Mikkelsen Sara of Kaamanan, who had been stabbed to death by Isaksen's shaman, was now at home in the cita of the Sokkis. Could they have behaved otherwise towards the man who had found Ellena's favourite daughter amongst the dangerous ravines of the Agjiet and brought her back to safety? He lived again the last moments of this adventure. It had happened not far from here, on the other slope of the sacred mountain. They had reached the crest of the hills, and suddenly beneath them they had seen the great herd, thousands of reindeer, spread out at the bottom of a large valley of snow protected from the wind. Paavi had pulled up his old grey reindeer, exhausted by the effort of the long journey, and the exhausted animal had lain down where it was, not wanting to get up again. What did it matter, for beside him Kristina, chastened and

[1] The name given to witch doctors in the far north of Europe and Asia.

40

ecstatic, was gazing fervently at the moving carpet of animals! The Finn had kept his promise!

Together, they both stood examining the herd they had come back to, and he could have wished that this moment would last for ever. But the dogs had scented them, and were rushing to meet them, barking; Chumbi, the black one with the white neck, had recognized Kristina and was making a great fuss of her. He leapt around her, but snapped furiously at the Finn's heels; and Kristina, delighted, called to him, 'Down, Chumbi, down,' feeling that she was protecting him—she, the wounded partridge, protecting a man who felt himself to have a giant's strength.

Then the herdsmen had started climbing towards them. Andis, Kristina's eldest brother, who during Simon Sokki's absence was responsible for the herd, was there, and Mikael Bongo, Karin's brother; and together they had carried Kristina to the tent.

She had slept for forty-eight hours on end, her sleep only interrupted by short intervals of wakefulness during which they made her drink reindeer soup and coffee; and each time she felt herself growing a little stronger. The men had given her the best place, at the back of the tent, on the right of the fire, and she lay there like a princess on a couch of birch branches and reindeer skins. She had become a little girl again, fragile and in pain, as though the effort of her flight had for a time exhausted all her strength, all the violence of her nature. Now and then Paavi came to sit beside her. Everyone knew about his passion for Kristina, but it was none of their business. As a true woman of the Lapps, Kristina would decide for herself who should claim her hand . . .

These two days of perfect happiness had passed like a flash of lightning. But the Finn could not stay with the great herd, for his place was at Suojaurre where he had to go on hunting, repairing the sleighs, getting ready to set out on the spring migration. Andis had told him to go:

'Why don't you take Kristina back to the hut? She has rested long enough now.'

'My reindeer is all in, just about ready to be slaughtered for meat!'

'You've got others in the herd,' the Lapp had said, cutting him short.

This was the first time that anyone had spoken to him of *his* reindeer! And he had felt the new blood coursing through his veins.

'Let's go and have a look at them,' the other added.

They had both slung their lassoes over their shoulders and put on their skis, for without them they would have sunk up to their waists in the thick, newly-fallen snow. With difficulty they had reached a hillock, cleared of trees and dominating the valley, from which vantage point they could hear, like the distant breaking of waves, the muffled sound made by the reindeer scraping away the snow. It was a confused symphony, composed of a thousand indistinct sounds, broken by the dry cracking of the animal's tendons, the stubbing of antlers covered with velvety dead skin against the trunks of the birch trees, the scraping of hoofs on rock, and the occasional dull grunt of an animal satisfied or glutted.

They had taken off their skis, and plunging up to their waists in the thick fall of snow they approached the herd, which opened and closed in around them so that they were like prisoners in the midst of a small clearing in a forest of hoofs, antlers, heads and hind-quarters, from which the globular, protruding eyes of the frightened animals shone out like little lamps. Then the excitement caused by their intrusion calmed down, and the reindeer, having recognized the smell of the herdsmen, took no further notice of them, merely withdrawing at their approach as if wishing to keep them at a distance. And into this void the herdsmen advanced, until all around them, in front, behind, to their left and to their right, all they could see was reindeer, facing towards them, advancing and retreating like waves breaking on the shore. Now and then, when one of them came within reach, Paavi managed to catch hold of it by the antlers,

42

clinging on to the maddened animal long enough to examine its ear-mark, then letting it go again.

Paavi already knew some of these marks, which he had been able to study at leisure in the ears of the sleigh-deer, and he had committed them to memory; for the first duty of a Lapp is to be able to recognize his mark, even when, as often happens in cases of theft, the thieves have modified it. But there was one strange mark that he had never seen before : in addition to the usual indentation cut in the lobe of the ear, a few of the animals had a mysterious star pierced through the cartilege . . . And all the animals marked in this unusual manner were exceptionally fine specimens. They were grouped around an old female, thin as a skeleton, who had lost one antler in a fight and was blind in one eye. She had a bell round her neck, like the big, grey leader of the herd, but it had been stuffed with moss to stop it ringing.

'She belongs to the Old Man,' said Andis. 'Her bell isn't freed until he gets here . . . and when he does get here, that's when we start.'

Paavi nodded his head and grunted. All through the winter he had been hearing talk of the Old Man.

'You'll soon be meeting him,' Andis went on. 'But you won't get to know anything more about him than we do.'

Then, as the Lapp was in the mood for confidences, they had squatted on their heels and talked about the Old Man. They were so still that in this familiar position they looked like two reindeer lying down, and the circle of animals unnoticeably closed in upon them, for their fur pesks gave off the wild odour that the reindeer confuse with the smell of other reindeer.

'The Old Man has been one of us for generations,' Andis continued. 'My father, grandfather and great-grandfather have all known him for as long as they can remember.'

Paavi smiled incredulously, and above his bushy eyebrows Andis' forehead wrinkled in a frown.

'The Old Man is ageless. From the beginning of time he has always turned up at the Suojaurre hut, and then we know it's time to set out. My father, Simon Sokki, would never start without having consulted him first.'

'That's all a lot of nonsense,' Paavi had cut in.

Yet even now, lying curled up alone in his snow-hole, he found himself trembling at the thought of the Old Man. He ought not to have blasphemed like that; perhaps Andis was right. And he could see his companion, deeply stirred, suddenly clutch the sheath of his long knife to indicate his indignation and anger. Whereupon Paavi, convinced of his good faith, had calmed him down and encouraged him to continue.

'The reindeer with the star are all his, then?'

Andis had remained silent for a long time before replying:

'Yes, they are his, and we never touch them, not even when we're in need of meat. For us they are sacred. The deer with the star are not animals like the others, you see. Never has a single one of them been eaten by wolves, stolen by men, died of illness, or been drowned crossing the fjord. If he had so wished, during all the centuries that he has lived amongst us his herd could have been the biggest of all, and he would be the absolute ruler over all the citas of the Samisks. But the deer with the star have never numbered more than sixty! Forty males and twenty females. Unlike us, the Old Man limits the number of both! One day when they'd both been drinking a good deal,' Andis continued, 'my father summoned up courage to ask him: "Why don't you do as we do, keep the females for breeding and kill off the males for meat?" And the Old Man answered him in a strange way: "If it ever comes to pass that I have to keep females to increase my herd, it will be because it's too late, Simon Sokki . . . too late for you and for all those who follow you. May that day never arise, for it will mean the end of the Samisk people!" What was he trying to prophecy? He's a shaman, Paavi! a shaman, I tell you! Maybe even a stallo[2]. I've often thought that he might be a reincarnation of the stallo of the Agjiets . . . the

[2] A spirit belonging to the mythological world of Lapp folk-lore.

one up there that changed a whole herd of reindeer into blocks of granite.'

Scared by his own words, Andis had lowered his voice. He had said too much already, and Paavi was too impressed to question him further. Yet later on the conversation had returned to the Old Man. It was clear that Andis, who looked upon the Finn as his superior, wanted either to convince him or be convinced by him. He took up the conversation at the point where they had broken off :

'He must be a shaman. How else can you explain him? He turns up at Suojaurre without warning, and for centuries we have waited for him. He says : "We are leaving, Simon," and Simon gives the order to start. That's all he says. We gather the reindeer, load up the sleighs and, when everything's ready, he takes his place at the head of the herd, leading the old doe with the bell, and immediately all the reindeer obey him, even Simon Sokki's big grey reindeer who has been boss of the herd throughout the winter. Then we set off, and the Old Man skis so swiftly that suddenly he ceases to be old. He can travel like this for days and nights without stopping, handling his long staff like a balancing pole. The women tie his pulka[3] to the long line of baggage-sleighs, and he never gives it another thought—it's the women's concern. He has stuck to the old-fashioned boat-shaped sleigh our ancestors used, and the only baggage he needs is a leather sack, a few reindeer skins, some tobacco, a pipe and a packet of flints. He spends the whole summer with us in our gammas[4], tanning hides, making lassoes and fishing. And it's he who decides when it is time to return, before the great autumn storms. Once we're back at Suojaurre, he inspects the great herd for the last time, selects fifteen animals above the number he has fixed for himself, ties them all to a long lead, and then, with his long staff and leading his reindeer, disappears towards the South ! But does he really go to the South? If so how comes it that no one has ever met him, either at Einontekio

[3] The old-fashioned type of Lapp sleigh, made entirely of wood.
[4] Huts of turf and stone, used in summer on the sea-coast.

or at Karesuando, at Inari or Karasjok! And how can you explain the fact that he never buys anything from any of the shops or markets?'

Andis was getting more and more worked up :

'You'll see, just you wait and see.'

'Bah!' said Paavi. 'With the meat, skins and sinews of fifteen reindeer, it's possible for a man to live, to feed and clothe himself. You could keep going a whole winter . . . and longer.'

But Andis was not convinced.

'But no one has ever met him. Once the migration is over, it's as though he disappears from the face of the earth and only comes back in spring. He's a stallo, I tell you!'

Then, as the Finn still appeared to be doubtful, Andis cut short the conversation :

'Come on, we'd better go and pick your reindeer.'

During the night Paavi got up. The dark forest of antlers spread out over the slope of the mountain. There was no sign of danger, everything was as peaceful as on that night when Andis had first shown him his own reindeer. But how far he had come in a few weeks! Then he'd been nothing but an outlawed rupes-hunter, barely tolerated by the powerful Sokki cita. And now, here he was, left alone in charge of the great herd. Quite alone. He trembled with pride. While the others were dancing and drinking in Viddakaïno, leaving the huts at Suojaurre deserted, he was alone in the vast luminous night, alone with the four thousand reindeer, that formed a moving fresco, a dark carpet spread out over the hillside. He was the master of the herd. True, this was only the result of various circumstances : Simon Sokki would never have permitted his being here, but Simon Sokki was far away in the South, planning his own downfall, and the others had been so anxious to go to the Easter festivities that they had suppressed their feelings of uneasiness and distrust. Pier himself had only consented unwillingly, but he was sure Andis and Ellena had had no qualms about leaving him in charge.

Why hadn't Kristina understood? Why had she been so upset? The future would prove that he had been right. But never would he experience a purer joy that he felt this evening. He watched his shadow, fantastically lengthened by the moon, stretching out over the herd as if it were really protecting the cita's reindeer against wolves and thieves, even against the Lapps themselves. He stifled his pride, the joy welling within him, and the beating of his heart was so loud that he could no longer hear the sounds of the night. But nothing happened, and the hours flowed by, stringing together night and day. Satisfied that the herd was all right, he went back to his dreaming again.

'Yes, we'd better go and have a look at your reindeer,' Andis had said. Then he had whistled through his teeth, and the deer, who had seemed to be listening to their conversation, scattered again to let them pass.

The herd had strayed into some clumps of dwarf birches and, as they followed them, they had to free themselves from the clustering branches, which caught in the fur of their pesks, bending like bows, then snapping off and throwing out a fine dust of irridescent snow. Beyond lay a huge clearing, where most of the herd were scraping away the snow. Amongst them was Simon Sokki's big grey reindeer, the leader of the herd, and the shrill tinkling of his bell reassured the others, scared by the approach of the herdsmen. The youngest ones leapt forward, forming a semi-circle around them, then merged themselves with the rest of the herd, which drew together from all sides to form once again a single impenetrable mass.

Andis and the Finn advanced very quietly, came to a halt and listened, subdued by the confused rumour rising from the herd, sustained by the deep chords of the wind blowing out of space.

'There are your reindeer, Paavi,' said Andis suddenly.

Paavi stood looking at them, motionless and silent: the great moment had come.

'Mikkel Mikkelsen Sara used to have thirty,' his companion continued. 'That'll be a start. We have made up his share of animals that were stolen. That's only fair, for he paid dearly enough for his loyalty to the cita. Look Paavi, thirty deer, twenty of them females in calf. That's not a bad exchange for the broken down old gelding that brought you amongst us. For a man who's fond of reindeer they're the basis for a big herd. And you are fond of them, aren't you, Paavi?'

The Finn had made no answer. He was too busy counting up his fortune. Already, with his skilled eye, he was registering the smallest signs that would enable him to recognize his deer amongst thousands of others; the shape and set of their antlers, the curve of their hind-quarters, the colour of their coats, their hoof prints and especially the mark in the right ear, the mark of his uncle, Mikkel Mikkelsen Sara, murdered by the shaman of the Vestfjellet, the evil genius of the Isaksens. This mark, which from now on was to be his!

But all that belonged to the past. As a result of Mikkel and his death, life had begun again for Paavi with the reindeer transmitted to him by his uncle. And he swore to himself that he would build up the herd. He had to, for himself and Kristina, so that one day he might become the master of the cita. It was as though his life had just begun, from that moment when he had first seen before his eyes the nucleus of what would later become the greatest herd in the whole of the Vestfjellet. And this proud ambition overwhelmed him, held him there, motionless, shut in upon himself, his eyes hardening; until at last Andis had shaken him by the arm.

'Come on, it's time you caught the one you are going to use to pull your sleigh.'

He untied his lasso and, having first carefully examined the animals, decided upon a five-year-old stag, a deep-chested animal which he had not once heard sneeze, a sure sign that it was free from worms. The difficulty was to get at it, for it was closely surrounded by the others and he would have to aim just right if he was to lasso it without getting his rope caught up in their antlers. At his first shot he missed, but the animals scattered a little and, at the second, he succeeded in getting the loop of his lasso over its head.

Andis looked on, squatting on his heels and smoking his pipe. Slowly, hand over hand, the Finn hauled on the long lasso stretched to breaking-point by the terrified deer, which hung back with its four legs firmly planted in the snow. When he got close to it, so close that he could feel the animal's warm breath on his face, he seized hold of one of its antlers with a skilled movement, bearing down with all his weight and exerting all his strength in an attempt to immobilize the reindeer. But in the savage struggle that ensued it was not always the man who had the upper hand. The animal fought to free itself, thrusting dangerously with its head, then suddenly, with a terrific leap, lifted the man clear of the snow, displaying a quite unusual strength and liveliness. Then, exhausted by the effort, the reindeer rested for a moment, mouth open, tongue hanging out, panting, and Paavi, by continuous pressure on the muscles of its neck, succeeded in twisting its head still further over. He was pleased with himself : he had chosen well and would have a good sleigh-deer.

'Come and give me a hand, Andis,' he called out. He had suddenly made up his mind. 'We'll castrate him, that'll calm him down.'

He was thinking of the return to Suojaurre, with Kristina still covered with bruises and unable to bear the violent shocks that an unbroken beast was bound to cause. This was a risk he could not afford to run.

'It's a pity to cut such a fine beast,' said Andis. 'Why, you could win the Viddakaïno races with it !'

The Finn shrugged his shoulders. Little did he care. The important thing was to get Kristina home safely. For a moment he had slackened the pressure on the reindeer's withers, and with a violent effort it managed to free its head and, catching him full in the chest, flung him several yards away into the snow. The shock of the blow broke off a tine from one of its antlers, and despite the thickness of his pesk Paavi lay for a moment completely winded. With a swift reflex movement, Andis flung himself upon the animal and mastered it.

'Let's get it over with!' Paavi said furiously.

He threw the reindeer on its back and hobbled its feet with a running knot so that it could not move. All this was the work of a moment. Then a kick in the liver knocked the animal out.

'Hold tight, Andis!'

He slit open the scrotum with the point of his dagger, cleanly drew out the testicles, and then, kneeling in the snow, his head buried between the animal's thighs, he bit through the ducts and blood-vessels, performing the operation as the Samisks had done it for generations. The job completed, he got up, wiping the blood from his face with a handful of snow and, as soon as they had untied the hobbles, the reindeer got to its feet humiliated and bewildered. From now on it would follow obediently.

Then they had returned to the tent where they had left Kristina. Paavi made ready the sleigh and laid the young girl in it on a pile of fir branches, and when he harnessed up the reindeer for the first time the beast, still weakened by the operation, scarcely attempted to struggle. It was going to make a good sleigh-deer, thought the Finn; and they had set off along the track that led to Suojaurre.

Ever since, he had dreamt endlessly about this journey with the young girl, and even now it seemed to have been only the other day.

On the way they had had to stop a number of times, for Kristina, still badly bruised, found the buffeting of the sleigh from the uneven surface of the tundra almost more than she could bear. To enable her to rest he had pulled up the sleigh, and sitting on the edge he had stooped over and taken her in his arms. And while the wind sang in the birches, for a long time they had remained, cheek pressed to cheek, listening to the rapid beating of each other's hearts. Then it was she who had drawn him towards her, kissing him passionately; and he knew he was caught. The snow, falling in fine flakes, covered their faces and, as it melted, ran down their cheeks like tears of joy. And they were happy, happy!

Throughout the journey he had been afraid of returning to the hut. What was Ellena going to say? And, later on, what would the Norwegian authorities have to say? But everything had passed off well. At the hut they had found Mikael Bongo, who had got back from the great herd two days ahead of them; and Kristina, who had been expecting to be scolded, had hobbled into bed, while Ellena finished cooking the marrow-bones, and Thor Risak puffed silently at his pipe and Karin, sitting near him, chewed away at sinews to make them into thread.

No one appeared to be upset. What did it matter why Kristina had decided to return to Suojaurre? Was she not free to return to her place in the heart of her tribe whenever she liked? A place that had always belonged to her, in the warmth of the hut among the members of her clan?

Then the Finn had joined the silent group of men, and as the red disc of the sun disappeared from the frost-covered panes of the window Ellena had set the bowls on the table, brought out the loaf of rye bread, and each of them in turn had got up, helped himself to soup and begun to eat. Only when they had finished their meal did they crowd round Paavi, forming an attentive circle beneath the lamp. Then he knew that the moment had come to describe all that had happened; from the day when he had set out to look for Kristina . . .

Such were the dreams that filled Paavi's head. Hour after hour, day after day, his thoughts drifted through his memory, perpetuating themselves in the wake of the setting sun. But it was no good living in the past. It was better to think of the present, of the herd for which he was now responsible. Kristina would not approve of Paavi neglecting his duty, even if it was to recall their love. But how could he know what Kristina was thinking of? She had gone off to Viddakaïno for the Easter festival and he had not gone with her. He was afraid of the snubs he might encounter there, and especially of Kristina having to share them. She must never have to blush for him. But he had not dared admit this either to her or to her brothers, for he, too, had his pride. He had simply proposed that he should stay behind to look after the herd, and Kristina, who had either not understood or not wished to, had shrugged her shoulders, angry and scornful. And since then, left to himself, the Finn, whose mind was usually calm and smooth as the pools of the vidda, had been a prey to bitter anxiety. He strove to reassure himself, and, to shorten the endless hours of watching, to escape the crazy images that aroused his jealousy, he took refuge in the eternity of his memories.

The setting sun had suddenly disappeared behind the high hills of the fjell. But a faint, almost imperceptible light still lingered over the empty expanse, prolonging the twilight, and when it finally disappeared the whole scene seemed to quiver before resuming its eternal aspect, grey and sombre as a dead country that had been abandoned by light and warmth. Later on a new light appeared here and there above the icy mountain-tops, soon to be followed by that of the first stars . . . And behind the clusters of grey cloud the sky became more luminous as the number of the stars increased . . .

And the Finn resumed his watch, puffing gently at his pipe, listening attentively to the rumours of the night . . .

CHAPTER FOUR

THIS time there could be no mistake: someone was coming. The dogs pricked their ears, but did not bark. Branches cracked in the distance. Somewhere a skier was approaching the herd. It could only be a friend, for he was taking no precautions; and now one could hear the sound of heavy breathing and the hissing of the snow beneath his skis.

Paavi climbed out of his snow-hole. Already the reindeer were becoming restless, drawing together in little groups then breaking away again. Suddenly the animals that were lying down chewing the cud got up. The whole vidda was astir, and the dogs, barking joyfully, set off at full gallop. It must be somebody from the cita coming to relieve him. But how could this be possible, for the festivities at Viddakaïno were at their height? Neither Pier nor Andis, nor even Ellena, despite the absence of Simon Sokki, had appeared to be anxious, or seemed in any hurry to return to the hut at Suojaurre. He could not make it out. Then, all of a sudden, he realized what it must be: they were worried about leaving him alone with the herd, they distrusted him. Maybe Simon had returned unexpectedly and, after bawling them out, dispatched one of his sons to find out what was happening. Yes, that was it, he was sure.

A figure stood out in the darkness against the luminous halo which, a little further down, revealed the slope of the hill, and now the moving shadow was coming towards him, escorted and guided by the dogs.

'Paavi!' a voice exclaimed.

And it was only then that he recognized Kristina. She came to a halt in front of him, and he stood there without moving while she took off her skis. Then she threw herself into his arms.

'Paavi, Paavi, you were right. Forgive me!'

'What's happened, what's the matter?' he asked, suddenly uneasy.

But instead of answering she pressed herself against him, burying her face in his furs, and despite the darkness he could see that her eyes were full of tears, shining like crystal. Then she smiled, and seeing her there so deeply moved, so slight a figure against his own, it seemed to him as though this was the little Kristina he had discovered after the accident, the Kristina he had rescued from the terrors of the Agjiet. Striving to prolong these memories, he made no attempt to explain her presence. Then he led her to his snow-hole, and there in the warmth, holding her in his arms, he let her calm down. It was not until much later when the stars were already whitening in the sky that she made up her mind to speak.

'You were right, Paavi. But I didn't understand. It took Dr Olafsen to convince me that you had made the right decision. Fool that I was, I nearly behaved stupidly.'

She told him how she had gone off with Per Bira, and as he thought of the rich young man galloping away with her in his sleigh, he clenched his teeth but said nothing. After all, wasn't it quite natural, inevitable? It was to avoid such incidents that he had been unwilling to go to Viddakaïno. But when she told him how Per had insulted her he unsheathed his knife :

'If I'd been there, I'd have cut his throat!'

'You wouldn't have had to bother, Paavi. I was ready to do it myself, but Bira's a coward.'

But when she told him what the young man had dared to say about Mikkel Mikkelsen Sara, Paavi's uncle, the old rupes-hunter, and how she had threatened him with her dagger, and how he had been so scared that he had taken her back to town at the gallop, the Finn gradually calmed down, gazing at her with pride.

The only thing that worried him now was what Simon Sokki was up to. Had they heard any news? Would he be back in time for the migration? But Kristina had heard nothing at Viddakaïno.

'There was no news at all,' she said, 'either about him or the others; nor about Per Oskal, the Lappefogden, who went with them. They are still at Tromsö. But Dr Olafsen thinks we ought to be on the look-out, he knows Simon and fears the worst. We must be prepared, Paavi! If only he gets back by the time the Old Man turns up and gives the signal to start! And maybe that won't be long, Paavi! I feel convinced that, once he has taken the great herd to the mountains of the sea again, he won't have the heart to leave it.'

'Do you really believe he won't get back in time?'

'If he was going to, he would have been here already. That's what everybody in Viddakaïno thinks, even if they don't actually say so. Ellena and the others are worried. They've decided to come back as soon as they can, directly the festivities are over. They're afraid my father may put off his return, and soon Thor will be coming to help you. It will be as much as the two of you can do to keep the herd quiet : their instinct is already making them restless, they want to get going.'

Suddenly they both experienced a moment of panic as they thought of the great herd on the march, of the huge mass of reindeer they would have to look after and guide, keeping them to the narrow route decreed by custom, between all the other herds of the vidda that would be travelling on either side of them. Then their confidence in their youth and energy, in their unity of purpose, returned to them.

'Listen, Paavi . . . now while the stars are looking down upon us, let's swear on oath never to leave one another again, never to forsake the vidda and the fjell.'

He looked at her for a long time, then kissed her.

'We've taken an oath, Kristina, and if anybody tries to prevent us carrying it out, he'd better beware. I haven't been guarding the great herd just for idiots to disperse it.'

He felt his anger rising as it had done previously when

he had discussed the future with Pier and Andis. They had both merely shrugged their shoulders, resigned, always ready to follow, to accept whatever the master decided. Well, this herd that he was now in charge of, he would defend, if necessary against its master!

Kristina stayed with him for five days, sleeping beneath the shelter of the upturned sleigh. He admired the skill with which she sent the dogs out to fetch back the strays, and her ability to foresee and calm the sudden movements of panic that sometimes affected the herd. She would have been able to take charge of the five thousand reindeer by herself. Each day they lit a small fire of birch bark to boil a kettle. Then for hours at a time they would lie side by side, motionless and dreaming, without either of them saying a word, their thoughts moving in the same direction. At other times their hearts overflowed, as they talked about the future, envisaging all the snares and traps that would be set for them, but in their own minds more and more convinced that in future it would be up to them to protect the herd.

Then one morning Kristina went off, as simply as she had come; and it seemed to the Finn that her short visit must have been only a dream. Yet the double track of her skis on the snow was still there, visible to his eyes.

'The others will be back before long,' she had explained.

Thor, who had been ambitious to win one of the races with his unbroken reindeer, and who had so lovingly helped Karin to harness hers, would be returning to the great herd immediately the results were declared, and without halting at Suojaurre he would cut straight across the hills.

'You and he will have to stay with the herd until the others come to join you,' she added. 'And until then, I'll do your trapping for you.'

Then he had begun to describe to her the best places near the river, and to tell her where he had set snares as he was on his way to take charge of the herd. But she had interrupted him:

'I know them all. Wasn't it I who pointed them out to you when you first arrived at Suojaurre?'

It was true, but he had already forgotten. Then, before she disappeared over the crest of the hill, Kristina had waved to him for the last time; and it struck him what a long way she had to go to get to Suojaurre. Maybe darkness would have fallen before she arrived!

Kristina had now taken up all the traps, at the same time taking advantage of her inspection to set more snares with a view to the next visit. She did this quickly and well: a slip-knot of thin brass wire attached to a bent birch-branch, and a few grains of barley or willow-shoots scattered on the snow. She knew just where to place her traps, as well as the Finn. Long ago old Mikkel Mikkelsen had taught her his secrets, enchanted to find the little girl, as she then was, so passionately keen about hunting. It was from him she had acquired the sixth sense that is essential for guessing which path the game will take; he had trained her to study their habits, to know how to judge the wind and the thickness of the snow, to decipher animal tracks. Now, had he still been alive, even Mikkelsen Sara himself would have had no more to teach her. As the Finn had said to her one day: 'On this job, you know all there is to know!'

She enjoyed the work since it left her free to think, for like all the people of her race she had a predilection for solitude, silence, interminable reverie; and as she went from trap to trap and from one bank to the other of the river Elv, her ceaselessly active mind kept returning to the Finn. Together they had watched over the reindeer of the great herd, and she smiled at the memory of those days of happiness; and she felt confident and at peace, for Paavi was with the herd, the reindeer were in good hands.

She was still keeping an eye on her surroundings, halting from time to time, stooping down to examine an animal's tracks or to set a trap. Then, feeling a sudden gust of wind, she looked up at the sky. It was rapidly filling with banks of cloud, travelling from east to west like the prows of mysterious ships, their long shadows racing across the tundra faster than the clouds themselves. It was time to make for home, for there would be a storm before night-fall and Suojaurre was still some five or six miles away.

Kristina straightened the shoulder straps of her knapsack, heavy with its load of snow-fowl; the sable and ermine were slung from her belt by the wires that had strangled them, and they dangled against her pesk like savage and sumptuous ornaments. A final glance at the sun was enough to tell her what time it was and the direction she must take. There was no point now in following the winding of the river; she must strike out across the tundra, following a scarcely perceptible track, used only by hunters. This would save her almost an hour's journey.

From the louder rasping of her skis on the snow she knew that it was already growing colder, but she tied the strings of her cap beneath her chin and turned up the fur collar of her pesk. The cold was her ally, hardening the snow wonderfully, and thus lightening her task. Who would have believed that spring was so near!

Kristina drove herself forward with her ski-sticks, travel-ling faster and faster. The cold, the cross-current of wind announcing the storm, the sudden gusts roaring in the snow-laden branches, the weight of her quarry on her shoulders, filled her with the intoxication of solitude, with boundless joy. She made rapid progress, though the track was scarcely visible in the forest and beneath the low, sheltering cover of the copse, while high overhead she could hear the loud roar of the wind twisting the tops of the trees. She was a daughter of the storm! This aeolian music matched the singing in her heart, and she journeyed on, light and tireless, despite the weight of her knapsack dragging more and more heavily on her shoulders.

Then suddenly, right ahead of her, the tundra came to an end, at the top of the steep slope forming the river's bank. Here the Elv described a large loop, almost com-pletely encircling the clearing where the huts of Suojaurre had been built. Though these were not yet visible, Kristina knew that at a certain point a break in the undergrowth made it possible to see the smoke from the houses, fleeing like blue spume before the wind; and she stopped in order to make sure that they were actually there, amongst the long streamers of snow suspended in the air. And there it was—a blue cloud, floating, unravelling itself, barely perceptible among the gusts swirling in every direction. It was enough to tell her that the others had got back!

She was in a hurry to join them, but to reach the camp she had to cross the frozen river. She looked over to the other bank, measuring the distance : it would mean climbing down to the level of the river, crossing that mass of powdery snow blowing across the frozen surface, and then scrambling up the other bank in the shelter of the undergrowth. In all, a few hundred yards to traverse, during which she had the impression of swimming in a new element. At this particular spot, a layer of icy fog, borne by the snow-laden wind, closed around her, burying her up to the waist, while her head and arms seemed to be floating in the blizzard. As the strength of the wind increased, it whipped up the snow like great ocean breakers, covering her for a moment or two with an impalpable dust that almost suffocated her. It became impossible to go on : she had to stop in order to get back her breath, and wait for a lull before starting again.

Once across the river, and having laboriously climbed the abrupt slope of the opposite bank, she was again protected by the trees; and as she rested in their comforting shelter she suddenly became conscious of her fatigue. Fortunately, the hut was not very far away : it was approached by a kind of narrow alley carved out of the tundra, a real woodland tunnel, within which the din of the storm was muted and the noise of the wind tearing at the tops of the birch trees could scarcely be heard. In the sudden calm that had succeeded the tumult raging on the nearby river she could hear familiar and reassuring sounds, the dry cracking of branches, the friendly rustling of her skis, the barking of a dog in the distance.

Then the branches parted, revealing a wide stretch of

open sky. She had reached the huge circular clearing in which the huts of Suojaurre, scattered here and there, seemed to be dancing in the storm, now hidden by whirlpools of snow, now appearing like a ship in distress, caught in the swelling current of a fjord. Here the wind blew in circles, hurling itself against the barrier of trees in an attempt to escape, twisting the snow into long cones that swirled through the air like waterspouts. All around, the wind roared its anger, yet high in the sky and clearly visible from here, above the dome of the Agjiet, glittering with ice, hung a cloud of snow swept from its summit by the wind, like the plume of smoke from an erupting volcano. But here in this wild spot Kristina was at home : everything was familiar to her, even the tempest.

For a moment she stood gazing at her cita's encampment. She loved the incredible muddle that surrounds the tents and huts of her people, where everyone leaves whatever he has no further use for and no one attempts to tidy them away; sledges with their shafts and harness lying on the ground just as they were left when the reindeer were taken out, and elsewhere, in the shelter of the sledges, turned on their sides to form a screen against the wind, the resting animals, tugging at the bundles of dried reindeer-moss that had been put down for them. There were carcases of meat, hung up to dry on poles, out of reach of the animals, which the storm had sprinkled with snow; and, here and there, antlers cut up for rubbish and piles of sawn logs formed pyramids upon which the workmen's saw or axe lay just as he had left it. Everywhere there were signs of the careless disorder that is usually found amongst the Samisks.

When she reached the hut she quickly took off her skis, leaving them where they fell and throwing her sticks into a corner, and was on the point of opening the door when she stopped, surprised and intrigued : an unknown reindeer, high on the hoof and deep-chested, still harnessed to a covered pulka, had been casually hitched to one of the poles for drying meat. The animal had recently come a long way, for its coat was still damp with sweat. But unlike its fellows, who had been startled by the girl's arrival and were restlessly moving about, reaching their heads into the air as far as their tethers allowed, it remained quite quiet. Kristina, always interested in the appearance of a strange reindeer in the herd, examined the beast more closely. The number of tines on its powerful antlers, which had not yet shed their winter velvet, showed it to be a ten-year old; and here and there shreds of skin, still attached to the bone, fluttered in the wind like bits of rag. It was a forest deer from the South, accustomed to people and their dwellings. Its thick grey fur was dark on the back, lighter on its chest and flanks, while its belly was covered with a kind of white fluff. Kristina went up to it and began stroking it, and as it made no attempt to move away she was able to examine its ear marks.

'Why,' she exclaimed, 'it's the reindeer with the star! It's the Old Man's! No one but he would dream of travelling in a pulka!'

She could have recognized the old patched-up sledge, loaded with its owner's slender baggage, amongst a hundred. Its hull had been reinforced with stays of birchwood, and the planks forming its stretchers had been renewed so many times that practically all that remained of the original vehicle were the runners, carved from the solid trunk of an arctic pine and not shod with iron.

So the man they had all been waiting for was here! Suddenly Kristina felt overwhelmed with joy. The Old Man had arrived, and soon they would be off! The long migration was about to start. From all around, thousands of reindeer, of men, women and children, would be setting out for the North. The whole of Lapland had begun to breathe again after the long torpor of the winter. This immemorial journey, from the steppes of the interior to the mountains on the coast and back again, was like the powerful regular breathing of their great country.

The Old Man had arrived! The Old Man had arrived! And Kristina danced about like a child, throwing her cap up in the air, almost frantic with joy and quite naturally the most ancient songs, songs that are not written down but handed on by word of mouth from generation to generation, sprang to her lips, and she burst into spontaneous improvisation :

'The Old Man is here,
Come from the country that no man knows;
With his starred deer as a guide
He will lead us to the sea.'

As the last shrill note of the yok mingled with the noise of the wind her joy was transformed into a feeling of uneasiness that caught her in the throat. What was the Old Man going to say? It was he who would decide their fate, he who would determine whether this migration was to be their last. He alone would be able to make Simon Sokki change his mind. But would he? Would he prove to be their ally or their enemy? Suddenly she felt apprehensive about meeting him face to face. This would not be like last year. Then she had been only a little girl who counted for nothing, for whom the Old Man used to carve toys out of blocks of birchwood. Would he now take her seriously, realize that she had more determination than all the others put together? If she had to fight she would have been glad to have the Finn there to support her, if necessary to protect her, for the others were of no account, mere weaklings, who would accept without question whatever Simon Sokki decided. But she would make the Old Man listen to her.

Quickly making up her mind, she opened the door of the outer room that was usually stacked with recently caught snow-fowl, frozen hard as stone. She carelessly threw the heavy sackful of game into a corner, shook the snow from her pesk and, using her knife, scraped down her stallers and ankle straps and all those parts of her clothing that were still covered with frozen snow. She must be neat and dignified, she thought, drawing herself up. It was important above all that the Old Man should no longer look upon her as an insignificant little girl! From inside the communal room she could hear snatches of conversation,

62

and the familiar roar of the stove. She opened the door and paused for a moment on the threshold, suffocated by the stifling heat; then, though she could scarcely see through the stifling fug, thick with steam from the kettle and acrid smoke from the fire, she greeted the new arrival:

'Bazza derivan!'

'Mana derivan, Kristina. Did you get a good bag?' answered a voice out of the shadows.

For a moment she shut her eyes, and by the time she opened them again she had become accustomed to the semi-darkness and could distinguish the people who were there. There sat the Old Man, bolt upright on a stool, alone in the centre of the room, while the others, squatting along the walls or slumped on the beds, formed a respectful circle around him.

He looked at Kristina, and his blue eyes, very clear, gleaming like carbuncles, deep in their sockets beneath shaggy eyebrows, seemed to glow from within. Kristina noticed that he had on the same old pesk, made from the skin of a white reindeer, from which almost all the fur had been worn away. His leggings, shiny with grease and dirt, fitted tightly to his skinny, bandy legs, and under his pesk one could see the blue koufte, as dirty as the rest of his costume, its high, stiff collar decorated with threadbare embroidery. From this collar, which was too large for him, his long neck emerged, thin and scraggy as a vulture's and joined to his chin by a fold of skin, beneath which his Adam's apple stuck out from a dirty silk scarf that had once been pink. His skin was like a mummy's, on which one could read the passing of the years, of storms and cold, written in long, deep wrinkles, gathering round his eyes, following the contour of his cheekbones and running towards his chin like tattoo marks. The latter was overshadowed by huge chapped lips, covered by an untidy, greying moustache, which concealed his almost toothless mouth but seemed to underline the aquiline line of his nose, etched with finer wrinkles.

They're right, thought Kristina. This man *is* ageless!

'Did you get a good bag, Kristina?' the clear voice repeated.

'Very good,' replied Kristina, throwing at his feet the mink and the ermine which she unhooked from her belt. Stooping down, he picked up the game, weighed it in his hand like a connoisseur, blew the fur against the grain, and once more looked at her with a gesture of approval. She lowered her eyes, fascinated by his limpid gaze that seemed to see and understand everything. Then, resuming his hieratical pose, he again fell silent, as though nothing had happened. His red cap, which he wore on the back of his head with the point falling like a scarf onto his left shoulder, revealed a fringe of grey hair, growing in a straight line across his forehead, almost down to his eyebrows. Every now and then he raised a short pipe to his lips, gave one or two puffs, then slowly lowered his hand again so that it rested on his knee.

Kristina had slipped into her usual place on the couch. From there she could watch the Old Man without flinching from his overwhelming gaze. She was scared, and at the same time filled with amazement. There were so many legends about this man that surely those who maintained that he was a shaman must be right! His silence and immobility were beginning to weigh upon the people of Suojaurre, who, as soon as they heard of his arrival, had all crowded into the hut and were now awaiting the moment when he was ready to speak. Only Ellena broke the silence, moving about, occasionally throwing a log into the stove, fetching bread from the cupboard, setting cups on the table; and her familiar movements helped to dissipate the spell surrounding the Old Man.

No one ever questioned him, they simply obeyed him, and though everyone knew that he would speak when the time came, no one could tell when that would be; they could only wait. They sat there, lost in their own thoughts, one sipping his coffee in little gulps, holding the sugar firmly between his teeth, another filling his pipe and lighting it with a splinter of wood from the stove. It must be getting late, for already the light from the fire was stronger than the lingering daylight. Except for the slow, regular movement with which the Old Man raised his pipe to his mouth, one would have imagined he had been turned to stone. Only the strange, light-coloured eyes rolled like agate marbles in their sockets, the vitality of his gaze contrasting sharply with the immobility of his body. He seemed to be scarching thc hut, cxamining not only thc objccts with which it was filled, but also the people in it, laying bare their innermost thoughts.

Outside the wind had died down. The roar, which had filled the tundra and sometimes shaken the hut, had grown fainter with the coming of darkness, and all that could be heard was the gay crackling of wood in the stove. Outside, the cold was already weaving its frost patterns on the panes of the small window, which now only admitted the faintest light. It was the pause after the storm. And when the Old Man knocked out his pipe on the side of the stool, everyone knew that he was about to speak.

'Ellena,' he said, 'and you other women of Suojaurre, the time has come to start baking the bread for the migration. The sleighs must be got ready, and the harness; the collars must be stuffed, the sleigh-deer rounded up, and messengers must be sent to the great herd to warn the herdsmen. The assembly point will be at Bastevarre. We must leave Suojaurre in two days from now.'

He had said all that was necessary; his orders had been given, and Simon Sokki himself could not have spoken better. The Old Man relapsed into meditation.

'Here you are, Ellena!' said Mikael, throwing a crumpled note on the table, and all the others followed suit.

She opened the trap-door leading down to the cellar and brought out some bottles of spirits, which the men passed from one to the other, taking deep gulps straight from the bottle, so that soon they began to show the first signs of drunkenness. The Old Man took his turn with the others, but the alcohol had no effect upon him; he changed neither his position nor his hieratical calm.

When the rest of them, humming and yokking, were beginning to get worked up, Ellena suddenly cut the orgy short.

'Come on now, get a move on!' she said roughly. 'It'll take you all of two days to get ready.'

They hesitated.

'Do as she tells you,' the Old Man said approvingly.

And so great was his authority that not one of them dared to protest. One after the other they stumbled out, and every time they opened the door a blast of cold air swept into the room.

'Get to bed the rest of you! We've got a hard day's work ahead of us,' she said, addressing herself to her sons, huddled in the corner. Without a word they climbed into their bunks, threw themselves down on their deerskins and immediately fell asleep.

The Old Man still remained sitting, quite upright on his stool, apparently feeling no fatigue despite the time and the fact that he had had a long journey. Ellena turned towards him, but he anticipated what she was going to say.

'Simon Sokki has written.'

'Yes? Then you've seen him? I thought he was still at Tromsö.'

'No, I haven't seen him, and I haven't been to Tromsö . . .'

It was always like this with the Old Man. He guessed what was going to happen, and forestalled it.

'Remember this, Ellena,' he said solemnly, 'a Lapp who's not back with his herd when it's time for the migration has already ceased to be a Lapp.'

He had said too much or not enough. But though her heart was heavy she had not the courage to ask him to go on. Besides he changed the conversation.

'It looks like being cold again for a few weeks, and that will make it easier going for the sleighs. First thing in the morning, Ellena, you must start baking the bread.'

She knew that he would say no more. She raked the ashes over the embers of the fire and then lay down. The Old Man was right: tomorrow would be a hard day for her.

For a short period the darkness was complete: from the

neighbouring room, which served as sleeping quarters, came the muffled sound of the boys' snoring. Ellena did her best to sleep, but could not. It was always like this before a migration : so much to think about, so many things to be done before they started, and this time, on top of her other worries, was the doubt as to whether they would return to Suojaurre in the autumn. She was already getting too old for this nomadic existence. Maybe Fru Tideman was right, and she ought to change her way of life. Then just as she was falling asleep, dreaming happily of Tröndelag, she heard the sound of stifled sobs coming from the neighbouring couch where Kristina lay. For a moment, upset by the Old Man's words, the young girl had lost heart. He had spoken clearly of what she herself feared : that Simon Sokki would never return to Suojaurre. Ellena shrugged her shoulders. Why worry? It was only a childish upset; her daughter had not yet made up her mind as firmly as she liked to pretend. Once she found out how pleasant life could be in the South, she would soon forget about their harsh existence in Lapland, about the reindeers and the Finn.

But Ellena was mistaken. Kristina had already pulled herself together and, clenching her teeth, was planning her counter-attack. She and Paavi would have all the summer to work out a plan of action. If only the Old Man would agree to help them! He alone could understand them—if he wanted to!

All night she scarcely slept. From time to time she furtively observed the Old Man. For hours and hours he had not moved, and was still sitting bold upright and utterly motionless. But now he was no longer smoking, both hands lay flat on his knees, and the slow rhythm of his breathing, faint and regular, showed he was asleep. Intrigued, the young girl leant over towards him. He was sleeping sitting up, his back still quite straight, his eyes wide open, like the reindeers' in the cold of the night.

Then, after a time which seemed to Kristina at once endless and too short, the morning light slid furtively and gently into the sleeping room, where living creatures and

67

inanimate objects alike lay stiffened by the cold. The light was not yet strong enough for her to be sure that it was morning : here and there it touched something for a moment, like the wooden panels that then disappeared again into the shadow; it awoke a reflection from the great metal bowl of snow standing on the stove; lingered for a moment on the shelves where the mistress of the house kept her personal treasures; then suddenly lit up the round copper face of an old alarm clock. Curious and indiscreet, the light peered into every corner, restoring life to an old fur pesk hanging from a nail, alighting on a bowl, a cup, and then, having completed its inventory, coming to rest on the parchment features of the Old Man, still asleep, with mouth and eyes wide open. At its delicate touch the mummy's face took on a golden hue, began to come alive again, as though the blood was starting to flow once more through the aged, knotted, dried-up body. This daylight summons restored his powers of speech, and without changing his hieratical pose by the slightest movement, the least quiver of a muscle, the Old Man began to speak.

'It's time to get up, Ellena!' rang out the eternally youthful voice. And as if by magic the whole hut suddenly sprang to life. Ellena leapt down from her bunk with a sprightly energy that belied her increasing plumpness :

'Pier, Andis, Kristina,' she shouted. 'Up you get! It's time!'

And because she felt they were not obeying her quickly enough, she went from bunk to bunk, roughly pulling off the covers, scolding them in her hoarse voice. One after the other the lads came in from the adjoining room where they slept, their hair unkempt, their heads still muzzy from drink; Pier even staggering a little. Kristina brought them a basin-full of snow, with which they energetically rubbed their faces, and this brief toilet completed their awakening. It was very cold in the hut. Andis tapped the thermometer hanging on a nail in the corner of the room :

'Only ten degrees inside! That means at least thirty below outside,' he estimated.

'The sleighs will run all the better,' said Pier.

They squatted idly on their heels, their backs against the wall of the hut.

'Damnation,' Pier exclaimed. An icy draught was blowing through a crack in the window on a level with his neck. Quickly he kneaded a piece of bread between his fingers and, using the point of his knife, sealed it up.

'There are holes everywhere in this lousy hut!'

'Maybe in a day or two you'll find it's better in a tent,' Kristina said ironically.

'Come on you, get the fire lighted,' Andis cut in authoritatively.

The girl shrugged her shoulders; she was not afraid of her brothers, who were only putting on airs because her father wasn't there. She went out, slamming the door, and a moment later returned with an armful of logs which she threw on the floor. Then, crouching in front of the stove, she laid the fire. This was an almost ritual performance: first the bark had to be carefully stripped from the logs, then the fine outer skin of the bark had to be peeled off to serve as tinder. As soon as she had enough, she opened the stove, raked the ash from the still warm embers, blowing on them until the tinder caught, then added some brushwood, and finally the logs themselves. The old stove required no coaxing and was soon cheerfully roaring away, the mere sound of it almost enough to warm the hut. It must have been very cold out in the tundra during the night, for in a few hours the frost had completely covered every metal object, door handles, pots and pans, and had lined the small windowpanes with sheets of translucent ice, etched with a fantastic variety of arabesques and flowers. But now the temperature in the hut was rising again as rapidly as it had fallen the previous evening when the fire had been allowed to die down. All that was needed now was to keep the stove well stoked, and there was plenty of wood.

The warmth restored the men to a sense of reality, and the Old Man, sitting like a mummy, reminded them of their duty. Feeling his eyes on them, they were more afraid of his silent reproaches than of Ellena's shrill nagging.

69

The day that was beginning was not like other days. They were about to leave Suojaurre for several months, perhaps for ever, depending upon what Simon Sokki had decided. This was no ordinary journey, like gaily setting out for a holiday at Viddakaïno. In two days' time they would be joining the great herd on the frozen lake of Bastejaurre, at the foot of the Bastevarre, and for six weeks, day after day, they would have to follow the reindeer, sleeping in tents, gradually eating up the long, long road that led to the sea.

Ellena distributed the pieces of raw, uncooked fish that constituted the morning meal; she had no time to cook. It was time to get to work, and she set them an example, sorting out the contents of chests, rolling up reindeer skins, exasperated by all these men sitting around watching her.

'Outside with you all!' she shouted. She needed the whole place to herself, for she had to pack up the entire contents of the house, leaving nothing but the walls and roofs. Everything else would be loaded on to the sleighs. She hurried about, shouting and railing at the boys. Oh, if only Simon Sokki were there, she thought. Then she turned on her son, Pier, who was already pulling a bottle of spirits from the pocket of his koufte.

'Put that away! Don't you realize we're leaving? Mikael will be waiting for you. In two days' time the great herd has to meet us at Bastevarre—that's what the Old Man has decided—and up there Thor and Paavi will be wondering what's happened to you.'

Suddenly she had recovered her authority, was speaking as mistress of the encampment, and Pier left the hut hanging his head.

'You, Andis, get the sleighs ready and check them over! And you, Kristina, see that the collars and back-bands are properly padded!'

At last she was left alone with the Old Man. He had lit his short pipe and the bitter smell of black tobacco filled the whole hut. He looked at Ellena, and she had the impression that he was smiling.

70

Outside, the morning cold struck the youngsters full in the face: it was a radiant morning, just the weather for the migration. Pier packed the haversack, roped his chest to his sledge and harnessed his reindeer. He was ready. The animal was pawing the ground, and he had difficulty in holding it in, clutching the reins close up to the bridle to avoid the dangerous thrusts of its horns. Andis and Kristina went over to their brother: it was a solemn moment, for he was about to join the great herd.

'Mana derivan!' they said, raising their hands in farewell.

'Bazza derivan!' Pier replied bravely, now quite sober again and conscious of his responsibilities. Then he sprang on to the sleigh and the reindeer leapt forward with a prodigious burst of speed. But it was only a false start, for after galloping a short distance Pier turned his sleigh about and pulled up in front of the hut. Then, standing upright, he turned towards the people of Suojaurre and suddenly broke into the yok that everyone was waiting for.

The song rang through the snowbound clearing like a challenge, and, in the distance, the voice of Mikael Bongo could be heard replying to him. Both men were improvising in the same tradition: the words they uttered like war cries, others before them had sung; they spoke of cold and hunger, of wolves and tempests, and of the slow advance of the reindeer, carving out the broad furrow of the migration through the snow of the fjell. Sometimes their wild song was touched by a note of passion, as it told of a reindeer, the finest of all, and of the bride they would find, dreaming upon the cliffs above the fjord, where the sun never sets!

Pier ended his yok with a piercing cry, raucous as the howling of an animal, and as he let go the reins his reindeer bore him away at the gallop in a flurry of irridescent snow, while on either side of the sleigh the dogs bounded and leapt like great balls of fur amidst a chorus of barking. The noise continued for a long time. Then at last peace and silence fell once again upon Suojaurre, and those who had stayed behind returned to their slow, patient work.

71

CHAPTER FIVE

THE Old Man supervised all the preparations, sitting on the doorstep, still apparently unmoving, as though immune to the bitter cold; yet his silent presence was enough to spur them all on. Besides, now that they were caught up in the bustle of departure they thought no more about being tired, and worked hard and swiftly; Andis showed no signs of the casualness he had displayed in the morning.

The baggage-sleighs lay around outside the hut, where they had been left in the autumn. They were not like the Finnish sleighs in current use, showy vehicles, light and elegant, gleaming with black paint: rustic, solidly built, they consisted of two heavy runners joined together by stout cross-stays, to which branches of birch were nailed lengthwise to form the deck. As they were to carry all the baggage belonging to the cita, it was important that the leather thongs which secured the shafts to the runners should be carefully checked, for it was they that took the whole weight of traction. So often had these sleighs been damaged, patched up, smashed once again, that practically nothing of the original vehicle remained.

Andis went from one to the other, trimming out a new shaft or fixing a fresh strap; and anyone watching him might well have wondered why all this work could not have been done during the quiet of the winter night. But logic is not the Samisks' strong suit. Why worry about the future? It is only the present that counts. What's the point of getting a sleigh ready in advance, when you can't be sure you will ever use it?

By midday, Kristina had finished looking over the harness. She had stuffed the collars with reindeer hair, sown into old, torn skins, using a long, bent needle with an eye big enough to take the sinews that served as thread. As the hours passed everything was beginning to take shape. In a huge cauldron, suspended from a metal tripod over a wood fire, tar was being melted, and the clearing was full of its aromatic scent, which delighted everyone, for it was a sign that spring had come. Next, Andis had to fix the iron runners to the sledges; a device that the Old Man disapproved of, preferring runners of unshod wood, which, provided they were well greased with reindeer fat, would slide over any kind of snow: in extreme cold the snow sticks to iron, and as the weather grows milder the runners get clogged with great lumps of ice.

'You'd do much better to stick to wooden runners,' he used to say. 'Iron's all right on a trail that's been hardened by constant use, but the soft snow you get during the migration is quite a different matter!'

They agreed: in the past it might have been better, but this was how they were going to do it.

Andis turned the sleighs upside-down, while Kristina, with a swab made of rag, tarred the iron runners to give them a good smooth surface.

'With plenty of tar, they'll slide all right,' said Andis.

He was in good spirits and smiling again, now that the sleighs were lined up outside the hut, repaired and shod. On each pair of upturned shafts Kristina had hung a set of harness that she had overhauled. All that had to be done now was to load up. Already Ellena had begun stacking some of them with reindeer skins, piling up sacks filled with a fantastic collection of useless objects which she nevertheless insisted upon taking with her. Preoccupied with the work in hand, no one paid the least attention to the biting cold that stiffened their fingers through the double thickness of their gloves, nor to their fatigue, nor to the passage of time; not even to their hunger. For Ellena had not prepared any soup: there would be plenty of time for that in the evening, while the bread was being made. Meanwhile, they had to make do with uncooked, frozen fish. She had cut up an enormous lavaret, and they were eating it with relish. Only Andis pulled a face:

'Raw fish again, mother! You might have changed the menu!'

But he was joking: he knew all too well that for a long time now hunger was to be their daily companion. Not that they would lack food, but simply that there would be no time to eat it: they would just have to keep going, gathering the reindeer, putting up the tent, taking it down again, but above all, keep going! Already their preparations had started up the intricate machinery of the migration and, if it was not yet running smoothly, nothing could now stop it, neither cold, nor hunger, nor exhaustion, nor tempests; not even if Simon Sokki were to change his mind and attempt to countermand it. From now on the reindeer were in charge: the great herd was on the move and they were bound to follow it, as they had done for thousands of years. They were in the grip of those obscure forces, which, year after year, drove them out on an endless journey that led nowhere; they had become wanderers upon the face of the earth; and so it would always be, as long as there were still reindeer and Lapps ...

And if they had forgotten this, the Old Man was there to remind them of it. He was their witness, ageless, coming none knew whence, set there to ensure that everything went on as it had always done! And, however lazy they might be in ordinary times, they could now think of nothing but setting forth, of journeying and suffering, for this was how it had to be.

Inside the hut, the stove had become red hot and was giving off a suffocating heat. With the back of her hand Ellena wiped away the filthy sweat that was trickling down her rosy-cheeked face, and went on stuffing senna[1] into a large sack. They would need plenty of it, for there was never enough to keep their feet dry inside their skallers. True, you could take it out of your moccasins every night and dry it, but when you had to walk for forty-five days through frozen snow—or worse, snow that had begun to

[1] A kind of long sedge-grass.

thaw—it was important to take particular care of this part of your equipment. She had already filled three sacks, but perhaps they ought to take a fourth. She heaved a sigh. This morning everything seemed to be falling on her. In ordinary times, Simon Sokki would have been there to give the orders and she would have obeyed him like the others, they would all have carried out their tasks without any argument. Having satisfied himself that everything was all right, he would have slung his lasso over his shoulder, harnessed his reindeer to his sleigh, and then, when everyone in turn had greeted him : 'Mana derivan, Simon Sokki,' and he had gravely replied : 'Bazza derivan,' he would have set off at the gallop.

Had there been time, Ellena would have felt despondent, for on this memorable day Simon Sokki was not there, and there was only the presence of the Old Man to remind her of their traditions. Hadn't he said that a Lapp who was not there when they were getting ready for the migration was no longer a Lapp?

Now, as the decisive moment drew near and they were about to leave Suojaurre to the wolves and foxes, Ellena was discovering how many things she had hitherto failed to notice. Their winter hut, well built and warm, the big clearing swept by the wind from the fjell, the birches of the tundra, astir with secret life, the wide, dead curves of the river which she had never seen flowing, since every autumn, by the time they had returned, they were already frozen solid again. At this time of year there were said to be plenty of salmon, and the kvaens and Norwegians made marvellous catches, whereas all they themselves ever got in the winter were one or two lavarets, caught with a hook and line through a hole in the ice, after waiting for hours in the freezing darkness, sheltered from the deadly wind only by a sledge tipped up on its side. Why should she suddenly feel overwhelmed with affection for this place to which she had been coming back for nearly thirty years? She loved this river, in the grip of the frost and invisible beneath the snow; it wound its way around Suojaurre like a fine avenue, free and untrammelled. She loved the pale sky of the fjell, with its procession of clouds floating like ships above the hills, and the distant mountains crowned by the sacred summit of the Agjiet! She discovered that she was deeply attached to Suojaurre, that she would miss the long winter nights, when gales made the timbers of the hut creak and everyone expected the roof to be blown off at any moment and be swept away like a handful of straw, high above the birches of the tundra prostrated by the wind. And suddenly the idea began to take shape in her mind that perhaps she would never again return to Suojaurre. Her heart beat faster. Until now, the only thing about the new kind of life they were proposing that had impressed her was its agreeable side : that it would be peaceful, regular, easy, free of danger. No more wolves, no more famine, no more stealing of their rendeer. All the year round she would be in a comfortable house, while the men took turns to herd the reindeer on the mountain. But how far they would have to go to attain this paradise, to that remote province of Tröndelag, which, for her, was situated at the furthermost extremity of the world. And it came to her that to get there would mean taking a journey from which there would be no return!

On the surface, however, nothing had changed. She was behaving as she had always done at this season of the year. When you migrate, you have to pack up everything, emptying the hut each morning as you do when you take down the tent and set out on the next stage towards the sea. The only difference is that here, in winter quarters, you stay a little longer : six months of waiting for the sun and the spring; and, until recently, it was the same tent that sheltered the family through the long Arctic night and the long days of summer. Nowadays, with the help of the Norwegians, the tent had been replaced by a wooden hut, comfortable but impersonal, and Ellena felt herself to be less attached to it than to the heavy, smoke-stained canvas tent, so often patched and mended, yet still serviceable. They were going away, and the doors of the hut would be left wide open : what did it matter if it was used by passing strangers? This house of theirs was nothing, it was the land itself that counted! And suddenly she realized that what had aroused her melancholy mood was the thought that she would have to leave this country of hills and lakes and marshes, into which, one day in May, already long ago, and in the middle of a great spring-time storm, she had been born. They had told her how the tent had almost been blown away, and how the men had braced themselves against the poles so that the women of the cita could help her mother to bear her child in peace. Despite these terrible memories, she loved the vidda stretching away into infinity, an infinity of vast open space, of sea, and desert, and steppes! The infinity of the heavens, the infinity of time, past, present and to come!

Here they had lived, remote from other men. For them, days divided into twenty-four hours had no meaning : there was only a long day and a long night, so that they lived three hundred and sixty-five times more slowly than other people! Were they prepared to launch themselves into the dizzy, thronging existence that was being suggested to them?

As the day wore on, the air seemed to grow more brittle with the deepening cold, and all around could be heard the noise of people getting ready to leave. Over there, in the second group of huts, where the Risaks and the Bongos lived, everyone was busy : Karin piling things into sacks; Andis and Mattis nailing up chests. There, as here, the women had long since ceased to worry about their appearance : their long, black plaits had come undone and hung about their shoulders, and their sweaty faces were grimed with soot from the stoves that they were dismantling.

Suddenly Ellena felt giddy : there was still so much to be done! She stared at the pile of reindeer skins she had taken out of store, the lumps of grease in the pots and pans, the bundles of sinews for making thread—all of which had to be sorted out and made up into loads. Kristina and the boys had already brought out their chests; hers would

77

be the last to be padlocked, after all the others had been loaded on to the sleighs. Like all the people of her race, Ellena set great store by the contents of her chest, though the total value of all the intimate objects it contained would hardly have amounted to more than a few crowns. But in a cita, where nearly everything is held in common, anything that belongs to you personally is priceless, for every memory associated with it has a dreamlike significance. Sometimes, when she was alone, Ellena would open her chest and tenderly handle everything it contained; and the other women did the same. Very rarely were they prepared to reveal their treasures to the public gaze. How could a stranger understand why one should prize so highly that yellowing snapshot taken in front of the mud-dried hut, those pieces of bark carved with reindeer earmarks, that threadbare silk scarf, once presented by an admirer? True, the chest might also contain a few banknotes and coins, but for Ellena these were of less significance. For her, money was something impermanent, something that came and went, something that merely enabled you to acquire real wealth—reindeer! Its value was only transitory. Once, someone had given Simon Sokki a splendid knife, with all kinds of blades and implements, and for a time it had amused him. Then the knife disappeared into his chest, since, for the work he had to do, Simon preferred his big Lapp knife, which was as handy for boring a hole in a shaft to take a strap as for cutting a reindeer's throat, or splitting a bone, or carving a block of wood. Yet occasionally he liked to bring out the elegant penknife to show to strangers, for the very fact that it was useless seemed to him to enhance its value. And Ellena felt the same way as her husband : that to be rich was to own things that served no useful purpose, that were superfluous.

Now it was time to start loading up, otherwise they would never be finished.

'You must give me a hand, Kristina!' Ellena called out.

And the two women got out the framework of the tent, and its canvas covering. It weighed a great deal, and had to be divided fairly between two sleighs. Tent, cooking apparatus and food were the women's responsibility; the men had to get ready the sledges and harness the reindeer, they were only concerned with the animals. Sorting out the various components of the tents was an extremely awkward job. First of all there were the three forked poles, which stuck out through the smoke-hole and supported the whole tent, so blackened with smoke and soot that they had become impervious to damp; Ellena could not remember ever having had to replace them. Then, to keep the skin of the tent apart, there were the two basketwork frames that had to be forced under the canvas and, to ensure that it was perfectly round and habitable, a dozen or so thinner poles that rested on these frames. The tent was completed by a moveable panel, forming the door, a hook and a chain for hanging the cooking-pot, and a kind of ladder, made from a forked branch, that they used for erecting it. When all this had been stacked on a sledge, the canvas itself had to be checked.

This, Ellena and Kristina laid out on the snow, so that they could make a final inspection of the heavy material, stiff with dirt and soot. It was made of sail-cloth and had been repeatedly mended; having been bought about fifty years ago from fishermen, it had originally been blood-red like the sails of most of the ships in the fjord. But of this original material practically nothing remained; it had been patched so often with different coloured materials that any appearance of uniformity was simply due to the layer of soot and smoke with which it was covered, and which had been exposed to years of rain, snow, sun and wind. A day or two previously the two women had mended the last holes, and the result of their efforts was revealed in the patches of brighter cloth with which it was now decorated.

'It's lasted a long time,' said Ellena. 'But I reckon this will be its last trip!'

Was this a veiled allusion to the possibility that was worrying them all, or simply a statement of fact? Kristina abruptly stopped working, and asked aggressively:

'What do you mean, mother?'

Ever since she had run away from school, Ellena had been afraid of her daughter's anger.

'I only meant that in the old days our ancestors used to make their tents by sewing reindeer skins together with sinews, and they never wore out: they would last a hundred years. Of course, it was hard work. My grandmother would spend a whole winter at it, and had three or four women working with her to get it finished. Still, canvas is more practical. And it costs practically nothing, as there's always a fisherman with an old sail to dispose of; or else you can buy one of those tarpaulins they use in the warehouses to protect fish-boxes. True, you've got to keep patching and mending them, but we can manage with this for another year.'

'I shall make the next one out of reindeer skins,' Kristina said casually.

But Ellena understood what she meant, and shook her head.

'You're in no position to criticize, Kristina. This will be the first migration you've made as a woman. Up to now you were only a child, our youngest one. You were spoilt, like any other child, and the migration was simply an outing for you. You could walk if you felt like it, but as soon as you wanted to ride any of the sleighs would give you a lift. You slept when you were sleepy, and ate when you were hungry. And there was always a reindeer skin for you to wrap yourself up in, and milk and sugar that I used to give you on the sly. But that's not what a migration is really like!'

'You're right, mother. But I'm not afraid of what has to be faced. You've been through it all, long before me.'

'You'll understand soon enough, Kristina. For the women, migration is no seaside jaunt, I can tell you.'

How could she make her mother realize that she was afraid of nothing? That, secretly, her heart leapt with joy at the thought that at last, like a true nomad, she was going to take her share in the free life that lay ahead of them? Nothing would ever make her change her mind. Already, unlike

80

the others, all the hustle of preparation, all the hard work of loading the sleighs, had filled her with a sense of peace.

By the end of the day, the hut was empty. Ellena kept going in and out, surprised by its spaciousness, for previously it had always seemed so crowded. Already it had become quite impersonal. After working outside, Kristina and Andis did not want to come indoors, and ate their meagre meal of frozen fish and coffee sitting on their sledges, outside in the wind and cold.

This was how it would be for weeks and weeks. Nothing could now prevent them from leaving, they had already started! They lay back on their sleighs as they would now have to do whenever they halted. The moment was inexorably approaching when the abandoned clearing would return to its summer solitude. The snow would rapidly melt, exposing the peat bogs, with their spongy mosses and swarms of mosquitoes, blown hither and thither by the wind, dark, humming clouds that would make life almost impossible for man or beast, even penetrating into the empty hut, abandoned to the foxes. But would it ever return to life again, when the first autumn snows began to fall, and when the ground, frozen to a depth of three feet or more, would once again make human existence tolerable? With a satisfied air, Andis contemplated the weary task of preparation that had been successfully achieved, despite all Ellena's complaints.

'It's nearly finished,' he said aloud. And he curled up on his sleigh like a gun-dog, pulling his cap over his eyes and determined to get some sleep. But, before he could doze off, he was interrupted by the trumpet-like voice of the Old Man:

'What about the stone? Why haven't you brought it out?' he yelled angrily.

They blushed, as though they had been caught in the act of committing a crime.

'The hearthstone he means,' said Kristina. 'We'd forgotten all about it.'

This was a large slab of granite, split along the grain,

81

and weighing well over a hundred pounds. It had been lying about all winter in the store room, and now, having carefully uncovered it, they carried it outside and, with two other flat but smaller stones, loaded it on to one of the sleighs. Both sides of the slab were blackened by fire, and it could be used either way up.

'It's come with us for forty years!' said the Old Man. He stood up energetically, and was stroking it as one might a piece of valuable material.

Respectfully the youngsters stared at the heavy stone which, from now on, laid on the snow in the middle of the tent, would constitute their fireplace.

Forty migrations, Kristina mused. In those days, what age would the Old Man have been? And suddenly becoming talkative as memories flooded his mind, he went on and on, while everyone listened in rapt silence.

'We discovered it, your grandfather, Aslak Sokki, and I, in a quarry on the island of Skjerpoy. It has acquired this surface in the course of its travels, but it was carefully chosen in the first place. That was the year your father was born. In those days everyone still used pulkas.'

Everything he talked about belonged to the past and had happened long ago. Andis shrugged his shoulders, but Kristina, looking the Old Man straight in the face, declared emphatically :

'It will make some more migrations yet, that old stone.'

The Old Man smiled, and she felt that his smile was for her as though it were she he had been thinking of . . . She began examining every sleigh, checking it over, giving orders : and, mechanically, Andis did what she told him.

'Change that shaft,' she said. 'Can't you see it's split? It wouldn't last ten miles !'

She was right. Andis started boring a hole in the branch of a birch tree, and five minutes later a new shaft had been fitted. Then it was a strap that had to be replaced, for most of the harness was made out of bits and pieces that had been used again and again, and very little of it was new. The collars were the one exception, owing to the skill that had gone into making them. A badly padded collar could injure a reindeer. The two pieces of which it consists must be polished and polished again, scraped and smoothed with the blade of a knife to make sure that it has just the right curve. Andis had spent hours and hours carving them, while his brother Pier, who was highly skilled, had painted them in bright reds and blues. The padding had been made by Kristina from bits of skin cut out of old pairs of trousers, then stuffed with reindeer hair and carefully sewn up. The job had been well done; even with heavy loads and in poor snow the reindeer would come to no harm.

By this time, twilight was filling the forests with ghosts and phantoms. The wind had risen rapidly as it did every evening, lowering the temperature in a few moments, sweeping through the clearing and covering the sleighs with a thick layer of powdery snow. There was still enough light to work by, and it was clear that the Risaks had not yet completed their preparations, for, from the direction of their hut, one could still hear bursts of conversation, the noise of a chest being nailed up, and then, drowning all other sounds, the piercing, triumphant voice of a man singing a yok about the migration.

Standing in the middle of the vast space in which he had lined up the loaded sleighs Andis was reckoning things out. First came the master's sleigh, ready for him if he turned up; then Ellena's and his own, then Kristina's, followed by the Old Man's pulka, and finally some dozen baggage-sleighs which were tied together in threes and fours, requiring only one driver.

'This time there's nothing else to be loaded,' said Andis, calling the Old Man to witness. But Ellena, who had overheard him, hurried outside and shouted :

'What about the bread and the stove, then?'

'What, mother?' said Andis, taken aback. 'You want to take the stove? It's just a waste of energy, considering we've got one at the gamma. Besides, think what a nuisance it will be! Don't you remember all the trouble Simon Sokki had when he was here?'

'I don't care! I'm not leaving anything at Suojaurre! Who knows whether we shall be coming back? Maybe *you* can tell me, clever boots?'

Andis hung his head. Nobody had ever been able to fathom his father's intentions, for he was continually changing his mind.

'We'd better load up the stove, Kristina,' said Andis, convinced, but no longer interested.

'As long as they've finished baking the bread,' she replied mockingly.

Let them load up everything and take it away; it was not of the slightest importance. She would have to discuss the whole question with Paavi, and until she had done that there was nothing to be done about it.

'You can start, Ellena, and I'll keep guard,' said the Old Man. He shut the door of the hut, leaving Ellena alone inside, as though she was to be cut off from the whole world. Nobody must disturb her while she was kneading the dough. Indeed, no one would have dreamt of doing so. From ancient times, this had always been forbidden, for an unclean presence could ruin the dough, and this was something they dared not risk. How could anyone be sure that, if a woman happened to enter the house, she would not temporarily be unclean? Rather than take any chance, the taboo, which in primitive times had been restricted to the female sex, was now extended to all human beings, even members of the family. So, until the following morning, Ellena would remain cut off from the world. The Old Man sat down outside the door, and everyone knew that he would not budge until the work was finished.

The others had settled down to spend the night outside, and it had already begun to look like a temporary camp. Kristina had lighted a huge fire, which she continually kept stoking, for there was plenty of wood. She had hung the big cast-iron cauldron on the tripod they were taking with them, and was cooking reindeer soup, while the others sat round in a circle, suddenly aware of being hungry as they smelt the boiling meat. To keep them quiet, Kristina handed round some more frozen fish, and the Old Man seated at the threshold of the hut, was chewing away at his portion. Despite the extreme cold and the falling snow, nothing would have persuaded him to leave his post. Squatting on the bottom step, huddled up in his furs, he looked like some domestic animal, and the illusion was accentuated by the presence of Chumbi, who lay curled up at his feet. The Old Man and his faithful dog allowed themselves to be slowly covered by the snow, which, flake after flake, delicately settled on them, after first dancing a wild saraband above the cheerful flames.

When it had grown quite dark and the flames of the camp fire were shooting high into the sky, the people from the neighbouring huts came to keep Andis and Kristina company. Earlier in the morning they had already brought flour and salt in proportion to their numbers, for Ellena was baking bread for the whole cita; a tiresome privilege, though one that she would not have dared to refuse, for it belonged by right to the mistress of the great herd. They arrived in small groups, like ghosts, for the rasping sound of their moccasins could scarcely be heard. Then, as they entered the circle of light, they uttered the usual greeting: 'Bouriz, bouriz,' and took their place in the silent circle, everyone giving himself up to his own thoughts, striving to penetrate the disturbing future that was awaiting them. No one dared to approach directly the question that was troubling them all; it was as though they had tacitly agreed to observe a truce. No one dared to admit what he was feeling to his neighbour. But if at that moment Simon Sokki had appeared out of the night, and announced: 'It's decided! We are emigrating to the Tröndelag,' all of them would have sprung to their feet in noisy protest. Doubtless the protest would have been purely formal, for they would do whatever Simon decided; he was the boss! They made no attempt to explain the almost superstitious feeling of fear they were all experiencing as the moment arrived to leave Suojaurre. Until that moment, they were free men, as Paavi had often enough told them; but what would they be later on? They brooded upon this for a long time, though it seemed to pass quickly. Then the lads started passing round a bottle of spirits, without any objection from the women, who even took a swig themselves! It was Martha Risak who set the example; hitherto she had remained silent, though, for her, every gathering was a pretext for drinking, laughter and singing.

She took a long draught; then, picking up an armful of wood from what was lying around, she recklessly flung it on the fire. She had overdone it, and for a moment it looked as if she had put the fire out; it was suddenly dark, and they could feel the night cold freezing their backs. But almost immediately a new flame burst forth, rose high in the air, crackling and flickering, lighting up the whole clearing—the people, the untidy camp, the dark background of the tundra. Revived, they listened to the cheerful song of the flames, which formed an accompaniment to the spritely dance of snowflakes, turning and twisting above the fire.

'You're wasting wood,' said old Martha Sokki-Bongo, the mother of Karin and Mikael. 'God grant we shall always have as much as we've got now!'

'What's the point of hoarding it?' Martha Risak retorted, cheeky as ever. 'Do you want us to leave it behind for the foxes?'

They laughed noisily, but old Martha shook her head. She hated to see anything wasted, having spent her whole life parsimoniously weighing out wood, meat, sugar. The alcohol was beginning to go to their heads, and gradually their superstitious fears died down as outbursts of collective laughter dispelled their misgivings.

'You'll remember this fire when we're crossing the fjell,' the old woman muttered.

'Plenty of time to think about that when we get there,' said Andis, irritated by her nagging.

They all knew what to expect when they were crossing the mountain : four days without firewood, without a shrub or a thicket, or even a dwarf juniper to light a fire with!

86

During the last migration they had had to burn one of the sleighs. But Martha was right. Since they couldn't take it with them, why shouldn't they use up all these logs they had split and sawn?

'Well, come on, then!' she exclaimed, suddenly exploding. She sprang to her feet and began hurling armfuls of dry wood into the flames, until the fire became an enormous furnace, giving out so much heat that they had to widen the circle.

Sparks flew into the air, fluttered among the treetops like fireflies, then disappeared into the darkness. Gusts of wind, ever shorter and stronger, followed one another in rapid succession, preceded by a muted roar like the sound of surf, produced by the wind forcing its way through the branches. The gale flattened the flames to a long carpet of fire, so that those who were in its path had to leap out of the way to escape being burnt. There were cries and shouts, partly of fear, partly of the hysterical veneration of fire that is common amongst the people of the North; and, as Martha relentlessly continued to throw on more and more wood, it was not long before the fire had got out of control and was leaping ahead, threatening to set everything alight: the forest, the camp, the sledges and the hut . . .

'Stop it, Martha, stop it!' yelled Kristina, who felt a religious fear of profaning the forest.

But Martha heedlessly went on with the sacrilege, throwing on branch after branch, dancing and singing; her tumbled hair floating over her shoulders.

'The devil's got into the girl!' said old Mrs Bongo.

'She's drunk,' declared Andis; and leaping about on his short legs, he finally managed to catch hold of her and throw her down in the snow, where the two of them rolled over and over to the delight of the onlookers.

'This'll quieten you down, you crazy creature!' he shouted, daubing her face with snow.

And, as though it had been awaiting this moment, the wind died away, and the flames flickered less wildly, rising and falling in a slow and regular rhythm that each time lit up a different part of the clearing, revealing here a sledge, there a resting reindeer, which suddenly emerged from the darkness, and as quickly disappeared again. For a moment, the firelight rested on the door of the hut, lighting up the Old Man, who, squatting on his heels and white with snow, was smoking his pipe, oblivious of what was going on around him. His sole concern was the task Ellena was occupied with; and every now and then her massive shadow could be seen through the small window, as she moved about or bent over her task.

The Old Man looked up at the sky. The stars were beginning to fade, the snow had stopped falling as soon as the wind died down, and the unbelievable cold seemed to accentuate that vague lightening of the sky, when it is no longer night and dawn has not yet begun.

CHAPTER SIX

THE thousands of reindeer belonging to the Sokki cita
slowly advanced towards the bald crest of the mountain.
Moving like the shadow of a solitary cloud they were making
for the North, driven by the mysterious instinct that deter-
mines the great migrations, a force against which the
herdsmen can do nothing.

Thor Risak and Paavi the Finn were angrily demanding
what had happened to Simon Sokki and why he was not
there to give the order to start. Time was slipping by; it
was already March 25. In two months' time the does would
be due to calve and, if there was much more delay, they
would still be on the move and the young calves would
get left behind for the wolves. Hadn't they suffered enough
losses already?—even if it was true that, despite the
thousand reindeer stolen by the Isaksens, the Sokki herd
was still one of the largest in the whole vidda.

Though the two herdsmen kept their thoughts to themselves, they had reached the same conclusion. Simon Sokki
ought to have come back! Only the leader of the cita could
decide when the migration should start. The situation was
serious. The herd, urged on by instinct, was already moving
irresistibly towards the coast and the mountains, and the
two herdsmen felt themselves drawn along by the powerful
current of the migration, which aroused in them primitive
longings, promises of savage enjoyment, as though they, too,
shared the restlessness that was tormenting the animals. It
was Nature herself that was responsible for this. The polar
night was rapidly giving way to longer and longer days,
the sun rising higher in the sky; already in a thousand imperceptible ways they were conscious of the changing re-
actions of the vegetation; the tips of the dwarf birches, on
which the snow-fowl were gorging themselves, were more

tender and, for days now, the feathery catkins of the willows had been bursting into flower, although the branches were still covered in a thick mantle of snow. Already these could be seen on every side—little tufts of down replacing the myriad flakes of snow deposited by winter.

The herdsmen were having difficulty in keeping the reindeer together. They kept straying towards the treeless hilltops leading up to the Agjiet, the sacred mountain away to the North. Ascending the southern slopes, the animals spread out over those to the North, and the men soon found themselves engaged in an unequal struggle, sending their dogs out to round up the reindeer, which formed such a serried mass that they looked like an immense cape of grey fur flung over the mountain, clinging to the surface of the snow, caught in the wind, fluttering, undulating, following the rounded contours of the land, hiding from sight, now a patch of gleaming blue ice, now the leprous stain of lichen where the snow had been swept away by the gales. The two men, muffled in their pesks, their big collars turned up and their richly embroidered scarlet caps, with the four tassels hanging down their backs, well pulled down, sped skilfully along on their skis, swinging from side to side on their short, curved legs, the swift movement of their hips aided by a long ski stick with a disc at the end; and now and then uttering a guttural cry scarcely distinguishable from the barking of the dogs whom they were urging to greater efforts. The reindeer formed an impenetrable mass, and the angry dogs flung themselves impotently at this redoubtable forest of thrusting antlers and sinewy, sharp-hoofed legs, occasionally sinking their teeth in an animal's hocks and being dragged along by the terrified creature, skilfully avoiding the dangerous horns, then, despite their masters' encouragement, suddenly turning tail, when a reindeer, bolder than the rest, turned to face them, and, rearing up on its hind legs, charged down upon them in a furious whirl of savagely kicking hoofs.

It was the does in calf that were most excited, their instinctive fears driving them on continually towards the

North; and with each fresh advance they succeeded in drawing the bulk of the herd a little further beyond the area within which the herdsmen were doing their best to contain them. They were irresistibly attracted by the forest, with its thickets of dwarf birch trees that stretched along the side of the mountain, forming a regular line beyond which glittered the snow-capped peaks of the Agjiet. Where better than in the forest could they hope to drop their young?

The barking of the dogs, the music of the wind, haunting as a dirge, formed a rhythmical background to the general stir of animals, men, dogs, branches and clouds. And this old, time-worn land, motionless for millions of years, suddenly began to move, to flow, as though brought to life by some cosmic influence. The time of day added to the sense of unreality, for the cold had become very acute, the daylight lingered on, and the sun hung above the crest of the hills, filling the whole sky with patches of mauve. The evening wind was blowing a spume of powdery snow over the surface of the earth, which immediately caught the rays of the sun, so that it looked as though the tundra was wrapping itself in a veil of ravelled pink silk; and, at the touch of its soft caressing light, the snowy, curving humps of the mountains took on the same colour, and the light moved as fleetingly as the shadows and the foxes. But this did not last long. A dying blaze of sunlight dissolved the snowy mist, and for a few short moments the tundra was on fire; everything took on the same tinge of colour, snow and rocks, reindeer and birch trees; the sheets of glittering ice on the mountains reflected the light like steel cuirasses, and the herdsmen's red caps stood out against the slope of the sacred mountain, brilliant as cranberries.

It was as though this fiery glow had brought the nervous excitement of the reindeer to a climax. What the herdsmen were especially concerned about was its effect upon the big grey animal. For this was a gelded male, which already had ten migrations to its credit, and round its neck was the bell worn by leaders of the herd. It kept leaving the others, head thrown back, antlers resting along its spine, sniffiing the air, trotting about, stopping, setting off again, skilfully avoiding the dogs; and in its wake other deer followed, one or two to start with, then more and more, until the movement became general, and slowly, steadily, still nibbling the tundra as they went, the whole herd began to move forward, pursued by the tireless men and harrassed dogs. And the herdsmen accepted it with resignation: this was as it should be! Since time immemorial it had been the deer who drew the men towards the sea in spring, and all the latter could do was to follow the herd, running behind it like the wolves and the wolverines—men, who for thirty thousand years and more have followed their wandering herds, living on them and for them, the oldest race of people on the earth, the Samisks who have come to be known as the Lapps. Thor Risak and Paavi dreaded the rapidly approaching moment when the herd would be completely out of control. But what could Simon Sokki expect? If he did not arrive soon it would be too late! Neither they nor the others would be able to restrain the massive strength of five thousand reindeer, driving a wedge into the snow and undergrowth of the tundra like the bows of a well-steered ship that can hold its course in the most powerful gale.

For the last two days the herdsmen had not allowed themselves a moment's respite. When the fate of the herd is at stake a Lapp can do without sleep. Vigilantly keeping watch in the biting cold, they were obliged more and more frequently to leave the snow holes they had dug in the lee of a snowdrift near the highest point of the mountain, a spot from which they could see the rounded summits, blue with ice and cold, far away on every side. Beneath them, the upward thrust of the dwarf birch trees stopped short two hundred yards from the summit, leaving a vast empty space, for beyond this line all vegetation abruptly ceased.

The deer had gradually emerged from the birch-covered tundra into this treeless area, and now floated on the wind-swept fjell like a raft driven by the currents, sometimes running aground on a reef of granite barely covered by the snow; and these isolated rocks formed little cliffs beneath which the lichen grew freely, thus giving the herdsmen a few hours peace, while the herd dug and scraped with their hoofs till their teeth and pliant muzzles could nibble at the moss that covered the frozen ground. Then, when they had had their fill, the deer would lie down for a few hours, sleeping and chewing the cud, and they were so well integrated with the landscape, fused with it, white as the snow, grey as the birch trees, that what had been nothing but a frozen empty waste took on the appearance of a new forest, sprouting spontaneously from the flank of the ancient mountain, a forest of branching antlers, swaying in the wind that blew from infinity and made the same sound as it did amongst the trees of the forest below. The big herd chewed the cud, lulled by its music, and the herds of men, motionless in their snowholes, dreamt away the time, squatting on their heels, protected from the cold and snow by their warm skallers stuffed with senna, their legs and thighs cased in the supple fur of their belingers, their bodies swaddled in blue cloth kouftes, and their long, broad knives hanging from their belts in sheaths made of tanned hide. The evening shadows grew longer, their fur pesks, flared at the bottom, formed little private tents from the top of which only the men's heads protruded, their faces hidden beneath red caps pulled down to their eyes, and the warmth of their bodies accumulated and increased until they felt it was good to be alive. But though they dozed contentedly, their eyes never strayed from the herd they were guarding which, by a thousand imperceptible signs, was already beginning to show that it was waking up once more. One animal would suddenly stand up, restless, head raised, sniffing the unknown smells borne on the wind, which the herdsmen vainly attempted to distinguish. Was it the scent of a distant wolf or of a scared blue fox! Or could it have been the sound of a snow-fowl's wings, disturbed from its nest by a blow from a reindeer's hoof? Thor and Paavi remained like this for a long time, waiting to see what would happen. They dreaded

93

the awakening of the old grey deer with the bell, for then once more he would start to draw the herd away towards the north, and a gust of madness would seize upon the animals, already trembling at the touch of spring. But when nothing happened, the herdsmen went back to their dozing.

Close as they were to one another physically, and intimately united by their common responsibility for the herd, a deep gulf existed between their innermost thoughts, and this was all to the good. Paavi the Finn had his worries, Thor Risak was full of his own hopes. The latter was recalling the Easter holiday at Viddakaïno. His head was still aching from the nights he had spent drinking and the sleepless days. It had been a magnificent spree; all day and night he had galloped about on his sledge drawn by his finest reindeer. The animal was superbly trained and superbly strong; qualities that are not often found in the same animal. He had entered it for the races. Two hundred sleighs had confronted one another on the frozen Elv. Major Thorp had set up a tent on the river bank, where the time-keeper was installed, and the course was marked out with red flags. A lot of tourists had turned up from the seaside towns, and they were enthusiastic about the heats. The huge frozen river was covered with a many-colour crowd, in the midst of which the hundreds of Lapps in their scarlet caps looked like a field of poppies, springing from the hard, wind-swept snow. The competitors had difficulty in controlling their restless and excited animals. And sometimes one of them would be dragged a considerable distance before he was able to scramble back again on to his sleigh. All the women were there wearing their Sunday caps and prettiest dresses, their shoulders covered with gay silk scarves, their bosoms decked with bronze jewellery glittering in the sun, and their slightly bandy legs sheathed in fur belingers.

Some of them had taken part in the race organized for women, in which, thanks to the care with which Thor Risak had made ready her sleigh, Karin Bongo had distinguished herself. He had checked all the thongs securing the sledge and the shafts knot by knot, the collar, the traces, and the double reins; and, when the time came, he had firmly held her reindeer by the head so that at the word 'go' she could take a flying leap on to the sledge. She had driven very well, and at a hundred yards from home was still in the lead, but a dog running out on to the course scared her deer so that it swerved aside. She had soon managed to bring the sledge back on the course, but this incident had cost her the victory and she had had to be content with third place.

Now, as he recalled the girl's disappointment, Thor Risak heaved a sigh. Poor Karin! He had done his best to console her, though in fact he was more upset than she.

'I'm going to kill that dog and win the men's race!' he had said. But she shook her head:

'Don't worry about the poor dog! Just win the race!'

And as she said this, he had seen that she was smiling at him with a face filled with tenderness, and he had suddenly realized that she was in love with him, that at last he had won her! He had overcome the long resistance with which the young girl had hitherto met his advances. All through the long night of winter he had patiently courted her with all the tact demanded by the fact that not only was he much poorer than she, but also the brother of Martha Risak, the wildest of all the girls! He used to meet Karin when she went to fetch water from the lake and carry her buckets back to the hut for her, full to the brim; he had always managed to be looking after the herd when she came to select an animal to be slaughtered for meat. Now he was reliving their first meeting in the hills. Karin had slipped in beside him in the snow-hole where he was keeping guard; he had put his arms round her to warm her and they stayed like this for a long time, huddled together, and that night he had made up his mind that she was to become his wife. He had waited all winter. Then Easter came with its revelry and feasting. When Karin had just failed to win the race he had taken her in his arms, exhausted and panting from her efforts, to console her. And feeling beneath her fur pesk the irregular beating of her heart, he had been overwhelmed with longing for her. But just at that moment, the starter had called out his name. Now he was determined to win for her sake!

He had taken his sleigh to be inspected by the jury, and his reindeer, frightened by the noise, arched its back, reared on its hind legs, striking out dangerously with its forefeet. He had had difficulty in holding it, and it took all his strength and skill to avoid the savage thrust of its head, for it had the wide-branching antlers of a deer that has reached its sixth migration. Scared by the shouting, by the people and the dogs, the animal rolled its protruding eyes and snorted wildly. The starter was already counting the seconds, and each one seemed to last a century. At last Thor let the infuriated animal go, and it had sprang forward with such a prodigious leap that the Lapp only just managed to catch hold of the sledge and fling himself face down upon it as it sped past him. Once he had sorted out the reins, he began to get the deer under control, though it was still galloping wildly, zigzagging, trying to escape from the course.

On his knees, firmly wedged at the front of the sleigh, Thor was now the master, and, realizing this, the animal calmed down and responded to his orders. The noisy crowd at the starting-post was now far behind them, and they were alone on the great frozen river. Thor talked to his deer, and, recognizing his voice, it fell into a steady gallop. It had all the qualities he had counted on for so long, a stout heart and sound lungs, so that all Thor had to do was to keep it going within its capabilities, sometimes urging it on, sometimes, when it showed signs of forcing the pace, holding it in. By maintaining that pace throughout the race, they covered the course in the best time, so that Thor became the winner of the biggest prize of the year. The thought of it made him purr with satisfaction. He could see the whole scene again, the cup being handed to him, not to mention a handsome sum of money; and the memory filled him with joy. He, the poor herdsman, had beaten all the best drivers from the citas both from the East and from the West; the unknown animal he had so lovingly trained had defeated the finest racing deer, belonging to the most important clans in Lapland, from Mattis Bira's to Aslak Siri's, and even Mattis Pentha's, who had been regarded as the probable winner. Thor chortled to himself : Mattis always wanted to go one better. He had insisted upon racing a deer recently taken from the herd, as yet ungelded and still completely wild. It had savagely turned him over in the snow, breaking the shafts, and then, as a crowning humiliation, slashed his face with a blow from its hoof as it struggled furiously, rising on its hind legs and striking out with its forefeet like a boxer at anyone who tried to get near it.

Mattis had lost and Thor had won! He had trotted slowly back to where Karin Bongo was awaiting him. It was as though everything had been arranged between them beforehand : he had tied the young girl's deer to the back of his sledge, she had got in beside him, they had wrapped the skins round their legs, and then he had driven her away, shouting with happiness as she huddled shyly at his side.

Then, with one arm round her shoulder, they had galloped all over the valley, crossing and recrossing the bridge over the Elv, stopping at Sara the kvaen's, where they had bought some spirits, plenty of it, since for once in his life, thanks to his prize money, Thor was rich; and they had drunk and drunk, and Thor had urged on his reindeer faster and faster, pulling out the bottle more and more frequently from his koufte pocket, then taking a swig and passing it to his companion, who had never once refused, for such has been the tradition ever since the Scandinavians first brought alcohol into the Samisk land. Drunk with happiness and aquavit—for often in the Arctic the two go together—they dragged out this interminable jaunt, which led them from one hut to another, always meeting friends as drunk as themselves, with whom they continued to drink until they no longer knew whether it was daytime or night. Many of the Lapps had already left Viddakaïno, and having done their Easter shopping and settled their accounts with John Haetta, had returned to their winter huts. Thor and Karin had stayed on two days longer, on the pretext of a baptism and two marriages, and the boozing had begun again. Karin, somewhat reserved to begin with, had displayed no fear now that he was with her. The hesitation she had shown all winter had disappeared. They made plans for the future, and reckoned up how many deer they would have in their herd. Thor did not have many, but Karin owned enough to make her a good match, especially as she knew herself to be well made and attractive, so that although amongst the Lapps good looks count for less than the reindeer a girl brings for dowry, she had this trump card in reserve. Martha Risak had been able to take advantage of this occasion. But Karin was convinced that Thor showed all the signs of becoming a great reindeer master; his skill in breaking them in, his infallible eye for a deer, just proved by his success in the Easter races, indicated that he was bound to become an outstanding connoisseur. Between them they would soon build up their herd. Besides, weren't Kristina and the Finn an example for them? The poor rupes-hunter, who, despite the execration of the Isaksens, was not afraid to sue for the hand of Kristina, the richest heiress of the Sokkis . . .

For a moment or two Thor let his mind wander. The herd was resting quietly, and the night was as peaceful as that marvellous night when they had returned to Suojaurre.

They had travelled from Viddakaïno to Galatina, stretched out side by side in the same sleigh. They had been caught in a great whirlwind of frozen snow that came scudding across the vidda, moving as swiftly as the sleigh. Still under the influence of alcohol, they had kept up their spirits by frequent recourse to the bottle, and the hours had slipped away, marked only by the regular click of the reindeers' hoofs on the frozen track and the sharp cries from the driver. Beneath the heavy furs, they had exchanged caresses, but though he had done his best to make them more intimate, she had energetically rebuffed his efforts.

'We'll get married next Easter,' she had said. 'Not before!'
And he had not insisted. Instead, he had urged on his reindeer with a savage cry that could have been heard a long way off.

'You sound like a wolf on the prowl!' Karin said to him.

But his only answer was an inarticulate grunt. And then, when the road ran downhill, he had broken into a headlong gallop, so that Karin had had to cling to him, terrified, yet transported with happiness.

Now he was thinking : still a whole summer, an unbroken day that lasts three months, and after that, the long winter night! He sighed. He did not share Karin's patient resignation when she said : 'A year soon goes by!' Sometimes he was worried : so many things could happen in a year. How could they know whether their plans would ever be realized! He hated it when she shook her head sadly, it was so unlike the Karin he knew, the precociously mature child, always gay and laughing. He knew what she was alluding to. Simon Sokki and his companions had not yet returned from their investigation of the Tröndelag. He was the leader, the cita's fate depended upon him, and if he decided to accept the Norwegians' proposal to emigrate, they would have to sell the herd and begin a new kind of life. Would it really be what they made it out to be, sweet and peaceful as a fjord in good weather?

Such questions continually plagued his mind, but, like most Lapps, he was not concerned to answer them. He lived for the present, and that was all that counted, for the past could not return and the future was in God's hands! So what? What was the use of worrying your head about proposals for some new kind of life, and dreading it as she did? On this matter she agreed with Paavi the Finn, who had warned them all. Like him, she thought that the men of the cita were too easy-going, too ready to accept the authority of her uncle, Simon Sokki. All the same, she did sometimes wonder about this stranger's behaviour! Although he had only joined the cita so recently, he had already begun ordering everyone about! She would rather it had been Thor, and she reproached him for being so spineless. But he refused to discuss the matter with her, though she had been prepared to go on all night.

He remembered the occasion. It had been a night as luminous as it was now. After leaving Galanito, where Maria Siri had given them boiling hot soup with plenty of marrow bones, they had alternately trotted and galloped until at last the exhausted reindeer had settled down to its own steady pace, its trembling nostrils drawing in the wind from the plain, which kept blowing the fine, powdery snow kicked up by its hoofs over the occupants of the sleigh. And he recalled the agreeable feeling of the cold, as it penetrated beneath the furs, damp with perspiration, where they lay huddled in each other's arms.

So intense was his memory of that long drive together that he suddenly felt as if he were suffering from an attack of fever. The over generous blood of his nomad ancestors coursed through his veins; his longing was the primitive instinct of the reindeer men, a violent current, surging up from the remote past, that reached its climax in the spring. He could not lie still, but rolled about like a young dog, shook his frost-covered pesk and leapt out of the snow-hole, noting the minutest details of the landscape, which he knew like the palm of his hand. But nothing could stifle the desire that was rising within him like the sap in the willows, thrusting up from beneath the snow. Then, as the cold grew more bitter, the fever died down, and he returned to his post feeling as though he had just awoken from a long, deep sleep. How many hours, how many days and nights had he sat here motionless, covered with frost like the tree stumps of the primitive forest! His thoughts, attuned now to the peacefulness of the night, followed an easier course. He had won Karin, now he was capable of anything! Soon there would be the long journey to the coast in the wake of the eager herd, and they would be able to soak themselves in the unending light of the great northern day, on the mountains by the shore, swept by the wind from the sea. He and Karin would make love amongst the whortle-

100

berry bushes, unseen by anyone but the huge eye of the sun floating above the waves! Of this he could be sure: for such was the Samisk tradition, approved by the customs of the cita and the warmth of their generous blood. Thus had their parents and grandparents loved one another long ago in the warm summer days. Karin had been right, a year soon goes by!

Beneath the thick, four-pointed cap they wear in the Oestfjellet, he sang softly to himself, nodding his head in time with the music; and his song was like the purring of a contented beast. But suddenly his heart overflowed, and he let out a wild, savage yell, hoarse and deep-throated as that of a wolf calling to its mate through the winter night. Then, soothed by this expression of his feelings, Thor returned to his dreams and, squatting on his heels, well protected by his furs, beneath the thick covering of windswept snow, he imagined Karin cuddled up against him, tender and submissive.

He awoke suddenly, breaking off his dream. From the valleys below came the cheerful sound of voices, and the barking of dogs and dry snapping of branches announced the approach of the sleighs. But it was still quite dark, and all he could see was the confused mass of the awakening reindeer, and the gentle slopes of the white mountains beneath the glittering vault of the sky.

'Here they come,' called Paavi, who was also bestirring himself. He could recognize their voices. Mikael Bongo, yokking at the top of his lungs, and Pier Sokki answering him from far away across the tundra.

Presently, with a din of crashing branches the two sleighs left the forest and headed straight up the steep, treeless slope leading to the summit of the mountain. The deer had moved forward in a succession of leaps, then stopped, heads lowered, panting, licking the snow to quench their thirst, their flanks heaving as they gasped for breath and their fur damp with sweat. They had made the long journey from Suojaurre without stopping. Stretched out face downwards on the leading sleigh, Mikael was singing away, and both he and his companions were obviously drunk. The yok flared up again, then died away in inarticulate phrases, but the meaning of their improvised song did not escape the herdsmen. It was the song of the great migration. At last the hour had come, and they would know what had been decided!

Mikael and Pier pulled up side-by-side in front of the herdsmen.

'The Old Man's here! We are starting . . .'

'And Simon Sokki?' asked Paavi.

'He has sent word that we are not to wait for him, but should obey the Old Man.'

'A fat lot that means,' grumbled Thor.

Of what was to happen they knew nothing, but this scarcely worried them. A new life was about to start that would last all summer.

'Let's have it!' Thor suddenly exclaimed.

Pier knew what he meant. From the inside pocket of his koufte he pulled out a bottle of spirits and passed it to his cousin. Thor and Paavi drank their fill, then drank again, until soon they were in the same condition as the others, and their voices joined in the songs of the newcomers.

When their thirst was quenched, Mikael took the lead, and the big, grey reindeer quietly followed behind him.

'Where are we to meet?' asked Thor.

'At the Bastevarre.'

It was a high mountain rising above Bastejaurre lake, which formed an outlier to the Agjiet, twenty miles west of Viddakaïno.

CHAPTER SEVEN

A L L night, alone in the hut, Ellena mixed flour, water and salt. Stripped of its familiar objects the empty hut seemed twice its usual size. Kneeling on the floor, the mistress of Suojaurre energetically worked the dough, kneading it with her fists, punctuating her efforts with a long-drawn 'Han!' She was by herself, while outside the others were singing, drinking and dancing, and every now and then a tongue of flame, shooting up from the fire, would shine through the window like the beam of a lighthouse. Her solitude she accepted, for the Old Man insisted upon her observing the tradition. With him guarding the door, no one would dare to cross the threshold! As though performing a ritual ceremony, she would stoop low over the mixing bowl, straighten up her body as she drew out the thick, sticky dough, then let it fall again, repeating the movements over and over again until the dough had reached the right consistency. It was exhausting work, but for hundreds of years the same ritual had been performed, and why should she seek to alter it?

She rested a moment, breathing quickly, and, with the back of her hand, wiped away the sweat that was pouring down her face. 'Yes,' she thought, 'things could change a lot if we didn't come back here. Fru Tideman has told me often enough how, in the Tröndelag, they have their bread delivered every morning! That would mean one job less to be done.'

She returned to her task, now kneading her memories and plans as energetically as the firm grey dough that she was working with her fingers. And the time went by, the too short hours of darkness giving way to long hours of dawn. Soon the first part of her job would be completed.

She counted the loaves. The stove was too small for her

103

to make really large ones, and she calculated that they would need one for each day. Allowing forty-five days for the journey, that would mean making forty-five loaves! She could not make as many as that, thirty would have to do. They would just have to ration themselves, for she was tired out and kept getting painful cramp in her arms. For the last few days they would have to manage without bread, or else send someone on ahead to the nearest port. As far as she was concerned she was kneading no more dough! Her woollen dress was stained with patches of sweat, and clung to her body. Besides, it was already daylight and there were other jobs to be done. She opened the door. The Old Man merely turned his head.

'It's finished!' said she, simply.

He let her pass and she walked over to the others, her hair coming down, her face dirty, her hands swollen. The last few hours had made her look ten years older.

'Come and sit yourself down, Ellena,' old Martha Sokki called to her solicitously.

She sat down beside the fire, and Kristina handed her a bowl of soup, which she drank greedily. Despite the bitter cold she felt as though she were stifling, and undid the neck of her dress.

The lads were sleeping on their sleighs, the dogs gnawing the bones that had been thrown to them, and Martha Risak had returned to her hut. Left to themselves Ellena and Martha Sokki-Bongo stared into the embers, glowing like a ruby that someone had dropped in the snow.

'Karin will stay and help you with the baking,' said Martha.

Ellena nodded her head, too exhausted to speak. The Old Man joined them and asked : 'When shall we be ready to start, Ellena ?'

'We shall be baking all day. I shall have finished this evening.'

'If we set out at night,' estimated the Old Man, 'we should reach the Bastevarre tomorrow.'

Karin and Kristina stoked up the fire and took it in

turns to see to the baking, which continued till evening. When they took the loaves from the oven they were still soft and smoking hot, but they stood them for a time in the frost, which soon hardened them, so that the boys were able to pack them into big sacks. The smell of warm bread hung in the air, and floated out over the tundra. Andis counted the number of loaves. Suddenly he broke off. 'What, only thirty!' But he stifled the angry shout that sprang to his lips. What was the use? His mother could not help it, her strength was exhausted. What she was expected to do was too much for one woman. None of the women ever had the energy to make enough dough. He worked it out : thirty loaves, thirty days—that would mean they would still be in the mountains. It couldn't be helped! The last few days of a migration everyone was always hungry. They would have to manage with reindeer stew and frozen fish. They would have all the summer to make up for it.

Towards nine o'clock of the second day everything was ready. The bread was packed, and it only remained to dismantle the stove; and for that Andis had to summon the men from the other families, for it was too heavy for a man to move by himself. The metal plates were still hot when they dragged it outside on rollers and loaded it up on the strongest of the sleighs. When this had been done, the Old Man himself came to make sure that it was properly stowed, checked all the straps and saw that the shafts and harness were strong enough. He appeared to be satisfied by his inspection.

'You want to be careful which reindeer you choose,' he recommended. 'Pick an old one that's nice and steady. A top-heavy load like this could easily upset.'

It was easy to imagine what might happen in the narrow gorges of the fjell.

Night had fallen by the time the long file of baggage deer arrived, shepherded by the dogs, who were leaping about in a tremendous clamour of barking and shouting men. The women rushed forward to meet them. All you could see in the darkness was a confused mass of antlers, heads and backs; a hundred reindeer was not many compared with the main herd they would be picking up next day, but everyone was in good spirits. The gathering of the lilleflock[1] was already a warning signal that the long journey had begun. All these animals had spent the winter apart from the others, restricted to a small lichen feeding ground half a dozen miles from Suojaurre. The owners had to go there and bring in one of the reindeer as it was required. In the main they were old animals, but strong and well-trained like those that had been gelded.

Now, everyone had to sort out his own animal and the darkness made this a long and difficult task. A dozen animals had already been caught when Mattis, who had brought them in, stopped, and pointing to a patch of sky towards the north, in the direction of the Agjiet, said: 'Look!'

Over the magic mountain the sky had just blazed up as though a fire had broken out, then the fire grew stronger, steadied itself, and soon it had become light enough to distinguish quite clearly the reindeer, the hut, the loaded sleighs drawn up in a line with their snow-covered tarpaulins.

'The aurora borealis,' said Kristina.

'At this time of year?' Karin remarked. 'That's strange.'

It was indeed astonishing. Streamers of fire criss-crossed in the sky and threw out incandescent elements that formed a shower of stars, lighting up earth and sky from east to west like a curtain of light. It was like some vast tapestry, woven of gold and silver thread, studded with precious stones.

'Nordlys! Nordlys!' shouted the Lapps.

'It's God who's sent him to us,' said Ellena, crossing herself.

The men seized the opportunity to catch the reindeer and harness them. They were singing merrily, for the aurora borealis was saving them a lot of time. It gave out a golden light, less harsh than the sun's yet more alive than the moon's; all the elements of which it consisted flared up, sparkled, died down, revived again, in an endless succession

[1] Small herd.

106

of fireworks. It was as though a curtain of flame was slowly dripping from the firmament on to the sombre mass of mountains and hills, and then running down them in a stream of rubies. This luminous veil was wafted by the breath of cosmic winds, and, as the phenomenon attained its fantastic climax, men and women all stopped working, gazing at the celestial display with conflicting emotions.

'If we're going to take advantage of it we must hurry,' said the lads. 'It won't last long!'

It was sufficiently unusual, an aurora borealis so late in spring! As a rule they occur during the long Arctic night, and the magic light that pours down hour after hour is like a benefaction from heaven. Despite their familiarity with the phenomenon, they were always moved by it, filled with admiration and gratitude and, at the same time, with pride, for they had heard that they were the only people on earth who ever experienced it. In other countries night was night, but here the Nordlys was able to transform the polar darkness into a sublime fairyland. For no other race in the world did the heavens adorn themselves with such splendour!

One or two of them, however, regarded the fiery glow in the sky as a warning. It was extremely rare for an aurora to occur at the end of the spring, and this one had appeared just as they were on the point of starting.

Ellena shuddered: things couldn't have been worse. It was a sign from heaven!

'We shall never come back now,' she said softly to Kristina.

'Will you be quiet!' the girl retorted bitterly, suddenly feeling forsaken and defenceless. 'Oh, Paavi, Paavi, why aren't you here?' she murmured.

He was the only one who could have interpreted the signs and given them hope; and she turned to the Old Man. He had seen it all, heard it all, yet he remained impassive.

'What can it mean?' she asked. 'Why should the Nordlys come now at this particular time?'

'Because in three days from now there's going to be a great storm!'

107

'And then?'

'Then?' he replied as though he had not understood what she meant. And that was all.

But to the others his meaning was clear : he was treating this phenomenon as belonging to the natural order of things. Everyone knows that the Nordlys gives warning of storms, they were satisfied with his explanation, there was no need to look for any other.

Disappointed, Kristina went off to her sleigh.

The aurora borealis died down, and a new day arose out of the short night; the fifty sledges of the Suojaurre, already harnessed and forming groups of five or six vehicles under the charge of one driver, were drawn up in the order sanctioned by custom on the trail leading to the Bastevarre. Each man held his reindeer by the head, doing his best to control it, but the restless animals reared and plunged, thrusting dangerously with their horns; and their impatience was beginning to affect the men. They ought to start. What was the Old Man waiting for? Yet no one dared to speak.

But at last he had made up his mind, exhaled a last cloud of smoke, stuffed his pipe into his koufte and got up. Immediately the whole scene changed, sprang to life, as though he had some secret power over their lives.

He put on his skis and made a quick tour of the clearing, swaying to the rhythm of his long ski stick, checking the harness, pointing out where a sleigh had been badly loaded. His harsh metallic voice rang out so that everyone could hear him as he gave orders, criticized, scolded, till it seemed to fill the clearing, reducing reindeers, dogs and people to silence. Scared and uneasy, no one uttered a word.

Whence did he derive his strength, this living mummy, skimming along with the grace of a young man on his long, narrow skis? His keen eyes missed nothing. Even if Simon Sokki is not here, thought Ellena, the Old Man is quite capable of taking charge. And when, at last, he was satisfied, he untied his reindeer and took his place at the head

of the convoy, ready to lead the way in his old pulka, with
its tapering prow like that of a viking ship.

'Let's go!' he cried, without looking behind him.

'Hang on just a moment,' Ellena called out in a voice
that was almost pleading.

The mistress of Suojaurre turned back, the door of the
hut had not been properly closed, and already the wind and
the cold were taking possession. A film of powdery snow
had already covered the beds, benches and tables, and
filled up the cracks between the floor boards. For a moment
Ellena stood listening. Instead of the familiar noises she
could hear new and disturbing sounds: the wind murmured in the gaping hole where the stovepipe had been;
the partition between the two rooms creaked; snow was
fluttering about in the draught. There was nothing to keep
her here. Suojaurre was a house without life, a heart drained
of blood. She must go!

Slowly she pulled the door to behind her. What was the
use of locking it. Thieves could break it open if they wanted
to and travellers in distress would be able to take shelter
there.

'Ellena,' the Old Man called impatiently.

Without hurrying she returned to her sleigh.

'We ought to start, Ellena,' said the Old Man.

She took her place in the string of sledges. Everything
had changed. In previous years it would have been Simon
Sokki who said, 'It's time we started, woman!' It was he
who used to get everything ready; the Old Man only intervened when difficulties arose. Simon was always bursting
with energy, hurrying about, swearing, losing his temper,
though no one was afraid of him, and, if they obeyed him,
it was simply because he was master. And when he calmed
down again he would pass round the bottle, restlessly moving
about from group to group till everyone was singing and
laughing, and the departure became a kind of holiday.
Today, thought Ellena, anyone would think we were running away. She had a feeling that she was turning her back
on a life that had been a happy one . . .

'Right!' she said to the Old Man.

He gave the signal, and as he stepped forward the movement was transmitted from sleigh to sleigh, from man to man, and reindeer to reindeer. Like a steamer that takes time to get under way, as though it had difficulty in tearing itself away from the quay, the migration had begun. Sledges that were too heavily laden promptly stuck in the snow, and, in order to pull them out, the courageous reindeer had to dig their broad, sharp hoofs into the snow to get a foothold, arching their backs to take the strain. Men and women hurried hither and thither, shouting encouragement to the animals, keeping an eye on the strings of sleighs and calling to the dogs, who leapt about barking, snapping at the hocks of the reindeer, as every now and then they turned on them with a sudden thrust of their horns and sent them spinning through the air, howling with pain. People bumped into one another, suddenly stopped, yelling and swearing. Then everything grew calm. In front, the Old Man led the way with his long, supple stride, and his well-trained reindeer followed him like a dog, drawing the light pulka, setting its hoofs carefully in the parallel tracks made by his master's skis. Behind him came Ellena, then Martha Bongo, followed by the youngsters driving the most heavily-laden sleighs, and by the time the last one had left, driven by Mattis, a broad pathway, hard and shining, stretched away into the forest.

The Old Man crossed the frozen river Elv and climbed the opposite bank, choosing the most favourable route and moving slowly. The migration had not yet found its proper rhythm, but the time would soon come when everyone would be able to keep going night and day, without thinking about it, almost automatically. As yet it was too early for this: progress was spasmodic. Deer would suddenly stop, and those behind taken by surprise, would overrun the sleigh in front, get tangled up in the breeching, and then have to wait until things had been sorted out before they could start again.

The Old Man was the first to reach the top of the slope.

Behind him straggled the long convoy. Some of the sleighs had overturned, scattering their loads. The sight of this confusion did not unduly worry him : this is how things always went when they were migrating ! The first stage was the critical one, for it was then they had to pay for inadequate preparation and careless repairs—with broken shafts and burst straps ! Only then order would be restored.

Fortunately, he thought to himself, the weather is favourable. The extremely hard frost facilitated the smooth running of the sledges. He examined the sky, and the appearance of the drifting pink-tinged clouds warned him of an approaching storm. The only question was, would it break before they reached the Bastevarre?

Before long the whole convoy had caught up with him. This was to be the first brief rest. The winded reindeer started licking the snow, and clouds of steam from their sweating flanks enveloped the whole caravan. After the strenuous climb, everyone was happy to rest for a moment, and they quickly broke up into groups, as the older ones sought one another out and the young men went in search of the girls.

From the top of the hill the wide clearing of Suojaurre, with its deserted huts, could be clearly seen. There was no sign of smoke from the chimneys, but the broad trail of trampled snow made by the passage of the convoy was plainly visible.

'Suojaurre, Suojaurre!' sang Mattis, and everyone listened admiringly to his improvised yok :

'Oh land of the wind and the snow,
When the sun tired out by its long summer's labour
Returns to its three months' sleep,
We shall come back to Suojaurre
And the night of a thousand stars !'

'Oh, shut up !' Kristina shouted, on the point of tears. 'It's no use challenging fate !'

But already the Old Man was summoning them to set out again.

'Come on, now! We've got to get as far as the Bastevarre tonight.'

Overhead, the filaments of pink light were already disappearing behind banks of heavy, greyish cloud, while all around them the hilly countryside stretched away to an infinity of snow and forest and lake—snow and forest and lake, repeated again and again.

PART TWO

THE WOLF OF THE BASTEVARRE

CHAPTER ONE

THEY had been on the march since dawn and were no longer conscious of fatigue.

In this endlessly repetitive landscape of lakes and forests, clearings and hills, time had ceased to count; the twilight of an Arctic spring dragged endlessly on, and though all day the wind had been tearing and scattering across the steely sky the long grey streamers that announced the coming storm, this now seemed to have disappeared behind the bald hills of the Samisk countryside. The huts of Suojaurre had long been left behind, and the men and women of Simon Sokki's cita tramped through the virgin snow of the vidda, while their sweat-drenched reindeer drew the sleighs over its frozen surface, occasionally arching their bodies in a tremendous effort to haul them free of a sudden patch of slush.

Above the convoy, as it wound its way through the undergrowth, hung a cloud of steam, formed by the warm breath of men and beasts. In these huge empty spaces, sounds took on the sharp, brittle quality of breaking glass, as though the cold were snapping off each separate syllable of the phrases exchanged by the drivers as their sleighs passed one another. Some were drunk and had started singing, and the brief, raucous notes of their yoks fell drop by drop through the transparent silence to dissolve amongst the furious barking of the dogs, who ran up and down through the string of sleighs, sometimes leaping right over the loaded vehicles and falling exhausted between the feet of the panic-stricken reindeer.

The first hours of the great migration are always the worst. Everyone suffers from the cold and the hunger, from the fatigue and lack of sleep, for hibernation in the close, warm atmosphere of the huts has weakened their powers of resistance, slowed down their reflexes; and it is not until they have been a long while on the march that they are able to adapt themselves once more to their new rhythm of living.

In front marched the Old Man, still maintaining the slow, regular pace at which he had set off. Hour after hour he continued with the same swaying movement, shifting his weight alternately from one short, curved leg to the other, driving his skis forward without apparent effort, and occasionally lengthening his stride with a long sweep of his ski-stick, driving it home now on one side, now on the other, like a man steering his punt on the peaceful waters of a canal. He still remained fresher than any of them, even when some of the younger members of the convoy were beginning to complain that it was time he called a halt, a few minutes rest, to break the long stretch between Suojaurre and the Bastevarre.

Most of the men, and some of the women, were still sleeping off the effects of the spirits they had drunk before starting. And, heedless of the wind and the cold, they drifted along, lying face downwards on top of the loaded sleighs. Those who had kept some in reserve, now emptied their last bottles of contraband alcohol, then fell back overwhelmed by a kind of drunken lethargy and leaving the string of five or six sledges they were in charge of to the discretion of the leading reindeer. But this did not last long : the runners would get caught in a rut and the sledge would overturn, throwing its driver into the snow. Heedless of their plight, those behind merely swerved aside, leaving the staggering driver to his own devices, as he disentangled his reindeer from the harness, tied it up to the sledge while he re-loaded, sorted out the traces and once more got it between the shafts . . . All the driver then had to do was to catch up with the convoy, shouting at the maddened creature, whose main desire was to rejoin the rest of the herd. Straining at the traces, it would struggle up the frozen slope and eventually overtake the others at the top of some windswept hill.

Presently, the wild enthusiasm with which they had started was overcome by fatigue. The cheerful yoks, the shouting, the exchanges between one driver and another gradually died down. Each man silently confronted his own exhaustion, which only he could overcome. The long convoy of reindeer and sledges seemed to glide ahead on its own, like a phantom caravan led by the ageless skier. But despite the endless space, despite the blinding glare of the snow which seemed to subdue the men, the dogs retained an extraordinary vitality: indefatigable marauders, they leapt about like mad creatures, barking and quenching their thirst with mouthfuls of powdery snow, for they knew the hunting season had returned, and occasionally one of them would break away from the train and dive into the woods in pursuit of a blue fox. Then it would come back to the convoy, shamefaced, its tongue hanging from its mouth and, leaping on to a baggage sleigh, would curl up on top of the load and go to sleep with its muzzle between its hind legs.

The route the Old Man was following was familiar to them all, and yet every time it struck them with the same sense of wonder as if it were leading them to an unknown land where happiness awaited them! Mysteriously as the shaman which he might well be, he had decided exactly what time of day the migration should start; they would only stop when he judged the amount to be favourable, and no one dared to dispute his orders. Yet, effortlessly gliding forward on his long, birch-wood skis, leading the reindeer with the bell round its neck, his ancestral pulka skimmed over the snow drifts like a kyak over the waves.

Behind him came Ellena, fat as a dumpling in her layers of petticoats and furs. Instinctively she had assumed the position of the nomads, sitting with her right leg folded under her, her left leg hanging over the side of the sleigh, the tip of her skeller skimming the snow, ready to jump out immediately if the occasion arose. She maintained this tiring position without effort, sitting bolt upright, her face, red with cold, exposed to the wind, yet protected by her cap, firmly tied under her chin. Five long, low baggage sleighs were attached one behind the other to her personal sleigh. Then came the men and women of the cita, each driver being responsible for several vehicles. As long as the track was flat and well-worn everything went well, though occasionally one of the lads, taking advantage of Ellena's absent-mindedness, would tie his reindeer to the sleigh in front and, leaving it to its own devices, jump on to one of the girl's sledges, slip in beside her under the furs and abandon himself to love-making.

The anarchy of departure had given way to a kind of well-ordered march, in which everyone had his place; the strongest reindeer naturally found themselves at the front, the laziest of the Lapps came far behind, while the Old Man kept an eye upon everything. The loiterers annoyed him, because he had to call a halt to enable them to catch up with the others.

The same landscape of hills and lakes still stretched away to infinity. The going was easy : frozen plains, where the wind carved waves in the snowdrifts, alternated with the smooth surface of glittering lakes. A thick growth of dwarf birches gave way to the forest, which scaled the hills, already shrouded in evening clouds. And these hills had to be crossed. Clambering up their slopes, reaching the top, sometimes took several hours, and then they would skim along between the snow and the clouds in a mist of cotton wool that deadened all sound. But once they were out of the cloud the sun would shine forth again and then, ahead of them, a denuded hillside swept down towards a fresh valley, drowned in the greyish tundra, suspended like a cloak over the undulating snow; then in the distance other lakes appeared, more forests, more hills, and clouds looking like mountains that lost themselves in still more clouds.

Somewhere in this desert was the Bastevarre, somewhere beyond the hills, icy blue and snowy-white, and sometimes grey with forest, that rose in tiers on every side as far as the eye could see.

To everyone's relief, the Old Man at last called a halt,

on the summit of a hill which had only been reached after a gruelling climb. Slowly the laggards caught up. The Old Man scanned the landscape, then fixed his gaze upon a particular point on the horizon that had attracted his attention. Facing them, on the other side of a broad valley, on the skyline, a large dark, moving stain spread out over the expanse of snow; it might have been taken for the shadow of a cloud, twisted by the wind's caprice, its shape continually changing, drawing out, fraying at the edges, dwindling away, and then, like some gigantic squid, shooting out its tentacles, clutching at the sides of the mountains, before withdrawing again and becoming once more a dark, motionless patch of colour.

There was no need for him to explain what it was: everyone realized that it was their enemy! With their thousands of reindeer spreading out like a provocation, they had come to jeer at the Sokkis. Andis was the first to hurl defiance at them, and his shrill, raucous yok carried his message of hatred and vengeance into the enemy camp. He broke off, and everyone listened. And presently, very feeble, yet, despite the distance, clear in the limpid air, could be heard the tribal war songs of the Isaksens.

Instinctively the men and women of the cita closed in around Ellena, who, with her hands raised to protect her eyes, was estimating the number of reindeer owned by the men of the Vestfjellet.

'How many do you think they've got?' she asked the Old Man.

'Eight thousand, at least!'

'And all stolen!' she spat out scornfully.

'It's no use worrying about them being stolen. The point is, they've got them!'

Not long before the raid the Sokkis had been the most powerful of the tribes. Now, they were weakened by a series of vendettas, whereas on the other hand fortune had smiled on their hated enemy, and the Isaksen's herd inexplicably prospered. Their reindeer now covered the top of the hill, and careful observation made it possible to distunguish them more clearly from the dark mass of the tundra with which they seemed to merge. The thousands of deer were straying about in a dense mass that looked like a carpet borne on the wind. A few feeble cries and insults were exchanged between the herdsmen across the valley. Then the Isaksen's herd withdrew beyond the horizon and disappeared from sight.

Meanwhile Simon Sokki's people remained rooted to the spot, bitterly submitting to the affront that had been offered them. The Old Man shook his head, their attitude boded no good.

'Look after your reindeer,' said he, 'take good care of them! During the next few weeks, our road will be parallel to theirs. The Isaksen's will be following the other valley to the coast; they're going to Kvenangen while we're making for Nordreisa. So look to your reindeer! Make sure that between their valley and ours there's always a range of mountains separating us, or a forest. Take care that our deer don't stray on to their territory, for any excuse to plunder us will be good enough for them!'

As luck would have it, of all the main migration routes sanctified by custom, the one that belonged to the Isaksens ran parallel to the Sokkis; for under Samisk law each family was allotted a succession of valleys, lakes and hills where the lichen was plentiful, so that all would have a fair share. But the law also decreed: 'Woe unto him who allows his reindeer to stray into his neighbour's territory!'

Deep in thought, Kristina, erect in her sleigh, stared at the forbidden hills with unseeing eyes. She could have cried with anger! Angrily, Karin said to her:

'They're trying to humiliate us. That's the first time they've ever been on that mountain. Their trail runs along the bottom of the valley, and doubtless that's where their sledges are. They drove their reindeer up to the top on purpose, for there certainly isn't any lichen there. Aiee, aiee, aiee!'

'One of these days I'm going to show them a bigger herd than they've ever had,' Kristina muttered. 'I'll show them thousands and thousands, and then it will be my cita's turn to crow over them!'

'You're talking like a child,' said Karin. 'You don't even know if we're ever going back to Suojaurre.'

'I don't mind whether it's Suojaurre or anywhere else, but I'm coming back to this part of the world in the autumn. Whatever happens, I swear I will come back.'

And standing erect on her sledge she towered above the horns of the deer, and her short, blond hair, escaping from her cap, floated in the wind. Her glance was hard and scornful, and she dominated all the others, who were sitting slouched on their sleighs, or squatting on their heels beneath their pesks so that they looked like human tents.

'You may be right, Kristina,' Karin conceded, obviously impressed.

The Old Man had already set off again and far ahead of them the string of sleighs, people and reindeer stretched out behind him. A wide area of trampled snow marked the place where they had halted, and from it, like a great, dark ditch dug in the snow, the way they had come stretched away to the south. For a moment the younger ones had hoped that the Old Man would order them to pitch their tents, but they were soon disillusioned. He continued to forge ahead with the same slow regular gait, and there was no indication that he intended to stop.

'Let him get on with it,' said Mattis. 'What's the use of hurrying? We shall all end up at the sea, just the same!'

'Oh yes, of course!' retorted Karin. 'It doesn't worry you if the does give birth on the way, that will simply mean less to get rid of, I suppose!'

'Stop quarrelling, children,' said Ellena. 'The Old Man is right. He knows what he's doing. It's still cold, and that means snow. Who knows what's going to happen to us during the next day or two!'

Her words turned their thoughts to the threatening storm. After the warning signs that had accompanied their departure, the aurora borealis, the red clouds and the driving winds, everything seemed to have quietened. Only the cold remained acute, and yet everyone knew from the slightest, most subtle signs that it was merely a lull, that they could not hope to escape the storm. The one thing no one could tell was whether the lull would last two or three days, or longer.

Kristina was the last to leave the hill-top. They annoyed her with all their arguments. Her brother Andis lagged behind, slowly mending a shaft, moving listlessly and uncertainly. He was in charge of the six sleighs that carried the greater part of their camping equipment.

'Why don't you pull yourself together,' she said angrily.

'If father had been here, I'm pretty sure we should have set up camp!' said Andis. 'There's more lichen here than at the Bastevarre! It's nine o'clock, and we've been on the go since dawn. Don't you reckon that's enough? The way the Old Man's going on, we shall have to put the tents up in the dark!'

'You needn't worry about that,' said Kristina, 'because we shall keep going all night. I can tell you that as sure as if I were the Old Man himself!'

'That's just what I'm afraid of,' said Andis sulkily. 'I'm absolutely starving!'

'Tighten your belt, then. You'll have plenty of time to let it out again later on.'

She was right and he knew it. There was no one like his sister, not even Simon Sokki, his father, for he could never make up his mind! Wherever did she get all this energy from?

'You ought to have been a man,' he flung at her irritably.

Then, leaping on the leading sledge, he let his reindeer go and started forward, drawing behind him the six thumping, zigzagging baggage sleighs, which followed in the ruts made by those that had preceded him like toboggans. Then, as no one else remained behind, Kristina let go the reins, and her gelding leapt ahead and began to overtake the others.

The descent was soon made. The convoy was strung

out for more than a mile, so that by the time the Old Man had reached the flat surface of a lake the last sleighs had scarcely left the top of the hill. So steep was the slope, that the weight of the loaded sleighs forced the deer to go at a gallop, with the result that some of them, getting caught up in the harness, ran off the track and plunged up to their withers in the powdery snow; and, in their formidable efforts to free themselves, their huge, round, staring eyes made them look like creatures out of a nightmare.

The twilight lasted for a long time; already at this season of the year it was never really dark, and the faint glow, enhanced by the glittering light from the stars, hung over the tundra for hours. Though it was not actually dark, nevertheless you could only just distinguish the difference between a copse and a clearing; and the continual half-light was depressing.

Occasionally, far on ahead, the tinkling bell of the Old Man's reindeer could be heard. And he, without forcing the pace, without slowing down, apparently tireless, kept thrusting steadily on his skis, drawing the whole cita in his wake. He was immune from hunger, thirst and fatigue; so remarkable were his powers of resistance that, to the Samisks, they had come to seem supernatural; and as the years went by his ageless personality struck them as being even more extraordinary. More than a shaman, to them he had become an envoy from God, a prophet, charged with the responsibility of leading them into a faraway promised land.

Later on, they arrived at a place between two lakes, where they had to clear a way through a narrow gorge blocked with snow and fallen trees. It was dark when they got there, and the terrifying silence was broken only by the noise of their coming, so that it was a relief to hear the silky squeal of the runners on the snow, the harsh crunch of a sleigh striking against a hidden block of granite or a buried tree trunk, the harsh breathing of the reindeer as they strained at their collars. But, in addition to these familiar noises, the men and women could also hear imperceptible night sounds that increased their feeling of dread. In olden days, this defile had been a death trap, and it took all the Old Man's courage to persuade them to enter it at night. Far above its deep granite sides, gleaming with ice, the sky glittered with stars, but in the gorge the wind whistled and howled. The Lapps were no longer talking and laughing. All they wanted now was to get out of the defile as quickly as possible, seeking towards the north the faint glow in the darkness where the Bastejaurre lake stretched away like a great fjord amidst its encircling mountains.

Halfway through the defile a sledge turned over in the slush, and the convoy found itself cut in two. It belonged to Martha Sokki-Bongo, and the old woman tried in vain to get it back on its runners. A shaft had broken, which meant that a new one had to be cut out from the branch of a birch tree, a hole bored in it with a knife and a broken trace mended with a length cut from a lasso. The men set to work, kneeling in the snow, their bare fingers red with cold, and all of them were thinking about those who had gone on ahead and by this time had perhaps emerged from the accursed gorge, while they were left behind, frozen, hungry, stupid with exhaustion, struggling to get this ill-fated sledge out of the hole where it had stuck.

This was the only incident and Martha Sokki, once more in control of her reindeer, drove it forward along the smooth tracks left by the others, and the others followed her. Further on the gorge widened out, and as a result the darkness lifted a little. Feeling more cheerful, Mattis and Andis began yokking lustily, and this brought some little comfort to everyone's heart. Soon they would be at the Bastevarre! They would be able to eat, drink and sleep!

Bringing up the rear, Kristina had dropped the reins and was dozing beneath her furs. Chumbi, her favourite dog, who was curled up at her feet, kept her wonderfully warm. She had merely laughed at the fears of the others, and had not deigned to get down to help old Martha. Everyone must look after their own affairs; she never asked anyone for anything. Proud and haughty, she stared up at the stars scintillating in the sky. She was not afraid of trolls or stallos, and delighted in the supernatural. All around her, constellations flared, and now and then, like a ball of fire, a falling star streaked across the firmament, where, despite the darkness, filaments of rosy, orange light had already begun to appear. The signs from heaven did not lie.

'The Old Man was right,' she thought. 'The storm won't be long now!'

The thought of it disturbed her, for the following day the main herd should be at the Bastevarre, and from then on they would have to protect the reindeer from blizzards, stop them getting lost in the fog and, above all, prevent some of them being instinctively attracted to the enemy herd which was following a parallel route behind the next range of hills . . . Yet though she was disturbed by the thought of losing a single one of her reindeer, she was reassured by the knowledge that tomorrow Paavi would be with her. This would minimize the risk, for Paavi himself was worth more than all the other men of the cita put together. With Paavi and the Old Man they could manage without Simon Sokki. Yet she could not help feeling angry when she thought of her father: he should have been here with them, instead of which he was perhaps already selling to strangers those reindeer that he had not allowed to be stolen from him!

The Old Man had reached the Bastejaurre. The great lake, trapped by the ice, was a continuation of a marshy plain, on which the poles put up for drying hay in the summer could still be seen. Birch woods covered its shores and crowned its occasional granite cliffs. And beyond it the naked, gleaming slopes, covered with melting frost and grey snow, stretched away to the grey clouds hiding the hills, so that the mountain of the Bastevarre seemed to rise endlessly into the sky, and all that was visible was its huge base encircled by the lake. The fresh snow, driven and polished by the wind, lay in irregular layers, gathered in restless heaps in the ravines; and wherever the snow had

125

been blown away one could see the leprous growth of the lichen.

'The reindeer will have plenty to eat,' Ellena exclaimed. And the Old Man nodded in agreement.

The sleighs had halted as soon as they had arrived, all mixed up together, and their exhausted drivers, stretched out on their loads, pulled their caps over their eyes and immediately went to sleep. It must have been about four o'clock in the morning, for already it was beginning to grow light, and imperceptibly the surrounding country was becoming visible. As yet all that could be seen were the great white slopes, thrown into relief by shadow, with here and there the darker patches of the tundra, and, almost unnoticed the stars had disappeared from the sky, leaving behind the single, glowing orb of the sun.

Above the place where they had halted, the breath of men and beasts formed a cloud of steam that gradually disappeared in the current of icy air that blew from the mountain, announcing the coming of a new day, a day which, once it had arrived, would remain for eighteen hours. Everyone was waiting for the Old Man's orders. He stood there, unmoving, his face expressionless, as though the tremendous journey he had just completed, in the course of which he had continually been blazing the trail, had in no way affected him. To him it seemed only natural that the younger people should be stretched out exhausted on their sleighs. Ellena, worn out, her face drawn, still remained full of courage, and after a moment's relaxation pulled herself together again. Her blue eyes, clear as quartz, rested sympathetically upon Kristina, who was the first to start unharnessing her reindeer.

Ellena, too, was awaiting the Old Man's orders. But she did not speak to him, for he had fulfilled his task, having brought the caravan into safety. And, vaguely, the plump woman regretted her husband's absence. He would have leapt about, woken up the youngsters, jeered at the laggards, stirred up the idlers and, in no time, the encampment would have begun to take shape. But she did not feel bold enough to give any orders herself. The combination of these last few exhausting days with all her worries and fears was weighing her down. Yet there was another woman ready to take her place, and the sleeping men were suddenly aroused by an angry cry, flung out like an order.

'What's the matter with you all? Do you think the wind's going to put up your tents for you? That the trolls will get the kettle boiling? In a few hours from now the main herd will be here, and we've got to have everything ready for them!'

Kristina went rapidly from sledge to sledge, waking up her brothers with a kick in the ribs, shaking Martha Risak and Karina Bongo, as full of the joy of life as if neither cold nor fatigue affected her at all. And they all began to stir, as though aroused by an explosion. They leapt to their feet, unharnessed their reindeer and led them away to the nearby lichen, where they crowded together, dragging the long leather thongs that prevented them from running away, and immediately began scraping away the snow with their hoofs, thirstily licking the snow, sniffing the wind . . .

The herd! The great herd! The mere mention of the word by Kristina had been enough to turn every one of them into a true Samisk again. Their collapse had not lasted long, as though they were throwing off the last traces of their long, winter confinement. Now they had done with hibernating; no more cosy huts, no more evenings drinking by the fire. The wind from the open sea was blowing around them, the piercing cold of the arctic night was weighing them down, yet the wind and the cold invigorated them, and each one of them realized that, from now on, their livelihood and that of the herd would have to be won from this great white wilderness. And so they began to come to terms with the snow, which henceforward was their element!

Ellena selected the spot where the main tent was to be erected, this was her responsibility as mistress of the cita; and Andis Sokki and Karin Bongo set up the hearth-stones on the spot indicated by her. Now, having regained her authority, she began distributing the jobs : two men were to collect wood—they had only to cross the lake to find plenty—while all the others would start putting up the tents.

Karin and Kristina were already unloading the long, forked poles, and had soon erected them, fixing the stays to support the smaller poles, which completed the framework of the tent. Then they sent the young men to fetch the heavy, frozen canvas, which had to be unfolded by sheer force, so that they had to take off their heavy mittens and work in thin woollen gloves, which gave them so little protection that, in a few seconds, their fingers grew numb.

Three tents would be enough to provide shelter for everyone, and it was not long before the three frames had been completed, standing in the centre of a circle formed by the sleighs and their loads.

As though it had been awaiting this moment, the wind suddenly started to blow, driving the snow across the surface of the ground so violently that it took their breath away and forced the Lapps to exert tremendous energy in order to get the canvasses unfolded and fixed to the frames. Now and then the wind would fill one of them like a sail, snatch it out of their frozen hands and blow it away, so that everything had to be started over again. But by now everyone was working with a will, as though the very violence of the storm was part of the natural conditions of life. It took nearly an hour for each canvas to be unrolled and fixed to the framework of the tent. The opening for the door was left on the lee side, and Kristina rapidly fixed the moveable flap, in order to prevent the inside from being filled with powdered snow. The two men who had been sent to fetch wood were now back, dragging behind them long faggots of birch wood, from which the girls picked out the smallest branches and began breaking them up for kindling. Then Karin, Kristina and Martha Risak made up six brushwood mattresses to keep them from contact with the snow, on to which they piled all the deerskins they could lay hands on, and beneath these frail shelters it was already beginning to be quite comfortable. The only thing that had to be done now was to fix the hook and chain for the cauldron and, to do this, Kristina, being the youngest and lightest of them all, propped up a rough kind of ladder, fashioned from a young birch tree, against the tent, which enabled her to drop the chain through the smoke-vent from outside.

To provide shelter, the men made a kind of rampart on the windward side by turning the sleighs on their sides, and stacking the scattered baggage inside it. Each of the three tents at once became the scene of great activity. Ellena and Kristina in the leader's tent, Martha Sokki and the Bongos in another, and Martha Risak in the smallest, which had been put up at some distance from the others as though to emphasize the poverty of its occupants.

Everyone knew just what had to be done. Kristina lit the fire with bits of birch bark, to which she kept adding fuel. The wet wood smoked terribly and, as the wind was driving the smoke downwards, the atmosphere inside the tents soon became almost unbearable, irritating the eyes and making everyone cough. But what did it matter, the fire and smoke meant warmth and life! Ellena hung the cauldron on the hook and filled it with snow, for they could not count on being able to pierce the ice on the lake which, just here, might well be six foot thick.

Gradually the disorderly bustle of installation died down. The men, having collected sufficient wood and finished putting up the rampart, hurried inside one after the other, opening and shutting the door flap. Then they took their places in order of precedence on the right and left of the mistress, the humblest of them squatting amongst the dogs close to the door, where there was a constant draught, the most favoured ones right away from it in the warmth. Already Ellena had assumed her traditional position, seated in the place of honour on a pile of reindeer skins, and leaving an empty space on her left for the master of the cita. Within easy reach stood the chest containing the crockery, and the sacks of bread, salt, margarine and dried fish, and she was busily cutting up a reindeer carcass, throwing pieces of meat into the pot, where a number of marrow bones were already simmering. And they all greedily inhaled the sharp, comforting smell of blood and fat, for the pangs of hunger were griping their stomachs.

One by one, those from the smaller tents came in and sat around in a circle, for Ellena did the cooking for the whole cita. They huddled against one another, the late comers lying curled up like dogs at the feet of the first arrivals, and as their furs slowly thawed the smell of sweat was mixed with the odour coming from the cauldron, and everything was so peaceful and homely that they felt that their existence was justified. Indeed, at that moment, nowhere else in the world could have been as comfortable as this tent, and they sat there, their faces, bronzed by the wind from the taiga, lit up by the flickering light from the fire, with nothing to do but wait until the meat was cooked and the soup was just right—and, above all, until the great herd arrived.

For the present, the wind played in the framework of the tent, making the canvas flap, and its sound, amplified as though by a drum, rolled away to unknown, distant places they would not see again, since for them there was henceforward only their marvellous tent beneath which they huddled like wild animals, happy and at ease, lulled by the storm raging outside. They felt no necessity to speak. They listened to the noises, distinguishing those that were customary and familiar—the shrieking of the wind, the flapping of the canvas, the groaning of the poles—from those that threatened danger, like the distant rumble of an avalanche, or the restless cry of a fox in a nearby thicket, giving warning that a wolf might be circling stealthily round the baggage deer. Then they forgot about eating and drinking and sank into a state of reverie, made up of well-being, repose, accumulated fatigue and relaxation, while the Old Man, squatting amongst them close to the fire, slowly puffed at his pipe, his eyes watching, all his senses alive, listening to the music of the wind in which he recognized the song of the world.

130

Then, all of a sudden, the dogs, who had been sleeping curled up amongst the furs, sprang to their feet, growling, and followed one another out of the tent. There could be no mistaking it, they were barking and yapping with joy, announcing the arrival of those they were all waiting for!

Andis, who was nearest the door, leapt outside, and they could hear him yelling into the wind: 'The great herd! the great herd!' And immediately everyone who was young and active enough hurried from the tent, leaving behind old Martha Sokki-Bongo who, taking advantage of their absence, came and squatted beside Ellena as she skimmed the soup.

'Get another potful ready, Martha,' said Ellena. 'The herdsmen will be hungry, and this is a great occasion!' Then she sighed: 'But why ever isn't Simon here with us all!'

CHAPTER TWO

'T H E herd! It's the great herd!'

Men and women hurried out of the tent, hallooing, shouting, waving and dancing about in the stream of powdery snow that the blizzard was blowing across the frozen lake.

As they came in from the south, the reindeer spread out over the slope of the Bastevarre, and like a huge, brown stain, the herd flowed slowly towards the waiting people, now spreading out, now closing in to form a gigantic furrow on the grey background of the tundra, now losing itself in the undergrowth in a confusion of reindeer horns and branches, now spreading itself out over the snow, then forming itself once again into a tight-packed triangle that advanced geometrically across the whiteness of the steppe, a vast shadowy expanse descending towards the lake.

'Tie the dogs up,' yelled the Old Man.

And immediately everyone fixed a log of wood to the running knot round his dog's neck to stop them rushing forward and spreading panic amongst the great herd. And all this was going on amidst the roar of the wind, the anger and the happiness of the men, the shouting and calling of the women heedless of the biting cold and the snow.

Before long the herd was so near that it was possible to distinguish individual outlines, recognize the man who was in the lead. They realized to their amazement that it was the Finn.

'What, him?' exclaimed Andis. He felt humiliated to see that it was neither his brother Pier who was leading in the deer, nor even Thor Risak, who as least belonged to one of the oldest families.

'And who did you expect it to be?' exclaimed Kristina. 'Thor Risak who let the reindeer be stolen? Or that irresponsible Pier? Or maybe Mikael, who's never happy unless he's driving a sledge?'

Andis did not insist.

Paavi was leading the herd and Kristina was radiant. He was the leader, the others had accepted his authority. She loved him, and she was fated to marry him. If it had to be, one day the two of them would set up the last clan in the country of the Samisks, and together they would drive the last herd, belonging to the last cita, through the unpeopled tundra.

She felt feverishly exalted. He was the extraordinary man that destiny had sent to them at the very moment when the whole spirit of the cita was disappearing, when everything seemed to point to the ending of a people, of all its beliefs and all its customs. And while the others ran out to meet the herd, she waited, standing erect at the entrance to her tent.

Paavi had brought the reindeer to the shores of the lake, and now, with the help of Thor Risak and Pier guarding the flanks, he was rounding them up in a suitable spot where there was plenty of lichen growing amongst the rocks. Behind, Mikael Bongo turned his sleigh aside and made for the camp.

As she watched the scene, Kristina experienced a strange emotion, as though she were already the real mistress of the cita. It was strong and fine, her cita!

And, indeed, the Lapps seemed to have recovered a new vitality and energy. They had forgotten about their hunger and fatigue, their well-warmed huts and the orgies at Viddakaïno. Here were four or five thousand reindeer that belonged to them, displaying the forest of their antlers, making a clicking noise with their thousands of delicate, nervous hoofs scraping away the snow: Why should they worry about the huts of Suojaurre, the merry evenings in the sauna baths, the expeditions by sleigh to the Viddakaïno festivities?

They had forgotten all about the Norwegian language and Norwegian ways that they had learnt at school and at

133

church! They were men of the reindeer, lost in the sacred mountains, and the roar of the wind was the thunderous voice of their gusty ancient gods! They surged around the herd, for was it not their livelihood as well as their property, since they lived not only for, but also on, the reindeer?

At this moment, maybe, they were obscurely aware of themselves as the survivors of the oldest race on the continent, conscious of the fact that they were still living in the same way as they had done in those remote centuries, when they had been the only people in this vast frozen land. They had survived the cold and the snow; this privilege of survival belonged to their race, was shared by no one else, and this was why they no longer suffered either from cold or hunger, or the vast white loneliness. They were masters of the tundra which for thousands of years, regular as clockwork, they had crossed from south to north, from north to south, following the rhythm of day and night, of the unique day and the unique night of the Arctic.

When the herd had settled down, and Paavi was satisfied that the deer were beginning to scrape away the snow and would soon be lying down chewing the cud, he summoned the other herdsmen and they made their way to the camp, where Mikael Bongo and his two sleighs had already preceded them.

While still some distance away, he saw Kristina waiting for him and his heart filled with joy and pride at the thought that he, the humble rupes-hunter, was now the master. When he got up to her, he stopped. The blizzard wrapped them both in a cloak of white snow, that clung to their legs and shoulders; and for a moment Kristina saw in his eyes the gleam of desire, and her heart beat wildly.

'Mana derivan, Kristina!' the Finn said, bowing solemnly to her as befitted the leader of the herd.

'Bazza derivan!' she replied, mastering her emotion.

Then she preceded him towards the tent, bearing herself like the mistress of the clan, and he was filled with admiration at her precocious dignity.

Mikael was already unloading the sleigh.

134

'I've brought some meat,' said he, throwing a frozen reindeer carcass at Kristina's feet. 'It was my turn!'

Freed from her domestic duties by old Martha Bongo, Ellena came out to greet the herdsmen, and Kristina disappeared.

'How's the herd?' asked Ellena, addressing herself to her son, Pier Sokki, for she, too, was affecting to ignore the Finn.

'There are none missing this time!'

'Well done! Now come and rest yourself. Andis and Mattis will watch the deer.'

Inside the tent, despite the limited space, Simon Sokki's place was still reserved for him, while the rest crowded in as best they could. Paavi and Kristina stopped for a moment at the threshold, and their eyes met.

'Sit next to me,' she said, under her breath. 'You've earned it.'

'Not yet, Kristina, not yet! I'm only a herdsman. You're still the chief's daughter, don't forget. You mustn't give up your rights.'

'You're right, Paavi. But, one day, our turn will come. I'll wait!'

She raised the door-flap, stepped over the bodies stretched out near the entrance and threw herself down on the furs in the empty place reserved for Simon Sokki. To the others, this was only the gesture of a spoilt child, for Simon often used to sit her down beside him in the warmth of the fire; and the Finn contented himself with the humblest position, near the entrance, where the biting cold came in every time the wind blew the flap open. He was not yet the master, and he knew it. He sat crosslegged, leaning against the damp canvas, while Karin Bongo threw an armful of green wood on the fire, so that a great crackling of sparks and bitter smoke surged through the tent and was drawn up towards the vent at the top. They were all exhausted and, although the members of the convoy were anxious to hear about the condition of the herd, the number of does in calf and all the incidents of the journey, they respected the newcomers' fatigue and waited in silence. Beneath the frozen walls of the tent, rocked occasionally by gusts of wind, they felt happy and contented. Those who were hungriest sniffed the aroma of the meat escaping from the cauldron, and to keep them quiet Ellena handed round marrow-bones, almost too hot to hold, which they split with the point of their daggers and then sucked greedily, covering their fingers and moustaches with melted fat. Next she handed round bowls of soup and, taking slices of meat from the stew-pot, put them into a large bowl so that they could all help themselves, voraciously gulping them down, and occasionally, when a piece was too big to be swallowed whole, cutting part of it off, close to their lips.

Already some of them, having eaten their fill or overcome by fatigue, had stretched out on their backs and fallen asleep with their mouths open, breathing rapidly, the grease trickling down their cheeks; while others lay down on top of those already asleep, who tossed and whimpered without waking up, so utterly exhausted were they by the long hours of work.

Ellena handed round bowl after bowl of soup, continually putting fresh pieces of meat into the cauldron, until everyone's hunger was satisfied. Inside the tent it was very hot compared with the outside temperature, and beneath their pesks everyone was sweating freely, though every now and then a gust of wind blew open the door and the terrible cold from outside quickly invaded the tent. Those near the entrance cursed and swore, jealous of those who were out of the draught. But little by little they, too, were overcome by fatigue and the frail shelter was wrapped in silence, a vague somnolence of well-being and satisfied hunger.

Only the Old Man, sitting crosslegged and upright, and the Finn, equally solemn at the other side of the circle, remained fully conscious. Kristina, snugly curled up, her feet protected from the cold by Chumbi, was sleeping peacefully, and her relaxed features, despite the moisture dripping from the canvas roof, wore an expression of carefree youthfulness.

136

Suddenly, the light filtering through the thick canvas grew dimmer, and simultaneously the noise of the storm increased. Outside, fine snow was falling, covering the sleighs and scattered baggage, blocking up the cracks and fissures that still allowed the cold to penetrate the tents. Now and then the Old Man glanced up at the smoke-vent, where, between the crossed poles, the sky could be briefly glimpsed through a gap in the clouds that were scudding overhead at a frantic speed, and so great was the force of the wind that not a single snowflake came in through the vent. Indeed, it seemed as though the mass of warm air and smoke served as a kind of cork, keeping out the wind and the snow and the cold.

For a while the Old Man listened to the snoring of the sleeping people and the singing of the wind, and his gaze rested on Kristina, sleeping innocently as a child, on the Lapps, drunk with fatigue and glutted with meat, on Ellena, who had fallen asleep as she sat, her mouth open, the ladle still in her hand, as though, even in sleep, she was still ready to serve the people of the cita.

'We ought to be getting back to the herd,' said the Old Man. 'In a few hours time, the gale will be so strong that it will be almost impossible to move.'

'Andis, Mattis!' cried the Finn authoritatively, giving them a kick with his foot. 'The Old Man's right! We mustn't let panic or wolves get a hold on the herd.'

The two Lapps leapt to their feet, slung their lassoes over their shoulders, stepped over the outstretched bodies, and, as they emerged from the tent, suddenly staggered as they caught the full violence of the wind.

'The Old Man's always right!' said Mattis. 'It's almost impossible to see the deer.'

They put on their skis and glided across the lake towards the dark mass of reindeer, barely visible against the grey of the landscape. The herd had not moved away. Many of the animals were lying in the snow, chewing the cud, so that all one could see was their heads and antlers. Some of them were scuffing up the snow in search of lichen, while others, startled by the arrival of the men, broke away at a gallop, but the dogs were sent after them and quickly brought them back.

Andis and Mattis contemplated the multitude of deer that belonged to the cita, but though both of them were thinking of the hundreds of animals that had been stolen during the winter, both of them kept their thoughts to themselves. The mere recollection was enough to reopen the wound in their hearts.

They separated, and each went to his post: Andis on the further side of the herd, almost on the edge of the tundra and the high snow-fields; Mattis in a snow-hole at the head of the herd, where he would be able to check the animals' instinctive movement towards the north. They had found disturbing tracks in the snow, but the recent thaw made identification difficult; they could have been a wolf's, or perhaps simply a dog's frisking about round the reindeer. In any case they were there to keep guard, and they would get no sleep. The gale might howl, the snow fall, the mist hide the approach, covering everything within its immense shroud, yet still they must keep watch over the reindeer and see that no one stole them.

On the other side of the Bastevarre, the Isaksen cita would be acting in the same way, and, to the west, the people belonging to yet other clans, who were also making for the coast, urging their herds along parallel trails that would never meet. Now and then a break in the clouds would light up the landscape, revealing in turn the summit of the mountain, the distant hills, the great frozen lake, where the three conical tents of the people of Suojaurre could be seen, each with its plume of smoke. To pass the time away, Mattis began counting them; one, two, three . . . but as he was trying to make out how many sleighs he could distinguish, a bank of thick fog suddenly descended, leaving him alone, hidden away in his snow-hole on the edge of the moving forest of deer, who strayed quite close to him without his being able to see anything of the animals but a dark mass.

The fog had stifled all sound, but occasionally a faint grunt, the clatter of a hoof or the sound of breathing, indicated the nearby presence of a reindeer, momentarily separated from the noiseless mass.

Then the wind started again, whistling, groaning, howling, and the whole earth was filled with the sound of the tempest.

The storm kept them at the Bastevarre camp for three days. It blew with terrible violence, sweeping across the tundra from west to east. The whole countryside was bathed in a translucent light, which cast no shadow because of the snow that was suspended in the air to a considerable height. In this opaque atmosphere, the temperature fell so low that, even in the tents, the cold was almost unbearable. The mist of snow filtered the rays of the sun and the wind robbed them of all heat, leaving nothing but a dazzling light, so blinding that anyone who left the shelter of the tents had to wear snow-glasses. On the Old Man's advice, Ellena cut down the spells of guard duty to twelve hours. This was the most that could be expected of the herdsmen, who were covered in a shroud of ice. Throughout their spell they scarcely left the snow-holes, which they had dug in front of the herd and on either side in order to be sure of getting warning of any unusual movement. Slowly, the herdsmen were completely covered by the snow, which protected them from the cold, and as they huddled in their fur pesks, gradually they became indistinguishable from the trees and rocks.

Each time the guard was changed, the newcomers made a complete tour of the herd, and on each occasion they came across the same disturbing tracks that Andis and Mattis had noticed on the first day. And although the herd remained calm, and this in itself was reassuring, they passed the information on to one another with a warning to keep a sharp look-out for the slightest sign of panic that might indicate the presence of wild animals.

Everyone, those in the tents as well as the herdsmen, was waiting for the storm to die down. The coldest time was about three o'clock in the morning, when dawn was beginning to break. It was almost as though the cold and the light managed to penetrate into the tent simultaneously. No sooner had the latter begun to make the worn canvas translucent, than the cold seemed to trickle through it, covering the inside with frost, and the sleeping people, stretching their feet towards the fire, were enclosed in a tomb of ice.

Men and women alike lay there waiting for the gale to die down, for the sun to start shining, for the Old Man to give the order to set out again. They were like hibernating animals, and their smoky lair was filled with the powerful odour of musk from the ill-tanned hides; a bitter, nauseating stench that came from the damp furs, the skins of the dogs, the sweat of human beings, and the sweetish aroma of cooking meat. Yet this stench and warmth all formed part of the intimacy and comfort.

The sleepers had done their best to protect themselves against the cold, stuffing up every crack with their chests, their furs and their spare garments. There was always someone awake to see that the fire was kept going continuously, to melt snow or cook the food, yet despite the heat, which made the hearthstone almost white hot, someone had only to raise the door-flap, a dog merely had to creep in from outside, and in a moment an icy draught drove out the warmth they had so carefully maintained, and they had to start all over again. Men and women lay huddled up together, so that all that could be seen was a solid heap of dark fur, broken here and there by the scarlet of a cap.

When anyone came in from outside, they immediately had to change the senna in their moccasins that had become soaked with sweat and fill them again with the dry grass, hanks of which were suspended from the framework of the tent. This was absolutely essential, for whether one's feet were warm and comfortable or one's toes frostbitten depended entirely upon the grass with which the moccasins were stuffed. They only interrupted their sleep to eat and drink, to fetch more wood from the great pile that the men had gathered near the entrance, to make up the fire, to listen whether the wind was growing stronger or dying down, to measure the passage of time by the long hours of daylight and the brief darkness of the night. Any other activity, apart from that of watching the herd, was out of the question. Few words were exchanged, as though everyone was striving to maintain his strength and energy. Some of them would have liked to have a drink, but no one dared to go and look for the spirits that were kept in Ellena's sleigh, for the mistress of the cita had sworn that no one should touch it until Simon Sokki turned up. And so, deprived of alcohol, they became morose and listless, and did their best to forget the storm and the passing of the hours in sleep.

CHAPTER THREE

PIER SOKKI raised the canvas-flap and crept into the tent, letting in an icy draught that made the smoky logs spluttering on the hearth burst into flame. The herdsman's arrival was greeted by a volley of oaths, but as soon as he closed the flap the swearing and the flames both died down. Pier had raced all the way from the herd to the camp without stopping; he was out of breath and very upset.

'There are tracks . . .'

'Take it easy, and say what you have to,' said the Old Man, without moving.

'It's a wolf!'

Everyone sat up, listening carefully, interested and anxious.

'Did you see it?'

'No, but there's not the slightest doubt! After the wind had died down, Mikael came across some fresh tracks. He followed them a little way, and found the spot where the wolf had been keeping a watch on the herd.'

'So what?' said Andis. 'Why did you have to wake us up? If he's there, shoot him!'

Pier Sokki was crestfallen.

'Mikael thinks we ought to double the guard! If the fog comes down again we shall need everyone we can get.'

The Finn had stood up.

'Mikael's quite right,' he said. 'We must be on guard. I'm going to see if I can track it down.'

He put on his warmest clothes and slung his cartridge belt over his shoulder.

'I'm coming with you,' said Kristina, but her words were greeted with a roar of laughter.

'A lot of use that'll be—a kid like her!'

'You'd far better stay and look after the fire,' said Ellena. 'That's a job for women. Aren't there enough men here?'

'If Kristina wants to come she can,' said the Finn, glaring angrily at the others who, once more indifferent or thoughtless, were burying themselves in their furs again. They were overcome by the somnolence, the passivity, that were the result of forty-eight hours of inaction. After all, if the wolves wanted to attack, wouldn't they have done so the first day?

Outside, while Kristina was putting on her skis, the Finn said to her gently :

'Your mother's right, you know. The proper place for women is in the tent.'

'Do you take me just for a woman, like all the others?'

'Your teeth are whiter than a wolf's, and you're always ready to bite.'

He was happy. They set out at a good pace, the Finn in the lead, Kristina skilfully making use of the tracks left by his skis.

As she followed behind him, she experienced a feeling of deep contentment. The blizzard whipped up the snow, and now and then, almost asphyxiated by the force of the gale, they had to turn their backs to it and wait for it to die down. And as they clung together during these brief pauses they knew that from now on they were but a single body, with a single heart and a single mind.

The Finn knew the spot well, for in the past he had been out every day, setting his traps here and there along the shore of the huge lake. He was making for the north, as if he had an intuition that it was from there the danger threatened.

'As the wind is in the west and the tents are to the east, the wolf must come from the north if he wants to make a surprise attack. They're intelligent brutes, the most intelligent there are in the tundra, and the most patient! Mikael's quite right, this one's been watching the herd for the last two days, just waiting for the right moment.'

They had to scramble up a small hill covered with trees.

Beneath them the heavy, deep snow was difficult, but it was as peaceful as a sanctuary. Now they were alone in the world, cut off by the storm and protected by the tangled branches. Sharing such silence, why should they talk? They were in complete accord with one another. Once the Finn stopped to wait for her, and when she drew level with him he clasped her savagely in his arms and kissed her. She was taken by surprise, his rough kiss tasted of salt and he bit her lips until they bled. Such happiness was almost too much for her. This man was her master! For the time being they were like the wolf and his mate in the hostile tundra, but the day would come when they would walk together at the head of their people!

They set off again. At the edge of the wood the Finn stopped:

'Look!'

Here, where the snow was not so thick, the zigzag tracks of the wolf were plainly visible; they led towards the herd, dodging from one clump to the next, occasionally breaking off, then starting again. Kristina could read the tracks as well as the Finn.

'He's going towards the reindeer!'

'I'm afraid so. Let's get down there.'

They took the shortest route, stopping now and then to examine the trail.

'You see, he comes in up-wind, from the north, so that neither the dogs nor the reindeer can smell him!'

Long before they reached the herd, the dogs set up a ferocious barking.

'Hurry, hurry!' said Paavi. 'Or we shall be too late, and the wolf will have attacked.'

The dogs howled and barked savagely and occasionally, above the din, the voice of the herdsman could be heard yelling:

'Voï, voï, voï!'

It was the twilight hour just before nightfall and, thanks to the wind, which was blowing up clouds of snow, visibility was nil. The Finn and Kristina increased their pace.

144

At last they came into view against the tundra and Mikael, who was the first to see them, shouted to them to hurry.

'The wolf has got amongst the deer!'

Pier Sokki, who had gone back to his post, was helping him to hold the panic-stricken herd, but the terrified animals kept crowding together, then drawing apart again in an attempt to get away. The essential thing was to prevent them from breaking away, for that would have been the end of the herd. Urging them on with cries and gestures, the herdsmen kept sending out the dogs, who were infuriated by the scent of the wolf, and they managed to keep the huge herd steady, turning on its axis like a constellation.

Immediately the Finn assumed full responsibility, and began disposing of his forces.

'You, Kristina, watch they don't break to the north! Pier and Mikael take the two sides. I'll see if I can get the brute out!'

He took off his skis, brushed the snow from his leggings and, taking up his gun, made for the centre of the herd. So scared were the reindeer by the strong scent of a human being that, although they were herded together by the dog, they opened up to let him pass; then they closed in again behind him, so that he was cut off in the midst of the herd, searching for the invisible enemy, which, hemmed in by a barrier of hoofs, was trying to get away from the dogs, while at the same time Paavi was caught up in the mass of frightened, tightly-packed animals that surged around him.

In contrast to the din made by the dogs, the men and the wind, the silence amongst the threatened animals was dramatic, for their only means of expressing fear was a faint grunting sound. Occasionally it was broken by the noise of an antler snapping off, or of hoofs cracking against hoofs. Then, as though a huge wave were surging through the herd, dozens of reindeer would suddenly rear up in the air, standing on their hind legs and beating the air with their forefeet, only to merge once more into the dense mass. The wave rippled through the herd, from one end to the other, marking the passage of the wolf beneath their warm bellies, for the silent invisible creature was protected by its victims, by the articulated mass of their bodies and the forest of slender legs. And the Finn was becoming furious, as now and then he collided with the lifeless body of a deer, lying with its throat torn open, or had to step over a mutilated creature, spilling its guts on to the ground and gazing at him sadly, its eyes already misted by death. Slinking along beneath the deer, the wolf ran hither and thither, managing to escape the sharp hoofs, tearing off here a lump of flesh, there a mouthful of fur, breaking a leg with a crunch of its jaws, instinctively refusing to leave the safety of this retreat, while all the dogs of the cita, howling and slobbering, waited for it on the outskirts of the herd.

There was a lull and, as a patch of clear water sometimes forms amidst the creaming waves, a wide space opened up around the Finn, a clearing of trampled snow surrounded by a fringe of terrified animals. Within this strange arena man and beast confronted one another. Though it was not afraid of the reindeer, the wolf was scared of the man, and it crouched, with open jaws and staring eyes, ready to spring. Thinking he would have time to shoot, the Finn raised his gun to his shoulder and pulled the trigger, but, at the same moment, for some mysterious reason the reindeer closed in as though to protect their tormentor, thus forming a screen between wolf and hunter. The charge of buckshot hit both the wolf, who let out a long howl, and some of the deer, who collapsed without a sound. Surrounded on all sides by the maddened animals, Paavi realized the futility of his efforts and made his way back to the edge of the herd.

The others had heard the shot.

'Did you get him?' said Mikael.

'Wounded him, probably,' said the Finn, without conviction.

'He's still there, then, in the herd?'

'If he's wounded, he'll try to escape.'

Again they set the dogs on, but these were not prepared to be parted from one another by penetrating into the mass

146

of reindeer : their ancient hunting instinct had been aroused and they formed themselves into groups, knowing only too well that a single dog is no match for a wounded wolf.

Paavi noticed with dismay that Kristina had remained at her post, quite alone and without any dogs !

'Kristina,' he yelled, 'look out ! He's wounded . . . he'll be trying to escape !'

He must have got away already, however, for the herd was already settling down again, like the sea subsiding after a storm. The endless twilight had fallen and it was already difficult to distinguish the reindeer against the grey sky that precedes darkness.

The Finn went over to Kristina, who had been following the drama from afar.

'He's got away,' she said. 'Look, there's a track !'

A long, intermittent trail of blood in the snow marked the desperate bounds of the wild beast. He had made for the first available clump of trees, passing close to the girl as he fled.

'I was very worried about you,' said the Finn. 'A wounded wolf is a dangerous brute, and you had nothing to protect yourself with !'

'I'd got this,' said she, unsheathing her dagger.

'Thank God you didn't have to use it.'

'Are you going after him ?' she asked.

'Drive the deer northwards,' Paavi ordered them. 'We've got urgent business to attend to.'

By the time they had cleared the scene of the slaughter, they could count their losses. The snow was red with spilt blood.

Three young deer had been killed outright, a dozen others were at their last gasp, with broken legs or torn-off feet. To force a passage for himself, the wolf had snapped indiscriminately to left and right with his terrible jaws.

'And what about these, Finn ?' asked Mikael. 'Are you booking them to the wolf as well ?'

He pointed to the three deer, lying mortally wounded by the hunter's buckshot.

'Not bad for one shot,' said Pier Sokki ironically.

They stood there, hostile, both of them more concerned about the deer the man had killed than about those slaughtered by the wolf.

The Finn shrugged his shoulders.

'Go and warn the others, Kristina. They'd better bring two sleighs to take the carcases back, and tell Andis and Thor to come and give us a hand cutting them up while it's still light enough to see. Be as quick as you can, for it's quite possible that the wolf, if he's still alive, or else his mate, will be back tonight to carry away the kill.'

They started to cut up the bodies. They slit open the bellies, threw the smoking entrails to the dogs, cut off the heads and stacked the jointed carcases and the antlers in the snow. They were covered with blood up to the elbows and despite the cold and the snow blown by the wind which clung to their faces, they were pouring with sweat.

'We shan't be exactly short of meat,' said Pier Sokki, still sarcastic.

The Finn dared not make any retort to this impertinence, for despite his youth Pier was Simon Sokki's son, whereas he was only the servant. He was boiling with rage, furious with the lot of them, and with himself, for the lads were right. He had made a mistake. You should never shoot at a wolf that has managed to get amongst the herd. No matter if by killing three deer he had perhaps saved ten, they would still blame him! But there was still a chance for him to save face by finding the wounded wolf, and already his imagination began racing ahead. He saw himself face to face with the savage brute, its jaws open, the great fangs projecting from the black gums, its tongue hanging out; and he could already smell its foul breath and hear its angry growl!

Summoned by Kristina, every able-bodied man hurried to the scene of the massacre. Only Ellena, Martha Sokki-Bongo and the Old Man remained in camp, having decided that there was no point in their moving. The latter sucked away at his pipe, occasionally spitting as he sat huddled up

148

on the furs close to the fire, dreaming and warming his calloused hands at the flames, listening to the song of the wind, the flapping of the canvas, all the mysterious sounds that pursue men as they wander about the tundra.

'The harm's done,' he said. 'All we can do now, is make use of what the wolf has left us.'

He made no attempt to blame the herdsmen in their absence, but he knew exactly how things had happened. The mistake they had made was to chase the wolf while it was inside the herd! The essential thing was to stop it getting there. But, once a wolf does get into a herd, the best thing is to let it be and, above all, not to set the dogs on, which makes it angry, in which case it starts slaughtering left and right and, in its efforts to escape, mutilates and wounds far more animals than if it had been let alone. Had they done that, it would have been content with one animal, which it would have killed properly, then furtively carried it off, creeping along on its belly through the forest of hoofs, for it was less afraid of being kicked than of being attacked by the dogs.

When Ellena heaved a sigh, he said :

'The wolf's got to live as well, Ellena. He takes his tithe, of course, but we're partners; as long as there are reindeer, there will always be Lapps and wolves following the herds! And don't you forget it, Ellena! Our ancestors were the first people to train wolves for hunting and shepherding. There are some people who do more harm than the worst wolves, you know!' And he spat into the cinders.

Ellena understood what he meant : he was alluding to the Isaksen's shaman.

'What a bitch of a life! Sometimes I wonder if Simon isn't right, and, if we shouldn't all be better off in the Tröndelag!'

'Don't say such things, Ellena. Why deny your own past and your own race? Don't you realize we're the last free people on the face of the earth?'

'A fine kind of freedom, when you have to suffer so much

for it,' retorted Ellena. 'I know something about the new kind of life, how comfortable it would be living in huts all the time, and every migration seems to be harder, more strenuous. We're just wanderers, like the reindeer and the wolves. The Norwegians are right! We could make a better kind of life if we chose to!'

The Old Man shook his head.

'Don't talk like that in front of Kristina! Hark at the wind, woman! Why, that's been the same for thousands of years; that's what brings us heat and cold, snow and thaw, according to which quarter it comes from. It does just as it likes, and that's what we want to do! It freezes and unfreezes the lakes, it drives the snow into the hollows and blows it away from the rocky slopes so that the deer can get at the lichen. You want to remember, woman, that our people are as old as this wind; we've been here as long as it has, and when it disappears so shall we.'

They could have gone on talking like this for hours. Ellena enjoyed being alone with the Old Man when she was able to unburden her heart in the secret hope that he would give her new reasons for hoping, for she had a shrewd suspicion that should they have to sell the herd and emigrate in obedience to Simon Sokki, it would be the saddest day of her life. But the Old Man signed to her to be quiet. He was listening carefully and above the angry roar of the wind he could distinguish the creak of the sleighs, the barking of dogs and shouting of men.

'They are back!'

The men unloaded the carcasses in front of the principal tent; the wind and blizzard had covered them with a layer of frozen snow, and they were shaking it from their furs like dogs.

The losses had been heavy: a dozen animals, young ones for the most part, including three does in kid, which they had had to kill, for they would never have survived their wounds.

Paavi was the last to arrive. He had stopped on the way to cut some birch poles, with which the others helped him to put up drying-racks where they could hang the meat, safe from the dogs and the wild animals of the vidda.

The Old Man had come out of the tent and was watching them work, silent automatons, their limbs stiff with cold, their faces reddened by the cruel wind, handling the carcases that were frozen hard as iron. He glanced up at the sky : twilight was slowly deepening, the squalls were succeeding one another at longer and longer intervals and, between them, the cold bit more savagely.

'Tomorrow we shall be able to set out again,' said he. 'Get all your work done this evening!'

Despite their fatigue, they did as he said. They were sad and resigned.

When their task was completed, they all assembled in Ellena's big tent. They came in one by one, after first brushing the snow from their pesks and skallers, but this made little difference; for there was almost as much snow inside the tent as outside. Soon they were all there, except for the two men in charge of the herd. They were worn out, and occasionally one of them would curl up in his furs and go to sleep. Because of the seriousness of the situa-ion, the Old Man had seated himself authoritatively in the master's place, while Kristina snuggled up against Paavi, who was smoking silently, morose and taciturn.

That evening the whole cita was experiencing a mood of bitterness. They had suffered a heavy loss, and it was only the heedless youngsters like Pier and Andis who were content to reckon that for the next fortnight they would have plenty of meat.

'Just fancy! Three does in kid, three!' exclaimed old Martha Sokki-Bongo. She was the hardest hit of all, for two of the animals due to calve belonged to her.

'What made you shoot, Paavi?' suddenly asked the Old Man.

'Anyone else would have done the same, if he had been in my place! The deer had drawn back, leaving an open space in the middle of the herd; and there was the wolf, all on his own, foaming at the mouth and showing his fangs.

I fired because I thought I should be able to kill him on the spot. But everything happened so quickly. Just as I raised my gun the deer moved in again, and as I pulled the trigger some of them got in the line of fire. It all happened as quick as lightning. My fingers were frozen stiff, and it was so bitter cold that my eyes were watering. I aimed badly . . . I know it was my fault.'

'And, as a result, you killed three extra!' Pier Sokki insisted pitilessly.

'But who was it who let the wolf get in amongst the herd in the first place?' Kristina demanded angrily. 'That was the first mistake.'

The herdsmen she was referring to hung their heads.

'You couldn't see more than about half a dozen yards!'

'Stop your squabbling,' said the Old Man in an authoritative voice. 'The trouble started as soon as the wolf got into the herd. Are you sure you found all those that were wounded?'

They described what had happened, how they had killed off the wounded creatures and gutted them while the storm was at its worst, and had had to leave part of the entrails behind, although the dogs had had a good bellyfull. On the other hand, they had skinned all the animals, and the hides, already stiff with frost, had been loaded up on one of the sleighs.

'Whatever is Simon Sokki going to say?' old Mrs Sokki-Bongo enquired anxiously.

'Yes, what will the master say?' Ellena's sons repeated.

'What can he say, seeing that he wasn't even there?' Kristina exclaimed disrespectfully.

Neither the Old Man nor Ellena rebuked her for this impertinence, for in their hearts both thought that she was right.

Already the heat and the sense of well-being were having their effect, making them all better tempered. When Ellena picked up the ladle and began filling the bowls they drank the soup, and they freely shared out the marrow bones and bits of blackened meat that she fished out of the pot

152

and laid on a plank of wood, picking them up in their fingers and greedily cramming them into their mouths. And soon everything had become normal once more, life was starting again. One after the other they succumbed to exhaustion, and fell into a brutish sleep, slumped on top of each other, immune from the wind and the cold. The smoke from the fire rose straight up into the air, passed through the vent in the top of the tent and dispersed in the bright, sparkling air outside. They had forgotten all about the cold and the wind. But while they slept, the Old Man still sat there, bolt upright and wakeful, occasionally studying the stars through the hole in the roof.

'We shall start at daybreak!' he said loudly.

'By daybreak everything will be ready,' the Finn replied.

'What? I thought you were asleep!'

'You know one thing, Old Man? I'm pretty sure the wolf was fatally wounded.'

'I don't doubt it. But what's the use of talking about what's over and done with? Tomorrow will be tomorrow, and today is already yesterday!'

Neither of them spoke again. They just sat there, unaffected by sleep, listening to the faraway sounds, and now and then throwing another log on the fire to stop it going out.

CHAPTER FOUR

PAAVI was the first to leave the tent. The wind had suddenly fallen, the sky had cleared and there were only a few stars still visible in the west. The biting cold made the frozen surface of the lake glitter and, on the slopes of the Bastevarre, a lot of fresh snow had fallen during the storm, bending the trees of the tundra beneath its weight. The big grey shadow of the herd stood out against the white expanse; the deer were either asleep or peacefully chewing the cud. From the tent, half buried on the windward side where the snow had drifted, men and women were cheerfully coming out into the newborn day, still almost numbed by the three days that they had spent shut up in the tent and cut off from the rest of the world. They shook themselves, examined the horizon out of habit, then set to work, for everyone had his special task during the migration and knew what he had to do.

Since they had taken care to unload the sledges as little as possible, they were soon ready, and stacking the tents was left to the last moment. This was the women's job; and before long the canvas covers had been taken off, exposing the framework of poles, from which the cooking pots were still suspended. The smoke from the fires dispersed, blown away by the fitful morning wind. Folding the tarpaulins was an arduous task, for the heavy material, frozen hard as iron, was made even heavier by the weight of frost, and the rough, icy material tore the skins from their hands despite the protection of woollen gloves. When everything had been stowed and firmly lashed and the sleighs were drawn-up ready to start, Ellena threw snow on the ashes, scraped them away and pulled out the hearth-stones, which the men carried away and laid them, still warm, at the bottom of a sleigh.

154

'Now we can go!' said Ellena.

'Your son, Andis, can take the lead,' said the Old Man. 'We'll meet again on the other side of the mountain. If the sleighs follow the trail made by the deer they'll run more easily.'

Andis had rounded up the hobbled deer and, with the help of Mikael and the women, was harnessing them one behind the other, despite a good deal of kicking and thrusting. Then, leading his file of sledges, he took his place at the head of the convoy. Kristina brought up the rear. She preferred to travel at her own pace and, as the youngest of them all, was allowed this privilege.

The Old Man and the Finn crossed the lake, gliding swiftly along on their skis, and soon caught up with the herd. Before their arrival the herdsmen had already rounded up the animals and led the Old Man's reindeer, as well as the doe wearing the bell who served as leader, to the apex of the triangle.

'Bazza derivan,' cried the herdsmen.

'Mana derivan,' replied the Old Man. Then, without another word, he took his place at the head of the herd, leading the doe with the bell, whose shrill sound rang out through the silence.

And once again the miracle was repeated. One deer started to follow, then two, then ten, twenty, a hundred . . . until thousands of deer were on the move, and like a huge ploughshare the great herd drove a wide furrow through the fresh snow, reached the smooth surface of the lake and set off towards the north. In the middle of the lake stood Andis, with all his sleighs drawn up in Indian file waiting for the reindeer to go by; and, when the last one had passed, the men stood shouting merrily and Mikael improvised a yok:

> 'Three days the wind has blown,
> Three days we had to wait
> In the tents of the Bastejaurre,
> And the wolf took his toll;
> But, despite his savage jaws

And the fury of his hunger,
Still Simon Sokki's deer
Outnumber the stars in the sky.'

And, like a challenge in the pure morning air, Martha Risak repeated in her clear, resonant voice: '. . . still outnumber the stars in the sky!'

The dogs galloped around the reindeer, barking, yapping, infecting everyone with their cheerful mood.

Paavi the Finn was the last to pass them, acting as the rearguard, and rounding up the laggards. He and Kristina exchanged a long look. Yesterday's worries were over, the young girl was radiant and her whole attitude bespoke her love and pride. The snow was firm, the sleighs ran easily, the bleak rays of the sun gilded the gentle undulations of the mountain, the wind had died down and there, ahead of him, thousands of reindeer huddled together, flank to flank and antlers interlaced, moved forward, accompanied by the muffled sound of pattering feet and grunting reindeer, and the curious noise of joints cracking beneath tightly stretched skin. The long fur carpet, bristling with thousands of forked antlers, stretched out in a triangle across the immense plain of the frozen lake. And the people of the cita, restored to happiness, sang of the marvellous reality of the migration!

At the northern extremity of the Bastejaurre a narrow gorge opened up: it ended in a wide valley that led to a low pass. Before starting the ascent, which threatened to be difficult, the Old Man called a short halt. Then he plunged into the defile, still skiing at the regular, monotonous, easy pace that never faltered, and behind him followed the deer, the men, the women and the sleighs.

When it came to their turn to enter the gorge, Pier Bongo and Paavi, who were in the rear of the herd, stopped, intrigued:

'Look, that snow over there is red,' Pier pointed out.

'The wolf must have gone that way yesterday,' said Paavi.

He was seized by sudden rage: perhaps there was still a chance of catching up with the wretched brute.

'You carry on with the others. I'm going to have a look.'

'Take care, Paavi, a wounded wolf is a dangerous creature!'

'So is a humiliated Samisk!'

Pier shrugged his shoulders and made no further attempt to stop him.

Paavi made for the pool of blood, staining the snow at the entrance to the copse. His hunter's instinct was awakened, and he noticed every detail: the wounded animal, curled up in a ball, had been surprised by the arrival of the convoy and fled. The tracks were fresh, the blood scarcely frozen. To follow the trail would be child's work. The Finn advanced slowly, all his senses on the alert. The animal had dragged itself on its belly over the deep snow, turning it red, but, on the frozen drifts, its claws had scarcely left a mark and the bloodstains were further apart. When the trail disappeared into a clump of trees, the Finn unslung his rifle and got ready to shoot. To follow it any further was risky. For a moment he hesitated, but at the thought of the slaughtered deer anger triumphed over fear. From that moment he became Paavi the Finn, the nephew of the great hunter, Mikkel Mikkelsen Sara, who had once killed the wolf of the Agjiet. Like him, he was going to attack the brute in its lair! All that counted now was the hunt: silently he glided forward, examining the ground far ahead of him, attentive to every suspicious sign, a clump of snow fallen from a branch, the faint sound of the wind blowing through a thicket, and keeping a look-out on both sides, for his uncle had warned him that a wounded wolf often makes a wide circle in order to surprise the hunter from behind.

Within the thicket the snow was deep and, despite his skis, he sank up to his waist in it, but nothing could stop him now: the scarlet thread, which kept appearing and disappearing, was leading him towards his destiny. He was no longer worrying about the risk, for he had an account to settle; the youngsters had jeered at him, and he was determined to bring back the killer's pelt! He knew it would take him a long time, for a wolf that has been disturbed can travel a considerable distance, even when mortally wounded. This one was making for the mountain. Would it be strong enough to get there? Now and then, when the tracks were clearest, the Finn could tell that its pace was weakening; the footmarks were heavy and uneven, halted occasionally, and the bleeding continued.

For a moment, as though moved by some presentiment, the hunter gazed around. The chase had brought him a long way and, beyond the gorge, he could see the herd scattered over the rising valley, followed by the sleighs. It would take him several hours to catch up with them. The sight of the cita, now so far away that they appeared as mere specks, seemed almost like a warning. He could still give up. No one tracks down a wounded wolf by himself; it is better to have a determined, well-armed companion. But his hesitation did not last long. Mikkel Mikkelsen Sara had confronted the wolf of the Agjiet quite alone, and he would do the same.

'I'll get this wolf if it kills me!' he swore. He consulted the sun, the wind, the sky, and all the signs were reassuring; there was no evidence of a storm and little chance of losing the trail.

He was surprised by the brute's powers of resistance, for it had certainly caught the buckshot full in the belly! Where did it get this fresh energy from? Probably it was looking for some lonely den where it could die in peace! The pursuit was unfair. Now the man was gaining on the animal: open spaces favoured the skier, but then he would have to make a detour round a clump of trees, and this once more slowed him down. Every time this happened he had to pick up the trail he had lost for a moment, and sometimes even make his way through the thick wood. To do this, to take off his skis, scramble through the snow, put them on again, free himself from the clinging branches, took time, but nothing could distract the hunter from his pursuit. He was surrounded by empty silence and blinding whiteness, and it seemed as though the usual inhabitants of the tundra, the foxes, snowfowl and various kind of waterfowl, had fled before the double danger of wolf and hunter.

The pursuit brought him to a deserted, silent valley, high enough up the mountain for the tundra to have died away. Above, all sign of vegetation stopped, and the naked rocks, glinting beneath their matrix of blue ice, formed a low cliff, where cavities and shallow eaves, difficult of access, were concealed by a dense thicket of arctic willow and birch. The tracks of the wolf led towards one of these shelters. The Finn halted, wiped the sweat from his brow and considered the situation. The wolf had been stopping more and more frequently, as one could tell from the impression of its body in the reddened snow.

The climax was approaching. Behind this curtain of trees, protected in the rear by the rock face, the wild animal was waiting for the man.

Paavi took off his skis, felt for the handle of his dagger, made sure that it slid easily in its sheath; then, holding his gun across his chest, he plunged into the undergrowth. The branches grew so thickly here that now and then he had to part them with his hands, like the bars of a moving prison; and within this cage he moved forward, yard by yard. Once more the Finn experienced fear. He was shut in by the gloomy silence, and would have been only too glad to hear the sudden growl that precedes an attack; anything would have been better than this waiting, this slow, dangerous advance. Why go on? The wolf, mortally wounded, could no longer do any harm. He might just as well leave it to its fate, for to follow it further was to risk disaster.

Despite the intense cold in the coppice, chequered by light and shade, Paavi was pouring with sweat. He kept hearing imaginary noises, and every sound seemed to be a threat. A branch fluttered in the air beside him, the snow piled up beneath his feet. The beating of his heart seemed to make a terrible din, like the rolling of a drum keeping time with his hurried breathing, which he felt certain could be heard by the animal he was tracking down, skulking invisible, yet there just ahead of him, only a few yards away!

He moved forward, taking his fear with him, yet managing to dominate it. He had to push aside the branches, climb over fallen tree-trunks, bend down, clamber, stand up again, and sometimes a birch tree, bowed down by the weight of the snow, would suddenly spring upright, striking him as it did so. A little further on, he got his foot wedged between two branches, which anywhere else would have been a trivial matter, but now, in order to free himself, he had to use both hands, dropping his gun in the soft snow, so that he could draw his dagger to sever the twisting roots. These simple movements, which he had made so often before, seemed to last a century, for all the time that he was making them he was at the mercy of the wolf. Gradually, as he advanced, the tundra began to thin out, and he picked up the trail again, still fresh and bloody. The cliff towered above the tops of the birch trees. He pushed ahead a few more yards, through a last clump of trees, and suddenly he found himself in a small open space between the forest and the cliff.

There was the wolf, crouched in the snow, facing him; an enormous beast, its lips drawn back displaying huge fangs, its fur standing on end, ears flattened, its front legs stretched out in a relaxed position. Its magnificent grey fur was stained with blood, and its entrails were escaping from a great wound in its belly. From its jaws a pink liquid dripped into a fetid pool.

It was an impressive encounter, lasting only a fraction of a second. But it was the decisive moment, and he must act swiftly . . . Gauging the short distance that separated him from the wolf, the Finn instinctively raised his gun and pressed the trigger. But no explosion follow the sharp click of the hammer. He ought to have fired again but there was no time, for uttering an agonized howl the wolf flung itself upon him, flinging him backwards with its weight, striving to get its teeth in his throat. Purely by instinct, Paavi raised his left arm, and this swift reflex movement was his salvation. The wolf's jaw closed like a vice on his forearm, which was protected by the thick fur of his pesk. Man and beast rolled over in the snow, locked in a savage hand to hand struggle, and, as the Finn was dressed in heavy furs, it was like an encounter between two wild beasts, in which first one, then the other, had the advantage. The Finn, hindered by his immobilized left arm, struck out with his free fist, got his arm round the wolf and finally succeeded in holding it down, crushing it beneath the whole weight of his body. It was a merciless dual, punctuated by the growls of the furious animal and the hurried breathing of the man. Eventually he managed to get his knee on the animal's throat and, in the few seconds that he was able to hold it still, he grasped his dagger. Just in time! His strength was ebbing and he was on the point of fainting, for the pain of his wound was growing more acute, as though his arm were being crushed. Mad with anger, he attacked his victim relentlessly; again and again he struck the brute in the neck, the chest, the back, and wherever the long, broad blade struck home the warm blood flowed, till he felt the wolf stiffen in a final spasm. Then, just as his grip was beginning to fail, its jaws opened and its head fell back, and the Finn collapsed in a heap on its still warm body.

Later, when he had recovered consciousness and got to his feet, his face was haggard and covered with blood, though whether it was his own or the wolf's he did not know, for he was aching in every limb, and his left arm had lost all feeling.

He examined his wound; the thick fur of his pesk and the cloth of his koufte had protected him. Only two fangs had deeply penetrated the flesh and, though he felt an intolerable sensation of burning, he was still able to move his arm despite his wound.

He could scarcely believe that it was all over. He experienced a tremendous feeling of fatigue, and, at the very moment when he should have been filled with joy, he was overwhelmed by an immense moral lassitude. The struggle had been too hard! Now the nervous tension was relaxing.

161

He had come through this fight to a finish without knowing precisely what had happened to him! During the struggle his gun had fallen into the snow. He picked it up, and checked it; the cartridge was still in the breach, the powder must have been damp. He was lucky to have escaped, for if the wolf had succeeded in getting him by the throat or the back of the neck he would have been killed immediately.

He felt thirsty, and ate some snow; and only then did he look at his defeated enemy: it was a well-built dog wolf, with a magnificent pelt. Hunter though he was, he could not help feeling a moment's pity as he thought of the bitch looking for her mate, and howling in the darkness. He had heard this sound once in the tundra, and it had impressed him profoundly. A wolf only has one mate, and remains faithful to her throughout his life. But almost immediately his thoughts turned to the reindeer that had been savaged and maimed, and to the welcome that would be waiting for him when he got back to camp, and his pity vanished.

Kneeling in the blood, he skinned the animal, rolled up the pelt and, having cut off the monstrous head, decided to take it back to the camp to show them. He tied it up in a bundle with his lasso, picked up his gun, put in fresh cartridges and staggered out of the wood. By the time he had found his skis again, the sun had already disappeared behind the mountains. The gorge lay like a bluish shadow in the darkening twilight, streamers of orange light lingered on the mountain tops, and away to the west a luminous band stretched away above the darkness. Retracing his footsteps, he found the wide furrow left by the passing of the herd. On the hard snow the going was easier. He forgot about being tired and, if it had not been for the stabbing pain in his left arm, all he would have thought about would have been his victory. He had killed the wolf of the Bastevarre! He would take his place in the sagas of the Sokkis, along with his uncle Mikkel Mikkelsen Sara and the wolf of the Agjiet. He improvised a yok, humming it between clenched lips, and the sound, like the humming of bees, formed an accompaniment to his long, ranging stride. He felt happy in just the same way that his remote maternal ancestors must have felt happy, those Samisk reindeer-hunters who thousands of years ago had challenged the wolves in single combat.

It was very late when he reached the camp. Though it was not yet dark, daylight had ebbed to a kind of shadowy luminosity in which it was just possible to discern the outline of the conical tents. The herd was spread out nearby, in a valley where the lichen was plentiful. It was a picture of a peaceful, happy people.

The slopes on either side of the valley were calm and silent, and even the evening cold was welcoming. The Finn halted, standing erect in the purple light like a conqueror. After so much savagery the evening peace was sweet to him. This encampment in the snow, to which henceforward he belonged, was utterly familiar to him; the scattered sleighs with their loads, and the great dark tents bristling with poles, lit up from inside by the flame of the fires. He could smell the scent of woodsmoke borne on the evening breeze.

The first stars shone in the sky, and for him they were like a signal. He let out the wild cry of the victorious hunter, and the dogs, hurrying from the tent, answered him by barking furiously. The whole pack galloped towards him, scattering the snow, then came to a halt and faced him, growling angrily. He was dripping with blood, and the hideous remains of the wolf hung from his shoulders. The dogs circled around him without daring to come nearer, showing their teeth, growling and barking; and he struck out with his ski stick to keep them off.

Inside the tents they had heard the hunter's cry. Listening to the sounds of the twilight, Ellena heard the barking of the dogs, angry and frightened.

'He's got him,' said the Old Man, taking his pipe from his mouth.

'God be praised,' exclaimed Ellena, suddenly growing pale.

They could hardly recognize the man who raised the

163

door-flap. Covered with blood, his pesk in shreds, his eyes burning with fever, he stooped down to enter and, in doing so, struck the feet of the sleeping people with his burden. Then he drew himself up to his full height, and in the glow of the fire, his shadow reached up to the frost-covered canvas.

'Here you are, Kristina,' said he, pushing the skin and the hideous head towards her; and they all expressed surprise and admiration.

'Why, it's as strong as the wolf of the Agjiet,' said Ellena, and for the Finn her words were ample recompense.

But Kristina noticed the blood that he was covered in, and the huge rent in the sleeve of his pesk, which was slit from top to bottom, revealing the torn blue cloth of his koufte.

'You are wounded, aren't you?'

'That's his blood, not mine.'

He was lying : his wound was beginning to hurt again, and his arm was growing stiff.

'Drink this,' said Ellena, passing the ladle to him, filled with soup.

They all stared at him, but no one dared to question him. By this time, those from the other tents had arrived, and as though in a dream Paavi could hear Mikael Bongo improvising in his powerful voice :

'The great black wolf is dead,
The wolf of the Bastevarre has paid his debt,
Killed by the hand of Paavi the Finn.
For your mother's blood has spoken, Paavi,
And now you are really one of our people,
You, who have killed the Bastevarre wolf,
That was decimating our herd
While the tempest raged on the Bastejaurre.'

He had done his best to master his fatigue, swaying on his feet, but now he sank down in their midst, and they made room for him so that he might stretch out at his ease; but even as he fell he was already asleep, mouth open, with the blood beginning to dry all over him, on his face and on his hands.

Staring into the distance, her lips pressed tightly together, Kristina listened to the last words of the yok improvized by Mikael. Then peace gradually returned to the tent, and outside the barking of the dogs died away.

CHAPTER FIVE

WHEN the Finn woke up he was bruised all over and feverish. His left arm was covered with congealed blood. Martha Sokki offered to dress his wounds, and as she was skilled in the use of herbs, Kristina had agreed to her doing so, though she herself had insisted on putting a linen bandage round the torn muscles. Then, as he was about to leave, she called him back :

'You're not going back to the herd!'

'I must.'

'Kristina's right,' intervened the Old Man. 'Stay with the baggage sleighs; Mikael Bongo can take your place. You're going to find it pretty hard going today, I don't mind telling you.'

Paavi did not insist. He had paid dearly for his victory, and was now physically and emotionally exhausted, as though drained of all nervous energy. Mikael had already harnessed the five reindeer to their sleighs and tied them one behind the other; the Finn had only to take the reins.

At dawn they set out on a week's march across gentle, well-wooded, undulating country, the valleys filled with a succession of lakes, connected by a stream, all the water still frozen. The richly wooded tundra made it impossible to cover long distances, but the lengthening hours of spring sunshine compensated for the bitter cold of the nights. As there was plenty of lichen on the sides and tops of the hills, the herdsmen had been told to let the reindeer graze as they went along, and they were content to urge the herd in a northerly direction.

Night and day no longer made sense! Time had become an eternity, dominated by the rhythm of the reindeer, so that whenever the herd instinctively stopped to chew the cud the whole cita, whether it was night or day, would come to a halt and, without troubling to put up the tents, the women would light a big fire, set up their tripods and start melting snow to make reindeer soup. The sleighs were drawn up in a square round the fire and everyone ate as the fancy took him, cutting off a hunk of meat and grilling it over the embers on his knife. Then those who were not on guard wrapped themselves up in their furs and lay down to sleep wherever they happened to be, pulling their scarlet caps over their faces.

The kind of country through which they were travelling stretched indefinitely ahead and, when they looked back, they could see a broad trail of trampled snow running away towards the south like the first parallel furrows of a ploughed field.

Paavi completed the greater part of the journey lying on an uncomfortable pile of cases and tarpaulins. Despite the slow speed at which the convoy was moving he would not have been able to keep up with it on foot; sometimes he was not even strong enough to hold the reins. When his sleigh happened to turn over, the whole string of six vehicles was brought to a halt in a confusion of twisted traces and scattered loads, and the sleigh had to be turned right way up and a new shaft trimmed out. But when, contrary to the usual custom, Martha Risak took pity on him and suggested helping him, he shook his head, and she continued on her way not wishing to humiliate him. This time, however, things proved to be too much for him. With only one sound hand he found it impossible to disentangle the traces in which his deer had got caught up and, by the time Kristina caught up with him, she found them both rolling about in the snow, struggling for mastery.

'Wait a minute,' said she, jumping from her sleigh.

She unfastened the traces, freed the animals' legs and, only when it had got to its feet and started grazing, did she summon Paavi to help her turn the sleigh right way up.

'Lift up the back. That's right . . . now heave !'

Before long, everything was restored to order once again

and Kristina, leaning against her white reindeer, began making excuses for him :

'You can't expect to do everything by yourself, with only one arm !'

'It makes me furious !'

'There will be worse things to face than this. Save your strength, Paavi.'

She had said what had to be said, and was already setting off again. He seated himself crosslegged on the front of the sleigh, whistled, slacked off the rein, and his reindeer heaved its heavy load out of the snow, while the other animals, tied on behind, strained at the traces and followed. Those who got left behind found the tracks made by the others already frozen, which made the going easier, and before long the Finn overtook Kristina's string of sleighs, caught up with the rest of the caravan and took his place again. At the tail end of the convoy Kristina, feeling soothed and proud, welcomed the warm touch of the sun on her face and surrendered herself to the reality of time. With eyes half-closed, she went on with her dream : they were alone, Paavi and she ! Alone in the great white country of which they were the masters, travelling endlessly across the vidda, free and happy, while their herd grew and grew, spreading out further and further, until it surged over the mountain slopes and choked the narrow gorges . . .

On the third day, since they were exhausted by almost sixty hours of uninterrupted travelling, the Old Man agreed to them putting up the tents in a depression well-sheltered from the wind. There was not much wood, but plenty of lichen, and the reindeer, who had had to graze as they went along, continually urged on by the herdsmen and dogs, would be able to take advantage of this splendid pasture.

Setting up camp had by this time become a simple matter and, as everybody knew what he had to do, in less than an hour the snow had been banked up, the tent-poles erected, the canvas covers stretched over the framework, the door-flaps fixed. All that remained was for the women to cover the floors with a soft layer of branches, to fix the hearthstone and suspend the cauldron. This last was Kristina's job, she being the youngest and lightest. Martha Risak assisted her by steadying the ladder, which was simply a single pole with cross pieces nailed to it, while she climbed up and dropped the chain through the smoke-vent. This made a metallic sound, which sounded strange in this world of wood and stone.

Meanwhile, the men who were not looking after the herd went off to look for wood, sometimes a long way from the camp—and on this particular occasion it was nearly two hours before they got back with their heavy load. This meant waiting a long time before the food could be cooked, so that by the time the old woman announced that it was ready most of them were already asleep, packed so tightly together that the sleeping figures looked like a great heap of fur, which gave off a powerful odour of musk and sweat.

The Old Man did not go to sleep . . . did he ever? He could remain squatting for hours on end without apparent effort, bolt upright, drawing at his pipe, his blue eyes fixed on some insignificant detail which helped him to concentrate, apparently indifferent, yet in fact listening to everything that was said and done both in the tent and outside, deciphering the messages borne to him on the wind, noting the slightest sounds that rose above the surge of the tundra : yapping of dogs, faraway cries, the raucous yelling of a man struggling with his reindeer.

The two-day halt they made here enabled everyone to make up for the lack of sleep and food. After the violent storm of the last few days, the cold, though still bitter at night, quickly disappeared at midday, and then the heat reflected from the snow became so strong that it tired the Lapps more than the cold. Already, in places, the snow was beginning to change, thawing, then freezing again, so that where the migration had passed there would now be a firm, slippery track across the vidda, until it disappeared with the final melting of the snow.

By the time they set off again, making for the big depression that leads to the mountains and the sea, they were

169

all once more in good shape. For Paavi, his wounds were only a bitter-sweet memory, revived now and then by a passing stiffness in the left arm. Once more he was back with the herd, the only place he liked, having handed over the heavily loaded sleighs to Mikael Bongo. Mikael, on the contrary, enjoyed driving the baggage sleighs. Occasionally there would be difficulties when the snow was very deep, or the going rough, or the trail badly made, but his whimsical temperament enabled him to put up with anything; and he thoroughly enjoyed the peaceful hours he spent, stretched out on top of the load, with the reindeer effortlessly trotting along over the smooth surface of a lake or down some easy slope, as though urged forward by their load. For Mikael was the bard of the cita, and these long sleigh-rides gave him a chance to improvize his poems. He would let his thoughts stray amongst the clouds, and lying face upwards to the sky, listening to the clickety-click of the hoofs, the whine of the runners and the barking of the dogs, from this natural symphony he would compose his yoks. Occasionally he would turn face downwards on the sleigh, so that all he could see was the round white quarters of his deer, the malicious flicking of its tail, and the great ark of its antlers, bristling with tines like the mandibles of a giant stag beetle. It was then that Mikael tried out his yoks; he started singing and if his improvization pleased the other drivers, they would join in at the top of their lungs. Each of them added something of his own, strengthened the theme, threw it back like a ball and, in this way, a new yok to the glory of the Sokkis became inscribed in their memories. Then, when everyone had exhausted both breath and imagination, Mikael would utter a short, high, strident yell, and they all fell silent again.

The sleighs wound their way along the trail, gliding towards the horizon with its hovering sun. And for all of them the hours flowed by, vague and indistinguishable, like the mistiness of dreams or the detachment of second sight.

Often, during these timeless hours, Kristina brooded over the utterances of the Old Man. They were simply links in an endless chain, added to all those that previous generations had rivetted together during their short spell on earth, and one day they would die, yet others would continue this endless chain; and in this way the race of the Samisks would be perpetuated, the oldest race in the world, the only one that would never perish if only they had the wisdom to go on living in the tradition of their people, to go on living, with the wind and the snow and the lichen and the reindeer!

It took the herd three days to reach the big circular depression of the Mollejaurre. It was surrounded by mountains, the highest of which were those barring the way to the north. The Old Man had scarcely allowed them to stop, resisting the pleas of the younger ones with the greatest firmness.

'Spring is early this year,' said he. 'What should we do if it began to thaw while we were still in the mountains, and it became impossible to pull the sleighs any further? No, we must take advantage of the easy going that God has granted us.'

The others did not insist.

Not once had the Old Man yielded his place at the head of the convoy. He was the figurehead of the ship, handling his ski-stick like a balancing pole, swinging along on his birchwood skis that were secured to his skallers by a single leather thong for all the world like some legendary guardian spirit. And his swaying gait, though far from swift to look at, was so regular that by the time night came the herdsmen were astonished at the distance they had covered. All day long, the old doe with the bell round her neck followed close in the Old Man's tracks, drawing the reindeer behind her. And while they quietly followed her, the dogs were dashing about, keeping the herd on the move, then suddenly stopping short and darting off in another direction, nose to the ground on the track of a white hare or a fox, to disappear into the undergrowth, despite the cries of the herdsmen calling them back.

Paavi was everywhere. Sometimes he would go up to the front to join the Old Man, and for an hour or so the two of them would trudge along side-by-side without saying a word, puffing out the smoke from their pipes in the keen mountain air. Then suddenly Paavi would notice a group of deer trying to break away and make for the hills; and immediately he would send the dogs after them, while he himself, driving himself forward with his ski-sticks, would round up the fugitives. Then, satisfied, he would drop back again to the rear of the herd.

This was the position he preferred. In front of him the wave of reindeer surged forward, horns entangled, muzzles covered with snow, bodies pressed closely together; and he never grew tired of watching all this wealth, for him the finest in the world. There were so many of them that it seemed as though he was driving a forest in front of him! And Paavi would swear to himself that the day would come when he, too, would be master of such a herd. Then he would stop for a moment and, looking back across the gentle, rounded contours of the land, would watch the long string of sledges, twisting and turning in the wake of the herd. And in this sight, too, he found reassurance, for to him it represented the Samisk people on the march, the ultimate meaning of his life.

Thus Simon Sokki's cita made its way forward towards the North, and, parallel with them, in other valleys, fifteen, twenty, thirty herds were drawing other families towards their summer quarters. Until they reached their destination, he would know nothing of all these other citas, for their paths never crossed. And so it had been since there had been Samisks on the face of the earth. Indeed, what he most feared was precisely that the reindeer, attracted by the scent of a neighbouring herd, might cross the invisible line laid down by custom, and get mixed up with those of another cita. This was how the tragedies of the vidda always arose; and in order to avoid such an occurrence the herdsmen never relaxed their watch, day or night.

Preferably, halts were made during the short night, for it was then that the reindeer grazed most readily. The Old Man would stop at the summit of a hill, where the wind continually swept away the snow and exposed the rocks and ice, and there they would bivouack uncomfortably. The baggage deer were simply unharnessed, without the sleighs being unloaded or the tents being put up, and they all crowded round the fire, while Ellena or Martha or Kristina set up a tripod and suspended the cooking pot from it. And the men waited patiently, squatting on their heels beneath their conical pesks, with their caps forming a scarlet circle. And the flames flickered to the rhythm of the wind, the song of the earth, and the night was so clear with all the stars lighting up the sky, and the cold weighed so heavily on their shoulders, that they dozed off imperceptibly into a lethargic sleep, and almost before they knew where they were the dawn of a new day had broken.

With the dawn, the cold suddenly returned, scorching their reddened faces more fiercely than the flames of the fire, and cutting their skins like a razor. They had to fight against it, moving about, drinking boiling hot coffee and eating hunks of meat grilled over the embers. Everyone spent the short night as he chose, some lying awake round the fire, others asleep, stretched out on their sleighs between two reindeer skins, curled up like wild animals, with their legs drawn up beneath their pesks and caps pulled down over their faces, jealously preserving the heat of their bodies. But though they looked like so many corpses, a shouted order from the Old Man was enough to revive them, to make them leap on their sleighs or go and look after the herd.

Sometimes these meals around the fire dragged on for a long time. They had difficulty in appeasing their hunger, which was accentuated by the prolonged hours of effort and the savage cold. Then their silence would gradually give way to chattering and laughter as they told one another stories or exchanged impressions . . . And in their interminable discussions again and again they would revert to recent events, the festival at Viddakaïno, the attack by the wolf and, above all, the unwonted absence of Simon Sokki which obsessed them.

Then the Old Man would butt in angrily :

'Why are you so anxious for him to get back? Isn't the migration going all right? You needn't worry yourselves—Simon Sokki will be here soon enough, and then everything will be changed.'

What he meant, they scarcely dared think.

'Are you afraid of him coming back, then?' asked Ellena.

He looked at them sternly, and they all lowered their eyes, unable to meet his steely glance. All except Kristina :

'I'm not scared of anything my father may do, Old Man, and well you know it !'

He turned his eyes towards her, smiled and said nothing.

A murmur of disapproval greeted the young girl's words. The head of the cita was not to be defied, and they knew they would all obey him as soon as he got back, whatever orders he might give.

'And what about you, Finn? What do you think?'

It was an attempt to make him give himself away, but Paavi avoided the trap.

'A rupes-hunter has no right to think, still less to express an opinion.'

'As if that worried you,' said Pier, shrugging his shoulders.

One morning, before starting again after a halt, the Old Man announced that the following evening they would arrive at the Mollejaurre.

'We shall need a good rest !' said Ellena.

They knew what she meant. At that point, they would encounter the mountains of the sea, and from then on everything would become difficult and dangerous : there would be little lichen for the reindeer, for the slopes of the mountains would be frozen hard; they would be threatened by avalanches and the height would make it ten times as cold; and if on their way through the gorges they had the misfortune to be caught by the mist and the blizzard, the terrified herd might well break away without their being unable to stop it.

'We shall rest for several days !' said the Old Man.

They all signified approval, and began getting ready for

174

the last easy stage of the migration. The dogs quarrelled over the last few bones, gorging themselves on the blood-stained snow, and while the woman loaded the sleighs the drivers caught the baggage-deer with their lassoes.

They set out in the glacial cold of dawn. And, as always happened, it was some time before the cita resumed its regular pace and rhythm; before each reindeer, each man and woman, each sleigh had become a part of the enormous, articulated column.

The rising sun touched the hills in the east, tinging the mountain snow a delicate pink; and, as they turned, urged by some obscure, age-old belief, towards the glittering star to receive the gift of its light and beneficient warmth, they could suddenly see, scattered over the crest of the mountain, the great herd of the Isaksens, which a chance break in the line of hills brought into view, following a parallel route. They were too far away for the herdsmen to shout at one another but, to the Sokkis, the vision of their neighbours, reviving so many ill-healed wounds, appeared as an insult. When the Isaksens had disappeared again in a fold in the mountain they started moving again, led by the Old Man and cheered on by the songs of Mikael Bongo. The great brown triangle of the herd cleaved a passage to the north like some giant snow plough, leaving behind it, clear and deep, the road along which the sleighs would follow. Paavi, guarding the flank, rounded up the straying deer. He was uneasy. Soon Simon Sokki would be back, bringing the ill-omened news, and once again he would have to defy him! For now he was convinced that the others would be ready to accept whatever the master had decided upon.

Before long the fringe of mountains could be clearly seen on the horizon; these were no longer gentle, eroded slopes, but, on every side, cliffs and spurs of rocks, rearing high into the air, a whole terrifying world, still made mysterious by distance, but into which they were soon to plunge.

And beyond that again was the country of the sea, of the fjords; a new world, which was no longer the world of the Samisks!

PART THREE

THE FJELL

CHAPTER ONE

I T was the wolf-hunter who first noticed the smoke from the camp beneath the wings of the aeroplane. They had just crossed the chain of mountains that runs along the coast, flying low, skimming the glaciers and peaks of Lyngen Fjord; and now, ahead of them, the huge Lapp plain, bathed in the blinding light of spring, stretched away towards the remote horizon, revealing an infinite succession of lakes and bare mountain tops, polished and shining, with the grey unvarying tundra, that followed the contours of the hills always at the same height, surrounding the lakes and accentuating their frozen whiteness.

'There they are!' exclaimed Sven Haraldsen, at the same moment turning the nose of his plane towards the blue smoke issuing from the squat, cone-shaped tents.

Per Oskal had lost his bearings. He had already flown over so many migration routes, marked by just such encampments with their haze of blue smoke! How was he to know where he was? The long trails of trampled snow could be seen from a long way off, one could scarcely miss them : they stretched away, parallel, from south to north, but as to recognizing which particular cita it was, of all those that were wandering about at this time of year, one would have had to be a Lapp—and sober at that, the Lappefogden said to himself bitterly, glancing over his shoulder at Simon Sokki, who was lying in the baggage-hold sleeping off his liquor!

'That's them all right,' the pilot confirmed.

Per Oskal shrugged his shoulders.

'I only hope you're right. I shan't know where I am until we land. From up here everything looks the same.'

'Everyone sees things his own way,' said the pilot. 'I have to be high up if I'm to get my bearings! And now hang on, we'll show them some fireworks!'

179

Without more ado he dived straight for the camp, straightened out at the last moment, climbed steeply and started to go into a spin, performing every kind of acrobatic manœuvre that his small, overloaded plane would stand up to.

Per Oskal did not fancy this at all. They had had a pretty bad shaking up coming over the mountains, and his stomach still felt squeamish.

'For God's sake take it easy, Sven, you can give your display after you've put me down. By that time, thank God, I shall be back on skis again!

Sven laughed, displaying a gleam of teeth as dazzling as those of the wolves he hunted.

'Can't be helped, Per. They enjoy it too much!'

Steadier now, the little aeroplane was cruising above the frozen lake at about 300 feet, and Per Oskal, feeling more cheerful, could distinguish the details of the countryside. Their arrival caused a sensation. The reindeer of the big herd dashed about all over the place, despite the efforts of the dogs to keep them together, and the herdsmen, who had recognized Sven's aeroplane, were waving to the pilot in the friendliest fashion. In front of the tent, perched on the sleighs, the young people were throwing their red caps in the air, and probably shouting with delight at the spectacle they had just seen, though the noise of the engine prevented the two airmen from hearing a sound.

'So, Per, you've really made up your mind?' Sven asked. 'You're going to advise them to emigrate to the Tröndelag?'

'Yes,' sighed Per, 'but it's a sorry business. If there was the slightest chance . . .'

'What? You don't really agree, then?'

Per Oskal shook his head. Yes, naturally he agreed, since Simon had consented. Simon was the chief, and whatever he decided the others would approve of. But there was the Old Man to reckon with, as well as the Finn! And not without emotion he thought of Kristina; what was *she* going to say about it? Hadn't he betrayed her trust in him? He suddenly felt overwhelmed with regret, with remorse. Although Sokki had appeared to be convinced, had he really made up his mind? Fru Tideman, who knew how changeable he was, had her doubts, despite his promises. Although he had pretended to agree with them, the Lapp had nevertheless insisted upon holding matters up : the matter could only be finally decided after the migration.

'It would be best if you stayed with him, Per Oskal,' she had suggested. 'You were there when he gave his word, and your presence at the camp would remind him of his duty.'

Per admitted that the agreement had been fully thrashed out; he had been scrupulously careful about that. In the circumstances, therefore, how could he have refused Fru Tideman's suggestion? That was why he had undertaken, rather thoughtlessly as it now seemed to him, to make sure that Simon would not go back on his word.

'We could come back again later on, if you like,' said Sven, who felt that he was still undecided. 'For once we land you know what to expect : the worst part of the migration is still ahead, a month in the fjell with nothing but marrow-bones and reindeer soup! You really are asking for it!'

'If only he would wake up,' said Per, turning round. But the Lapp was still snoring, his face hidden in his furs.

'Your acrobatics haven't had much effect on him!'

'For anyone who's used to being jolted about on a sleigh, anything else seems dead calm,' said the pilot seriously. 'And now we're going in to land!'

'Get on with it then,' said Per Oskal in a resigned tone of voice.

Sven Haraldsen made straight for the water-hole, clearly visible in the middle of the lake, with the path made by the women fetching water leading up to it. The little aeroplane landed without difficulty, gliding gently along on its broad skis, which carried it as far as the camp. Having stopped the aeroplane head-on to the wind, Sven shut off the engine. The silence of the vidda after the roar of the motor was impressive. Sven, accustomed by this time to the steady drone of the pistons, was more conscious of it than anyone else. Every time he landed in this lunar landscape, a kind of anguish filled his heart.

'It's like being on the moon, Per,' said he. 'How do you manage to live in all this monotonous snow? All I want is to get the engine going again!'

'And yet you keep coming back to it! How do you explain that?'

The pilot hummed a little tune. Per Oskal was right. This solitude scared him, yet at the same time he loved it.

'Because here I am free,' he admitted.

'And I, because I have the feeling of being in control of things here,' said the Lappefogden. 'But that's just kidding oneself . . . here more than anywhere else.'

They took off their safety belts and jumped out of the machine.

'Here comes the reception committee!' said Sven.

The youngsters from the camp were running towards them waving their arms and shouting with joy. Per Oskal recognized Mikael, Pier, Andis, Kristina and Karin, and went to meet them, but the Lapps displayed some hesitation.

'Per Oskal here?' Kristina said under her breath. She felt a kind of choking feeling, and remained rooted to the spot. What was the meaning of this visit? They were expecting Simon Sokki but it was the Lappefogden who had come to see them. Not for a moment did it strike them that some accident might have happened. No! Perhaps everything had already been decided, and Simon Sokki had stayed behind to prepare for their arrival, and had sent Per Oskal to break the news to them!

Kristina made as though to retreat, but Andis caught her by the sleeve. He guessed that something was worrying her, though he did not see things as clearly as she did. Besides, the Lappefogden had always been a friend to them.

'Per Oskal is one of our friends. You know Fru Tideman

182

and the Pastor wanted to prevent him from being a member of the commission! If it's all fixed up, it's because it's going to be to our advantage.'

'Even our best friends could betray us without realizing it,' said Kristina.

'Per Oskal will have to go back when the pilot does. You don't imagine he's going to stop here.' said Andis. He had not considered this eventuality.

'In any case we can't let him go until we have found out what has been decided about the Tröndelag!'

Sven advanced, smiling, Per Oskal following a short way behind him, and everyone started murmuring the welcoming 'Bouriz, bouriz!'

'It needs a nose like a gun-dog's to track you down,' said Sven. 'I expected to find you further south. You must have been making good time!'

'With the Old Man, there's not much dawdling about,' said Kristina.

The pilot turned back to the aeroplane :

'Better wake him up, I suppose!'

'I'll see to him,' said Per Oskal.

Intrigued, the others followed him. Leaning over into the cockpit, Per Oskal vigorously shook the heap of grey furs, which suddenly came to life. From beneath the red cap came the sound of belching and grunting; an arm freed itself from the heap, and a hand appeared and pushed back the cap, revealing a man's bewildered face, with a bristling moustache and eyes puffy with sleep and drink.

'Simon!' exclaimed Mikael.

'Simon!' the others repeated.

There was a general burst of laughter, but it was not lacking in respect. They were all suddenly happy, relieved that the master was back and that everything would now be as it should be. Looking rather hang-dog, he managed to scramble out of the aeroplane, swaying as he walked.

'Had a good sleep, Simon?' said Sven.

'Where are we then?' the other grunted.

His gaze turned from one to the other. He was hardly

awake yet, and, trying to make out where he was, he began looking for landmarks, the bare crest of a hill, blocked by the trunk of a solitary birch tree, the frozen creek of a lake, and gradually his prodigious visual memory began to reassert itself, for it had been upset by the speed of the flight as well as by the sleep and drink.

'Mollejaurre already? The Old Man hasn't wasted any time!'

'You can trust him for that,' said Andis.

'And how's the lichen?'

'Plenty of it.'

'And the reindeer?'

They muttered something that was meant to be reassuring. No one was anxious to tell him about the massacre. He had caught sight of the great, grey blotch of the herd, and now he could think of nothing else but the reindeer covering the tundra, which reminded him of the wealth and power of his clan. He gave free vent to his happiness; broke into a short, piercing yok; pulled off his cap with a swift gesture; began scratching his head in his familiar manner; then, putting on his cap again, he clapped the youngsters on the back, and everyone started laughing. Simon Sokki was really back again, cheerful, bold, impulsive, and probably as quick-tempered as ever. They hadn't managed to change him at Trömso. For an instant Kristina felt her hopes reviving. Simon Sokki had not given in. But what was Per Oskal doing here with him?

Simon Sokki suddenly remembered his guest:

'Come on into the tent! I know my Ellena, she's sure to have some coffee and soup ready.'

The two Norwegians were dying with hunger, and did not have to be asked twice. As they reached the camp, they saw the Old Man waiting for them, standing outside the principal tent.

'Manna derivan, Simon Sokki,' he said ceremoniously.

'Bazza derivan! How's everything been going?'

'We'll talk about that later on, Simon. Your guests are hungry.'

184

Simon Sokki entered the tent first, took his place on the right-hand of Ellena already busy with her stew, sniffed the familiar greasy smell of the soup, squatted on his heels and signed to the others to take their places. Everyone sat or squatted in a circle, according to rank or age, the older ones furthest from the entrance, and each time one of them sat down you could hear the creak of the branches beneath the reindeer skins. Sven Haraldsen and Per Oskal found themselves squeezed up near the opening, where, despite the door-flap, the wind and cold were most noticeable.

Ellena passed round the bowls of coffee. They drank slowly, sucking the liquid through lumps of sugar held between their teeth, and, as the time for exchanging news had not yet arrived, they all remained silent, thoughtfully observing one another. Outside, the usual breeze droned through the dwarf trees. High in the sky, the shafts of the sun shone straight down, and within the tent the heavy condensation seemed to accentuate the translucence of the canvas. Kristina put some green wood on the fire, which gave off a thick smoke. Someone coughed.

'Look out, Kristina!' a voice grumbled. 'Do you want to smoke us out?'

She laughed, and mischievously added another branch.

'If you go on like that I shall take you back to the Agjiet!'

'I shall go back there one day, Sven, whether you come with me or not,' she said calmly.

'You wouldn't be afraid to?'

'The stallos are part of our life,' she replied.

Sven looked at her sympathetically. He realized what Per Oskal had meant when he spoke about her strength of mind. He knew quite well what she was implying, but no one else picked up the allusion.

Simon Sokki ate greedily; anyone would have thought he had had nothing to eat for a week. The truth of the matter was, the Norwegian food, which was all he had had since leaving Viddakaïno, did not altogether agree with him;

like all Lapps, what he really liked was to devour a great
bellyful of meat and soup, and then spend hours blissfully
digesting it, curled up in his furs, lulled by the harsh song
of the wind.

When he had eaten his fill, he asked sharply :

'What's been happening while I've been away?'

They all looked at one another, without daring to speak.
Seeing their embarrassment, he looked at the Old Man : he
was not there. Probably he had gone back to the herd,
feeling that, now the master was here again, his role as
leader was completed.

'The Old Man will tell you all about it later on,' said
Ellena. 'There's no need to worry our guests with it.'

Immediately, he began to feel uneasy. They were hiding
something from him. But Ellena was right, it wouldn't do
to talk in front of strangers. He counted up those who were
sitting around. He knew where the others were : Martha
Risak and Thor had gone back to their tent, and his sister,
Martha Bongo, would be cooking in hers.

'Is the Finn with the herd?'

'Yes, with Mattis.'

He was fond of his nephew, and approved of the two
of them being together. Ever since the business of the raid
he had lost confidence in Thor Risak—a herdsman who
could sleep while his reindeer were being stolen ! Mattis was
quite different, a sensible lad, always on his toes. If he and
the Finn were together, everything would be all right ! He
nodded his head contentedly.

Several minutes elapsed before anyone spoke. Per Oskal
was listening to the invisible music of the great open spaces.
It made him feel happy, yet at the same time intimidated
him. Although it was not the first time that he had shared
the life of the Lapps, he was aware that being with a cita
during a migration would bring him into much closer
contact with their nomad existence. Perhaps they would
reveal themselves to him in a new light? But what was immediately worrying him was the fact that the people of the
cita did not appear to be aware of the decision that had

been taken; and, contrary to his hopes, Simon seemed to be in no hurry to inform them.

A sudden powerful squall set the canvas flapping and drove the smoke back into the tent so that it was almost impossible to breathe.

'Open the flap, Per,' said Sven. 'It's stifling in here.'

Per Oskal was nearest to the entrance. He raised the flap, and an icy blast swept away both the smoke and the warmth.

'Hi!' exclaimed the pilot, suddenly concerned. 'While I'm sitting here dreaming, a blizzard has started. Come and give me a hand, Per and Mikael. The lake is not very long, I shall have to take off quickly.'

They all hurried out to watch the manœuvre, while Sven took his bearings. The hum of the engine awoke echoes in the mountains, and the wind from the propellor, sweeping across the lake, raised a cloud of snow that hid Per Oskal and Mikael from sight as they hung on to the wings, waiting for the signal to let go. They knew what to do, for this was not the first time Sven had taken off like this. The pilot fastened his helmet, adjusted his goggles and, leaning out of the window, yelled :

'By the way, are there any wolves around here?'

'There were,' said Mikael laconically, 'but there aren't any more !'

'So you don't need me? Then I'll go eastward. They sent me a message that several packs had been seen in the Vestfjellet.'

'Good hunting !' they called back to him.

The pilot pressed the starter, while the Lapps clung to the wings to prevent the aeroplane from moving. Then Sven signalled to them, and they dropped into the snow, while the little aeroplane leapt forward at full throttle, taking off in the shortest possible space and quickly beginning to gain height. Overhead, the pilot made a farewell turn, flew over the camp, waved his hand, then passed above the herd, dipping his wings, and finally, turning to the east, disappeared behind the mountains.

When the flurry of snow caused by his departure had

settled down again and the sound of the aeroplane was no more than a distant hum, the people of the cita slowly returned to their tents.

Per Oskal went with them. In the excitement of the take-off, the Lapps had forgotten all about him. Now, they began looking him up and down as though it was the first time they had seen him.

'So you're staying with us, Per Oskal,' asked Kristina.

He could feel the girl's uneasiness.

'Simon Sokki has asked me to!'

He was lying. It was he who, at Fru Tideman's suggestion, had given the Lapp the idea of taking him along with him.

'You intend to go back to Viddakaïno on skis?' said Kristina.

Her hopes rose once more. Per Oskal was an outstanding skier and he often used to visit the camps in this way, pulling his small, very light, sledge behind him to carry his camping gear.

'No, I'm coming with you as a herdsman!'

This was obviously not the reason, since there were plenty of them without him. She was about to protest when Simon Sokki, who had been listening to their conversation, authoritatively cut it short.

'Per Oskal is staying with us. You can't have too many hands when you're crossing the fjell. He'll drive the sleighs and take his turn watching the herd.'

The young girl shrugged her shoulders. It was too soon to find out what he was up to.

Per Oskal left the group and walked off through the camp. He needed to straighten out his ideas. Suddenly he felt terribly alone. Simon Sokki seemed to have completely forgotten everything that had happened at Trömso, and Kristina was keeping him at a distance. As soon as he had arrived she had guessed why he was there: to help them to accept the idea that this was to be their last migration. But what Kristina did not realize was that he now lacked confidence in his mission. He no longer knew what he was going to do or what was going to become of him.

188

Here, in the middle of the fjell, amongst the tents of the nomads, in the poignant and unaccustomed atmosphere of the migration, he felt bewildered and ignorant. Here, the Lapps were no longer the same people. These were not the Lapps from the coast that he had known as a boy, with whose children he had played and whose language he had eventually learnt to speak. He had suddenly come to realize that his contact with the life of the Laplanders, which he had thought to be so close, was really only superficial. Of the real nomads he knew nothing.

He could no longer be sure what was right and true. How could he hold it against Simon Sokki, then, that he had forgotten his promises, when he himself might already be on the point of betraying his mission?

In the slowly fading light, the mountains had begun to disappear; they knew that the sun had set, and that a new storm was brewing. Per Oskal, recognizing all the warning signs, calculated that Sven Haraldsen would just have time to land at Viddakaïno before the blizzard started.

No one seemed to be concerned about him now; they were all busy at their various jobs, heedless of his presence. Simon Sokki had made up his mind, and they accepted his decision.

The only person to show any interest in him was Martha Risak; after all, he was a new man, and she knew all the others. When she accosted him, he smiled bitterly.

'Where are you going to sleep, Per?'

He shrugged his shoulders.

'Why not come in with us, then? Our tent is the least crowded.'

In fact, the only people in it were Martha, her brother Thor when he was not on guard, and Mattis, her nephew. Per Oskal put down his haversack in the place she pointed out to him.

'There you won't be in the draught from the door!' she said.

'Thanks, Martha,' he said, for he knew that had he been in Simon's tent he would have been given the worst place.

She stared at him so hard that he felt flustered. He lowered his eyes, went outside and took a deep draught of the icy air.

He had made up his mind.

'Since this is how things are, I may as well live like a Laplander! Martha, show me where you get the wood from, so that I can make myself useful.'

He had already put on his skis, and was soon making for the tundra. Now the only thing he worried about was to cut wood and bring back as much as possible. From now on, he was simply one of the many cogs in the machine that was driving the migration to the North, to the North and the mountains of the sea, where Simon Sokki would at last make up his mind as he had promised.

CHAPTER TWO

S I M O N   S O K K I suddenly halted.

'What was the point of slaughtering all these animals?'

Andis, who was accompanying his father on a tour of inspection, was too frightened to speak. Simon pointed to the tall drying-poles, bent beneath the weight of reindeer carcases. There were still at least a dozen of them. More than one reindeer at a time was never killed during a migration!

'Come on now! What's happened?'

And when Andis could not help displaying alarm, he raised his fist and said:

'I'll make you tell me, whether you want to or not.'

Andis was accustomed to these sudden, terrifying outbursts of anger, and decided it was better to speak up.

'It was a wolf, father . . . that got into the herd.'

'Who was looking after them?' asked Simon. 'That useless Thor Risak, I suppose!'

He had never forgiven him for allowing the herd to be raided.

Andis hung his head:

'Your son Pier, and Mikael Bongo.'

Simon looked amazed, for these were the very ones he had the greatest faith in.

'And how many did it kill?'

He could easily imagine what had happened. It was just one of those things, a normal episode in their lives, and with his usual fatalism he was already beginning to calm down. If anything like this had happened to Mikael, it must have been a pretty bad storm.

'During a blizzard, eh? How many did it kill?'

'The wolf itself accounted for ten of them!'

'What d'you mean?'

He did not like the tone of Andis's voice.

'The Finn killed the other three! He fired when he was right in the middle of the herd, like any greenhorn. It was lucky he didn't kill any more.'

'The fool,' said Simon. 'If what you're saying is true, he'll have to repay me for the three reindeer and if any of them were does I'll insist upon him giving me a calf every year for the next ten years.'

He was no longer upset, he had begun to calculate. If the Finn had made a mistake, he would have him at his mercy. He'd have to stop his swaggering about; and he'd lose all his influence, over Kristina in the first place, then over all the other members of the cita, who were only too ready to look up to him as a leader.

'Get back to the herd, and send the Finn and the Old Man here.'

'Who's to take their place?'

'You.'

'But it's not my turn . . . it's . . .'

'Do as I tell you.'

Andis went off feeling thoroughly disgruntled.

It was late in the evening when the Finn and the Old Man returned to the camp. The blizzard that had been threatening all day had just started, and they had gathered the herd into as compact a space as possible to make it easier to keep an eye on them. It was nearly dark, and the fires in the three tents could be seen shining through the canvas, so that in the flurry of snow and wind they looked like tiny glowworms.

The Finn had watched the arrival of the aeroplane from a distance; he had seen the Lappefogden get out, followed by Simon Sokki, and had felt sure that, from now on, everything was going to be different.

'This means *our* time's up, Old Man,' he said.

'The future will be whatever you make it, believe me!'

Andis had refrained from telling them why the master wanted them, and both of them assumed that it was because he was going to announce the great decision.

192

As soon as they arrived in the tent they found Pier and Mikael, Kristina and Ellena, Per Oskal and one or two others already assembled, and they could see from Simon Sokki's expression that things were going badly. The master merely grunted in response to Paavi's respectful greeting. Then, after a few minutes of general silence, Simon got down to business.

'You must be a pretty good shot, Paavi! Well done! It's not often anyone manages to bring down three at one go!'

The atmosphere was already becoming tense. They all knew how coldly audacious the Finn could be, and how proud he was: was he going to answer back? Per Oskal, sensing the drama in the air, listened with an impassive expression. This was no concern of his, he must remain neutral. The Old Man leant against the frozen canvas, drawing on his pipe, his eyes far away. Everyone was waiting to see how the Finn would react.

Paavi felt the hot, angry blood rising to his head. So that was why they'd all been called together, to hear him insulted publicly! He clenched his fist, and was on the point of giving vent to his anger when a glance from Kristina calmed him.

'I suppose Mikael and Pier have told you how it happened, master?'

Simon was taken aback. He had not even troubled to ask them. In his sullen anger he had summoned his people around him without explanation. All he knew about the incident was what he had learnt from Andis.

'What Andis has told me is enough for me,' he growled.

'Don't you think, Simon, it would be better to get to the bottom of the business, before passing judgment?' said the Old Man.

Kristina heaved a sigh of relief. Perhaps it would be possible to prevent Simon Sokki from losing his temper. Mikael started to speak, and did so in generous terms. He admired the Finn, and he knew that Simon would listen to what he had to say.

'The storm lasted for three days while we were in camp

at Bastevarre. There was such a strong blizzard, and the night was so dark, that it was impossible to see anything clearly! When we discovered its tracks, the wolf, scared by our presence, took refuge in the middle of the herd. We were trying to drive it out, when the Finn arrived and started to help us. At the risk of getting himself ripped open by the terrified reindeer, or trampled underfoot, he went straight into the middle of the herd!'

Simon was listening; he could imagine exactly what had happened. He, too, had once acted just like the Finn, and been knocked over by the reindeer, trampled on and so seriously wounded that it was several weeks before he recovered. He could appreciate the man's courage.

As Mikael continued, Pier nodded in agreement. He was trying to justify the shot, but at this point in his account the Finn interrupted him.

'What Mikael has said it true, Simon, but I must admit I was wrong to shoot. It was a mistake. Mikkel Mikkelsen Sara always warned me: "Never fire when you're in the middle of the herd". But it seemed to me to be such a splendid opportunity, for all of a sudden, the reindeer opened up, leaving a big empty space, and there I was, face to face with the wolf. Unfortunately just at that moment they all closed in again.'

He stopped speaking, and the others respected his silence. Per Oskal realized that nothing was going to happen: now that he was confronted by the facts of the situation, Simon's wrath had collapsed of its own account.

'As a result of my carelessness I killed three reindeer. You can pick three animals from my herd to replace them.'

He was on the point of getting up and leaving the tent. He felt the need to be alone. It must have taken a considerable effort for a man of his class to have to admit his mistake publicly.

'There's more to it than that,' said the Old Man. 'Describe what happened afterwards!'

And as Paavi remained silent, Kristina hurried outside, snatched up the head and pelt of the big grey wolf from

194

beneath the cover of her sleigh, and threw them down at Simon Sokki's feet.

'He certainly hasn't told you everything, father.'

Simon's gaze wandered from the wolf-skin to the hunter's expressionless face, rested for a moment on his daughter, then on Ellena, who was clutching the cross she wore round her neck, and finally turned to the Lappefogden.

'Why he's as big as the wolf of the Agjiet,' Simon Sokki exclaimed with a sharp whistle. Then he felt the thickness of the fur, noted where the knife had slashed it, and with a brusque gesture of astonishment enquired:

'D'you mean to say you killed him with a knife?'

'Show him your arm, Paavi,' said Kristina. 'Is there anybody else here who would have had the courage?'

'Kristina is right,' said Simon Sokki, nodding his head, 'and you, too, Old Man! Andis didn't tell me everything.'

He reflected for a moment or two, while outside the wind moaned, causing the tent-poles to creak and the canvas to flap violently. Everyone was waiting for the master's verdict.

'In this business, all of us are responsible,' said Simon Sokki. 'The herdsmen's negligence was due to the storm, which made it difficult for them to do their jobs; and if it hadn't been for that the Finn wouldn't have become involved. If he killed three reindeer in order to destroy the worst killer in the Bastejaurre, he may well have saved dozens! The losses must be shared by the whole cita, and those the dead animals belonged to will be excused from contributing to the meat supplies. Any does that were in calf will count as two. I have spoken!'

He had suddenly become quite cheerful, and was stroking the wolfskin with the greatest satisfaction, continually admiring its size, the colour of its fur and the length of its fangs. He turned to Per Oskal:

'Well, what did you think of my judgement?'

'Wisdom itself, Simon Sokki! If only all your people would sort out their differences like that, I shouldn't be needed any more.'

'And now, what about us all celebrating the death of the

big, grey wolf? Let's have a look at what you've got in that fourth sledge of yours, Ellena!'

They all knew what this meant: the fourth sledge contained the supply of illicit alcohol. They would drink to celebrate the master's return, the Finn's hunting and the presence of the Lappefogden.

As if the wind had carried the news throughout the whole camp, in no time at all the whole cita was assembled, everyone crowding into the restricted space as best they could. Those who sat with their backs against the frozen canvas could feel the bitter cold even through their furs, those in the centre scorched their hands and faces at the fire, but everyone was happy; peace was once more restored to the camp. Kristina crept over to where the Finn was sitting. She had regained all her confidence, and he began caressing her gently, more moved than he cared to show. Bottles of aquavit passed from hand to hand, and by the time they had swallowed a few mouthfuls they were not ashamed to be seen sitting clasped in one another's arms; and thus they remained, without moving, content to listen to the noise of the wind, the spluttering of the fire, the occasional sound of raucous voices. Yoks broke out spontaneously, died away, were taken up again: while Mikael, who had made himself a kind of guitar with a box and some copper wire, accompanied them with a tune he had composed for the occasion.

Per Oskal, slightly drunk, felt himself drifting far away into time and space. He had no means of comparing what was now happening with anything in his past life: this evening he was living with primitive people, sharing their life, their occupations, their songs. What was he doing here? It was only with an effort that he could recall the purpose of his mission. Yet what mission could he possibly fulfil, with these people from another age, another epoch, lost in the heart of the vidda, with nothing between them and the icy wind blowing from the fjell but a thin sheet of canvas? Had everything that had been said, decided, promised at the Trömso conference been forgotten? Here was Simon

Sokki with his cap pushed to the back of his head and his face flushed, already half-drunk, and all these people breaking up into couples and fondling one another quite naturally, and no one worrying about anything except the warmth and well-being provided by the liquor and the fire. What did they care if a storm was raging outside?

And gradually Per felt himself succumbing to the mood of carefree happiness.

'Should I ever really become a Lapp?' he asked himself.

The question was soon answered for him: someone had slipped down beside him, a hand sought his and their fingers intertwined.

'Martha!' he exclaimed breathlessly.

She smiled at him, with a gleam of white teeth. He turned to look at the others, but no one was paying the least attention to them, neither Ellena, lying round and plump in Simon Sokki's arms, nor Thor with Karin, nor Kristina clasped in the Finn's embrace.

Yes, in the Finnmark there were two distinct worlds, two races, two civilizations. And what could all the comfort and security that people wanted to provide them with add to the happiness of these people, living contentedly in their snowy desert, shut in by the cold and the storm?

There was nothing, he told himself, no one, that could ever take the place of such moments of happiness. They had fire and furs to keep off the cold, tents to shelter them from the snow, thick soup and aquavit that lent beauty to everything and awoke the fires of passion. They asked for nothing more. Certainly, nothing that would have meant sacrificing some part of this complete freedom.

'It's splendid to be alone, isn't it, Martha?' he said suddenly, seeking her lips, which she freely yielded to him.

'We'll make a real Lapp of you yet,' said she.

And he did not tell her that the reason he was here was to turn them into real Norwegians. Why should he? What was the point?

No one had noticed the Old Man leave the tent. He had drunk just as much as anyone else, but without turning a hair. Then he had got to his feet, stepped over the huddle of bodies, and gone out into the night and the storm to have a look at the herd. That was where his place was. As though by instinct, he found his way to where Andis was squatting in his snow-hole, slipped in beside him and lit his pipe.

'Why aren't you with the others?' asked the young Lapp.

'Because my place is here.'

He sat bolt upright, probing the darkness, listening to the music of the wind and all the familiar noises of the herd whose musky smell filled him with delight, the oldest perfume known to mankind. And through this smell, the Old Man felt himself linked with those immemorial times when, on nights like this, his ancestors had gorged themselves on the warm blood of living reindeer, sucking it from the veins in their necks.

CHAPTER THREE

T w o days after Simon Sokki's return the blizzard was still blowing. The previous night an aurora borealis, exceptional at this time of year, had lit up the whole sky and, for some hours, everything had been transformed, taken on a new beauty, as the herdsmen watched the great herd, caught up in the general conflagration, assuming the strangest colours, that turned from rose pink to yellow, to blue, like the animals in the apocalypse. When daylight broke it was accompanied by a terrible cold, which turned the herdsmen into statues of ice, though those who remained in the tents managed to keep reasonably warm by constantly making up the fire.

Simon had had a consultation with the Old Man.

'We ought to get going,' the latter had recommended. 'Already a number of the does are getting restive; it won't be long before they start calving down.'

'Aren't you afraid of the storm in the mountains?'

'It may well go on for a week. The aurora borealis is a warning that never lets you down. Would you prefer to see your whole herd calve before we reach the sea?'

This business of calving was a constant worry for the Lapps: if any of the does had their calves before reaching their journey's end, mother and calf had to be left to their fate; and the chances of finding them again in the autumn were minimal.

'Why couldn't you put the young ones on the sleighs?' Per Oskal suggested.

They looked at him in amazement. Didn't he know that if a human being so much as touched a newborn reindeer, the mother would smell them and leave the calf to starve?

Every day the Norwegian was making some new discovery. Though he had thought he knew everything there was to know about the Lapps, he was now beginning to realize that, fundamentally, their real selves only emerged in the course of these long migrations, which took them from the middle of Lapland to the mountains of the sea. Everything else was simply a façade that they assumed. Here things were much simpler : hunger and cold, the herd, wolves, life and death! And all these problems that beset them had to be resolved; they had to live, and, in order to live, or even to survive, they had much too much to do to start worrying about additional problems. As to this Tröndelag business, they had scarcely mentioned it, not even Kristina or the Finn. After the first evening's drinking bout, everyone had gone back to work, waiting till Simon chose to call them together. Apparently he did not regard the time as being opportune, however; and when Per asked him about it, and tried to insist, he had answered :

'For the moment, Per, the only thing that matters is getting the herd to the sea. Once we are there it will be time enough to start thinking about making up our minds.'

'But you promised, don't forget!' Per had thought it as well to add, anxious to carry out his side of the bargain.

'And what makes you think I shan't keep my promise?' said Simon, breaking into the familiar form of address that he always used when he wanted to appear on friendly terms with anyone. 'Don't you see, Per, that the migration is the one big thing in the lives of our people? If it weren't for that, there'd be no need for you to lecture me, nor Fru Tideman and the Pastor, either! The day we cease to be nomads we shall be Norwegians like you and the doctor! What will it matter to me then, whether we live in the Tröndelag, or whether life's better there than at Viddakaïno? But our life here, which probably strikes you as abnormal, is our real life!'

While this conversation was taking place, Simon was making a tour of the sledges and tents, moving through the blizzard like a ghost, or rather, like some monstrous animal, bandy-legged and covered with fur. Though the force of the wind was terrific, he scarcely seemed to notice it. How on earth could they set out again in weather like this?

Suddenly he said :

'The Old Man's right, the longer we wait, the worse the reindeer will suffer ! Take down the tents, and get the sledges loaded.'

'He's crazy,' thought Per Oskal.

But already his companion had disappeared into the impalpable mist, shouting to wake up those who were still asleep; and the Lappefogden found himself alone, isolated in the midst of the din and bustle of the cita.

No one had raised any objection. For two days they had been eating and drinking, gorging themselves; and now they understood perfectly well the motives behind Simon's order. Already one or two does had begun trying to break away from the herd, and it was becoming increasingly difficult to prevent them.

Per Oskal helped them to strike camp. Everyone—men, women and youngsters—was already busily at work. In less than no time the tents were taken down, and the wind was scattering the hot embers. Groups of people were folding the heavy, frozen canvas and stacking the poles and stays on the sledges. Others were taking down the drying-poles, loading the carcases on to the pulka kept for this purpose, and despite the apparent confusion everything was being done quite methodically. Now and then the wind was so strong that they had to turn their backs to it and wait until it died down before they could get on with their work.

Even Per Oskal forgot all about the cold; though he had been turned into a block of solid ice, he did not even feel it. He was amazed to discover the prodigious qualities of these people, who had adapted themselves by hundreds of years' experience to the daily struggle with the elements.

The herdsmen had rounded up the main herd, and either the Finn or Andis or the Old Man was looking after it. The reindeer, held in check by the dogs, crowded around the camp, and, for the first time, Per Oskal noticed the tremendous din produced by this mass of huddled bodies; the

201

rubbing of their frozen coats, the rattle of their antlers, like the sound of the wind in a ship's rigging. Flurries of snow filled the air, wind and fog swirled round the reindeer; then, suddenly, it would become clear again, and the whole scene would be filled with ghosts, restlessly moving hither and thither, charging down upon one another, bending their bodies, lassoing the draught-reindeer, who had joined the rest of the herd in an attempt to avoid capture. The oaths of the herdsmen and drivers, the reindeer kicking and thrusting dangerously with their antlers, the dogs rushing about helter-skelter, the rapid orders shouted by Simon Sokki— all this created a bewildering scene, a whirlpool of figures, at the heart of which Per Oskal stood rooted to the spot, incapable of any reaction, absorbed in his thoughts.

'Come and give me a hand,' a voice called. 'It will warm you up.'

Martha Risak appeared from the cloud of snow and, in her frozen pesk, with her frosted hair escaping from beneath her scarlet cap and her fur leggings pulled up over her short skirt, she seemed to have emerged from some other age, from a time long gone by, infinitely remote, and had it not been for her mocking voice, endlessly in quest of a man, he would not have recognized her. Suddenly he felt ashamed of his idleness.

'You're right, tell me what to do !'

'We'll fix my tent on one of the sleighs. Take care now, these thongs easily break when they're frozen. Make sure the tarpaulin is properly tied.'

And he obeyed this young woman, who, in the midst of the storm, appeared so slight, yet was able to move about in it as freely and easily as if it were her natural element.

'What about the wood?' yelled Simon Sokki. 'Have you got enough?'

'We have three sledges fully loaded,' said Mikael.

They all knew that they were about to confront the fjell, and that for three days if everything went well, a week if the storm continued, they would not see another tree, not even a bush, only the wilderness of ice and snow and rock.

202

Per Oskal realized that gradually everything was being sorted out. In a moment of calm, which cleared the powdery snow of the blizzard, it was possible to make out the vague outline of men and reindeer; the wind blew across the surface of the earth, and all one could distinguish were heads, shoulders, human figures like moving tree-trunks, all mysteriously borne on the waves of snow; and then, more clearly discernible, the sleighs drawn up in order, ready to set out. In some cases the reindeer had already been harnessed up, but one Lapp was still rolling about in the snow, struggling to control his animal to the accompaniment of a hail of blows and kicks. In front of them, the main herd was gathered on the surface of the lake, most of the animals lying down and chewing the cud, muzzles to the wind and completely covered with icicles. Where the large tent had stood, nothing now remained but the still glowing hearthstone, on which remained a metal stew-pot filled to the brim with meat and soup, and each of them, before going to his post, went up to Ellena, who handed them sugar, coffee and a portion of meat, which men and women ate standing up, heedless of the storm.

Per Oskal followed their example, and before long his fingers were sticky with melted fat, which was also running down his cheeks. He was experiencing an intense physical pleasure : the hot soup and meat warmed his whole body, so that he no longer felt the cold or the force of the wind. Indeed, he suddenly realized that he had become at one with it, that, like the Lapps, he could move about in it, exist in it, work in it, and when he caught sight of Martha Risak, carefree and content in the milky half-light, he even experienced a pang of love.

He was no longer a foreigner, and this abrupt and complete change surprised him. Now, everything here had become part of his life; like Simon Sokki he was worried at the thought that the does might calve-down before reaching the coast; like the Old Man, he was carefully estimating the amount of wood they were taking with them; like all of them, now that he was approaching the fjell, he no longer did so in that rational state of mind which would have made him calculate the danger and the risk, but in the sure conviction that he would suffer from cold and hunger, and that this was something necessary and predestined, an inherent part of his life!

It was with an almost religious feeling that he confronted these mountains, which they had to cross to reach the sea; and he was no longer scared by the storm, since he knew that now he was with the people of the wind and the storm. Already, in his unconscious mind, strange shapes of spirits and gods were beginning to take shape, and nature itself was once again taking on its ancient mystery. This conception of the supernatural was so completely in tune with the uniqueness of the position in which he found himself, with the dramatic grandeur of the countryside, that he felt a sudden gust of fear. With an effort of will to rid his mind of every idea that was not related to action, he asked to be shown which was his string of sleighs, and started to harness the reindeer.

Mikael had caught his reindeer for him, but left him to see to harnessing it himself. Per Oskal had done this often enough, and he did not feel self-conscious about it. Like every Norwegian who lived in the Finnmark, he used to join in the Easter festivals of the Lapps every year, taking part in the races, and often being well placed. But then it had only been for sport. Today, it was quite different; now he had to lead his own life, it was as though he were entrusting his very soul to this sledge.

Everyone was now wondering about the difficult stages of the journey that lay ahead; all that remained of the drinking, wrangling and singing was a bitter taste in their mouths. Everyone was busy: lassoing reindeer, harnessing them, checking the loading of the sleighs, giving or receiving orders; but at last everything was completed, and they were ready to start.

At that moment, it seemed to Per Oskal that he was leaving behind everything which, up till then, had constituted for him life, beliefs and civilization. The cita was sweeping him along with it, in the same way that it was itself being drawn forward by the great herd. Now he was about to become a nomad amongst nomads, a Lapp amongst Lapps, to play his part in this great movement of men and reindeer and sleighs; and the huge bulk of the cita would surge forward through gorges of cruel, blue ice, up steep slopes covered with dangerous patches of driven snow, over gentle hillsides terminating in precipitous cliffs; and all he would be able to do was to keep going, on and on, without seeking to understand, the prisoner of all these people, bound by the same fate!

He had a sudden feeling of vertigo, as though he were plunging into a bottomless void, journeying back through time, to the beginning of all beginnings.

CHAPTER FOUR

BORNE upon sixteen thousand hoofs, the four thousand grey, white and fawn reindeer trampled the snow, forming a moving carpet that rippled in the wind.

Per Oskal had been given the job of guarding one flank of the herd, which drew out into a triangle behind the swaying figure of the Old Man. The Lappefogden was an excellent skier, well-known throughout the whole country as a long distance runner, and Simon Sokki knew what he was doing when he gave him this position, where he would have the responsibility of keeping the animals together and rounding up any of them that broke away. It was an exhausting job, for the cita moved slowly and steadily, sometimes travelling for eighteen hours on end, with only an occasional short halt.

They were approaching the mountains and Mollejaurre already lay behind them, but as they had been gaining height, the frozen lake was still visible, and if they looked back they could see its elliptical white shape standing out against the grey birches of the tundra.

In front of them, domes of ice gleamed in the sunlight. These were formidable mountains, with sheer smooth sides, where here and there sharp spurs of granite projected from the sombre covering of ice. The wind played ceaselessly with the snow, whipping it up into powdery columns, whirling like comets, through which the sun showed dimly; and the terrible cold in those shadowed areas was in violent contrast to the warmth on the sunny slopes.

It was a stiff climb. The draught-reindeer were hard put to it, and Simon Sokki, who was with the Old Man at the head of the herd, took charge of the convoy. They were climbing dead against the gradient, the reindeer advancing in a series of leaps, then stopping, heads down and tongues hanging out, their flanks heaving as they gasped for breath. Some of them lay down, and in order to get them to their feet again the Lapps kicked them hard in the ribs, a cruel but effective method. Getting a ride on a sleigh was now quite out of the question : the drivers had to struggle along in the snow, sometimes sinking up to their waists, and the next minute, without warning, trying to get a foothold on the livid ice, hard as diamonds, which suddenly appeared where the wind had swept the snow away.

The pass was still a long way off, and high above them; and already, after the short spell of calm weather, there were all the warning signs of another blizzard. The reindeer felt it coming, and tried to break away. Again and again the herdsmen had to bring back the in-calf does who, to avoid the climb, sought to get back to the tundra.

Simon Sokki was getting furiously angry.

'We're already behind,' he declared. 'We've lost a whole week!'

And no one dared remind him how long they had waited for him in vain, at Suojaurre !

As to the Lapp Congress at Trömso, he said never a word, and Per Oskal realized bitterly that it was useless to try to revive his interest in it so long as he was preoccupied with this arduous journey, which made him conscious of himself once more as a nomad leader. At the moment he had only one idea : to get to the coast before the does began to calve, and thus to assure the future of the herd.

And after that, when they reached the mountains of the sea, there would be the fjords to cross, the fish to be caught and dried to supplement their food supplies, and the women would be busy gathering senna, the fine, silky grass which they used for stuffing moccasins. But all this still lay a long way ahead, and what immediately confronted them was the necessity of scaling these heights with heavily loaded sleighs that kept turning over and foundered reindeer that had to be replaced by powerful stags, which could only be tamed by the cruel method of castration.

The Old Man was still foraging ahead, and when the

mountains closed in to form a defile, the herd tapered out like a long, grey serpent, leaving behind it a trail of trampled snow that made the going easier for the rest of the convoy.

Beyond this defile was another, then a gradual descent that gave everyone a breathing space; then yet another climb, shorter but more difficult, blocked in the middle by a stretch of blue ice, a kind of petrified waterfall.

The reindeer had skilfully avoided crossing it by scrambling higher up amongst the steep rocks on either side, where they were continually pursued by the dogs, but the sleighs were obliged to stick to the track, so that eventually they had to get across the stream of glittering, diamond-hard ice.

The sun had disappeared in a last burst of light, and all around the mountains were turning from blue to grey, though in places where the ice persisted, they still shone like mother-of-pearl. As the brief night closed in, it was impossible to see far in the overpowering darkness; yet it was still possible to distinguish the clear outline of the rocks against the faint light from the sky now studded with brilliant stars. Now and again, clouds still touched by the rays of the sun, which had already disappeared behind the horizon, streamed across the firmament and disappeared.

Per Oskal, his task made easier by the narrowness of the defile hemming in the herd, stopped at the summit of the pass, where he encountered the full force of the wind, and could feel its icy blast scorching his face and gradually coating his eyebrows and moustache with frost. The Old Man had called a halt at a spot where the pass levelled out, and the harnessed reindeer were already lying down in the snow, chewing the cud. The herdsmen, temporarily unwanted, retraced their steps, but the sleighs were not yet in sight.

'We'd better go and see what's happened,' said Per Oskal, speeding away like an arrow, leaning forward with knees flexed and skis close together.

But the others only shrugged their shoulders. This was no concern of theirs: today they were with the herd, tomorrow they would be with the sleighs; everyone must look out for himself.

Half-way back, the Norwegian stopped at the edge of a cliff, overhanging the narrow defile, and what he saw terrified him. The sleighs were locked together, one behind the other, with a bunch of Lapps clinging to each load, trying to ease the reindeer's burden, cursing and swearing, with the blizzard swirling around them as the gale whipped up the snow. The whole convoy was straggled out down the slope, according to the weight of the load. Exhausted reindeer were lying stretched out on their sides, while men and women hurried about in an apparent confusion, which nevertheless concealed a passive strength, an amazing instinct of survival. To Per Oskal they looked like those heroic armies of ants that struggle along with burdens too heavy for them, ten, twenty times bigger than themselves, exhausting themselves, scrambling over obstacles, rolling back to the bottom, and continually starting all over again. There was the same disproportion in this battle between the men and reindeer and the mountain. Simon Sokki was going from one to the other of the sledges in difficulty, heaving with all his strength on the long leading reins, and, as he urged them on, you could see the animals arch their backs as they strained, desperately stretching out their muzzles towards him, rolling their lidless eyes, which protruded with terror. The courageous brutes dug in their hoofs, trying to get a foothold in the ice, fell on their knees, got up again, and once more struggled ahead. As soon as the sledge was clear of the obstacle, its driver immediately left it in order to go back and help the others, and the exhausted deer would at once lie down, and begin nuzzling at the snow and sneezing. But most moving of all was the contrast between the shouting and swearing of the little black men in their fur clothing, and the silence of the harassed reindeer, submitting to their calvary without uttering a cry, incapable of expressing their agony . . .

The baggage-sleighs had been saved. But, in some cases, it had been necessary to jettison part of the load, and all kinds of objects had been left lying about in the snow that would have to be collected later on. This worried Simon Sokki.

'The loads were too heavy, you should have brought more sleighs.'

'And where should I have got them from, Simon Sokki?' Ellena retorted angrily. 'We brought all we had. Don't you remember that we lost four during the last migration?'

Simon Sokki quietened down: it would not do to quarrel with Ellena. Besides, he knew it was his fault. Several times during the past winter he had set off to Viddakaïno to buy sleighs, only to return with a load of aquavit!

Around him, the men were beginning to grumble. Had it not been for the atavistic fear inspired by the head of the cita, they would have protested, for they knew very well that Simon Sokki was responsible. But it was no use now to start blaming anybody. A decision had to be taken. They had been on the march for thirty-six hours without a halt, and they were still only at the beginning of the ascent! And the gathering clouds warned them that sooner or later the storm would break out again.

Per Oskal, who had now reached them, saw that Simon was hesitating. There could no longer be any question of reloading the sleighs to their full capacity; and this meant that the surplus goods would have to be left behind.

After a short silence, Simon said:

'We'll leave the hearthstones.'

The others stared at him, trying to guess what was at the back of his mind. Was this to be the last migration, then? Some of them felt their hopes rising again, for, since his return, Simon had made no reference whatever to his trip to the Tröndelag; the whole business seemed to have been buried and forgotten. Mikael Bongo immediately started heaving the heavy, granite stone out of his sledge. But, almost before he could move, Kristina sprang forward:

'Stop, Mikael! You can't touch the ancestral hearth-stone!'

She confronted him, brandishing her knife, and her blue

eyes blazed with anger in a face that seemed suddenly to have aged.

'Stop, I tell you!' she repeated, as he made another attempt.

Around them, the others formed a circle. Then, all of a sudden, there was an extraordinary silence. The young girl had defied her father and, faced by her determination, Simon had remained speechless. A murmur arose from the little group; everyone was waiting to hear what he would say.

To leave the hearthstone behind would be tantamount to abandoning the cita! In that case, there would be no further need of explanation; they would do whatever Simon decided. Without intending to, Mikael had brought things to a head: he had forced the master to declare what was in his mind. Simon Sokki slowly walked over to Kristina and pushed her out of the way.

'Go on, Mikael, do what I tell you!'

But when Mikael still hesitated, seeking approval from the rest of them, the Finn strode forward:

'Hang on a bit, Simon Sokki! Don't do something you may regret! Here's the only man who can advise you,' he said, pointing to the stooped figure of the Old Man, who, thrusting with his ski-stick, was speeding towards them as quickly as he could.

By the time he reached them he was out of breath. He took one look at the sleigh, at the sacred stone, at Simon, Kristina, the Finn, Mikael and all the other members of the cita standing around, and allowed an appreciable time to elapse before saying anything. He was trying to make up his mind, and the effort of concentration brought a look of inspiration to his face.

'You see all these mountains, Simon? You know their names and history?'

'Of course,' said Simon, clearly ill at ease.

'That one up there is the mountain of the wind where, when the storm rages, only the men of stone can stand upright! And the one facing it is the mountain of the sunset.

From its summit, where our ancestors built an altar to the reindeer, you can already see the sea! Away to the north, in that frozen, inaccessible region where none of us has ever been, are two other peaks, from which, so they say, on certain summer nights you can watch the trolls dancing in a ring! And up there, at the top of the pass we've got to cross, is where our ancestors used to offer sacrifices to the stallos of the mountain. If the snow hasn't filled the hollow between the rocks, you can still see the great heap of reindeer antlers, which proves how long we have been using this road.'

The Old Man seemed to be transfigured. It was as though he had suddenly grown taller, dominating them by his height, as well as by his authority. The echoes of his voice, borne on the wind, seemed to grow louder. There were muffled, rumbling noises, followed by short silences, and these produced a kind of reverberation which, to all of them, sounded like the rhythmic beating of the magic drum.

Mikael was so scared that he had already covered up the hearthstone again with the tarpaulin and was tying it down. And everyone was thinking to himself: The Old Man is right, it would be sacrilege to leave the hearthstone of our ancestors in this sacred spot!

The women crossed themselves and, as they prayed, begged the stallos to take pity on them. Already their spirits were beginning to rise again. At all costs they had to cross the pass! Without waiting for further orders, those who had managed to get their sleighs over the stretch of ice were preparing to start.

'Wait, all of you!' thundered the Old Man. 'The loads must be fairly shared out!'

Daunted by his voice, they all obeyed.

'We shall have to leave the firewood behind! You've got two sleighloads of wood, Simon Sokki. You'll have to take it off, and then reload both with whatever won't go on the other sleighs.'

'Fair enough!' admitted Simon Sokki. 'If it hadn't been for you, I should have committed a crime.'

212

'Why, Kristina has more sense than all the rest of you put together! I tell you, your daughter is inspired!'

The young girl was standing a little apart, awaiting the decision precipitated by her action. Her proud, disdainful glance rested on each of them in turn, and they all lowered their eyes, ashamed. At her side stood the Finn, with a grave expression on his face, ever ready to protect her against any hostility, but no one seemed to be worrying about her any more. The Old Man had aroused the wrath of the stallos, and they had to get away from this groaning mountain; then, since Simon Sokki had signified his approval, they began dragging the carefully hoarded supply of wood from the sledges, and not one of them so much as thought of asking himself how they were going to light a fire!

The Old Man was right, the wood was unnecessary! Per Oskal watched the scene with amazement: he still had a lot to learn about the Lapps.

High up above him, on the mountain of the wind, the great stone stallo stood undaunted, as though it was the wind's master!

In the time it took to change over the loads and share them out between the available sleighs, the short night had passed almost without his having noticed it. The Lapps had set about their task with the same frantic energy, the same determination, that they had displayed when trying to get the fully-loaded sleighs over the frozen waterfall. They seemed to be completely immune from both hunger and exhaustion. All of them, including the women and youngsters, tugged and heaved, yelling and swearing, heedless of the squalls of snow that covered them from head to foot, so that they looked like the stones their ancestors had erected to serve as guardian spirits, and felt themselves to be a part of the eternal landscape.

Having managed to drag one sledge as far as the pass, Per Oskal felt worn out, and decided to join the herdsmen, who all this time had remained squatting on their heels in their usual position, looking like little cones of fur set up in the snow. Half asleep, they awaited their orders, casually keeping an eye on the herd, which was lying down covered with snow, though here and there an old stag stood on guard. Per Oskal was hungry and thirsty. Several times, like the reindeer and the dogs, he had eaten some snow, but instead of allaying his thirst this had only caused a terrible burning sensation in his throat. One after the other, the sleighs were beginning to arrive at the head of the pass, and presently Kristina appeared, leading her white reindeer, with the Finn hanging on to the load to prevent it from being flung off. The young girl seemed to be no more affected by the strain than the rest of them, and Per Oskal could not help admiring their reserves of strength. Indeed, he felt rather humiliated—he, the giant Scandinavian, the famous athlete of the Finnmark, compared with these little men of another race who remained untouched by cold or hunger or fatigue.

By the time the whole convoy had reassembled, it was already broad daylight. The dawn had lit up the mountains, but the last touches of colour had faded away in the sepulchral light. Before long, the three highest peaks were shrouded in heavy cloud, billowing around their summits. Per Oskal was frozen to the marrow! Never before in his life had he experienced such cold: the temperature must have fallen to about thirty or forty degrees of frost! The piercing cold penetrated his fur clothing, and he felt as though he were suddenly enclosed in a framework of hardening muscles, as though he were suffocating. He longed for a big fire, and remembered all the wood they had left behind, all those logs and branches, so patiently collected, that were now lying at the bottom of the ravine. How were they going to cook their food, or melt snow for drinking? To have thrown away the wood now struck him as monstrous, yet, when the Old Man ordered them to, no one had shown the slightest hesitation. And now, once again, here they all were, stretched out on their sleighs or squatting in the snow, their faces reddened by the cold, yet their eyes alive, heedless of the storm.

Per Oskal admitted his anxiety to the Finn :

'How long will it take us to get through the mountains?'

214

'Three or four days, if everything goes well!'

'And how are we going to manage without wood?'

'According to the Old Man, a bit further on there's a ravine where there are a few birch trees! If we don't hang about, we ought to get there in two days' time.'

'Two days!' exclaimed Per Oskal.

The Finn looked at him, laughing. He pulled himself together, and got to his feet.

'When do we start?'

'As soon as we've eaten! Here come the women with the food.'

Ellena, Martha and Karin were moving from one group to the other, distributing portions of dried fish and raw reindeer meat, frozen hard, and everyone was ravenously chewing this curious form of nourishment.

Like all Norwegians, Per Oskal looked upon fish as his natural food, whether fresh or dried; nevertheless he felt some hesitation about eating fish that was frozen so hard that it was as transparant as crystal, almost like amber. If he tried to bite it he would break his teeth, yet the few mouthfuls of food he had already swallowed were making his stomach writhe with hunger; he hardly dared think how long it was since he had last eaten. Opening his knife, he cut the fish into small cubes, which he allowed to dissolve in his mouth, and the salt juices of the fish, far from increasing his thirst, allayed it. Gradually, as he went on eating, standing there with his back to the wind, he felt his strength beginning to return. All around him the Lapps were savagely devouring their ration, now and then mixing a handful of snow with the food, and Per Oskal began to realize how it was that they were able to manage without water and without fire.

CHAPTER FIVE

THE Old Man had given the signal to start.

Over the mountains the storm lowered. It was not one of those swift, raging blizzards that suddenly appear out of a clear sky, and in a few moments make the air almost impossible to breathe; but a spell of relentless bad weather that had settled down over the fjell, with a ceiling of low, threatening cloud that hung over the caravan, intensifying the hostile aspect of the place.

Sullen rumblings reached them, coming from above the mist, and the older ones shook their heads anxiously. It must be the snow, piled up on the higher slopes that was breaking away and forming unpredictable avalanches. They would have to move fast if they were to escape from the narrow corridor they were in.

Ahead, blazing the trail, went the great herd. The reindeer, also worried, were beginning to force the pace; these mountains were as hostile to animals as they were to men. Instinct urged them on, towards the north, where the hills were not so high and they would find cover amongst the birch trees, and plenty of lichen protected by the thick covering of snow.

Presently the going became easier. As far as Per Oskal could judge, from what he could see of the base of the mountains emerging from the fog, they were now in an ancient glacial trough, a kind of arena, enclosed on all sides by rocky cliffs, and the level ground probably marked the boundaries of an ice-age lake. Within this arena, swirling air-currents made breathing difficult, but to everyone's surprise the Old Man decided to halt there. He had led the herd along the face of a cliff swept bare by the winds, and there the reindeer immediately set about scraping the snow away; they had found lichen and the anxious faces of the Lapps relaxed—the reindeer had been saved.

'We shall stay here until dawn tomorrow,' declared Simon Sokki.

They found themselves in a kind of vague twilight, and even Per Oskal could not be sure whether day was beginning or ending, for, by the time it reached them, the light that managed to filter through the mist was faint and discoloured.

Simon Sokki gave the order to unhitch the sleighs. But as it would take too long to lasso the draught reindeer when they wanted them again, they turned them loose with their long leather halters trailing behind them to stop them straying too far from the camp. Then they all sat around on their sleighs.

Some crept beneath the tarpaulins and furs, and immediately fell asleep. Others stayed where they were, almost dropping with fatigue but too tired to sleep. Ellena proceeded to hand round a second helping of frozen fish and, this time, Per Oskal ate it with relish. As it melted in his stomach, it seemed to give him fresh warmth and vitality; never before had he experienced a sensation like this. Then, his hunger satisfied, he looked around till he found a spare place on one of the sledges, pulled back the tarpaulin, climbed in underneath it and went to sleep, heedless of the blizzard which gradually covered him with fine, powdery snow.

He awoke to find the camp in a state of animated bustle. Already, without waiting for orders, the Lapps were reharnessing the reindeer, while the Old Man, having put on his skis, stood leaning on his long stick, waiting to set off. The reindeer, refreshed and in good fettle, scrambled to their feet without difficulty, pricked their ears at the shrill tinkling of the bell, stretched their silky muzzles towards the north and slowly, with long, easy strides, extricated themselves from the deep snow and took their place in the convoy.

This time, Simon Sokki was hoping to get as far as the big lake on the other side of the mountains without making another halt, for there they would be able not only to have a few days' rest, but also to graze the herd and see to the in-calf does. After that, they would still have one more pass to cross; then the descent to the sea would begin, and the migration would be over!

As soon as they started to climb, they were caught in the fog. It was still the same treeless kind of country, a naked world of snow and ice and blue granite crags. Behind them, every now and then the fog lifted and, far away in the distance, they could see high above the clouds, the summits of the three mountains of the wind, and on the highest of them the stone stallo, an enduring monument. Up there the sun was shining, so that it was like some extraordinary apparition; the marvellous soft light seemed to belong to another world. But it was not to last for long. Soon the clouds closed in again, and once more everything became cold and hostile.

The first flakes began to fall as they reached the higher slopes—wide, desolate plateaux where the wind dogged their footsteps, with pyramids of stone stretching away into the distance, that had stood there for thousands of years to mark the course of the migration. Soon everything began to merge, clouds and snow, earth and sky; and, had it not been for the fresh track left by the herd, they would have felt cut off from the world, utterly alone in this desert.

Per Oskal had returned to his position on the flank, and was gliding along on his skis in a kind of a trance. The life he had hitherto led no longer seemed to make sense; he had passed beyond the stage of fatigue, of hunger and thirst. The weary hours at the start, when he had staggered along almost asleep, bleary-eyed and swaying, had yielded to a state in which he was oblivious of time and distance. He was discovering that, instead of driving and looking after the herd, as he had supposed, he was like his companions, under the protection of the reindeer! What would become of him, if it were not for this huge mass of vitality surging forward, drawing him along in its wake like a straw caught in the wind? For all of them, the reindeer meant an assurance of life; meat, warmth, everything, came from them!

218

And when he brought back a straying animal, he felt, through some vital reflex that he was now rediscovering within himself, that it was not merely a matter of restoring an animal to the herd, but actually of preserving a part of his own life.

Everything was now swallowed up in dense, cotton-wool mist, and his skis kept sinking in the fresh snow which never stopped falling. Of the herd itself, all he could see was a kind of shadow, a grey mass, distinguishable from the mist by its fluid, almost unreal movement, and by the tangle of antlers, the undulating backs and haunches, the scuffing of hoofs in the snow, and also by the strange, composite sound, produced by the cracking of joints and the breathing and grunting of the animals, which he could distinguish like some kind of supersonic music above the roar of the wind.

Assailed by all these noises, some of them deafening, some scarcely audible, which to him now represented life, he experienced a sudden feeling of terror: the roar of the storm was heralded by an unexpected silence, a kind of empty lull. Could this be a warning of coming catastrophe? Then, somewhere high up in the mountains, there was a loud crack like a cannon-shot, the snow started to move, and soon it was flowing down the invisible slopes with a curious sound like the whistling of silk. The noise grew louder, turned into a roar and, for several minutes, continued, like the shattering rolling of drums.

He knew at once what it was, but some curious force held him motionless and silent, though all his senses were on the alert. A sudden icy blast covered him with powdery snow. Then he yelled:

'Look out, it's an avalanche!'

Voices that sounded a long way off came to him through the opaque wall of fog; men were calling to one another, shouting at the top of their voices, and the dogs were barking!

Urging himself forward with his ski-sticks, he hurried to the front of the herd where a state of confusion seemed to be raging. The avalanche, starting at the top of a sheer cliff, had swept past the northernmost edge of the herd. Instinctively, the terrified reindeer had tried to escape in the opposite direction, but many of them, taken by surprise, had been knocked down and, though several managed to get up unhurt, the herdsmen were already busy digging out the one or two animals that were completely buried except for their antlers.

Then suddenly someone shouted out :

'Hi, Thor ! What's happened to Thor ?'

He had been guarding the flank just at this spot, and must have been caught by the mass of moving snow. Per Oskal sprang forward. In the fog, it was difficult to locate the exact path of the avalanche, but his long experience, combined with the wisdom of the Lapps, proved invaluable. The buried reindeer indicated where the search should start, and they all began probing the snow with their ski-sticks, and every now and then succeeded in freeing a half-stifled animal. Some ten minutes elapsed, however, before they discovered Thor Risak, lying in an inert heap beneath the piled-up snow, wrapped in his pesk : he was already purple in the face.

'He's dead,' groaned the men.

And the women gave vent to their distress in a wailing lament.

'Not yet,' said Per Oskal. 'Just leave him to me !'

The others drew back, and watched him incredulously as he carried out artificial respiration; and before long Thor began to show signs that he was slowly reviving. The colour came back to his face, he opened his eyes and, though still suffering from shock, gradually regained consciousness, and was regarding his rescuers with a dazed expression on his face.

'The reindeer ! The reindeer !' he muttered. He was doing his best to speak, to explain to them what had happened, but Per Oskal ordered him to keep quiet.

'Later on, later on.'

They gathered that he had been the first to hear the loud

crack as the snow broke away, and had at once sent the dogs out to turn the reindeer away from the path of the avalanche, thus certainly saving the greater part of the herd. He himself, on the other hand, had not been able to get away in time and, with five or six of the most stubborn animals, had been buried beneath the mass of swirling snow. He had had the presence of mind to pull his pesk over his head, and this had prevented his lungs from getting choked with the snow; but then he had felt himself sinking deeper and deeper, and, by the time the others found him, he had probably only just passed out.

Per Oskal got them to put the herdsman on a sledge, and felt his pulse. Very feeble at first, then far too rapid, gradually it began to beat normally. Meanwhile, the Lapps stood about watching him attentively, their red caps forming a brilliant circle round the Norwegian and giving a strange note of gaiety to this desolate scene.

The Lappefogden turned to Simon Sokki:

'He'll be all right now, but a good swig of aquavit would do him good!'

These words were greeted cheerfully by the onlookers, and when someone pulled a bottle out of the deepest pocket of his koufte and handed it to the herdsman, the incident was soon forgotten. Everybody looked upon Thor's restoration to life as a miracle, with the result that the man who had performed it, whom they already regarded as a friend, though one to be kept rather at arm's length, now acquired a quite new prestige. Like the doctor, he was able to restore people to life!

'Here, you'd better have a drink yourself,' said Pier, who had hitherto been the least friendly of any of them.

Per Oskal did not wait to be asked a second time, he felt that now he had advanced a considerable step on the long road of friendship.

The danger of further avalanches, however, still remained, and was all the more to be feared as the fog, which was getting thicker, made it impossible to locate the danger points. They must get going again as quickly as possible.

But the Old Man was still busily engaged at the spot where the avalanche had occurred. He had noticed that the dogs had continued obstinately scratching at the snow and were now showing signs of great excitement. Could it be that someone was still buried beneath the snow? He checked up the members of the cita, but no one was missing. Then, suddenly, the dogs uncovered the body of a reindeer; unable to escape the avalanche, it had been violently knocked down and broken its ribs.

'We must be off,' Simon Sokki decided. 'It's no use hanging about here any longer. You, Mikael, cut up the deer! Per Oskal, you get back to the herd! The rest of you see that the animals don't straggle. The valley we shall soon be entering is very wide, and we shan't be troubled with avalanches there, but there will still be plenty of danger from people, as well as from this fog!'

From what Simon said, they knew that they must now be near the place where their route and that allocated to the Isaksens were very close to one another.

'Don't worry,' said Thor Risak. 'We'll keep an eye on everything.'

'Oh no, you won't! You'll ride on one of the sleighs. You need a good rest,' Simon Sokki insisted. 'Someone else can take your place.'

The Old Man was already moving off, and they could hear the shrill tinkling of the bell, so different from the noise of the elements. The stream of reindeer disappeared into the mist and the sleighs were once more drawn up in line. Mikael had cut up the reindeer in no time, and, as they were leaving behind the head, the paunch and all the guts, there were only the four quarters, already frozen hard, to be carefully stowed on the meat-sleigh. The ravenous dogs quickly flung themselves upon the warm entrails, and soon nothing was left to mark the spot but a patch of red, churned-up snow, already nearly obliterated by the swiftly falling flakes.

Once more the march was under way.

The ghostly caravan wound its way across the wide

222

plateau and, though the sledges travelled more easily here, this also increased the danger of getting lost in the fog. It was becoming more and more difficult to hold the reindeer together : they kept trying to turn aside, and both dogs and herdsmen had their work cut out to keep them on the course decreed by the Old Man. The light filtering through the clouds showed that it was still day, but as it gradually grew fainter, Per Oskal calculated that night must be drawing on. He strode along with his lissom, mechanical gait, accompanied by the silky swishing of his skis. Through the moaning of the wind he strained to pick up the reassuring and familiar noises of the caravan, the muffled sound made by the reindeers' hoofs, the stifled barking of a dog, the disturbing cry of a herdsman. Occasionally someone called out, warning him that a deer had broken away, and the voice seemed to come from so near that he would turn round expecting to find its owner just behind him, only to discover to his surprise that the voice heard through the fog belonged to someone who was some hundreds of yards away. But everything had a kind of unreality : when he thought he was climbing he found his skis taking him downhill, and when he thought the road was level he would suddenly crash into a hillock, invisible in the universal whiteness. Where had all the others got to? Simon Sokki, Mikael, Thor, Kristina? And where was Martha?

This extraordinary existence, which was a continuation of man's age-old struggle for survival and gave rise to all the primaeval fears and hardships and pleasures, this return to the most primitive kind of life, was something to which he had completely surrendered, and he realized that he was engaged in a redoubtable experience. It was no longer an official mission, but an adventure, and it seemed quite likely that his superiors, as well as Fru Tideman and himself, had made a profound psychological error. The kind of man he had become under the stress of this new reality was no longer the same man that had been at Viddakaïno or at Trömso! He had become a nomad amongst nomads, and who could tell what opinions he would hold, how he would behave, when, at the end of the migration, the time came for Simon Sokki and his people to take the promised decision . . .

He bumped into the herd, which had abruptly come to a halt. What was happening? He could hear the sound of voices, of orders being given, and hurried to join the Old Man who was arguing with Simon Sokki.

'We are stopping here,' cried the latter.

'What, already?'

'It's two hours since the avalanche,' Simon Sokki pointed out.

How quickly the time has gone by!

Simon Sokki explained:

'The Old Man is quite right. We are in the middle of a big depression, and there are three valleys leading out of it; but with this persistent fog we could easily take the wrong one, and then we should run the risk of our herd getting mixed up with that of the Isaksens, which may well be in the neighbourhood by this time. So it's best to wait until the visibility improves.'

'But there isn't any wood, and apparently no lichen,' the Lappefogden objected, not unreasonably.

'I know. It will take us another two days to get to the tundra, but the reindeer can manage with what they ate yesterday, and as for us, there's plenty of meat.'

Per Oskal lacked the courage to add: 'But how are we going to manage without any fire!' Suddenly, he felt an overwhelming need of fire, more for the sake of the light, perhaps, than the warmth! Without a fire the fjell was their enemy, like some lunar landscape, like a country where man had never existed!

Did Simon Sokki realize what was passing through his mind? He turned away towards the drivers who were now beginning to come up, and they, too, were surprised by this unexpected halt.

'We're stopping here, and we'll use one of the sleighs for firewood.'

Everyone was shocked: a sleigh is a very personal

224

possession. Andis, obviously annoyed, was the first to speak :

'Well, it's not going to be mine! It's as good as new!'

Whereupon everybody fell to pointing out the defects in his neighbour's sleigh, arguing angrily, yet knowing very well that, once Simon Sokki had made up his mind, they would all obey him. The Old Man cut short the argument :

'You can burn my pulka. It's all patched together anyway, and I haven't got many personal belongings. They can easily go on another sledge.'

At this, there was a general outcry. Surely to burn the Old Man's sleigh would bring bad luck upon the cita. It was out of the question for anyone to lay a finger on him, or his reindeer, or his sleigh. The women especially were violently opposed to his proposal : Kristina offered her own, while Ellena, scared that they were about to commit sacrilege, suggested they should take hers. But Andis was not convinced, and he attempted to persuade the others.

'Since the Old Man himself has offered it, that's not the same as taking it.'

Simon Sokki realized that he would have to show his authority; and, turning to the Old Man, he said :

'You are our guest, and no one is going to touch anything belonging to you. You led our cita in my father's time, and in my grandfather's, and probably long before that. Your old pulka is no more worn out than you are. We are very grateful, but you must stick to it! . . . Martha Bongo, didn't one of your runners get broken when we were crossing that ice?'

'I mended my mother's sledge straight away,' Mikael Bongo quickly intervened, 'and now it's as good as new.'

'A sledge is never as good as new, once it's been mended. But you don't have to worry on my sister's account; during the summer we'll make her a new one. There's plenty of strong, supple birchwood growing on the island.'

He had spoken.

They brought up all the sledges and turned them up on their sides to give protection against the wind. Then they

225

hauled Martha Sokki's old crock into the middle of the square and began smashing it to bits. Before long, Kristina was cutting shavings from one of the shafts, while Martha Risak and Ellena Sokki set up the hearthstone. Soon a clear, bright little flame was flickering in the wind, and everyone shouted with joy. The flame grew bigger, and although it was still daylight the pale light from the fire lit up the tanned, weather-beaten faces so that they shone like those of the statues in church. But when the youngsters began stoking the fire too energetically, Ellena intervened:

'That'll do,' said she. 'Go easy with the wood. Who knows how long we shall have to stop here!'

They accepted the rebuke, and contented themselves with a more modest blaze. She had dragged her sledge near to the hearthstone, so that it could serve both as a seat and serving-counter; the snow in the cauldron was already melting, and the pieces of fish and reindeer flesh that Karin and Kristina were grilling over the flames were already beginning to crackle, giving off a smell of hot fat, which tickled the palates of the onlookers and gave a pleasant edge to their appetites. There was no question of putting up the tents, for they were not really camping here, and as soon as the fog cleared they would be off again. Then, as the gale began to blow more violently, the men set about strengthening the wall of sleighs, and they all huddled close against it, well wrapped up in their furs, warming their hands and faces at the fire. Soon there was enough boiling water to make some coffee and, for the first time in several days, they were able to have a hot drink, and they could feel its comforting warmth running through their bodies. They sat wherever they chose. Per Oskal had slipped in beside Martha Risak—had he sought her out or was it mere chance? Whether or no, the young woman pressed her body lovingly against his, and despite the roaring of the wind and the biting frost, he felt completely happy. Never could he remember having felt so utterly content!

He watched the day fade imperceptibly into night, then, covered with snow, fell asleep, curled up in Martha's lap, their furs huddled together so that they looked like two wild animals.

Towards morning, by the time they had eaten a large meal of fresh meat and drunk innumerable cups of coffee that scarcely compensated for the dehydration of their bodies, the snow started to fall again in huge flakes. To set out now was out of the question. The herd had gathered round the bivouac of its own accord, and as they chewed the cud, standing up or stretched on the ground, the animals seemed to be keeping guard over the human beings.

CHAPTER SIX

M OS T of the men, exhausted by the accumulated strain of more than three weeks on the move, were sleeping heavily, their caps pulled down over their faces; others remained awake, from time to time feeding the fire, just enough to make sure that it did not go out. For them it was a form of happiness just to be able to dream away the time like this, propped against the uptilted sleighs that protected them from the wind, their faces glowing from the heat of the fire, while the snow continued to fall, gradually covering them, until all that could be seen of them was the white shape of their bodies almost indistinguishable from the surrounding background. When the men pulled out their bottles of aquavit Ellena had said nothing, they had had a hard time of it. As they greedily gulped down the harsh spirit, each man offered Per Oskal a swig, so that before long he found himself getting happily drunk.

At regular intervals the Old Man took a turn round the herd, then came back to the tent to get warm. He and Simon Sokki discussed the weather and which direction they should take, and both of them were worried.

'This'll be the last fall of snow this winter, Simon,' the Old Man predicted. 'It's going to cause us a lot more trouble on the last stage of the journey. What with fresh snow, thaws, avalanches, it will be bad going for the sleighs.'

Simon Sokki sighed. His secret weighed heavily on him : maybe the moment had arrived to tell then what had been decided at Trömso, at the Lapp Congress? Now that they were in the heart of the fjell, shut in by the storm, perhaps they would have a better appreciation of the very different kind of life that was being offered them. Simon had already drunk a lot and when that happened he lost all sense of discretion and easily got excited.

228

'It's a real bitch of a life, this!' he exclaimed, appealing to the company. 'Year after year having to go through this torture all over again, with a good chance of dying a miserable death! And what for? Just you tell me that! Why, simply because we have to follow the herd! Sometimes I can't help asking myself if our race hasn't had its day.'

The others knew what he was getting at. They drew closer, waiting to hear what he would say, and their scarlet caps formed a kind of double corolla, with the fire in the centre like a giant pistil—a bright red flower against the darkness of the mountain!

'What are you grumbling about, Simon Sokki?' Thor Risak suddenly demanded. 'It's no good getting impatient. This is to be our last migration, isn't it? Why don't you tell us what was decided?'

The others regarded Thor Risak in amazement; he was standing up to the master, and Simon Sokki was saying nothing. Thor Risak had almost been killed, he had felt himself going under, life being extinguished like a candle. They had thought he was dead, yet here he was among them, like a ghost; he could speak out boldly.

Simon Sokki examined his companions; his inquisitorial glance turned from one to the other, trying to plumb their souls, and in all of them he discovered something different: their eyes betrayed uneasiness, hostility, silent approval, reserve, distrust.

'They none of them know exactly what they do want,' he thought to himself. 'If I let them chew on it for a bit, they'll come round to my way of thinking.' And he felt both relieved and reassured.

There was a long silence. At last, Ellena spoke.

'Tell us about the Congress,' she said. 'What are you waiting for?'

She leant over to put a piece of wood on the fire, bent down to blow it, sat up again, then went on blowing as if keeping time to the leaping of the flames. Having done this, she resumed her hieratical position, sitting bolt upright with her legs crossed beneath her, while the snow on her cap suddenly began to melt and run down the wrinkles on her face so that they looked like concentric tattoo marks round her eyes, cheekbones and mouth.

Towards the back, hidden by the prow of the sleigh and huddled close together, the Finn and Kristina waited anxiously.

'I really am scared this time,' whispered the girl. 'Did you see the others? They all agree with him, they'll say yes!'

'Don't worry! I'm still here!' the Finn muttered under his breath; and, to reassure her, he kissed her on the mouth, slipping his hand round her waist; and Kristina's fear was transformed into a long, passionate tremor.

'Speak up!' Ellena repeated. 'The time has come!'

The master still hesitated; he seemed to be trying to put a name to these bundles of snow, the men and women of the cita whose faces he could scarcely distinguish. He would have been glad to have had Per Oskal at his side, but the Norwegian was guarding the herd; on the other hand, he was delighted that the Old Man was not there, for he would never have been able to stand up to him. The two of them, as well as Andis, were taking their turn on guard, and all three had gone off into the fog. That left the Finn and Kristina. But the Finn was only a servant, and his daughter—well, his daughter would damn well have to obey him!

'You are right, wife. You're entitled to know what was decided back there. Pay attention everyone, and I'll tell you what happened.'

It was as though all the scarlet caps, all the faces petrified by the wind, all these bodies weighed down by their heavy, frozen furs, simultaneously leaned forward towards the flames in some kind of initiation ceremony. It was still snowing hard, and as the flakes fell on the fire they melted with a hissing sound. Beyond the huddle round the fire, it was possible to see about ten yards, enough to reveal the few reindeer that were still standing up, mounting guard over the rest of the herd who lay around covered with snow;

through the noise of the wind, you could hear the sound of their jaws chewing the cud, their rapid breathing, the occasional sneezing of an animal infested with worms—all the familiar sounds of sleeping reindeer.

Simon Sokki was about to speak, soon they would know what their fate was to be. But it had to be done in the traditional manner.

Mikael, sitting with his eyes half-closed, begun humming a yok. The words took shape on his lips, the song rose into the air, swelled up like a stream in flood, then suddenly died away in a long drawn wail that faded away into the moaning of the wind. His improvized song told of the migration, of the trials and joys of life in the cita, the fight with the wolf, the avalanches; and now they were all beginning to tremble with emotion, for he was about to announce the coming of the messenger, and his voice was gaining strength :

'Speak out, Simon Sokki, speak !
Since the world began we have travelled like this,
From the cold of the vidda to the mountains of the sea,
Crossing the inaccessible fjell,
Feeding on reindeer and snow,
Snow people endlessly journeying !
Are you the last chief of our clan ?
Is this the last of our migrations ?
What news do you bring us, Simon Sokki ?
We are poor in silver and gold,
But rich in our thousands of reindeer ;
We are free to wander the earth,
Though prisoners of cold and of snow,
We know all the ills that assail us
And the happiness rooted in custom.
What news do you bring, Simon Sokki ?
Are the new joys as good as the old ?
This fabulous country you come from,
Far to the south by the sea,
They say that it's good to live there,

That the reindeers thrive and grow fat,
That sickness and pain are unknown,
That our children will learn how to read,
And that there we shall live at our ease,
Fishing and hunting by day,
Dreaming all night in our huts.
But what of the savage enchantment
Of this life we're leading at present?
Does it mean we must lose it for ever?
Does it mean we must cease to be Samisks,
Huddling round camp fires for warmth,
Hearing the song of the wind
As it lulls our reindeers to sleep,
To whom we owe warmth and life.
Speak out, Simon Sokki! Your people
Await the news you have brought us!'

The master got up, and as he stood there, his pesk covered with wind-blown snow, he looked like a statue of white marble, dominating the circle of men and women who formed a barrier against the wind and cold. Erect beside the fire, he made a gesture with his hand, and Mikael broke off his song.

Simon chose his words carefully:

'The whole business was finally agreed at Trömso,' he began. 'First of all we all went to the Tröndelag. It's a fine part of the country, with high mountains, considerably higher than these, running down to fertile plains, where there are no mosquitoes. What they are proposing is that we should live like the Swedish Lapps, on the other slope of the mountain. There would be one big common herd that the herdsmen would look after during the summer and, in addition, the possibility of rearing sheep and cattle in the valley.'

'Why not pigs as well?' Martha Risak broke in.

Far from laughing, everyone looked at her furiously, and she subsided into silence.

'The women will have plenty of work!' Simon Sokki

went on. 'The fishing is good, and there are canning factories as well. We shall be able to double or triple our income; and, on top of that, there will be no more migrations; at most, a changeover from summer to winter pastures, like there always is wherever there are mountains.'

They could scarcely contain themselves, yet they knew they must not interrupt him. He had such a flighty mind that he was quite capable of forgetting what he had said almost as soon as he had spoken. But though they did not interrupt him, everyone was longing to discover how things were going to work out and what was going to become of the herd. Kristina was trembling with anxiety, despite the reassuring presence of the Finn; this man would be able to overcome the others' fear of the master.

'Lastly, the parish church will be only five or six miles away and, as the shopkeepers are all Norwegians, we shan't have the kvaens exploiting us any more!'

A long murmur of approval showed that this was a sore spot.

'. . . And, besides, we shall have schools, hospitals, doctors . . .'

Suddenly he was interrupted by a loud noise coming from the direction of the herd : something must have gone wrong. The herdsmen came running up, and as their vague forms emerged from the mist they began shouting and gesticulating to attract attention. Per Oskal and the Old Man arrived first, skiing swiftly, and pulled up in front of the circle of Lapps.

'Thirty reindeer have disappeared in the fog, Simon Sokki. Shall we go after them?'

'Thirty, you say? Which way have they gone?'

The Old Man shrugged his shoulders.

'You can hardly make out the tracks, but they are still quite fresh. Per Oskal and I were making our rounds when we noticed a kind of trail in the freshly-formed snow, going towards the east! It was obvious that it must have been made by the deer. We followed it as far as we could, but the fog was too thick, and at the first patch of ice we got to all trace of them disappeared. The wind is blowing a gale, and has covered up the tracks.'

After a moment's reflection, Simon Sokki said anxiously :

'To the east, you say? That's bad!'

'At first I thought they might have gone back the way we have come, like the does when they're due to calve, but they haven't. They're making for the east.'

Everyone immediately realized the danger, and there was a long-drawn murmur. To the east, only some ten miles or so away was the trail allotted to the Isaksens. The reindeer must have got wind of the other herd, and gone off to join them.

'Damnation!' exclaimed Simon Sokki. 'We shall have to get them back!'

'In a fog like this, and with such a gale blowing?' Mikael objected.

'I'll go myself,' Simon Sokki energetically decided. 'Ellena, put up a sackful of dried meat, and some powdered coffee and sugar.'

'Your place is here, Simon Sokki,' the Old Man insisted. 'You've been away too long already. I'll go and find your reindeer, and Per Oskal can come with me. I shall certainly need him.'

It was clear what he meant : the Lappefogden would act as judge. He was the only man who could settle their differences and perhaps avoid a row. Besides, he was their friend.

'You're right,' Simon Sokki said approvingly. 'Wife, load up the Old Man's sleigh, and the rest of you get out there and round up the herd! But first we must take a count, and find out how many we've lost.'

234

CHAPTER SEVEN

Two draught reindeer were lassoed, and harnessed respectively to the Old Man's pulka and Per Oskal's lightweight sleigh. The Norwegian felt proud that he'd been chosen. The Lapps crowded round him; he was sharing in their life, in their troubles!

Now he was involved in one of the dramas of the tundra. Compared with the disappearance of thirty reindeer, the question of their future counted for little! The Samisks live only for the present. As far as he was concerned, since he was now one of them, Simon Sokki's explanations could wait; the first thing was to find the reindeer. The whisper was going round that they must have reached the Isaksen's herd; if that was so, the old clan feud was bound to break out again. He asked himself what his real function ought to be. Instead of helping to break up their nomadic way of life, surely his first duty was to insist upon the law of the tundra being respected! It was up to him to see that further clashes did not arise in future.

They were equipped for a difficult journey under exceptionally cold conditions, and the second fur pesk that each of them had put on made them look huge, and restricted their movements. Simon Sokki gave them their final instructions and they were ready to start. There were signs that the end of the storm was in sight. Here and there, shafts of light pierced through the fog and lit up people's faces. Higher up, the sun would be shining. Then there was a sudden burst of cold, and the wind swept away the low-lying clouds, revealing a small, deserted plateau surrounded by mountains. The reindeer were lying down facing the wind; they had survived the blizzard in their usual instinctive way, by pressing closely together, forming a huge mass of necks and antlers. Their bodies were completely covered with snow, so that the four thousand antlered heads looked like so many trophies of the chase laid out on the snow. Never before had Per Oskal witnessed such an amazing sight. Herdsmen and women were taking advantage of the lull in the storm to count the reindeer, and when they came back to the little group that was waiting to set out they informed them that thirty animals were missing.

'We'll find them, Simon,' said the Old Man. 'I know where they'll have got to.'

'Maybe they've already been killed and cut up,' said Simon Sokki.

The thought of this spread a feeling of gloom amongst them, for they all knew, having done it themselves, how easy it was to bury a skin and, especially, the ears, which carry the clan's mark.

'They won't have had time,' said Per Oskal. 'The Old Man says the reindeer have only recently got away.'

'When deer are determined to get away, they travel fast and cover huge distances,' insisted Mikael.

'Make a thorough search,' advised Simon Sokki : 'check the herd, the drying poles, and any newly-slaughtered animals. Make sure there aren't any secret caches. The Isaksens are a cunning lot !'

'If you let me go with them, Simon, I promise you I'll find the caches,' the Finn proposed. 'Besides, I've got an account to settle.'

In his excited state of mind Simon would doubtless have agreed, had the Old Man not intervened.

'It's no use paying off old scores, Paavi, you are much too tied up with the Isaksens! Your presence would only make matters worse. Leave it to me, I can deal with that shaman of theirs! His magic spells and filters have no effect on me : besides, he's afraid of me. With Per Oskal's help, I shall be able to manage. The Lappefogden is the law; he represents Norwegian justice, as well as ours. But in the tundra, it's clan law that counts. That's right, isn't it Per Oskal?'

The other gravely nodded assent.

'All the same . . .' the Finn persisted.

'Get back to the herd, Paavi,' Simon Sokki cut him short. 'The Old Man knows what he's up to.'

'How you've changed, Simon Sokki,' exclaimed the Finn. 'Six months ago you'd have charged me to exact vengeance for you. This Trömso trip of yours has turned your head.'

'Are you insinuating . . .' Simon's anger was rising, and he was beginning to shout.

Kristina intervened.

'Come on, Paavi, let's go and have a look at the herd.'

He gave in . . . he always did when he was with her.

When they had gone some distance, she began scolding him gently :

'This isn't the time to have a row. It's essential for you to remain with the herd. They won't be back for a week, and by that time we shall have crossed the fjell, and have to start parting the does. And I want you to be there. Aren't you the future master of the cita ?'

'What cita ?' he asked, slyly. 'Don't you realize that everything has been decided already ? Once we get to the coast, and the others see how comfortable the huts are, and all the boats in the fjord, and the tourists, it will be enough to make the whole lot of them want to go to the Tröndelag.'

'Simon Sokki hasn't yet told us everything . . .'

The Old Man was waiting, standing beside his ancient, patched-up pulka. Per would follow in his tracks, driving a black gelding with huge antlers, using two reins instead of a single one like the Lapps. Martha Risak went up to the Norwegian who was doing his best to control his restless, excitable animal. He felt her slip a bottle of spirits into the pocket of his koufte.

'Take it ! You'll both need it.'

The Old Man gave a whistle, and the two reindeer set off at a gallop, accompanied by delighted shouts from the members of the cita. The drivers swiftly leapt onto their sleighs, where they sat erect, one leg folded beneath them, the other trailing in the snow. They had to climb a long, steep slope, which disappeared into the dense fog. The reindeer soon slowed down to a walk.

When Per Oskal managed to look back, the depression where they had spent the night was already filled with mist, and the banked clouds rose to meet them, engulfed them, deadening every sound.

By common accord, the two men jumped off their sleighs and, to ease the reindeer's load, put on their skis. And as the slope grew steeper, the Old Man started tacking from side to side to make the ascent easier. Before long, they could tell from the wind that they had reached the pass; it was blowing a gale and slowing them down. Per Oskal would have been glad of a moment's rest! The additional effort was exhausting him, and though he was regarded as one of the outstanding long-distance skiers of the Finnmark, he had to struggle hard to keep up with the steady pace set by the Old Man. Wherever did this ageing creature, tough as one of his own sleigh shafts, find the strength to keep going? They were all like this, women as well as men: neither time nor the elements seemed to make any impression on these nomads, hardened from generation to generation over the centuries. For Per Oskal, the Scandinavian, it was humiliating. To take his mind off it, he tried to discover where they were.

When they left the bivouac the Norwegian had quickly marked the position on his military map, and each time the Old Man changed direction for reasons known only to himself, he made a note of it. It was impossible to tell what guided his steps; he would work round a hill, appear to be making south again, then suddenly, when the fog was so thick that they could scarcely see one another despite the few yards that separated them, he would stop, sniff the air, note the direction of the wind and change course. Sometimes he would stop his sledge and begin scraping away the freshly fallen snow from the top of a frozen drift.

'They passed this way scarcely two hours ago,' he would announce.

Per Oskal was reduced to silent admiration. He thought of all the courses he had taken on orientation and topography, of all the books he had read; and he had to admit that if it had been left to him to choose their route they would probably have still been going round in circles in this vast desert where everything looked just alike.

'We shall find them, all right,' said the Old Man, as though conscious of his anxiety. Far behind them, they could hear the sound of furious barking and Per Oskal gripped his rifle.

'You won't need it, Per! Anyone behind us will be a friend,' said the Old Man. The barking drew nearer. Vainly they peered into the fog, they could see nothing. Then they heard the quick breathing of a trotting reindeer, and the encouraging cries of the man who was driving it shattered the enveloping silence. Suddenly, as though a curtain had been torn aside, a sleigh appeared and drew up in front of them, and out of it jumped Andis Sokki, looking very pleased with himself and escorted by Chumbi and Lumba, his two favourite dogs.

'Father sent me,' he announced.

'All right, then you can follow us,' said the Old Man. 'Doubtless your father has his reasons.'

Per Oskal could scarcely conceal his surprise, though he had the sense not to ask any questions. But Andis was only too ready to explain.

'There had to be someone who could speak in the name of the Sokkis,' he said, in a cocky tone of voice.

The Old Man muttered something to himself. He did not like Andis. He was lazy and quick-tempered, the image of his father, but without the older man's good qualities. It would have been better if it had been Pier Sokki, especially if he had had the chance to speak to him beforehand, when the Finn suggested coming, for instance.

Per Oskal understood: Simon was making good an oversight. If there was going to be any trouble with the Isaksens, neither he nor the Old Man would have the same authority to discuss matters with the master of the hated cita as would the son of the Sokki's chief. And, as though he was able to read his thoughts, Andis went on :

'From now on, it's going to be me who gives the orders! That's what father said.'

'As you like,' said the Old Man, roaring with laughter. 'You take the lead, then, and show us the way to Isaksen's herd.'

Andis looked crestfallen, and began stammering. But the Old Man was anxious not to show him up, especially in front of a stranger.

'Unless, of course,' he added, 'you'd rather follow us until we get there. Your reindeer's pretty exhausted.'

He was right. Almost as soon as he had caught up with them, Andis' reindeer had lain down in the snow, and was now puffing away, its sides heaving like a blacksmith's bellows.

'All right then, Old Man, perhaps you'd better lead the way,' said Andis, suddenly overcome with humility.

They made a short halt, and Per Oskal never succeeded in discovering whether it was day or night; there was always the same translucent light, that seemed to ooze through the fog. He made an effort to remember; it ought to be night-time, yet what about the moon? True, during these last few days of bad weather he had forgotten all about it!

The trail now ran downhill, towards the east, from which Per Oskal concluded that they were about to emerge into the great valley of the Kvenanelva, which extended north-wards, parallel to the one they had just left. They had been on the go for some fifteen hours, alternately trotting and walking, when suddenly the clouds overhead parted, and a great wall of mountain, brilliantly lit up by the rising sun, appeared for a moment, only to fade away again; and once more they were plunged into their silent universe, where every sound was muted by mist and snow.

But the Old Man had had time to recognize the mountain.

'That was Boeccegoeldhaldi!'

This was the Isaksen's sacred mountain! Every now and

240

then, the shaman would climb to its bald, ice-capped summit in order to perform mysterious sacrifices, to which no one was admitted. Stirred by this sudden glimpse of the holy mountain, Per Oskal thought to himself that probably up there would be a reindeer altar like the one on the Agjiet.

This was the holy place of the enemy tribe, the temple where all their traditions were preserved. And suddenly it struck Per Oskal that what the Samisks sought in places like this must be the same thing that, all over the world, attracted man to the heights: to the mythical mountains of Greece, to the mountains of the genii in the Sahara, to the god-mountains of the Himalayas, and to Mount Sinaii! Here Thor was present, there Buddha, elsewhere Jupiter or Christ on his cross; everywhere a manifestation of God!

The sight of the holy mountain seemed to have hypnotized the Old Man. He had leapt from his sledge, and was struggling forward with rapid strides, dragging his pulka behind him, which swung from side to side over the snow-drifts like a drunken ship, while Andis and Per Oskal followed, sometimes on their skis, sometimes, when the nature of the road made it possible, taking a short rest on their sleighs.

All Per's attention was concentrated on the sleigh immediately in front of him; though only a few yards away, it could only be seen through the dense fog like some vaguely deformed object, now gigantic, now suddenly dwarfed. Occasionally the track led steeply downhill, forcing the reindeer irresistibly forward so that they had to arch their backs and dig the points of their hoofs into the hard ice, while the men were obliged to take off their skis. Elsewhere there were crevasses in which they sank up to their hocks in the snow, and could only extricate themselves by a series of wild plunges. In this powdery, elusive snow, which never melts, the Lapps struck out with both arms, like a swimmer against the current, and when they managed to emerge from the dangerous spot it was only to find themselves slithering about on snowdrifts, the surfaces of which were wrinkled by the wind like a breaking wave.

The pursuit continued, endless and exhausting, and as the hours flowed by Per Oskal lost all sense of where they were or how many hours they had been on the go, continually leaping on and off their sledges, putting on their skis and taking them off again, or, when the gradient permitted, having a brief ride on the sledges.

Yet the tireless, hypnotic figure of the Old Man continued to forge ahead, until even Andis would call out angrily.

'Aren't you ever going to let us have a breather?'

But the Old Man paid not the slightest attention. Since the brief mysterious glimpse of the sacred mountain, they had been unable to see anything of the country around them. Only by the angle of their sleighs could they tell whether they were going uphill or down, and every now and then, blinded by the fog, they would plunge into a huge snowdrift, or drive straight over the top of a hard mound of snow several feet high, and find themselves lying at the bottom, with their sleighs overturned, their loads scattered, and their exhausted animals tangled up in the harness.

When this happened, they had to stop for a time, and the Old Man would hand them a lump of dried meat, which they gnawed ravenously, and pass round the bottle from which they all took a swig. Then, revived by the sharp burning sensation of the spirits, Per Oskal would suddenly find himself only too ready to forgive the smugglers he had so often condemned.

'In the old days,' the Old Man told him, 'if you were thirsty, you used to slit open a reindeer's jugular vein, and drink the blood! It was better than alcohol, because the strength it gave you lasted much longer.'

Per Oskal felt convinced that, if anyone had given him the chance to suck the blood from a reindeer's vein just then, he would have been prepared to do so. He was experiencing a kind of intoxication, a strange feeling of fatigue and an almost irresistible desire to sleep. With an effort, he looked at his watch and calculated how long they had been travelling. Twenty-seven hours, almost without a halt! He

242

would never have believed that the human body was capable of such an effort. And all this merely to retrieve a few reindeer! What chances were there they would ever find them?

The Old Man, however, appeared to be quite confident.

'They're with the Isaksens' herd. It's the only place on this route where there's any lichen, and their instinct will have led them straight to it. It's not just the attraction of other reindeer, but hunger as well, for the animals are starving and they won't stop until they have found some lichen.'

They set off again, and had been travelling for some time when suddenly they emerged from the fog. Beneath the low clouds stretched the wide valley of the Kvenanelva, which just here formed a succession of small lakes, surrounded with birch trees; and here and there on the slopes of the hills one could see where a considerable herd of reindeer had been scratching away the snow. The Old Man pulled up his sleigh, and signalled to the others to do the same.

'The Isaksens' herd has passed this way. They can't be far off now.'

His keen eyes were searching everywhere to discover the slightest trace of them, and, when this failed, he borrowed Per Oskal's field glasses and before long called out that he had seen something.

'There they are, behind that hump! You can't see the herd, but they've posted sentries on the crest of the hill. I can just see the steam coming from their snow-holes.'

For a moment they were at a loss. If they were to make straight for the camp from their present position, the enemy would be able to see them from a long way off, which would give them plenty of time to hide the lost reindeer. The essential thing was to take them by surprise. The Old Man cursed the fog, for it had gradually risen so that the light no longer came from above, filtered through the clouds, but seemed to be creeping in underneath them, in long, bright shafts that temporarily restored life to the dark snow and dead rocks.

'We'll go back,' said he. 'They can't have seen us yet, for we shouldn't have discovered them if it hadn't been for Per Oskal's glasses.'

They crouched down behind the crest of the hill, and the Old Man signalled to them to wait. He had handed over his reindeer to Andis, and now he was climbing through the snow with all the agility of a young trapper, disturbing the snow-fowl who clumsily fluttered away, circling towards the foot of the hill, and then settled down behind a hillock. When he had found a suitable observation post, he took out the glasses again and examined the lie of the land with the skill of an old hunter; luckily both the camp and the herd were hidden by the skyline. He knew the spot; a low cliff rose from the frozen bed of the Kvenanelva, then came the slopes covered with lichen, the men down below, close to the water, the reindeer higher up and, right at the top, the sentries. By the time he got back again he had already made up his mind.

'We're going to slip into the valley through a gorge I have just spotted, then we shall continue along the left side, where we shall be hidden from the sentries by the overhanging slope and the tundra. Unless something very unforeseen happens, no one from the camp is likely to go back that way.'

Andis approved, but Per Oskal expressed astonishment: 'What's the point of behaving as though we wanted to take them by surprise? Wouldn't it be better to whip up our reindeer, make straight for the camp, and demand a straightforward explanation from the Isaksens?'

The two Lapps burst out laughing.

'Do you really imagine they're going to wait, instead of making off with their booty or hiding it? If they reckon they've got time to, either they'll kill our animals and cut them up, or else they'll destroy the earmarks and we shall have the devil of a job proving that they were stolen.'

Per Oskal was worried. To do what they proposed was surely behaving as though they were enemies? Was he justified in doing so? It was his responsibility to settle disputes and, if necessary, to act as judge. Could he behave as though he were a member of a clan, of a cita? He hesitated, and the Old Man strove to convince him.

'I know just what you're going to say, Per Oskal, but don't you see there's law, and there's custom. Supposing we, the Sokki clan, found ourselves with thirty reindeer belonging to the Isaksens, and they sent a delegation to us, what do you think we should do?'

'You'd give them back the reindeer that belonged to them, wouldn't you?'

'That sounds easy enough, but lost reindeer are lost reindeer, and custom is custom. If you're going to give an animal back, it must be alive and it must have an earmark. Besides, it wouldn't be breaking *your* laws. At the most, we shall just have decided to turn up without attracting attention to ourselves, and in this fog it's impossible to pick and choose which route you'll take, isn't it? By keeping in the lee of the hills, we shall simply be sheltering from the wind. The important thing is, to get close up to them without being seen! What happens after that will be your business, and I promise to give you a free hand.'

Per Oskal was taken by surprise:

'You give me your promise?'

'When you were appointed Lappefogden, it was by agreement with all the tribes. The Isaksens will accept your arbitration.'

'And supposing they don't agree to my being involved in this business?'

'In that case we'll act on our own account.'

Per Oskal shrugged his shoulders:

'As you wish!'

They crept through a narrow gorge, the bottom of which was filled with the black ice of the stream on which sleighs and reindeer slithered about, but thanks to the skill of the drivers they reached the valley without too much difficulty. They decided to cross the river at a bend, and reached the other side where the sleighs were able to run easily, as the snow had been trampled down by the recent passage of the Isaksen's caravan. They trotted along, followed by the dogs, who, exhausted by their long journey, ran with their head down and tongues hanging out, and before long they reached the point where the valley widened out, which was marked by a kind of narrow gorge that gave on to a plateau filled with harsh light. The camp was the other side of this. Above their heads rose the little cliff.

'We'll get down here,' said the Old Man, and plunging into the tundra he began to climb the wooded slope, at the top of which they expected to find the sentry. When they were fairly near, they muzzled their dogs to prevent them from barking. Presently the Old Man signalled them to stop; through the branches, less than five hundred yards away, they could just make out the small white cone of the herds-man's pesk buried in his snowhole, with his red cap standing out vividly against the greyish-white of the fjell.

'Come on,' said the Old Man. 'It's all right, their dogs haven't smelt us yet.'

They were no longer bothering to hide themselves. They unmuzzled Chumbi and Lumba, and the two dogs, delighted to be free again, sprang towards the man, barking furiously. Behind them, the Old Man whipped up his reindeer and as the three of them advanced at a fast trot, suddenly the herdsman stood up on the summit of the hill, uttered a long, surprised shout of warning, and then, gun in hand, awaited their arrival.

'Mana derivan,' said the Old Man solemnly, while still a few yards from the herdsman.

'Bazza derivan,' replied the other.

And while Andis and Per Oskal repeated the words of greeting Sven Isaksen haughtily looked them up and down.

'What brings you here on our territory? Have you come to spy on us, to find out how many deer we have? If so, take a look around! The Isaksens are the wealthiest cita in the vidda, and they're not afraid of anyone! Ten thousand well-picked reindeer, and in a week's time they'll all be down by the sea.'

It was, indeed, an impressive sight. The Isaksen herd was six thousand animals larger than the Sokkis', and the mantle of reindeer clinging to the hillside, chewing the cud as they trudged through the snow, produced such a profound effect that young Andis, despite his humiliation, could not take his eyes off them.

'We're not here to quarrel, Sven,' said the Old Man. 'Thirty of our animals got away in the storm, and we've tracked them down as far as here. Probably they've got mixed up with your herd by mistake?'

'Really?' said the young Isaksen. 'I suppose they came here of their own accord, to put themselves under our protection! Everyone knows how we look after the weak! One of these days, the way things are going on at present, every herd in the vidda will have got mixed up with ours. It can soon happen, can't it, Andis?'

His pride hurt by the other man's derision, Andis sprang forward, knife in hand, the herdsman raised his rifle.

'Stop, you young idiots,' said the Old Man. 'You, Sven, there's no need to start showing off! Your clan's record isn't as good as all that. Have you forgotten the reindeer the Germans took from us, after you'd told them where to find them? This time Andis is here to claim his own property. You know the law: if the reindeer are with your herd, and alive, you must hand them over straight away.'

The young Isaksen was obviously impressed. He knew the Old Man: people said that neither poison nor knives could harm him, and even the shaman of their tribe spoke respectfully about him. It had been a mistake to insult him.

'You speak wisely. Go on down to the camp. There you'll find both my father and the shaman,' he said sourly. 'They're the only ones that can decide anything, and until then no one's going to look at the herd ... Voï, voï, voï!'

He had set his dog on to the three draught-reindeer, terrifying them and making them rear, so that they broke their traces and rolled over in the snow. Meanwhile, Chumbi and Lumba, attacking in their turn, had roused the animals in the Isaksen herd, who, waking from their torpor, quickly began to panic.

247

'Call off your dogs, call them off!' shouted Sven, worried by the turn things had taken.

'Don't you start that nonsense again, then,' said the Old Man, 'or I'll kill those dogs of yours with my own hands!'

His anger was so frightening that Sven Isaksen realized it was better to climb down, and with considerable difficulty they managed to separate the dogs. But their furious barking had by this time awoken every echo in the valley.

CHAPTER EIGHT

THE camp had already been alerted, and men, women and children poured out of the tents. The most active ones had started scrambling up the slope and were urging on their dogs: 'Voï, voï, voï!' The whole valley rang with the sound of shouting and barking. High up above them, Sven Isaksen and the Old Man still confronted one another, observing a kind of truce, while at some distance from them Andis held on to the dogs, and Per Oskal attended to the reindeer.

Thor Isaksen, followed by his shaman, was advancing at the head of his men, and behind them came the youngsters, armed with rifles and clubs. The situation was beginning to look ugly.

'Soon it will be your turn to take a hand, Per Oskal,' the Old Man observed quietly. 'It doesn't look as though they're prepared to listen to reason.'

The Norwegian was uneasy; so far he had never been directly involved in a quarrel between Lapps. Usually, by the time they called him in, the Tribunal of Ancients had been summoned, and all he had to do was to give a ruling on a matter that had already been discussed. But now he was right at the very centre of the drama, and was beginning to discover how violent and stubborn the Samisks could be; all this raiding and thieving of reindeer was an integral part, not only of their lives, but of their whole history, and woe to the dispossessed tribe! A man who loses his reindeer is simply a miserable wretch, who is on the way to becoming an outcast.

Thor Isaksen was out of breath from the climb. He was a big, fat man, and beneath his plump, good-natured appearance, he concealed an extraordinary cunning, which made him feared by all his rivals. His powerful position was due to double-dealing rather than to ability. His evil genius, the shaman, followed close behind him, and this was the first time Per Oskal had seen the witch doctor, who had been accused of more than one murder, beginning with that of Mikkel Mikkelsen Sara, Paavi's uncle.

He was a tall, withered-up, bandy-legged creature, whose flat nose bore witness to his Mongol ancestry; he had high cheekbones and heavy, black eyebrows that overshadowed the deep eye-sockets and half hid his treacherous, cruel gaze. He was like some malevolent gnome, and Per Oskal regretted that neither the existing laws nor the fears and superstitions of the Samisks made it possible for him to arrest him as the common or garden criminal that he knew him to be. The shaman glanced at him defiantly, but prudently remained in the background; he was quite aware that his magical gifts depended upon the beliefs and superstitions of the Samisks, and that the Norwegians did not believe in them. The tall, fair-haired Scandinavian impressed him by his air of resolution and his height, as well as by the searching way he looked at him and the reputation for kindness and justice that he had won throughout the vidda.

'So you're at the bottom of all this?' said Thor Isaksen, surprised to see him, or at any rate pretending to be.

'You know quite well why Andis, the son of Simon Sokki, is here,' said the Old Man.

'But what about *him*? What's *he* doing here with you? Does it mean he's already taken sides? Does it mean you've become my enemy, Per Oskal?' demanded Isaksen, in passable Norwegian.

He spoke Norwegian in order to show off, but Per Oskal quickly undeceived him:

'Speak your own language, Isaksen, we shall understand each other better. Do you imagine it's by sitting on my backside in an office that I learnt to speak Samisk as well as you do? I'm here to help Simon Sokki get back his reindeer, just the same as I'd help you if you were in trouble. Thirty reindeer escaped in the storm! The same thing might very

250

easily happen to you, Isaksen, and if it did, what would you think of a cita that tried to keep your property?'

The other shrugged his shoulders.

'The Sokkis are no good as herdsmen, it's well-known! But if that were to happen to me it wouldn't be long before I got my property back. That's right enough, isn't it?' he asked, turning to the sly, withdrawn shaman, to his son Sven, even more arrogant than himself, and to the rest of the herdsmen who had now arrived on the scene.

'Sure enough!' said Andis. 'You're all here, but there are only three of us.'

'Two,' Per Oskal mildly corrected him. 'I am here as arbitrator, don't forget.'

Then he continued, addressing himself to Thor Isaksen:

'Have you already forgotten the thousand reindeer you stole? Didn't I allow that matter to be treated as an affair between Lapps, and do everything I could to prevent Norwegian justice from interfering? If it hadn't been for me, where would you be today? Do you suppose the Norwegians would have let you keep the reindeer you'd stolen? Do you imagine that shaman of yours would still be here defying me instead of serving a life sentence as he deserves?'

He walked over to the shaman, who drew back.

'Don't you start interfering in my business, you damned Lappefogden!' the sorcerer swore between his teeth. 'You'll pay dearly for it if you do!'

'That's enough of that,' said the Old Man. 'Per Oskal is a friend of ours, and a friend of our whole race. As for you, shaman, you impotent wretch'—here he spat into the snow—'don't you try laying a finger on him! He's under my protection, and anyone who is under the protection of the Old Man is not to be touched!'

They all nodded approvingly.

'Sven Isaksen has refused to let us look over the herd,' the Old Man went on. 'He was quite entitled to do so, but now it's you we're asking, chief. Do you refuse?'

'I'm not asking you, I'm ordering you,' Per Oskal cut in emphatically. 'Be a man, Thor Isaksen. Play the game!'

251

Regretfully, the master of the Isaksens submitted:

'Let these men look through the herd, but see that they tie up their dogs first.'

'Good,' said the Lappefogden, 'and see that your herdsmen round up your huge herd (at this recognition of his power, Isaksen smiled with satisfaction) and make sure that not a single animal gets away.'

Quickly, the Old Man and Andis began examining the herd, preceded by Thor Isaksen. The surging flood of reindeer opened to let them pass, then closed behind them, and both of them were wondering how many of these animals had been stolen, and how many of them had false earmarks.

They had been through two-thirds of the herd, when suddenly Andis caught sight of the lost animals. They had instinctively kept together, forming a smaller herd within the main one.

'There they are,' said he.

'They must have got mixed up with our lot during the night,' Isaksen observed casually. The moment had arrived when he would have to make an attempt to save face.

'Naturally,' said the Old Man. 'They must have turned up during the night, when your herdsmen were asleep!'

Isaksen disregarded the insinuation. Andis was counting the reindeer. There were twenty-eight, all bearing the double earmark, their owner's and that of the cita; two of them belonged to Martha Sokki, others to Kristina and, amongst them, were two marked with the star. As the Old Man approached, these two came up to him of their own accord and began licking his hands.

'And what about these, Isaksen? Would you have kept them, too?'

'You know very well we wouldn't,' the other replied sullenly. 'We should have driven them away from the herd and left them in the fjell. Nobody kills animals belonging to the Old Man.'

'I'm glad to hear it,' said the Old Man, satisfied with the answer. 'Bring them on, Andis.'

He tied a bell round the neck of one of the reindeer with

a star, Andis caught one of the does with his lasso and the little flock started to follow them. When he had separated them from the main herd, Andis anxiously counted them again.

'There are two missing,' he said grimly. 'It was thirty we lost!'

'Probably the wolves got them, on the way,' Sven Isaksen commented ironically.

'The wolves that got our reindeer are a damned sight crueller than the wolves of the tundra. Wait here a minute, you lot!' Andis exclaimed, and leaping on to his sledge with surprising agility, he whipped up his reindeer and went off at a gallop, straight down the slope towards the camp.

The Old Man realized what he was up to, and shouted after him: 'Stop, Andis, stop!' but the Isaksens, taken by surprise, leapt in pursuit of the young Lapp.

'What's going on?' Per Oskal asked the Old Man.

'Quick, quick, we must get to the camp or there'll be the devil to pay!'

Thanks to the start, Andis was the first to reach the camp, creating a great commotion amongst the dogs and women and children who rushed out of the tents. Quickly he started to examine the drying poles. Hanging from one of them were two reindeer, freshly skinned and not yet completely frozen, drying in the cold air of the vidda.

'What about these two? Do you mean to tell me they belong to you?' yelled the young Samisk.

'Check the earmarks,' said Sven who, being swifter than the others, had by now caught up with him.

It was not the moment for joking. Andis pulled out his knife and Sven, taken aback, did the same. But instead of starting a fight, Andis shouted furiously:

'Hang on a minute, Sven, and we damned well *will* find the earmarks.'

He called to his dog: 'Seek, Chumbi, seek!'

And the dog, to whom he had thrown a piece of meat, ran after him, sniffing at the snow. It led him straight to a clump of nearby birch trees, where the freshly churned-up snow indicated that something had been hidden.

'Fetch him out, Chumbi, fetch him out!'

The dog began digging away the snow, and soon revealed two pelts covered with blood, and two heads from which the ears had been removed. As Andis stooped forward to control his dog, Sven jeered:

'Reindeer without ears! A fat lot of use that is!'

'Get on, Chumbi! Seek, seek!' Andis repeated.

Once again the dog started digging and, right at the bottom of the hole, hidden beneath the antlers of previously slaughtered animals, he brought to light two pairs of ears.

As Andis straightened up, he found himself face to face with Sven who had a knife in his hand and an evil expression on his face.

This time the theft had been proved. Now they would have to pay handsomely. What was Andis, backed by the Old Man, going to demand? In reparation, Per Oskal would probably insist upon three for one, six reindeer for two! Sven knew his father would never forgive him for such carelessness: if you are going to cut off any ears, they should be burnt, not just hidden away!

Beaming all over, Andis drew himself up and turned towards the group of men that was coming towards them: it consisted of Thor Isaksen, burning with hatred and no trace of his previous good-nature, the Old Man and Per Oskal, slowly leading the three sleighs. The rest of them straggled behind.

'Here's the proof, Lappefogden! Now it's up to you to give judgement,' said Andis, throwing the ears at Per Oskal's feet, the irrefutable proof of the Isaksen's crime.

But, in the time it took him to turn round, Sven had sprang upon him and struck him a violent blow with his dagger. Andis felt a burning pain in his back, spun round and fainted away.

Already his assailant was some distance away, skiing swiftly, protected by his fellow clansmen, who formed a human barrier between him and the Lappefogden.

Preoccupied with the wounded man, Per Oskal shouted :
'Have him taken to your own tent, Isaksen, and tell the
women to boil up some water !'

His voice had a note of authority that none of them had
previously heard . . . Feeling utterly crushed, they all hurried
to do as they were told.

This was the first time in the history of the Lapps that a
crime had been committed in the presence of the Lappefogden. Sven Isaksen had put himself in the wrong, and
this created a difficult situation for the cita. The wounded
man was carried into the tent and laid on the reindeer
skins. They took off his pesk, his koufte and his thick
woollen underclothes, exposing his naked, muscular torso.
The knife had struck slantwise, so that the blow, deadened
by his furs, had glanced off a rib, but there was a long deep
gash, and a good deal of blood had been lost. Per Oskal
washed the wound with boiling water, then, pulling out
the bottle of spirits that Martha Risak had given him, he
disinfected it. When he had finished, he swallowed a mouthful himself, for he felt badly in need of a drink. Then he
turned to face the circle of Lapps, who crowded round him,
waiting anxiously.

'Fortunately, it missed any vital organ. You're lucky,'
he added, 'otherwise, Thor Isaksen, you'd have had to come
with me to answer for it !'

There was a general sigh of relief.

He asked for some clean rag. The women produced linen
chemises from their chests, and began tearing them up into
bandages. The wound would need one or two stitches, but
Per Oskal hesitated to use the materials they offered him—
thread made from reindeer sinews and a fine bone needle !
At this point, however, the oldest woman of the cita came
forward.

'I'll see to it,' said she. 'You've done what you can. You
can leave the rest to me.'

She had an expert knowledge of herbs, and he allowed her
to prepare a plaster with which she covered the wound,
having first drawn the lips of it together; then she fixed a

roughly-made bandage and put on Andis's clothes again. Except for the blood on his clothing and the pallor of the wounded man, who was now opening his eyes, there was little to indicate what had taken place. By this time Per Oskal had managed to get him to drink a few drops of aquavit, he was already beginning to recover.

Once more the Old Man assumed command.

'Lay him on his sledge.'

Per Oskal found it difficult to decide what attitude he should adopt. He had witnessed an attempted murder, and he would have to report it to his superiors; yet somehow he felt instinctively that the matter was beyond his competence.

'Your son behaved very badly, Thor,' said he severely. 'Weren't we your guests?'

'My son was provoked, Andis also had a knife.'

'But that's no excuse for Sven!'

'You must decide.'

Everyone was waiting for the Lappefogden to give judgement. He gazed round the camp, which was almost a replica of the Sokki's; the same tents, with the same smoke issuing from between the crossed poles, the same smell of food and confusion of sleighs, with the same scattered loads and piles of antlers and drying meat, and dogs wandering about looking for a bone to eat. He turned from one to the other, from the sly old women to the hostile youngsters, proud and arrogant; from Thor Isaksen, now somewhat reassured but with no trace of his earlier well-fed joviality, to the Old Man standing upright and clasping his long ski-stick, the one man whom they all felt would be able to settle the dispute, while he, Per Oskal, responsible to his government for administering justice to this strange people, stood there hesitating, more doubtful than ever of his ability to discover the truth.

The would-be murderer had not returned, and there was no point in following him; he could not escape from the fjell, the vidda, the migration; he was the prisoner of these vast open spaces, where he could only hope to get a livelihood from the reindeer! He would be able, if he so chose, to remain in hiding for the rest of his life, since no one would think of denouncing him, not even, indeed least of all, the members of the Sokki clan! The risk he would run would be a much greater one : a stab in the back one winter's night that would avenge the man he had wounded, even though he had failed to kill him. The law of a life for a life would still remain in force, and nothing could hinder it.

The shaman had disappeared at the same time as Sven. Per Oskal felt disappointed, he would gladly have arrested the fake witch doctor. But then he realized that it was all to the good, for what would happen to him, if he had had to take the shaman with him as a prisoner across these vast expanses of snow? He knew only too well : no one would have helped him or backed him up, not a single Samisk would have come to his assistance or given him food, not even those who were most devoted to him. In their eyes, the shaman was beyond the law, like the Old Man.

It was at this point that Per Oskal reached a wise decision.

'What would you do in a case like this?' he asked the Old Man.

'I'd insist on the tribal law being carried out: the Isaksens should give us six reindeer in place of the two they've killed, and three of them should be does; and, in addition to that, four reindeer to compensate for the attack on Andis. Provided that they do that, everything will be as it was.'

'Do you accept that, Isaksen?' asked the Lappefogden. 'If you agree to the proposal put forward by the Old Man nobody will hear anything about this, either at Trömso or at Hammerfest. I give you my word!'

Thor Isaksen sighed heavily :

'Do you promise my son won't be arrested?'

'Have I ever gone back on my word?'

'Never, never!' said the Lapps with one accord. 'Accept his offer, Isaksen, and peace be with you.'

'In that case,' said the Lappefogden, 'my decision is that the Old Man's ruling shall be carried out. You, Thor Isaksen, get back to the herd and select the reindeer yourself.'

It was getting late, clouds were banking up over the hills, and moving towards the camp, forming a dense ceiling half-way up the slope, beneath which the immense plain stretched away into the unknown.

Per Oskal took charge of Andis' sleigh. The young man's condition was improving, and as he passed the tents, they all murmured:

'Mana derivan, Andis, mana derivan!'

To which the Old Man replied on his behalf: 'Bazza derivan, bazza derivan! Peace be with you!'

To Per Oskal, the climb back to the herd seemed long and hard. The Old Man was once more in the lead, striding ahead at his usual speed and puffing away at his pipe. With him, this was a sign that he was highly satisfied. He had triumphed over the Isaksen's shaman, he had imposed his will, and provided the Sokkis did not attempt to avenge themselves, order would be restored for many winters ahead. But that was a matter for the future, and all that concerned him was the present.

Thor Isaksen made no difficulties about selecting the ten animals from the thousands of reindeer in his heard. He picked out alternately fat ones and thin ones and, as agreed, two does in calf, which the Old Man immediately marked with the Sokki earmark, leaving it to Simon to allocate them to those who were entitled to them later on.

Then he secured the ten animals one behind the other with a lasso and tied them to his sledge, for otherwise they would not willingly have left the main herd. Meanwhile, Per Oskal had rounded up the other twenty-eight animals that belonged to them, and as the Old Man took the lead, automatically the reindeer with the star in its ear and the doe wearing the bell lined up behind him, while the dogs leapt about wildly, rounding up the strays. From a distance, the herdsmen watched them go, and before long Thor Isaksen was the only man left on the crest of the hill, watching with rage and disappointment as the little convoy moved off into the greyish light and disappeared into the tundra. When they were no longer to be seen, the master of the Isaksens gave his orders to the new herdsmen, whistled up his dogs, put on his skis and returned to the camp. He had only gone a few hundred yards, when he heard the howling of a fox across the tundra. He turned his head, shouted in reply, and waited. Whereupon, very slowly, Sven Isaksen and the shaman emerged from a thick clump of trees.

'They've gone, then?' enquired the son anxiously.

'I've paid for your carelessness. It will take us years to wipe out this shame.'

'You don't have to worry, Thor Isaksen,' said the shaman. 'I've prepared a filter, and I shall sprinkle it on the road in front of their herd. All their animals will fall sick and die, and you'll be able to take on their men as herdsmen!'

For a moment Isaksen looked at the shaman with a feeling of hatred and vengeance, but his eyes faltered before the other man's glance.

'Only the future can tell whether you're speaking the truth, shaman. Have you forgotten the dressing-down the Old Man gave you?'

'Pshaw!' muttered the shaman. 'I've got something that will put that right!' And he spat on the ground three times.

CHAPTER NINE

THE Old Man kept them going most of the night, but towards daybreak they had to stop; Andis was showing signs of fatigue. They realized that for three days they had had practically nothing to eat or drink. Although they were still on territory allocated to the Isaksens they decided to make a halt; there was plenty of lichen where the wind had driven away the snow, and the animals were starving.

As there were too few of them to keep a proper watch, for greater safety they tied the reindeer together with lassoes to prevent them from wandering away. They were especially careful to secure the Isaksen animals, since the main herd was still near enough for them to take the first opportunity of returning to it.

The fog had cleared, and they found themselves in a wide, treeless trough between two ice-covered mountains. The pass was a dangerous short-cut, though well-known to the Old Man, and it would enable them to get back to the Sokki camp before the final stage of the journey and the descent to the sea. Here the wind never stopped blowing and it was quite the worst place to camp, but, according to the Old Man, it was the only one where they would find any lichen and the animals must be their first consideration.

In a small ravine Per Oskal discovered enough arctic willows and dwarf birches to make a fire. Sheltered by their upturned sleighs, which protected the wounded man, they decided to eat their fill. The icy wind pierced through the double thickness of their furs, but with the help of a big tarpaulin they managed to erect a kind of screen which gave them additional protection. Patiently they set about making a fire, twig by twig, and before long its flames were flickering in the darkness like a will-o'-the-wisp. Per Oskal kept stoking it up, while at the same time he melted snow in the cauldron suspended from a tripod. Despite the excessively low temperature, this evening his mind was at peace and he felt unusually happy; above the continual whistling of the wind he could distinguish all the familiar noises of their little herd. They were returning as conquerors, with eight deer more than they had expected to! Simon Sokki would be pleased, and Per Oskal was impressed by the good sense he had shown: had he allowed the Finn to come with them, there would certainly have been a battle royal and people would have been killed or wounded. Andis had behaved like an idiot and he did not carry much weight, but his blunder had turned out to be to their advantage.

A couple of hours elapsed, filled with this sense of inner peace; and by the time they were able to drink the hot soup and ravenously devour the pieces of meat they had cooked, even the wounded man had a good appetite.

'You'll soon be on your feet again, my lad,' the Old Man told him. 'This knife gash will have earned you four reindeer!'

Andis felt very pleased with himself. He would be the hero, the one who had dared to attack the Isaksen's camp single-handed, and he was already beginning to think of how he would describe the incident. It delighted him to imagine the endless summer days when he would visit the girls in their turf huts and, sitting on the mountains of the sea, carpeted with red cranberries and looking out over the fjords and the open sea, dotted with red sails and clouds of spray, tell them of his exploits.

After spending a considerable part of the night eating and drinking, they all three sank into a deep sleep. They knew that, for the time being, they were in no danger; the Isaksens had been temporarily neutralized.

The short night was over long before they set off again; the weather had changed, the sun had suddenly become much warmer and it was more and more difficult to make their way through the soft snow. The sleighs did not run so well, and, after struggling through the patches of slush,

261

they ran into stretches of hard ice and rocks, where the reindeer had difficulty in keeping their feet. But they were no longer constrained by their unending pursuit, and the Old Man was taking the return journey easily; they travelled by short stages, interspersed with brief halts, usually where there was lichen for the reindeer. Besides, it was becoming more and more difficult to drag the sleighs along, and they adopted the habit of sleeping by day and travelling by night, when the surface of the snow began to freeze over again. Per Oskal was living in a dream. He had forgotten all about his mission, and if, occasionally, the thought of it ruffled the surface of his mind, he quickly dismissed it. He was engaged in a timeless journey and, from now on, he was sharing the fortunes of the Samisks.

One morning as they were about to descend a steep, exposed slope, the Old Man halted abruptly : over large areas the sun had completely melted the snow, revealing the short, reddish arctic grass. Here and there crocuses had started to shoot, and the snow-fowl, their white winter plumage already speckled with brown, were flying about looking for somewhere to build their nests, choosing those places where the mixture of snow and grass would enable them to make use of their protective colouring.

'It's time we were there,' said the Old Man. 'The warm winds have started, and we shall have to look out for the does—they'll be calving down prematurely.'

Then, seeing that Per Oskal looked worried, he added :

'Tomorrow evening we shall be back with the cita !'

'Tomorrow evening we shall be home !' Andis chimed in.

It struck Per Oskal that he was beginning to think just like them. For him, too, returning to the camp would be returning to everyday life. The cita, with its thousands of reindeer, its tents, its dogs, its men, women and children, was now the one spot on earth where the fire burning on the hearthstone spelt home. All the forms of civilized life, the idea of the nation, of political frontiers, of cities and comfort, all this was now done with. Per Oskal, the Norwegian, had but one desire : to get back to the Samisk camp, slip into Martha Risak's tent, suck a marrow bone, drink the black soup, recount his exploits over a bottle of aquavit, then fall asleep on the reindeer skins and, when summoned by the head of the clan, be ready to set out once more with the reindeer.

He understood better, now, what gave this people their strength! For them, their fatherland was wherever the herd happened to be; and, once it was destroyed, what would become of them? Yet this was precisely what he had been sent here for: to persuade these people to break up the cita and become a part of the great mass of Norwegian settlers. He felt himself beginning to tremble with indignation. After the honourable part he had played, from a sense of justice and of friendship for the Samisks, was he now to help destroy the people he loved? 'Tomorrow we shall be back with the cita,' the Old Man had said; and Per Oskal had felt in his heart the same shock of pleasure, the same feeling of relief as his Samisk comrades. It was as though he, too, was returning to his distant fatherland. Besides, wasn't the ruling he had given based on Samisk law rather than on Norwegian? He ought to have arrested Sven Isaksen and the shaman on the spot, and insisted upon the others helping him! He would be criticised for having failed to do so, he might even have to give up his position. When they came to hear of what he had done, what would the Lennsmann, Pastor Brombdal and Fru Tideman have to say . . . ? And yet, in this sunlit morning, where, on every side, spring was already triumphing over the snows of winter, Per Oskal's soul was at peace. It was as though tomorrow he would be going home, to that undefined, ever changing country, that fatherland, whose extent and frontiers had never been determined, the heart of which was a herd of reindeer, ever on the move, around which for thousands of years man had gravitated . . .

Per Oskal rose to his feet and stared out over the fjell. He felt strangely excited, and began to improvize in Samisk a triumphant yok, about the loss of the reindeer and their recapture, the victorious struggle with a hated enemy and the heroes' return to camp, leading behind them the living ransom for the crime that had been committed!

'So that's how you feel,' commented the Old Man. 'You're becoming one of us, then, Per Oskal.'

'Get cracking,' he replied, 'I'm longing to get home.'

For a moment they looked at one another. On the Old Man's face there was a ghost of a smile, and his eyes were clearer and more limpid than ever.

For the next twenty-four hours they travelled beneath a cloudless sky, for the night had almost ceased to exist, an hour at most, a kind of bluish half-light that made it possible to see the stars; yet, when the sun was at its zenith, the heat became stifling, and the soft snow slowed down the sleighs considerably. The air was full of the breath of spring, and, as they descended into a new valley, the patches free of snow became more frequent, then streams began to flow, and greedily they stooped down to the running water, scooped it up in their hands, and bathed their faces! So tanned and scorched were their cheeks that they looked as though they were made of pottery, gleaming in the rays of the setting sun, which disappeared behind the sky-line of mountain peaks for a while, came into sight again a little further on, then gradually rose once more until it was clear of the horizon.

Now, on every side, the snow-fowl were flying about, with their speckled plumage and their crops bursting with the first green shoots; and everywhere fresh tracks were appearing in the snow, blue and silver foxes, ermines, martens, and once, to their consternation, the broad, sharp-clawed footprints of a wolverine, most terrible of enemies to the reindeer, at last beginning to emerge from its long winter sleep.

The further north they went, the deeper the valleys became and the higher rose the mountains, most of them covered with glaciers, though the slopes facing to the north and west were covered with dense forests of birch, spreading out like grey fur almost to the summit. Gradually it was becoming more and more difficult to find a way suitable

264

for the sleighs between the patches of ground where the snow had already melted.

At the bottom of the valley, a wide stream ran between muddy banks and stretches of marsh, which, in summer, would be covered with senna, the grass they used for their moccasins. In some places, great lumps of ice were swirling along in the current, while elsewhere, where the sun had not yet reached, the water was still frozen and it was possible to cross the river on foot without danger. The breath of spring was affecting both men and beasts, and they all seemed to have taken on a new life. The Old Man was monotonously humming a yok, and as his high, shrill voice did not carry, he seemed to be singing to himself—which, perhaps, was precisely what he was doing!

After passing through a short defile, the valley widened out once more, and here they found the broad trail made by the recent passage of the main herd. The cita of the Sokkis could not be much further now! They reached a bend in the valley, a place where, between mud banks, the river wound its way across a large plateau, still covered with snow, and Andis was the first to spy the swarming mass of the herd, the tents and the plumes of smoke fluttering from the forked tent-poles, and all around the usual confusion of sledges lying on their sides, their loads scattered on the ground and the ceaseless coming and going of men, women and children.

Almost at the same moment they had been seen from the camp, and there were shouts of happiness. Andis wanted to get up from his sleigh, and Per Oskal had to calm him.

'You must keep quiet, or you'll open up that wound of yours again!'

'But when father sees me, I want to be on my feet!'

'Not yet, you're still too weak.'

Disappointed, Andis decided to send his dogs ahead as messengers:

'Get on out, Chumbi! Get on, Lumba! Tell them the good news.'

265

He unleashed his dogs, who immediately dashed away, while he laughed like a child to see them bounding across the snow like balls of black and white fur to meet all the dogs of the cita which hurried out to greet them.

It was to the accompaniment of their barking that the three men entered the camp. They were quickly surrounded by the younger folk, Per, Mikael, Martha, Karin and Kristina, all terribly excited.

'But you've come back with more than we lost!'

And immediately they all began trying to find an explanation. Either they must have stolen some reindeer on the way, or they had found some that had been lost by other people? Probably the latter, for the Norwegian wouldn't have allowed them to steal.

The Old Man pulled up his sleigh in front of the first tent, got down and made a sign to Per Oskal to do the same. Walking slowly, they advanced to where Simon Sokki awaited them, standing outside his own tent.

'Mana derivan!' said the master. 'Did everything go off all right?'

'Take a look at the reindeer, Simon Sokki! We've brought back thirty-eight. We insisted on them paying blood money!'

'What do you mean?'

And as he caught sight of his son, lying on the sleigh and trying to smile, Simon rushed towards him, exclaiming:

'What's my son doing there? Why doesn't he come to greet me?'

Painfully, Andis got to his feet, his face drawn with the effort, then pulled himself together and, staggering, took a few steps, to meet his father.

'You see, father, Isaksen missed hopelessly! Why, it's just a scratch, but I got four reindeer for it all the same.'

So there had been trouble! They would all have liked to hear the whole story straight away, but they mastered their curiosity: the first thing to do was to look after the travellers who seemed to be almost at the end of their tether, and as they led them towards the camp fire they

266

all started asking about the route they had taken, the weather and all the little incidents of the journey. But no one dared to raise the main question.

Ellena had at once put a couple of huge logs on the fire, which was already smouldering on a smooth slab of stone in the open air, and they all seated themselves around it, having first made up a bed of reindeer skins where the wounded man could lie down. They sat in pairs, Martha Risak squatting beside Per Oskal and taking his hand; as they exchanged smiles, Per Oskal realized that he found her attractive as well as beautiful. Affectionately, he began stroking her hand and she gazed at him, at first in surprise, then smiling.

Kristina and the Finn congratulated the newcomers:

'You picked out some fine animals to bring back!'

They were delighted to think that now they would have some of the Isaksens' reindeer in their herd. The Finn felt a sharp pang of jealousy; he ought to have been in on this exploit.

'We shall have as big a herd as ever,' said Kristina. 'You wait and see.'

'Hang on a bit, let them tell us what happened.'

But first of all they had to eat and drink, which was a protracted business; and no one seemed in a hurry to speak. Simon Sokki knew how to loosen their tongues, however.

'I reckon they deserve a drink for getting the reindeer back, don't you, wife?'

Ellena understood what he meant. She quickly produced some aquavit, and before long they were all drinking happily. It was clear that they meant to make a night of it.

'Come on now, Andis, tell us what happened,' Simon Sokki said at last.

Everybody fell silent, but Andis looked from the Old Man to his father, then to the Lappefogden, and not a sound issued from his lips; after looking forward with such pleasure to describing his exploits, now he did not know how to begin! He was beginning to feel that maybe it was not

267

he who had played the chief part in all this business! The others encouraged him:

'Come on, Andis, tell us! You didn't get that knife wound for nothing.'

'Your son, Simon Sokki,' said Per Oskal, 'drove straight into the Isaksen's camp at the gallop, all by himself . . .'

He was interrupted by a chorus of exclamations that expressed amazement, surprise and admiration.

'Silence, let him go on!' Simon Sokki interjected.

'. . . It was he who discovered the cache where they'd hidden the skins and ears of the reindeer they'd killed! But that wasn't the start of the story. I think the Old Man ought to tell it. After all, he was in charge of everything, and it was he who once again put the Isaksen's shaman in his place.'

Without realizing it, Per Oskal was taking sides: he was no longer the impartial arbitrator, but simply one of the herdsmen belonging to the cita of the Sokkis who had helped find the stolen reindeer.

Now the Old Man took up the tale, and as he spoke they all began reliving the incidents, committing them to memory, singing the opening phrases of a yok, growing more and more excited as the Old Man soberly described the various happenings, occasionally appealing to one of his companions to confirm what he was saying. He told the whole story, in-including his own words and actions, as though it were all something that he had simply watched happening. For example, he said:

'. . . then their accursed shaman went up to the Old Man, but it was enough for him to look him straight in the eyes and the shaman retreated.'

While he was speaking everyone kept laughing and shouting to express their approval of his story. He stressed the part played by Per Oskal: how he had settled the differences between them, and promised not to take the matter before the Norwegian courts; and then how, thanks to his medical skill, he had been able to treat Andis' wound!

'From now on,' he said, gravely pointing to the Lappe-

268

fogden, 'he's become one of us. He carried out the law of the vidda!'

'Yes, yes, now he's one of us!' all the Lapps repeated in chorus, and Per Oskal, who by this time was pleasantly drunk, felt that he was entering upon a new phase of his existence.

'You see,' Martha said to him, 'now you're one of us!'

And she held him close, looking at him passionately, but by now he was already far away. He was dreaming of the mountains and frozen deserts he had just crossed, and it seemed to him that he had been travelling for centuries. He had forgotten everything else: his little white house in Viddakaïno, and the fisherman's hut beside the Alta fjord where he was born, and where his parents still lived. He felt himself steeped in snow, in lichen, in reindeer, as though this country of the Samisks was *his* country.

A faint light still lingered on the snow-covered crests of the mountains, and the sun's disc lay low on the horizon, enormous, flaming, yet giving out no heat; it sank to the bottom of the valley, burst fourth above the topmost peaks, disappeared for a moment or two behind a spur of rocks, then shone forth again, rising slowly above the horizon and announcing the birth of a new day almost before the previous one had finished dying. And almost imperceptibly the snow, which had turned from pink to blue, from blue to grey, suddenly flushed once more.

The sun's course was eternal; night had ceased to exist.

Per Oskal, intoxicated by the spirits he had drunk, by fatigue, and by too much food eaten on an empty stomach, listened to the wild songs they were singing, that seemed to stem from the very heart of the fire, whose flames twisted and turned in the icy blast of a new day.

As he listened to them singing their yoks, his own name frequently recurred, mingled with the short, poetical phrases improvised by the singers, and he knew he had been admitted to the sagas of this eternal people.

PART FOUR

THE MOUNTAINS OF THE SEA

CHAPTER ONE

By midday the heat became stifling. The melting snow gave beneath the weight of the sleighs, and when they had to alight the men sank up to their waists into the soft, watery slush.

This last climb to the pass leading to the sea was interminable. A narrow valley, between high cliffs still gleaming with winter ice, led them gradually upwards. The herd, which had left the sledges behind, was strung out behind the Old Man. Per Oskal was walking with him. Their journey in search of the lost reindeer had brought them closer together. Now there was a kind of complicity between them, as if the Old Man had guessed the progressive change that had taken place in the Lappefogden's outlook, transforming him into an ally.

Where the reindeer had passed, churning up the deep, powdery snow, there was now a stream, which added its voice to the sound of running water that could be heard on all sides; and, at times, as it made its way between the ice and rocks, it was like blood coursing through the veins.

The reindeer climbed eagerly, already beginning to smell the odour of the sea, and instinctively aware that they were nearing the island where they would find lichen in plenty and an abundance of grass. A shout from the herdsmen behind him made the Old Man stop. At the top of his voice, the Finn, who was bringing up the rear, yelled a warning: a white doe was calving. It was one of Kristina's, and handing over her sledge to her brother, she rushed forward to give a hand.

'Too late!' said the Finn. 'It's already over.'

A new-born calf, bright-eyed though still unable to stand, was lying in the snow while its mother licked it clean.

'We'll pick it up in the autumn, on our way back.'

She nodded in agreement, yet she could not help thinking of all the wolves and wolverines, all the eagles and the men!

The calf was already trying to stand up, but its slender legs were too long and too weak, they kept splaying out like those of an ungainly spider.

Per Oskal, who had turned back, now came up with them.

'What a shame!' he said. 'The poor little thing will never be able to keep up with us. Why not try putting it on your sleigh?'

'We should have to wait a good time before doing that,' said she. 'If anyone were to touch it now, its mother would smell us and refuse to suckle it.'

'What are you going to do, then?'

'Leave it with its mother. She's the only one who can possibly save it!'

Meanwhile, the Old Man was growing impatient; they had to keep going. There had already been quite enough premature births.

'You go on ahead,' said the Finn. 'We shall have to drive the mother and calf away.'

This was not easy, for the mother was unwilling to leave the herd, and the dogs had to chase her a considerable distance away. The doe kept turning back, anxiously calling to her calf, which swayed, tripped, fell down, scrambled to its feet again, struggled towards her, then, almost giving up, lay down in the snow once again, but finally managed to get to its feet. While all this was happening, the herd had reached the pass; now it was obvious that they would never be able to catch up.

'We shall just have to pick them up in the autumn,' said the Finn.

'Do you think they'll still be here, Paavi?' Kristina asked dubiously. And for the first time, there were tears in her eyes.

'Don't you worry,' the Finn assured her. 'I'll manage to slip away from the island somehow. After all, nobody's going to shut us up there. The Old Man has shown me the way.

274

Come on now, get back to the sleighs; I must catch up with the herd.'

He climbed easily, springing from rock to rock, avoiding the streams, seeking out the spots where the snow was still hard, and before long he had caught up with the rest of the herdsmen. When he looked back, he could see small black specks clearly visible on the snow, stretching away along the bottom of the valley towards the south, and made a note of the direction.

'We should be able to find them somewhere near Mollejaurre,' he estimated.

Andis was with the baggage sleighs; as he was still too weak to walk, they had made him up a comfortable bed of furs and tied him to it. His cousin Mattis was leading his sledge, but, though he took great care to avoid the bad patches, they sometimes sank through the hard layer of snow into the wet slush beneath, and the reindeer had to haul the sleigh out of the stream of icy water that flowed between the snow and the frozen earth. Every time the reindeer, arching its back, suddenly sprang forward, it shook the wounded man violently, and now and then he would let out a groan.

'Take it easy,' Mattis said to him. 'Tomorrow we shall be on the island, and you'll have all summer to get strong again. This is the last bad stretch. Tomorrow it will all be over!'

Kristina, who was just ahead of them, was bewailing the loss of her white doe and its calf.

'We've been hanging about too long—first of all for father, and now for you! Four does have calved already. We ought to have been on the island by this time.'

Mattis sighed.

'What a bitch of a life! Thank God it's for the last time!'

'Do you really think so?' said Andis. 'You know what father is, always changing his mind!'

'This time it's been too much of a good thing. The Norwegians are right, we're crazy if we keep on in the same old way.'

'Shut your mouth,' Kristina snapped. 'It's only because he knows you'll all agree that Simon Sokki is giving in, you cowards!'

Her cheeks were flaming with anger. The two lads laughed and began making fun of her; whereupon, Kristina furiously whipped up her reindeer and, with the five or six sleighs she was in charge of tied on behind in Indian file, she quickly left them behind and caught up with the rest of the caravan.

'Leave her alone,' said Andis. 'It's the Finn who's setting her against us. But, when it comes to the point, she'll do whatever father decides.'

'Do you really think so? I don't!'

They had started to climb again, and were taking it easy, for Andis was finding every jolt increasingly painful.

Simon Sokki had handed over his sleigh to Mikael Bongo; he must be at the pass by the time the Old Man and the herd arrived. He scrambled up the slope with surprising ease for a man of his age, seized by the sudden frenzy that seemed to have effected both animals and human beings as they drew nearer to the sea. Already, through the sickle-shaped opening of the pass, a new landscape was visible, consisting of lofty, needle-sharp peaks, surrounded by big glaciers, flowing towards the fjord. Before them lay the whole coast-line of the Arctic Ocean: the islands, the fjord lying between its steep cliffs, with clumps of dwarf birch trees covering the bottom slopes. This was quite different from the dense scrub of the tundra, and, in places, the plantations of pine trees, forests almost, emphasised the greater mildness of the climate. Wherever the land was ploughed the fields were enclosed with fences, and scattered about amongst them were one-storied houses, red, white, yellow and blue, standing like so many lighthouses on every rock and promonotory. At the centre of these was the main settlement; the post office, the little church with its pointed spire, the landing stage and wharf, the racks for drying fish, and the big boathouse. All this created an impression of peaceful stability, but all around, on the open sea, in the

276

fjord and the channels between the islands, there was a ceaseless coming and going of hundreds of fishing boats, while the broad-beamed steamers coming in to land and the wash of the ferry boats produced an extraordinary effect of intense activity, punctuated by a sound that was strange and disconcerting to the ears of anyone arriving from the vidda, the phut, phut, phut of innumerable engines, likc the beat of a feverish pulse, which seemed to betoken a thirst for life, a fear of losing time, of death, of the precariousness of existence.

The herdsmen were assembled at the top of the pass, and all of them, from the youngest to the oldest, experienced the same emotion. Before them lay a new world, where the people who lived in it rushed to meet their fate as if they knew that they were already condemned; and this new world was simply a narrow strip of land, running along the shore and sometimes no more than a hundred yards wide. Yet this narrow strip of inhabited land was Norway, the country of the sea, completely different from the wild empty vidda they had just crossed, the country of eternity.

Before them, a mighty mountain range towered above the sea, rising almost from the shore on the other side of the fjord. Although, geographically, it was a peninsula, joined to the mainland by a rocky isthmus, narrow and almost impassable, it was always known as the island. To the north, towards the ocean, the granite spurs and glaciers abruptly came to an end, but the island itself was a 3,000-ft. high plateau, still covered with snow, which, in the summer, provided the reindeer with an extensive area of abundant lichen, exposed to the winds and free from mosquitoes. This was why, from time immemorial, the Lapps belonging to the Sokki cita had been swimming their herds across the eight hundred yards of sea in order to spend the summer there.

It was here that they had built their huts of stone and turf, low, rounded structures, completely enclosed except for the entrance and a hole to let out the smoke, in which, for centuries, the cita had lived throughout the summer.

It would have been possible for the Lapps to reach the

island by land, but as the fjord ran inland for some forty miles, forming an almost inaccessible canyon, this would have taken them another month . . . They therefore preferred to risk the short but dangerous sea-crossing, since it provided them with rich, isolated pasture land, safe from raiders and thieves.

Simon Sokki went over to Per Oskal.

'This is your country then, Per,' he said affectionately.

'My country and yours!'

'D'you realize what you're saying?'

Per Oskal did not answer, he was too moved. In a few days now, his mission would be completed, and he would have to leave these people with whom he had lived so intensely for the last few weeks. Across the fjord, he would find once more the pretty little white houses, the pastor, the lennsmann, and the fishermen, all Norwegians, and it would suddenly be as though an insurmountable wall had been erected between the Samisks and himself.

'You're right,' he said presently. 'This country along the coast isn't yours, Simon. That's your land, over there!'

They both turned their heads, and before them stretched a succession of lost valleys, frost-bound and treeless, of snow-capped mountains and high plateaux, the outlines of which, receding into the distance, gave some intimation of the vastness of the vidda.

'That's your land,' Per Oskal repeated. 'The island over there is simply a temporary port of call. You were here long before us Scandinavians, and yet for more than three centuries we have been settled all along the coast. When the first Scandinavian fisherman came to this desolate spot, it was because the fishing was almost miraculously good. But his descendants have built this chain of wooden houses, and now, in every one of them, a family lives and manages to make some kind of living from fishing, and pigs, and milk. And, for all of them, it means the same peaceful, precarious existence. Like you, they learnt what the long arctic night is like, with the storms and blizzards and loneliness, yet they never went away; this thankless land became their father-

278

land. These folk are my kith and kin, Simon Sokki, but not yours; they have never been into the interior, into your real country, that land of mountains and plateaux that goes on for ever. They think they know your people, but in reality they haven't the slightest idea of what you are like. Even for me, it's only through making this long journey with you that I've come to understand you.'

'Since this business with the reindeer, Per Oskal,' said Simon Sokki, 'you haven't been the same man; your attitude towards me seems to have changed.'

The Norwegian looked embarrassed. Of course he had changed, but he found it odd that Simon seemed to be reproaching him for it. He had hoped that the development he had undergone would have brought him closer to the Sokkis, and to Simon, restored to his old self. Was this all a mistake? Had Simon ceased to be the nomad he once was? Had he, despite all his hopes, changed in quite the opposite way to himself during the migration? He feared it might be so.

'What d'you mean, Simon? I have never felt so close to all of you in spirit as I do now, as a result of sharing in all your setbacks and troubles. There have been times when I have felt as though I had really become one of you!'

And when Simon hung his head, without making any reply or giving the least sign of agreement, he felt worried and, like a man seeking refuge in words to avoid listening to his companion say something he is afraid to hear, he suddenly burst out:

'I can't explain it exactly. I feel as if I had reached the frontier of a new world; and that after a journey that has been going on maybe for centuries—how can I tell, since time no longer exists—suddenly I find myself confronted by the signs of a civilization that seems utterly foreign to me. Look, everything is different! The country we've come from is not the same as the one we're going into.'

And, in fact, everything was different. The air was full of salt spray and the wind was blowing with the mildness of summer, and the Arctic Ocean itself, cut up into thousands of fjords and bays, presented nothing but a calm, black surface, and it was only by looking far out towards the distant horizon, where the sun was already sinking, that you could make out the white line of foam, the swell of the open sea. All around, sheer mountains, most of which had never been climbed, thrust their granite spires up into the greyish sky; and mysterious islands floated upon the waves, covered with snow like giant icebergs, and those that were furthest away seemed to be drifting out towards the open sea.

'Tomorrow we shall be there,' Simon Sokki said grimly, pointing to the island. 'We've only got one more obstacle to overcome, a hard one in all conscience—crossing the fjord. And I swear to you, Per Oskal, on my word of honour, this will be the last time my cita has to face that ordeal.'

'Have you thought about it seriously, Simon?'

'What more do you want? Fate has been pretty hard on us : all those animals killed by the wolf, then the avalanche, the reindeer we lost, my son wounded. And God knows how many more reindeer will be drowned tonight while we're crossing the fjord, not to mention the calves born too early and all the does we've had to leave behind.'

He shook his head.

'No, it's been too much of a good thing!'

'But, Simon, every year it's the same; for thousands of years there have been avalanches, wolves and thieves! Why should you change your attitude now?'

'Have you forgotten that they gave you the job of convincing me that we ought to emigrate?'

And as Per Oskal did not answer, the Lapp continued :

'What finally decided me was Andis getting wounded like this! We can't just allow the matter to drop, we have to avenge ourselves. If Andis was to try to get out of it he'd lose face, and so should we. Look you, sometimes I wonder if it wouldn't have been better if you'd done things the Norwegian way, and taken Sven Isaksen and the shaman to court at Hammerfest...'

Per Oskal was indignant :

280

'But I thought you approved of what I did!'

'So did I at the time. But now I keep telling myself that the vendetta will have to start all over again, that blood must pay for blood, and I'm sick and tired of all these crimes and thieving. Fru Tideman was right, they were all right! And now it's me who has to start trying to convince you, Per Oskal the Lappefogden, the man that Fru Tideman sent to win me over! What are you going to do? What are you going to say to your superiors?'

Per Oskal felt completely at a loss. Could he, without going back on his word, speak as his heart dictated? Could he say:

'No Simon, don't go, stay here as chief of the clan. Go on leading your cita from the sea to the vidda and from the vidda to the sea, year after year. If you don't, it's your race you'll be destroying. Tomorrow it'll be too late! The people from Tromsö and Viddakaïno, maybe even from Oslo, will take away your great herd, and you'll be nothing but a pawn in their hands, a prisoner on the island, without hope of escape.'

But after a moment's silence, he said:

'You see those houses, Simon? Well, they belong to my people. I was born in just such a house, on the fjord at Alta. Every summer I used to see the cita of the Vestfjellet come back and take possession of their huts on the mountainside; as a kid I used to play with the little Lapp children, they were my friends. Every autumn they would go away, and I used to long for the spring to come again, the wonderful day when the herd would appear on the mountains, as we're doing today. Then the time came when I, too, went off into the interior, and because I knew you well, because I spoke your language, I was made Lappefogden; and it was my job to settle your disputes, to decide matters as far as possible in accordance with your traditions. And this is what I always tried to do, until the day I heard them offering you the mirage of the Tröndelag and an easy life. Everything they promised you, Simon Sokki, they will carry out! You'll get a new house on the fjord, and there you'll stop; and on the mountains there'll be a proper herd, shared in common with other citas and run on modern lines. You won't have to budge again. You'll be tied to the seashore, your children will go to school and to church, you won't have to put up with any more hard winters out on the vidda, there won't be any migrations and, as you said just now, you won't have to run any more risks! Your life will be pretty much the same as that of the Norwegians, and later on your children, who will never have heard of the migration, will settle down properly, and then . . .'

'I know what you mean. Maybe you're right. Anyhow I'll think it over again. But isn't what you're saying to me just the opposite of what you ought to be saying?'

'It's my heart that's speaking to you, Simon, and that should suffice. My ideas have changed a lot since that day when the aeroplane dropped me at Mollejaure. I feel as though I have lived a hundred years in less than a month, and that everything has become different. The country ahead of us is my homeland. In the past, when I used to look out from the sea towards the mountains, I tried to imagine the untamed vidda where you and your people have always lived, and for me that country was one great wilderness. But today, as I gaze out there, what do I see? I see things with new eyes : the cosy little white houses—just like the one they'll build for you in the Tröndelag—the fishermen's boats, the swift ships bringing newspapers, mail and food, the shops, the church ! And everything seems to me quite new, unknown. From living with you folk, I have completely forgotten what I used to be like before I knew you. If I go down to the fjord I shall regret it ! I feel as though, now, my life is with you, because, in some miraculous way, you have preserved throughout the centuries your freedom and your independence. And so you see, Simon, I have to ask myself this question : have I really the right to ask you to come and settle down with us? Isn't it perhaps the Old Man, and Kristina, and the Finn, who've got hold of the right end of the stick? I know that, for you, existence is dangerous, but would you be able to put up with the invisible chains that our civilization forces us to wear? And if you couldn't, might not your attempt to achieve happiness only make you unhappy?'

Once more Simon was shaken! Could he be sure that, looking at the fjord with its crowds of people and all the activity of the fishermen and sailors, he had found an easy, peaceful life that seemed to him to be the picture of perfect happiness? Or was it all an illusion?

CHAPTER TWO

'THE Lapps! The Lapps! Here come the Lapps!'

The children were racing along the beach like mad creatures, singing and throwing their caps in the air; the women came out of their houses, laughing and calling to one another :

'The Lapps have arrived! We've got the little black men back again!'

Some of the men started putting on their skis, and the entire population of Sorreisa crowded on to the beach, for the arrival of the cita was one of the great events in their humdrum existence. Indeed, they had been expecting it for several days and had been surprised by the delay, for a rumour had got about there had been a fresh quarrel between the tribes, even that some tragedy had occurred in the course of the migration; and the elders of Sorreisa, anxiously shaking their heads, felt sure that Simon Sokki must have been at the bottom of it. Early in the morning, a look-out had seen through his field-glasses the thousands of reindeer, spreading out like a grey stain across the snow, and soon the news had spread all along the fjord, borne from house to house by telephone, so that now, from every direction, from the town itself, from isolated dwellings hidden at the end of secret bays, from the fishing grounds, from little wooden landing-stages, groaning and creaking with the play of the tide, people had put to sea, for every available boat would be needed to control the reindeer while they were swimming across the arm of the sea.

Everybody's eyes were glued to the slope of the mountain, trying to discover some further sign of their arrival amongst the thick undergrowth.

'Look, there's a sledge!' someone exclaimed.

It needed an eagle eye to spot it, as it threaded its way

through the thick clumps of birch and pine. It was coming down the mountain side at a gallop, and the driver was not sparing his reindeer. He came on at full tilt, uttering shrill cries, heedless of obstacles, crashing through the dwarf trees, snapping off the branches, guiding his reindeer with demoniacal skill, as it leapt over the great blocks of granite half hidden beneath the snow and plunged through the undergrowth. They could tell which way he was coming from the increasing noise, by watching the tops of the birch trees bending over and straightening up, again, by listening to the barking of the two black dogs that were driving the herd, and, above all, from the sound of the man's voice, as he intoned his triumphal yok, greeting his Norwegian friends and expressing all the intoxication of speed, all the joy of difficulties overcome, all the pride of arriving like a conqueror, on this shore where they had been awaiting him for nearly eight months.

'Here he comes, here he comes,' cried the children, as he emerged on the little alluvial plain where the herd would eventually be gathered.

And Harald, the postman, who had recognized him from the distance, called out:

'It's Simon Sokki! Why, Simon, you still drive like a born leader!'

But Simon was still too far off to hear what he said, and went on singing his yok at the top of his voice.

'They do say this is the last time they'll be coming here,' a fisherman's wife said shyly.

'Well, there have certainly been plenty of telegrams about it,' said the postman, adding, as he remembered his official position: 'Though, of course, I'm not allowed to say anything about it.'

In fact, it was already an open secret, for, in the Great North, everything soon gets known, and throughout the winter the government proposals had been discussed in every household, all the details of the Trömso conference had been followed with the greatest interest and everybody was wondering anxiously whether things would turn out as planned.

'If they do go, it's going to be very lonely here for the rest of us!'

'Why, what use are they to us?' someone enquired sceptically. 'We only see them for four months in the year; the rest of the time they disappear into the vidda! Honestly, I don't think it's going to make all that difference!'

'But they bring the spring with them! They bring us the sun! If they don't come back any more, maybe the sun won't either!'

'Oh, shut up,' said the husband of the woman who had first spoken. 'Don't tell me you're getting as superstitious as the Lapps?'

But she was simply expressing the general opinion, and everybody supported her.

Simon Sokki pulled up his sleigh in front of a group of the leading people, nimbly jumped down, tied his reindeer to one of the runners, and, straightening his cap, advanced towards the Norwegians, who greeted him effusively, repeating again and again the 'Bouriz' of welcome. His pesk had been torn by the trees, which, in places, had rubbed off all the fur, so that he looked as though he had been skinned. Swaying slightly on his bandy legs like a bear, and covered from head to foot with reindeer skins, the man whom they had been thinking of all through the winter as a brother now struck them as nothing but a savage. They greeted him almost with embarrassment, as though, as civilized people, their conscience reproached them for having allowed him and all his people to spend the entire winter living in the snow. It was the same every time they came back, but this feeling of uneasiness very soon disappeared as they crowded around the new arrival and began asking him questions:

'Aren't you very late this year, Simon Sokki?'

'Have things been going badly?'

'No setback, I hope?'

'No, no, God be praised! At least nothing much! We had a bit of trouble with a wolf, and there were one or two premature births . . . Just the usual run of the mill!'

But he said nothing about the business with Andis.

'We have let all the fishermen know,' said the manager of the fish factory, Trygve Per, 'and they have all turned up. I advise you to cross the fjord tonight, about two o'clock. It will be slack tide then, and practically no current. You will have a good half-hour ahead of you, more than you need to get the reindeers across, at least across the main channel where the current is strongest.'

Simon Sokki agreed; he had complete confidence in his friend. The crossing was not without risk : if you left it too late, the reindeer would be swept out to sea by the ebbing tide, if you tried to cross when the tide had started to come in, the young ones would be drowned in the backwash! This gave him two hours in which to bring the herd down from the mountains. He took off his red cap and began waving it in the air and shouting; it was soon apparent that those who had remained behind understood the signal, for there were signs of great activity amongst the reindeer and they began pressing forward through the opening of the pass.

'Here's a letter for you,' said the postman.

Simon Sokki turned it over and over in his fingers.

'D'you want me to read what it says?'

'Usually I get Kristina to,' said Simon proudly. 'She can read and write as well as any of her teachers, but she's right at the back with the sleighs.'

'Would you rather wait until she gets here?'

'No, you tell me what it says.'

'Nothing serious. It is from Fru Tideman, and she says that she'll be at Sorreisa in three days' time and will see you on the island with the minister in charge of Lapp affairs in the south!'

'In three days' time . . .' Simon Sokki breathed again. He had been afraid she might be there already, and would catch him while he was still fresh from travelling, without giving him time to consider. She was always doing that kind of thing.

'Tell me something,' said the postman. 'It's still on, this

business of you going to the north Tröndelag? I thought the idea had been dropped.'

'No, it's still under discussion, but so far nothing has been decided.'

'That's good. It would be a poor look-out for us if you stopped coming here year after year! It would be like the whole district suddenly losing its soul.'

Without realizing it, he had put the matter in a nutshell. For what would happen to the people living by the fjord without the herds in the mountains and the picturesque huts of the summer camp? They realized that, although these people were not of much use to them, they nevertheless justified their own isolation!

'They're starting to come down!' the youngsters suddenly shouted.

And Simon Sokki agreed:

'They're going to follow the stream!'

Whereupon everybody began getting out their field glasses.

Up at the pass, the Old Man was giving his final instructions.

'Take it easy, and see that they don't bolt! If they panic, they may throw themselves into the sea and drown. I'm going on ahead with the Finn. The rest of you spread out on either side of the herd, to stop them breaking away. And look out how you go, the track's very narrow, full of great boulders and precipices. We can lose the lot that way, if you don't take care.'

The Old Man had already taken off his skis, and now started on the descent. Leaving the sledge trail, which wound its way through the forest of willows and birches, he took a short cut, following the course of the stream, which hurtled down to the shore, where it ended up in a small alluvial plain separating the twin hillocks on which the shops and dwellings of Sorreisa had been built. This was the route the reindeer had to take, for here the waters of the stream, and, in spring, the glaciers, had cleared the trees from the side of the mountain, leaving a broad, negotiable corridor. Half-way down, the stream was blocked by huge rocks, forming a waterfall, and here and there you could still see great chunks of unmelted snow and sheets of ice. They continually had to watch the reindeer in order to prevent them from knocking each other over in this narrow defile, filled with the ceaseless roar of running water, and what made their task all the more difficult was the excitement of the animals now that they could smell the sea. Those that attempted to hang back were forced ahead by the veterans, powerful stags and old does, still carrying last year's antlers, who were making the journey for the seventh or eighth time, and who now trotted along from side to side, raising their muzzles to sniff the breeze, drunk with spring, pawing the ground, leaping in the air, then, all of a sudden, closing in to form a dense block of animals that at once had to be broken up. Occasionally a whole batch of animals would break away and plunge into the undergrowth, while the Old Man yelled and stormed :

'Get on after them ! Fetch them back !'

Then the herdsmen would shout to their dogs, 'Voï! voï! voï!' and off they would go, leaping from rock to rock, skilfully avoiding the patches of melting snow and slush, but occasionally missing their footing and falling head over heels into a pool of water, only to scramble out and dash off again . . . 'Voï! voï! voï!' The roar of the stream, the barking of the dogs, the shouting of the herdsmen, drifted down to the spectators, crowded on the shore below, in a savage murmur, that blended with the noise of the waves, as they broke on the shore regular as a man's breathing.

In front came the Old Man and the Finn, holding the animals back. But once the herd had entered the gulley, everything seemed to sort itself out, and, from below, it looked as though the forest itself was flowing down to the sea, the grey herd of reindeer filling the treeless space with their thousands of antlers, hardly distinguishable, save by the fact that they were moving, from the boughs of the birch trees swaying in the wind from the sea. And where the reindeer had passed, rushing down the hill like a waterfall, nothing remained but a trail of dirty snow and slush. Once the reindeer reached the plain, however, they quickly calmed down; there the snow was still deep, and it was no use their scraping at it with their hoofs and sniffing, for no lichen grows in the marsh. As a result, they soon drew together again and, apart from a few of the older animals, restlessly wandering about like sentinels, lay down in the snow chewing the cud, half asleep in the overwhelming heat.

Without quitting their posts, the herdsmen exchanged friendly greetings with the Norwegians; they had suddenly become as shy and restless as their animals, and for the Norwegians it was matter for astonishment, recurring every year, to watch these people and their herd surge down from the snowy wilderness like a river in spate.

It was more than an hour later when the first sleighs began to emerge from the trees, for though they had followed the same narrow path taken by Simon, they were all heavily loaded and, as each driver was in charge of a dozen sleighs, they were often delayed; loads were frequently upset, and men and animals got so bogged down in the soft snow that it was not easy to extricate themselves. By the time they eventually arrived, they were all worn out and dripping with sweat, their fur pesks torn to rags, their hands blistered, their faces tanned and shining from the sun, yet so alive and cheerful that to the tall, fair Scandinavians they looked the same as ever : the strange little black men, the Lapps!

Now that they were all there, they followed in the course of the sun, which seemed to be suspended like a phosphorescent disc just above the surface of the sea, so that its mild light cast elongated shadows. High above them, the mountains were still pink with the rays of the setting sun, but already a new dawn was breaking, another day was beginning almost before the previous one had faded.

The incoming tide flowed swiftly through the narrow channel, and they noticed how quickly the water was rising, causing occasional whirlpools, flecked with foam, while the breeze from the sea whipped up the waves, making a splashing sound; and this worried Simon Sokki, because, when the sea was choppy, all too often the reindeer would swallow the water and drown.

At last, the moment they were waiting for, when the tide stopped flowing, had come : the waves died away and the sea became quite calm.

'Now's your chance, Simon Sokki,' Trygve shouted.

He gave a loud whistle, and dozens of little motor boats converged on the shore, forming a semi-circle facing towards the beach. The rattle of the engines drowned the noise made by the herd, by the men's cries and the barking of the dogs. One boat detached itself from the others, and came ashore in the centre of the little beach.

Simon Sokki climbed aboard and signalled to the Old Man to join him. The latter, still leading the reindeer with the bell round its neck, scrambled through the sea up to his knees in water, followed by the animal, which drew back its lips as it sniffed the salt odour of the sea. The salty smell seemed to awake half-forgotten memories of the island across the water, with its rich pastures blowing in the wind!

'Now, start calling the herd!' said Simon Sokki.

The Old Man started ringing a bell he was holding and the sound immediately caused excitement among the herd. Herdsmen and dogs had been gradually driving it towards the beach, and by now it formed a wall of bodies, tightly pressed together : the animals, reluctant to enter the water, hesitated, then, driven on by the weight of those behind which could not as yet see the sea, advanced a few steps further.

The oldest deer were in front, and some of them, having crossed the fjord several times before, instinctively began to make for the island, where they knew they would find plenty of lichen and fresh water throughout the peaceful arctic summer.

Before long, one of them entered the water.

'Go on ahead!' Simon said to the man in charge of the boat.

Slowly they drew away from the shore, and the rope with which the Old Man was leading the bell-deer tightened, forcing the animal to plunge into the water, where it started swimming vigorously, keeping alongside the boat and within sound of the Old Man's voice, who kept calling to it encouragingly, at the same time rhythmically ringing his bell. Soon a compact mass of several hundred reindeer were swimming shoulder to shoulder, escorted by the little boats, which did their best to keep them together, for if any of them got separated they were likely to drown. One of the Lapps was on each of the boats, directing the operation and also ringing a bell.

Most of the young animals, however, were too scared to enter the water, and were still running round, pursued by dogs and men, with the result that the leading animals had almost reached the middle of the fjord, where the current was strongest, while the last of them were still on the beach.

'Voï! voï! voï!' yelled Simon Sokki. 'Set the dogs on them. In another thirty minutes the tide will have started to ebb. We've got to hurry.'

Eventually the whole herd had taken the plunge, and the flotilla closed in behind, following them as they swam towards the island. Low on the horizon the great disc of the sun was gradually rising out of the waves, turning from evening purple to morning gold. The threatening shadows of the mountains stretched across the grey waters of the fjord, and the noise of the bells contrasted strangely with the chug-chug of the engines and the churning-up of the water caused by the swimming animals. Gleams of sunlight sparkled in the wake of the boats, played on the surging antlers of the reindeer, on the thousands of swimming heads, on the triangular wedge formed by the great herd as it ploughed its way through the sea and seemed to be swimming towards the sun, drawing men and ships onwards towards the mysterious island, whose sombre hostile outline stood out against the sky, tipped with the silver and ivory of glaciers glittering on the peaks of the mountains.

The boats scurried about, going from one exhausted animal to another, to enable the Lapps to get their lassos round their necks or antlers and haul them back to the herd before releasing them again. In this way the reindeer were given fresh courage, and would start swimming again with renewed energy, whereas those animals that got left behind would immediately start to sink, from fright rather than from exhaustion.

Presently the veteran reindeer reached the opposite shore, but behind them the rest of the herd stretched out for four hundred yards or more, and the laggards were still struggling in the middle of the fjord where the current was strongest. The number of these was increasing, and the Lapps rang their bells louder than ever, coaxed the animals by calling to them; and they seemed to understand, to take courage from the presence of the herdsmen and their dogs, for they kept as close as they could to the boats.

Nevertheless, despite all those precautions, a number of them were drowned. A yearling doe disappeared beneath the water right under Per Oskal's eyes: he watched it sink, its eyes suddenly glazing with fear, and the exhausted animals near-by showed signs of panicking. This was the one thing to be avoided, at all costs! He managed to catch hold of a youngster by its horns and drag it aboard. And the same business was repeated in every boat, as herdsmen and fishermen desperately struggled to save as many animals as possible. But it was impossible to tell what was happening right in the middle, for there the reindeer were so tightly packed together that they resembled a floating raft.

Eventually, however, the last reindeer reached the island and scrambled ashore, but they were so exhausted that some of them fell back into the water and lay there for a time, their heads drooping and their eyes misting over. Others, however, feeling firm land beneath their feet, acquired fresh energy and trotted out of the sea, stopping a moment to shake themselves and dry their shaggy coats, then setting off again, heads high, to start the ascent; they could smell the summer pasture, and were making straight for it. At last only some thirty animals remained on the beach, some of them too weak to move, others, as one could tell from the feebleness of their movements and the look in their eyes, already at the point of death. The latter just stood there until they collapsed, then lay on their sides, scrabbling in the sand with their sharp hoofs until, suddenly stiffening in a final spasm, they stretched out their necks and died.

The men now began counting the herd. The losses had been considerable, twenty animals having been drowned, all young ones, and another dozen lying on the beach, dying of exhaustion or already dead. These the herdsmen put out of their misery, and at once started skinning them.

'You see, Per Oskal, our summer grazing costs us a tidy bit!'

The Lappefogden nodded his head, Simon Sokki was right, he ought to take Fru Tideman's advice: this way of life belonged to another age. To lose thirty or forty reindeer every year, getting the herd across the fjord, was an expensive way of feeding them during the summer.

The Norwegians were greatly upset, but most of the Samisks were already hard at work rounding up the herd and calling to their dogs, and they all appeared to be blithe and unconcerned. They were ready to pay this death tax without complaint, as their ancestors had done for perhaps ten thousand years. Now it was all over, and they were going to enjoy a peaceful existence until the autumn storms started once again.

'Listen!' exclaimed Per Oskal, 'they're singing!'

It was true enough, and as Simon Sokki listened to them he shook his head. On previous occasions he would have been the first to begin singing of life's triumph over death, of the arrival at the summer feeding-grounds, of his people's eternal existence . . . But since the Trömso conference he was no longer the same man. A new virus had infected his blood, and he was gradually becoming aware of a different kind of life, tuned to the rhythms and obligations of civilized people. He, who had always lived from day to day, had heard them talking about the future and, from that moment, he had lost all peace of mind.

'Once I used to be just like them,' he said sadly. 'They are singing because they live in the present, and because they know that their only purpose in life is to carry on our race. But now I realize that we've got to go on living tomorrow, and all the days and years that come after. I used not to worry at all, Per Oskal, but ever since I started talking to your people I've been worried to death !'

Someone called to him from the beach, and slowly he turned away. The bustle of the little boats, bringing the loaded sleighs and the remaining members of the cita, was almost over. All that now remained on the mainland was the sleigh where Andis was lying, which Mattis had driven right up to the edge of the sea. The young man was in pretty bad shape; coming down from the pass had shaken him up, reopening his wound, and he was running a temperature. The fishermen surrounded him sympathetically.

'Why not stay with us this evening, Andis, and have a decent bed?' said one of them.

'Those huts are damp, and still full of snow. That's not going to do you any good. You'd better spend a few days with us and look after yourself,' proposed another.

Any of them would have been only too glad to put him up, but Andis refused. He even refused the invitation of Susanna, the plump kvaen, although she was a Lapp by birth.

'I know how to use herbs to make plasters and medicines. If you let me take care of you, you'll soon be on your feet again. There's plenty of room at our place, now Peter's dead,' she said with a sigh.

Peter, the kvaen, who used to keep the Sorreisa store, had died of alcoholism during the winter. He had always supplied the Lapps with whatever they needed and, like his opposite number at Viddakaïno, he had also been a money-lender and made himself useful in a dozen different ways. And as everybody depended upon him for spirits, sugar and coffee, they were prepared to put up with the exorbitant rates of interest he charged. He was as dependent on the Lapps as they were on him, for throughout the summer they used to let him have reindeer meat, which he sold in the towns pretty well everywhere along the coast of the

Finnmark and the Troms. The news of his death came as no surprise; Andis had already heard about it while he was still far away in the vidda, for in that vast country news travels fast, despite the lack of communication.

'It's not much of a wound,' said Mattis. 'An old stag caught him in the back with one of its antlers . . . ripped him up like a knife!'

And they pretended to believe him, for it would have been impolite to ask any further question.

Then Trygve Per, the manager of the fish factory, suggested having the wounded man taken on board his ship, but Andis firmly refused, though he agreed to let him take him across the fjord. But when he tried to stand up to go on board, his legs would not carry him, and if it hadn't been for Mattis' help, he would have fallen down.

'It's obvious you're too weak,' Trygve grumbled. 'Why not let us look after you?'

'He's got his own reasons,' Susanna intervened. 'It's his own business, so just let the lad alone. I'll bring you some herb medicine this evening, Andis.'

'You and your old woman's remedies,' Trygve exclaimed angrily.

But he did not insist. He, too, came from that strange country where everyone respects other people's freedom, and he realized that there are some wounds it is better for other people not to see.

'Right you are then, Andis, I'll take you over to the island.'

The huts had been built many centuries ago, on a high granite mound, three hundred feet high and overlooking the sea, which made it possible to keep an eye on the pasture as far inland as the foot of the glaciers. A track led from the temporary village to a creek, where, all through the winter, the Sokkis kept a small boat drawn up on the beach, which in the summer they used for fishing. The Old Man had led the herd to the foothills where the lichen was abundant, and the animals were slowly beginning to regain their strength; already some of them had started picking out the reindeer moss, which, now that the snow had melted, grew in great silvery patches on the rocks. Everywhere there was plenty of fresh water, and far away in the distance they could hear the roar of the streams made by the melting glaciers. High in the sky, the sun seemed to be suspended above the topmost spur of rock, and its vertical rays made the sea gleam like platinum. In every direction, fishermen's craft could be seen, moving about the fjord, and their sails, white, yellow and red, studded the grey waters with gay touches of colour.

The huts, made of mud and stone and covered with turf and dried grass, were shaped like small domes, and from a distance they looked like a collection of ancient tombs, built high up where they could be seen. During the winter they had become filled with snow, and Simon Sokki set everybody to work clearing them out. Through the single opening, so low that you had to stoop to get in, the men were sweeping out the snow and, though this meant hours of hard work, nobody grumbled; they were there for the whole summer, and on the big fire that was already burning out of doors, the women were cooking chunks of meat and fish and taking them round to the men while they worked. Those who were not busy sweeping out the huts were erecting drying poles, on which, out of reach of the dogs—there were only a few foxes and no wolves on the island—they could hang the skins, the bladders of lard, the tendons, and whatever else would be needed during the summer for work or food. Everything was going ahead at a steady pace, for now, after the exertion of the migration, they had nothing to do but rest, look after the calving animals and collect supplies of meat, fish and dried grass for their moccasins.

Presently the first hut was clear of snow and a fire had been lighted inside it; and the smoke that rose high into the sky announced to all the inhabitants of the bay the rebirth of the stone village. The Lapps installed themselves in it just as though they were in one of their tents. The women gathered branches to form an insulating layer between the earth and the reindeer skins, while the men collected firewood. As the smoke began to rise from hut after hut, songs of joy could be heard on every side. They laid Andis down in the most comfortable of them, and in the evening, when the midnight sun seemed to be floating on the ocean, Susanna the kvaen arrived with some herbs, from which she made a plaster that immediately soothed the pain of the wound.

'A real pretty gash, and no mistake,' she exclaimed admiringly.

Andis smiled at the compliment. He was determined to get strong again as soon as possible, for he knew of other huts in the neighbourhood, where there were plenty of attractive girls, and he had every intention of describing his exploits to them in the warmth of the long summer days, as they lay stretched out at ease amongst the cranberry bushes. A fine summer was already on the way.

'What are you doing here, Per Oskal?' Simon Sokki suddenly asked. He was inspecting the huts and had found the young Norwegian squatting beside the fire in the one belonging to Martha Risak. 'I thought you'd be with your own folk. Didn't the manager invite you?'

Per Oskal shook his head :

'I'm stopping with you till it's all over . . . and who can tell when that will be !'

'Fru Tideman will be here in three days' time,' said Simon Sokki.

Per Oskal sighed, but made no response, and Simon crept out through the low entrance, leaving him alone with Martha Risak.

'I shall soon be losing you, Per,' she sighed.

'If you stay on with those who remain behind, you'll have me with you for always.'

She looked at him in surprise. Could he really mean what he said?

298

CHAPTER THREE

A L L the reindeer had been gathered in a flat, marshy hollow just below the huts. Simon Sokki had given orders that they should be parted into two separate herds, males and females, and taken to different grazing grounds. The purpose of this was to prevent the stags from disturbing the does while they were calving, and as more and more of them were doing so every day this had ceased to be a cause for anxiety; now that they were on the island all the calves could be kept. The entire cita was engaged in this job, herdsmen, women, old people and dogs. It was a great occasion; they had overcome all the difficulties of their long journey and were free to busy themselves with easier tasks throughout the pleasant hours of almost endless daylight. Safe from wild animals and human thieves they no longer had to worry about the safety of the herd.

Everybody needed help, so they split up into couples again: Thor Risak lassoed the deer while Karin Bongo helped him to separate the does from the stags; Kristina and the Finn bustled about without leaving one another for a moment; Per Oskal and Martha Risak got on like a house on fire.

Gradually signs of progress became evident; the two herds grew larger, the main one smaller. Parting the animals was easy; at this time of year the males had lost their antlers, though in some cases the new ones could already be seen, little knobs on the top of their skulls, covered with velvety skin; on the other hand, as they still retained their slender horns, the females could be recognized at a distance. The whole business was carried out to the accompaniment of merry shouting and the continual noise of barking under the supervision of Simon Sokki, who stood at the top of the granite mound like some motionless red gnome. The

Old Man stood beside him, watching what was happening, giving advice and puffing away at his pipe. The Norwegians from the fjord had all gone off to work, so that there was nobody about apart from a few tourists taking snapshots and a bunch of fair-haired lads playing truant, who were helping the Lapps, working with a will, and yelling and shrieking with delight in Samisk as well as Norwegian.

'Look, that's just how I used to be!' Per Oskal said to Martha Risak.

He had suddenly remembered his boyhood at Alta. Every spring he, too, had awaited the arrival of the great herd from up country and, just as these lads had done, managed to cross the channel on the sly in order to join the children of the Samisks with their dogs and reindeer.

'Do you regret those days?' asked Martha.

'It's only now that I realize how little I have changed. In my heart I was always one of you, even if I did belong to a different race.'

'And now it will soon be over!' Martha sighed. 'And yet . . .'

She diverted her sudden anger to a huge stag which, snorting loudly, was trying to get back to the herd from which they wanted to separate him.

'You had better catch him, Per, or we shall have to start all over again.'

He lassoed it skilfully, and clung on to the rope trying to bring it under control. It was a hard struggle, and several times he was thrown to the ground. The rest of the Lapps interrupted their work for a moment to watch him.

'I see you've made considerable progress in the art of catching reindeer,' said a voice from amongst the onlookers. Surprised, he looked over his shoulder : it was Fru Tideman, looking very tall and distinguished in her long, black seal-skin coat.

'Let him go,' said Martha under her breath. 'I'll look after the reindeer, you see to her !'

He handed over the lasso to her and awkwardly approached Fru Tideman. In spite of his height, he seemed

300

to have adopted the Lapp way of walking. He swung from one foot to the other, and his heavy, red cap, pushed to the back of his head, revealed a mane of hair that had neither been washed nor brushed for the past month. His fair, straggling beard stood out in sharp contrast to the tanned, burnt colour of his cheeks. A broad Samisk belt, studded with silver, hung low on his belly, and over his koufte he wore the bulging garments which, though indispensable to a real nomad, would be quite useless to an office worker. When he was within a few feet of Fru Tideman he suddenly felt abashed, and his friends the Lapps who were looking on, were deeply concerned on his account, for beneath Fru Tideman's polite behaviour they could sense her mounting anger.

'Did nobody tell you I had arrived?'

'I was expecting you, Fru Tideman, but meanwhile I had to finish my job.'

'Catching reindeer, I suppose?' she said ironically.

'Wasn't the purpose of my being with the Sokkis to help them?'

'But was this how you were supposed to help them, by parting reindeer? Weren't you entrusted with a more important responsibility? I assume all these people are prepared to set out for the south! Have you explained to them properly what we intend to do with them?'

'To tell you the truth, Fru Tideman, I have scarcely had a chance to. We have had all kinds of difficulties on the way, wolves, straying animals, avalanches and a terrible storm. You can't very well organize a meeting, huddled in a tent in the middle of a gale.'

Gradually he was beginning to recover his composure.

'This is Mr Nylsen, the Minister for Lapp Affairs,' said Fru Tideman, introducing her companion. 'He has come with me in order to assist in carrying out the project that we all have at heart. There are one or two questions he would like to put to you.'

Per Oskal looked the newcomer up and down. He was a tall, smooth-faced functionary, with a thin, freshly shaved face, wearing a gabardine skiing costume and a fur cap with ear flaps. Everything about him was neat and clean. With his clear, penetrating gaze, he was observing the spectacle of four thousand reindeer running round in circles pursued by the herdsmen, as though it were some folklore display at Bygdoy. Per Oskal was immediately aware of his hostility. This was probably the first time the man had been in the Finnmark. The Lappefogden knew the type only too well, one of those officials who carry on all their business by telephone and written instructions, without ever leaving their office, and look upon the people they are responsible for as so many hundred problems to be filed away in a card index.

'Mr Oskal,' he enquired loftily, 'what precisely happened between the Sokki cita and the Isaksens? We received information from the police at Kvenangen. I understand that there was some quarrel about a theft, and that Andis Sokki was stabbed by Sven Isaksen. But I would like to hear what really happened. To begin with, why did you not intervene? By this time the guilty man ought to be in prison, awaiting trial!'

His words were received in complete silence, which seemed to create a vacuum in the sky above the sea, where the red and yellow sails rose and fell. Presently, speaking very slowly and weighing his words, Per Oskal said:

'Nothing occurred, sir, that falls within the competence of Norwegian justice. I was appointed Lappefogden by the government: don't forget that my function is to act as arbitrator when differences arise within the Council of Ancients. That is just what I did. And by mutual agreement, Per Isaksen and Simon Sokki, despite the fact that they detest one another, are satisfied that the matter has been settled.'

'Settled? Settled?' Fru Tideman could not help interrupting. 'Do you really consider that attempted murder can be disposed of as simply as that? In the first place, where is the wounded man?'

'What man?' intervened Simon Sokki, who up to now had remained silent.

'Come, come, Simon . . . your son, of course! Only three days ago he was still so weak that he couldn't even get up from his sledge!'

'Pshaw! Just a touch of frostbite. You don't want to believe everything you hear from the kvaens. Anyhow, there he is.'

And, indeed, there he was, in the middle of the herd, whirling his lasso round his head, shouting at the top of his voice and urging on the dogs. Per Oskal had the greatest difficulty in concealing his amazement. How on earth did he manage to be there, apparently quite fit again, when only a few hours earlier, Susanna, the fat kvaen, had been applying herb plasters to his festering wound?

'Hi, Andis, come here a minute! In Oslo, they seem to think you're dead!'

One or two of the nearby Lapps began to laugh, and their amusement spread like a trail of gunpowder, though only they knew what they were laughing about. It had been Kristina's idea; she had seen Fru Tideman clambering up the footpath and had hurried off to the hut to fetch her brother.

'Come on, quick! Fru Tideman's on her way, and she certainly knows what's happened. Per Oskal has done what he can for us, now it's up to us to help him. Get up, you've got to make an effort.'

As he stood up he started to sway and, to keep him going, she had given him a huge glass of aquavit. And now, here he was, yokking away at the top of his voice, while Simon Sokki, slyly pretending to be embarrassed, said in a low voice:

'You'll have to excuse him, Fru Tideman. He's been celebrating the end of the migration, and I'm afraid he has had a drop too much to drink!'

'So what's all this people have been telling me, then?' the official demanded severely.

Fru Tideman made an evasive reply; something had to be done to allay his suspicions.

'It must be as Simon Sokki says . . . probably some trades-

man they owe money to has been trying to get his revenge !
A silly squabble . . .'

Fru Tideman felt relieved. She herself was prepared to be
severe with Per Oskal, but she was not going to have him
criticized by a man from Oslo. The latter was not one of
them; he had never had to endure the arctic winter, the
endless night, the loneliness; he didn't belong to the Finnmark. True, he represented officialdom, and he believed
that the government's ideas for the Lapps were the same as
Fru Tideman's, but that was as far as she was prepared to
collaborate with him.

'It is time we put an end to these squabbles, these per-
petual rows,' Nylsen went on, beside himself. 'At least my
coming here has done one thing : it has convinced me that
we are fully justified in trying to break down this clan spirit,
these tribal customs,' he concluded, assuming an air of self-
importance.

Now that the danger seemed to have been averted, the
Lapps returned to their work and went on parting the two
herds. Per Oskal had to explain the purpose of this operation.

'But is it really necessary?' said the official, shaking his
head. 'The whole herd already practically belongs to the
State !'

'As a matter of fact, sir, this herd still belongs to Simon
Sokki, *de facto* as well as *de jure* !'

'But what makes you suppose that we don't intend to
arrange matters fairly and generously? Believe me, this
whole business is costing us a great deal of money ! Though,
naturally, not as much as maintaining the present system—
all the sanitation, schools, police, law courts, with all the
dozens of officials, who just for the sake of a few thousand
people belonging to a bygone age, have to spend their whole
life in Lapland, cut off from civilization !'

'This country happens to be *our* country, sir, and we love
it,' Fru Tideman observed drily. 'But what's the use of arguing? You know that I approve of your plans, and all that
we now have to do is to explain them carefully to the Lapps.
I suppose they are aware of what's on foot, Per Oskal?'

'It was not for me to lecture them, Fru Tideman, but I can give you my word that they will choose quite freely, for I've made no attempt to influence them. They have been talking the matter over between themselves for a long while now, and they've all made up their minds.'

As he stopped speaking, he could not help thinking of Kristina and the Finn and the Old Man; he felt sad at heart, for he knew that the great moment was approaching.

By this time the separation of the reindeer had been completed : the does and young calves would remain near the hut throughout the calving period, and the stags would be taken to the mountain, where the Finn and the Old Man would look after them until August. Then the two herds would be reunited, for by that time it would be nearly autumn, when the rutting season begins.

But would the great herd really be reunited this autumn?

'Simon Sokki,' said Fru Tideman, 'I want you to call a meeting of the whole cita—everybody. Mr Nylsen has an important announcement to make to them, as you know. We are going to carry out the agreement we reached at Trömso, so it is important that everyone should be present.'

'We are all here, but I've got to send the stag herd to the mountain straight away, and the Old Man and the Finn will have to take them.'

'That won't matter, Simon. After all, neither of them are members of your cita.'

'Some of the reindeer belong to them, though !'

'But so few.'

'As you like . . . They may as well go !'

Simon Sokki went round to all the huts telling everyone to come outside, and presently the whole cita was squatting on the turf, forming a circle round the Scandinavians, waiting with an air of apparent passivity to hear their fate.

'Does everybody understand Norwegian?' the official enquired.

'Not all of them, unfortunately,' said Fru Tideman, 'but Per Oskal can interpret for them.'

Nylsen glanced at him suspiciously.

'Wouldn't it be better if you were to do the interpreting, Fru Tideman?'

Per Oskal sprang to his feet :

'Mr Nylsen, you seem to forget that, as an official, I took an oath of loyalty ! I regard your lack of confidence in me as a personal insult.'

'Now, now, Per Oskal, there's no reason to get so upset,' Fru Tideman intervened. 'Pay no attention to him, sir ! This last month has been a very gruelling experience for him !'

'All right, then, Per Oskal will interpret,' said the Minister, taking a typewritten document from his portfolio, which he proceeded to read aloud :

'As between the Department for Lapp Affairs of the one part, and Simon Sokki, recognized leader of the cita of the Sokkis, of the Risaks, the Bongos and their relations, of the other part, the following agreement has been entered into pursuant to the decisions of the general meeting regarding the status of the Lapps, which was held at Trömso in the spring of this year.'

As he read, Per Oskal was translating each paragraph word for word, and this gave the Lapps time to grasp the real meaning of the agreement.

'In order that the Lapps may no longer be obliged to accept conditions of life which are inappropriate to modern Christian civilization, and, in particular, the seasonal nomadism, which takes them every spring from the interior of the Finnmark to the sea and back again every autumn, and which is the source of such hardship to the Lapps as the loss and theft of their animals and the dangerous and precarious existence of their families due to storms, avalanches, etc., the Department of Lapp Affairs proposes to the members of the said cita of the Sokkis that they should emigrate to the district of the North Tröndelag, where the extensive grazing at present unoccupied will enable them to pursue more rational methods of reindeer breeding, and, in addition, to increase their income by rearing sheep and cattle.

'To this end the Norwegian government shall place at the disposal of the members of the cita of the Sokkis houses similar in all respects, i.e. design, dimensions and amenities, to those of the Norwegians of that province, which houses have already been built, close to the sea and forming part of an existing village; and, furthermore, shall provide each household with a motor-boat, suitable for fishing either in the fjord or in coastal waters. In return for such provision, the Samisks, for their part, shall undertake to settle in the Tröndelag, and there live in full and friendly association with the Scandinavian inhabitants, their brothers, both spiritually and by religion, if not by race.

'It is further agreed that, upon arrival in the Tröndelag, each family shall have at its disposition a herd consisting of thirty does and ten stags, which animals shall be selected with special regard to their breeding potentialities, and shall constitute a common herd; that this herd shall graze the mountains overlooking the sea, which, in all essential respects, are similar to those in the Finnmark, and shall be looked after by the herdsmen of the cita, employed as agricultural workers. During the winter, the herd will be brought down to a small inland valley, well-sheltered and abundantly provided with lichen, where it will remain within easy reach of the village, thus sparing the members of the cita the rigours of the annual migration and enabling them to accept gainful employment throughout the year, either as members of the fishing fleet or as self-employed fishermen, using the boats provided for them by the government.

'In the event of there being any shortage of lichen, the feeding of the herd will be fully guaranteed by the government, which hereby undertakes to dispatch by air, as is done in Sweden, such hay and lichen as may be required.

'Every year, in autumn, official buyers will select from the common herd those animals to be slaughtered, and these will be conveyed to municipal slaughter-houses, where they will be paid for at the official rate then obtaining. It is further agreed that all requisite efforts shall be made to ensure the production of high quality meat, and that all

307

unsuitable animals shall forthwith be slaughtered and the bodies disposed of.

'In compensation for the fulfilment of the above terms, the Department of Lapp Affairs shall forthwith take over the entire herd belonging to the cita of the Sokkis, now on the island, at a valuation to be arrived at on the basis of an inventory, made on the spot by an accredited official in the presence of the chief of the cita. Each reindeer shall be paid for at the official price, currently obtaining in the Finnmark and based upon its weight and condition. After deducting all expenses involved in purchasing the herd, building the houses and organizing the journey to the Tröndelag, and in the purchase of those does and stags to be selected for the future herd, the balance of the money remaining in hand shall be paid, either in cash or in kind, to the head of the cita, who shall be responsible for dividing it between the members of his clan in accordance with customary procedure.'

Having concluded his reading, the government official folded up the document and put it back in his briefcase. Per Oskal had interpreted it clearly, and, while he was doing so, the expressions on the faces of the Lapps had reflected a variety of emotions. To begin with, they were delighted at the thought of having a house beside the sea like the Norwegians; and not only a comfortable house near school, church, shops and doctor, but a boat as well! But, when it came to the conditions regarding the dispersal of the great herd, they all began to look extremely downcast. At that very moment the stags driven by the Old Man were slowly disappearing towards the mountains and were already no more than a greyish triangle, fading away in the distance!

There was so much grumbling that even Simon Sokki felt obliged to protest.

'But they promised me we should be able to take the whole herd with us to the Tröndelag,' he said.

'I am quite aware of that, and the possibility was considered at head office,' the official interposed. 'But it would be a mistake to repeat past mistakes. You must realize, though, that it would not be easy to move the herd by ship. I am not as ignorant of Lapp affairs as some people appear to think'—he was obviously addressing the Lappefogden—'and I realize that to pack thousands of reindeer into a ship's hold would be a risky business, that could only result in enormous losses. But, apart from this, our aim is to establish a new breed consisting of reindeer reared in the forests, which are much heavier animals, produce a high proportion of meat, and which, if necessary, can be fed on hay. One of these animals will provide twice as much meat as any of your steppe reindeer, which have to be kept continually on the move in search of lichen. In a few years' time you will have built up a splendid herd, but what you must realize above all is that you will be getting a regular income from the annual sale of the surplus animals. We estimate that, with a herd of no more than five hundred reindeer, your standard of living will be considerably higher than it is at present with all these thousands of useless beasts.'

'Steady on!' exclaimed the Lapps, deeply shocked.

'By that, I mean animals that are at present bringing you in nothing! And don't forget, either, that your children will be able to learn a trade, so that later on they will not all be forced to become herdsmen. They can just as easily become fishermen or skilled tradesmen—even schoolteachers and engineers, why not? And, on top of that, your wives and daughters will be able to find well-paid jobs on their doorsteps, in the fish canning industry. From every point of view, it is in your own interests to accept our proposal.'

'But what about our herd?' Thor Risak insisted stubbornly.

'We shall have paid you for it in cash, and although we are determined not to allow the size of the herd to increase indefinitely, there will be nothing to prevent you from buying more reindeer under our supervision. The point is, your reindeer will be productive, not just represent so much intangible, useless capital.'

Everybody felt that this was going a bit too far and, taking off their caps, they began scratching their heads.

Per Oskal had to explain the position once more, and, though he could not repress a feeling of dismay, he did so as honestly as possible.

'If you look at it objectively, there is no reason why you should not accept what the government is proposing. If you do, I feel sure that it will depend entirely upon yourselves whether or not you become fully integrated Norwegian citizens, leading peaceful, contented lives like the rest of my compatriots. Moreover, also quite objectively, the offer they are making you is from your point of view very satisfactory. It means that you will be at once set up in houses that belong entirely to you, with your own fishing boats, and a small stock of carefully selected animals that will be regularly attended by government vets, so that you will have every opportunity of showing what really skilled stock-breeders you are. Mr Nylsen is right : your children will have the chance of becoming fishermen, school teachers, engineers, clergymen ! They will be real Norwegians.'

'But what is this country they want to send us to really like ?' asked Mikael Bongo.

'Much like it is here. The fjords run deeper inland and are less affected by storms; the mountains are twice as high, but the valleys are very sheltered, with fine pine forests; and there are some places on the coast where you'd think you were living right in the south of the country. And of course the polar night is forty days shorter than here, so that the spring comes that much earlier. There are bilberries and cranberries growing on the mountains and, with the money from your reindeer, you'll be able to buy sheep, pigs and cows. And you'll be able to do all this because you won't have to leave your homes, except to go up into the mountains from time to time, two days' journey, to keep an eye on the herd.'

The sun was near the end of its daily journey, and seemed to be resting on the sea. For two hours it would skim the tops of the waves, and then, once more, begin its long climb through the heavens. With the departure of the stags, the does had calmed down and were now peacefully chewing the cud in the deserted coomb, some of them already suckling their new-born calves. To the south, one could see the glaciers flowing between the jagged spurs of granite.

Though they had all had their say, Ellena, conscious of the unspoken opposition, decided to express her own point of view publicly. To everybody's astonishment, she said :

'The Minister is right! We must go! What kind of existence do we have at present, always wandering about in this wilderness of snow? Do you want more children to be born like I was, in a tent, in the middle of a tearing blizzard? Must we spend our whole lives looking after the herd, up all night right through winter, just to protect it from thieves? What's the point of going on in the same old rut, year after year? If you decide to go to the Tröndelag, Simon Sokki, I shall go with you!'

'So will I, so will I,' Karin Bongo and Martha Bongo chimed in, while Mikael Bongo added :

'It's right, what she says!'

But Simon Sokki signed to them to be quiet.

'Don't be in such a hurry. You ought to think it over,' said he. 'If you come back tomorrow, Mr Nylsen, and you as well, Fru Tideman, we'll let you have our answer : yes or no.'

'But what d'you mean, Simon Sokki? It's too late to refuse now! Your houses are all ready, and I've brought the money with me. I rely upon you. All that's necessary is for the Lappefogden to approve the sum you suggest, and I will pay you immediately.'

'Your wife is looking at the whole question very sensibly, Simon Sokki. She sees it from a mother's point of view, and wants to spare your children a lot of suffering,' said Fru Tideman.

Simon Sokki had recourse to his usual gesture : pushing back his cap and revealing his balding forehead, covered with unruly strands of hair, he conscientiously scratched his head. Clearly he was perplexed.

'This thing is, Fru Tideman, I had never really thought

about the possibility of leaving the herd behind! For us to go elsewhere, to change our country, that's right enough, we're used to travelling about. But the herd is another matter—it's our whole life. What should we do without it? You talk about us having a few dozen reindeer, but that's ridiculous. Our neighbours would lose all respect for us. In this part of the world it's only really poor people who own less than a hundred reindeer!'

Fru Tideman was becoming exasperated, and turned on Per Oskal:

'I thought you would have made them understand that, in exchange for the reindeer, they're going to be given money, and that with the money they are going to be able to buy whatever they like! There are plenty of Norwegian peasants who haven't got as much in their bank accounts as they will receive from the sale of the surplus reindeer. What more do they want? They'll have money, a home of their own, a boat—not to mention regular jobs and a scientific method of farming!'

'Fru Tideman is quite right,' Nylsen said irritably. 'It looks as though we shall have to provide for these people's happiness in spite of them!'

'Will you really be ensuring their happiness, sir?' Per Oskal asked respectfully. 'That's a question I've been asking myself for months now, and I still haven't been able to make up my mind.'

On the hill where the huts clustered together like mole-hills they had lighted big fires, around which the Lapps sat in circles, gravely discussing the proposals that had just been put before them. The night was as light as the day had been, and, despite a few hours of semi-twilight, the sunlight was already beginning to flood the earth again after only a brief interruption.

'What are you going to do with *our* reindeer?' Simon Sokki suddenly asked.

'Well,' the official replied hesitatingly, 'we shall dispose of the herd to whoever cares to make an offer. It's simply a question of supply and demand.'

312

Per Oskal and Fru Tideman understood Simon Sokki's reservations; it would never do to leave him in this unsatisfactory state of mind.

'The point is, sir,' Per Oskal interrupted, 'Simon Sokki is utterly opposed to his herd being purchased by other Lapp families. For his reindeer to be sold to buyers from Oslo, and in the meantime to remain the property of the State, is one thing; but, from his point of view, it is quite another matter if, while you encouraged their cita to emigrate, their herd can be bought up on the side by their hated enemies; for example, simply go to increase the size of the huge Isaksen herd.'

This was an aspect of the question which had not been considered at Oslo. Nylsen was embarrassed; obviously it was easy enough to transport twenty, even a hundred, Samisks and settle them down elsewhere, but to dispose of four to five thousand reinder was a very different kettle of fish . . . especially if one didn't happen to be a Lapp!

'This does not fall within my province,' said he, 'but if Simon Sokki wants some reassurance, I am quite prepared to give him one : during the normal slaughtering period his reindeer will remain State property. Furthermore,' he went on, appealing to Fru Tideman, 'it is in no sense our intention to break up one cita in order to strengthen the power of another. If this Sokki experiment comes off, our aim will be to move all the other citas to the Tröndelag!'

'If that's the position,' said Simon Sokki, 'I shall go and talk to my people.'

They were all gathered round the fires, the midnight sun drove a flaming path across the ocean, tinting the glaciers and lighting up the whole country of the north. The discussions that followed were enlivened by the production of some bottles of aquavit. Before long everybody would be in a better frame of mind.

'We had better stay here,' said Fru Tideman. 'If the matter is not settled today, Mr Minister, it never will be.'

'Mr Minister,' a little red-faced man suddenly intervened. He was dressed in a Lapp koufte and skiing trousers, with

313

a black cap with ear flaps, and hitherto no one had paid much attention to him, taking him for one of those casual labourers who are employed for hay-making or fishing or repairing the roads. 'What do you say to a drink, Mr Minister?'

'Whatever d'you mean?' said Nylsen, taken aback.

'Why,' said the little man, 'I know the best way of reaching a decision.'

'What's that?'

'If you agree, I suggest it would be a good idea if, on your behalf, I was discreetly to give Simon Sokki a few bottles—just as a present, naturally!'

'But what you're suggesting is not permissible! I engaged you as an expert, to deal with the question of payment for the reindeer because you are not related to any of the families in the Finnmark. But to act illegally like this . . .'

'It's not a question of breaking the law! It's simply that a decision like the one Simon Sokki has to take will be all the easier for a drop of drink! I know these Lapps, the ones from the Troms are just the same as those from the Finnmark. They'd give the shirts off their backs for a bottle of aquavit! Obviously, you can't pay them for five thousand reindeer in bottles of spirits . . . unless, of course, you want to rid the Finnmark of all its Lapps in record time.'

'I must say you live up to your name, Rieban! I knew you were a cunning fox, but I'm afraid that in this case you may make things very awkward for us. I don't want to know anything about where you get this alcohol from.'

'Don't worry,' said the half-breed, 'I shall buy it from Simon Sokki himself, or rather from Ellena!'

And, miraculously, bottles did in due course appear, while Simon Sokki was engaged in winning over his fellow-countrymen. The most difficult question to deal with was that of abandoning the herd. They had all envisaged setting out for a new world with joyful hearts, but the idea of leaving behind them these thousands of reindeer, which they had just brought all the way to the sea with such difficulty, and which, for as long as they could remember, they had

314

been protecting from wolves, tempests and thieves, filled them with an intense feeling of sadness.

Ellena Sokki was the most determined to go. She knew how much they all looked up to her, from Simon Sokki to the members of the other families, like the Risaks and the Bongos.

'It's all very well for the men to refuse,' said she vehemently. 'Apart from the herd, what else do they do? It's us women who have to stay alone in the huts all winter, who have to look after them and bring up the children. I am all for going to the Tröndelag, and leading a decent life like everybody else.'

'Really, mother,' Kristina exclaimed passionately, 'you shouldn't say such things, I beg you! All these proposals are just so much bait, and before three months are out you'll be wishing you had never given up your old life. We belong to a different race from those people,' she added, pointing contemptuously to Nylsen and Fru Tideman, but particularly to Rieban, a suspect creature whose baleful role in the whole business she recognized only too well. As soon as he saw a group of people engrossed in discussion, he would go up to them, offer them a drink and start talking about the Tröndelag . . . he'd been there, the mountains were simply covered with lichen, spring and autumn storms were quite unknown, the reindeer were content to live all the year round in the same area, so that it was only a few hours journey from their winter quarters to the summer grazing; and he was never tired of pointing out the attractions of a settled life, always plenty of money, and, as a result, always plenty of spirits. She knew perfectly well how treacherous he was, ready to swindle his masters as well as the Samisks. 'You can easily get across the mountains into Sweden,' he had told them, 'and that means that all through the summer the herdsmen can do a nice bit of smuggling on the side.'

'I beg of you mother,' Kristina continued bitterly, 'change your mind before it's too late, otherwise there'll be only one thing left for me and the Finn . . .'

315

She was standing in the middle of the circle, with her back to the fire, silhouetted against the radiant morning sky.

'As for you, Rieban, how much a head are they paying you for our reindeer if we accept? Why, the man's nothing but a crook.'

She spoke in Samisk, with great vehemence, and Nylsen, who had been trying to understand what she was saying from her angry gestures, was surprised when he saw them all hanging their heads with a guilty expression on their faces; even Simon Sokki remained silent.

'Who is that girl, Fru Tideman?'

'The most intelligent of the lot, but also, unfortunately, the most difficult to convince. She should have been my best pupil, and indeed she still could be! But the fact is, Kristina Sokki is a regular wildcat!'

'Is she trying to stir them up against me?'

'Not you particularly. She knows the influence her mother has over the cita, and that if Ellena agrees all the others will follow her—and Ellena does agree.'

'And so . . . ?'

'Simply that Kristina does *not* agree, and she is a very forceful personality. She embodies all the spiritual energy of her people, so that sometimes I can't help admiring her and fearing her. What would you say, Per Oskal?'

'During the migration, she never expressed an opinion one way or the other, except by implication. It was as though she was confident that the occasion would never arise for her to have to make a stand.'

'See if you can't convince her.'

'It would be better if you were to try, Fru Tideman. If I did, she would know that my heart was not really in what I was saying.'

'You have gone over to the enemy, Per Oskal,' said Fru Tideman sadly. But she was not the woman to admit defeat. She got up, and her tall, proud figure dominated the slim young girl, who abruptly stopped speaking, overcome with fear and respect.

'You have caused me a great deal of worry, my dear Kristina,' she said, 'and yet of all the little Lapp girls in the Viddakaïno school that have passed through my hands, you were the one I was fondest of, the one I thought I should be able to count on to carry on my work. You were the most intelligent and the most courageous. It only took you a few months to learn to read, write and do your sums, in Samisk as well as Norwegian. Now I am appealing to you, Kristina : I need you in the Tröndelag. You are the one person who can really help to transform the nomadic Samisks into properly settled Lapps. You could educate your people and turn them into peaceful, happy folk, leading a life free from danger. Your example would convince the others, and your good qualities would make the Norwegians, who all too often know nothing about them, appreciate the real virtues of the Samisk people, for though they are so different from the Scandinavians they are very lovable. I want you, Kristina, to take my place in the Tröndelag, to be responsible for visiting the people in their homes, helping them to settle down and persuading the parents to send their children to school . . . There's a marvellous job for you to do. It might well be you who eventually saved the Samisk people from complete extinction !'

There was a long silence, during which everybody kept their eyes on Kristina and Fru Tideman.

The young girl was shaken; she looked around for someone to support her, but, apart from one or two perhaps, all she could see in their eyes was their complete acceptance of what Fru Tideman had said. The Old Man and the Finn were away with the herd. She was alone. She looked up at the mountain, where the clear-eyed Old Man would be herding the reindeer, while the Finn would be wondering what was going on down below. What would he say if he knew that she had given in, had yielded to this moral blackmail and allowed herself to be seduced by these appeals to her vanity? Her hesitation did not last for long. Stepping back a few paces, as though to emphasize the distance between herself and Fru Tideman, she looked her adversary up and down in a way that reminded the older woman of the proud, fearless glance that had so often provoked her during the preceding winter.

'All you have said to me, Fru Tideman, might well satisfy some people. You have already succeeded in convincing my father, Simon Sokki, who is unable to resist either money or alcohol; and you have won over my mother, who is exhausted by the strain of the migration. Nevertheless, I remain convinced that their weakness is only temporary. As for the rest,' she went on, eyeing them contemptuously, 'they just follow like sheep. If Mr Nylsen cares to put down his money, he will have won. But don't count on me, Fru Tideman. If, from now on, the cita is to be disbanded, so be it! Let them all go to this wonderful country, where apparently everything is to be had for the asking! But I'm staying here, and my reindeer belong to me. Nothing will make me leave the cita! If the others want to go, let them, and good luck to them!'

In a sudden burst of anger she kicked savagely at the fire, and everybody had to jump out of the way to avoid the blazing embers that shot in every direction.

'Go on! What are you all waiting for?'

Completely dumfounded, Fru Tideman turned away and went over to where Nylsen was standing, a little apart, with the half-caste, Rieban.

'This youngster is capable of ruining everything. We must act quickly. Per Oskal, I want you to interpret what I am going to say without any comment. That's an order: we are going to start counting the herd. Rieban, who is a reindeer expert from the Troms, will value the animals, though naturally if we can reach a friendly agreement, all the better. The Lappefogden, Per Oskal, will supervise the operation. In a few hours' time we shall split up the herd according to the families they belong to. The herdsmen must gather all the animals into two separate herds, keeping the stags and does apart. While that is being done, Simon Sokki will receive a payment on account of what is due to each individual. Be so good as to hand him the money, Mr Nylsen.'

The Minister realized that it was necessary to force a decision, and was already opening his capacious briefcase, stuffed with bundles of hundred-kroner notes. On the Finnmark market, at this time of year, poor quality reindeer were fetching about three hundred crowns. He therefore decided to pay the master of the cita, immediately, the sum of 250,000 crowns on account, reckoning the herd at between four and five thousand animals.

Everybody was busy trying to work out the figures; they had never seen so much money in their lives. So their huge herd meant that they would all be rich men. This was part of the bargain that they had not properly understood. In the past, when they needed money to buy some alcohol, they would sell as many reindeer as was necessary, but as soon as they were in a position to buy others to increase the size of their herd, they were only too glad to hand over these pieces of paper which seemed to be of very little use to them! And now, all of a sudden, here was an official, Nylsen, offering them the prospect of a new kind of life in the concrete form of an enormous wad of banknotes, which represented no more than a sixth of the total value of the great herd!

'You'd better fetch your chest, Simon Sokki,' Per Oskal said to him quietly.

And into this wooden chest, gaily painted with primitive designs, Simon began stuffing the bundles of banknotes, alongside all his personal treasures: a penknife, an old calendar, some other beautifully made but quite useless knives, a few photos, some tobacco, his pipes and a variety of shoddy goods.

Occasionally he would finger a bundle, trying to count it, but soon giving up in despair, in the hope that Kristina would come and help him . . . but Kristina had disappeared. Helpless, he turned to Per Oskal, who assured him there was no need to worry, that no one was trying to cheat him of a single penny.

319

'But whatever you do, don't trust Rieban. He's already been paid for valuing the reindeer, and he's not entitled to another cent!'

With a crestfallen expression, Simon Sokki admitted that Rieban had promised to increase the valuation provided he would let him have twenty reindeer and smuggle them away from the main herd.

'Hang on a minute,' said Per Oskal, springing to his feet.

Rieban had disappeared, but the Lappefogden knew where to find him and, hurrying from hut to hut, eventually discovered him, lying on the ground half drunk, with a bottle of aquavit in his hand.

'Come on out, I want a word with you!'

His voice was ice cold, but the look in his eye was even more glacial, and Rieban gave in.

'What's the trouble, Lappefogden, anything wrong?'

'That's enough of that! I know what you've been up to, and I'm warning you that I'm still the judge here. You've been taking advantage of Simon Sokki's gullibility. You've managed to steal some of his reindeer and promised in return to over-value the herd. That's already quite enough to send you to prison.'

'I come from the Troms, so you have no authority over me. I shall do what I like, and Mr Nylsen will back me up—and that's a good deal more than I'd dare to say if I were in your shoes! I don't fancy you're going to be Lappefogden very much longer . . . ha ha!'

He laughed sneeringly, but Per Oskal quickly seized him by the throat.

'One more word out of you, and I'll knock your block off, you swine! It's precisely because I soon shan't have any further responsibility for the Lapps that you'd better look out. But in the meantime, just you behave yourself, see! I don't give a damn for you or anyone else!'

He gave him a violent shove, and Rieban fell on his back in the wet grass.

Per Oskal returned to the others. Nylsen had almost

320

finished counting out the money, which Simon Sokki was still stuffing into his chest, while Ellena looked on greedily, for a part of this hoard belonged to her and other members of the cita, who were wondering whether it was going to be shared out straight away. Each of them knew the exact number of deer that belonged to him, and all they had to do was to work out the amount due to them.

'Kristina, Kristina!' Ellena called . . . But Simon Sokki shook his head.

'It's no use counting on her, woman. We'll get Per Oskal to help us.'

But this was contrary to all tradition: counting the reindeer from the great herd, and settling up for them, was a matter for the Samisks, and 'what was the use of calling in a foreigner?' as Martha Sokki-Bongo remarked.

'And who's going to work out all the sums for us?' retorted Simon. 'You? Mikael? Mattis? There's not one of you can read, let alone do arithmetic. Kristina's the only one . . . Or would you rather we asked that damned half-breed from the Troms?'

This suggestion was loudly rejected by everyone. Simon Sokki was right, they would have to appeal to the Lappe-fogden.

The position was explained to him; it would mean a fairly long job, he was perfectly willing to undertake it but he would have to inform his superiors. Nylsen, however, raised objections and suggested his confidential employee, Rieban. Per Oskal explained that he had already tried to swindle them, and though Nylsen did not seem to be convinced he eventually gave in, for he was not at all anxious to become involved in this tribal bargaining.

'I shall stay on here for another two days,' said Per Oskal. 'When do you intend to move the cita?'

'The mail boat will be calling here for the purpose in three days' time. There will be room on it for everyone, and four days from now they will all be in the Tröndelag.'

'By then we'll have everything sorted out,' said Per Oskal. 'I bid you good-day, sir.'

'There is a rather more unpleasant matter we shall have to discuss, Mr Oskal,' Nylsen drily observed.

'That will be quite unnecessary. My letter of resignation will have reached the Ministry before you get back to Oslo, unless, of course, you decide to have me recalled for serious dereliction of duty . . .'

'But look, my dear Per, have you really thought the whole matter over?' said Fru Tideman.

She went over to him and, for the first time since he had known her, held out her hand to him. He was discovering an unknown Fru Tideman, no longer an austere, sternly overbearing lady, but a sad, distracted woman, whose eyes were full of tears . . . Fru Tideman was actually crying.

'Don't force the issue! Nylsen is very impulsive, and here he feels completely lost. But I am sure he won't do anything. He doesn't like rows, and besides, who will he find to take your place? Who else is there that knows the Samisks as well as you do?'

'But since there won't be any Samisks left, Fru Tideman . . .'

'I am sure that as long as there are people like Kristina and the Finn, and now you, my dear Per, there will always be Samisks! Maybe you are right, but isn't it going to make you very unhappy?'

'Fru Tideman, my dear friend, if only you'd stop trying to make other people happy according to your own personal idea of happiness! I think I have discovered mine. No, really, I assure you, I shall not be unhappy . . .'

Nylsen and Fru Tideman slowly walked away, down the footpath leading to the landing stage, followed by Mattis Sokki, half-carrying Rieban, who, by this time was completely drunk and whom he had been told to see on to the boat. It had eventually been agreed that Mikael Bongo should remain on the island until the great herd had been completely and properly disposed of. In this way the responsibility would not be left in the hands of the man from the Troms, and they could all feel sure that none of the reindeer would be fraudulently transferred to other citas.

The sun had passed its zenith, and a new night was

already beginning; it sank lower and lower in the sky, till it almost rested on the sea, turning the waves to flame; then, once again, it started to rise. The fishing boats were leaving the fjord, making for the open sea. The mountains were boldly silhouetted against the sky and the brilliant light that shone from behind the topmost peaks emphasized the vastness of the vidda. Then, gradually, the mountains of the sea disappeared from sight, and the whole countryside was bathed in the soft light of the unending day.

CHAPTER FOUR

THE bitter-sweet midnight light drenches the sunlit night. In the huts, the women leave everything in a muddle: what's the use of tidying things up, of sorting out skins, of filling bladders with melted fat, of tanning the superfine velvet from the muzzles and cheeks of reindeer in order to make skallers? In a couple of days, the long black hull of the mail boat will draw alongside the landing stage, and they will all go aboard on their way to the Tröndelag.

For the last two days they had conscientiously been counting the reindeer in the two herds, supervised by Per Oskal, who insisted that the whole operation be carried out according to the rules.

'Of course,' he said to Simon Sokki, 'I know the size of your herd, pretty well to the nearest reindeer. But, don't you see, they mustn't be able to criticize me afterwards.'

Already he was saying 'they', as though he was talking about foreigners.

The previous days a serious incident had occurred. Kristina had suddenly turned up while they were counting her animals.

'You can leave my reindeer out of it,' she had said, 'as well as those belonging to the Finn and the Old Man. They have made up their minds not to go with you.'

Though everyone had expected this, Simon Sokki had still tried to persuade her to change her mind.

'So you really mean to leave us, then—me and your mother and brothers, and all the people of the clan who have been living together for centuries . . . ?'

'But it's you, father, that's deserting the vidda and the herd! It's you that's breaking up our cita! The Finn and I are determined to create a new one without you.'

'But however are you going to manage? With such a small herd you'll be miserable!'

'The reindeer will have calves, we shall have children, and everything will start all over again.'

'Think of all the wretched winters that lie ahead of you.'

'Anything is preferable to the comfortable slavery the rest of you have chosen. Go, go, go! It's too late now to change your mind, you've already accepted their bribe.'

She drew herself up like a fury, yet, though she was on the point of tears, her eyes remained dry and gleaming, and the others, already beginning to obey her, drove her reindeer to one side.

When she had calmed down a little, she went on:

'What will you do with the money, father? I know you! Instead of working, you'll just drink it away! In a few years' time you will be nothing but ghosts, wandering about in your fine houses that will already be falling into decay. Do you really believe the Norwegians will ever accept you? Rubbish! They believe they belong to a superior race, and you are never going to convince them that you are their equals, whereas, until now, they couldn't really do anything to harm you—you were free men, obeying your own laws, following your own traditions! You were beyond their control, as I was that winter night when I escaped from the school at Viddakaïno.'

Simon Sokki shrugged his shoulders. He spent his whole time counting and re-counting the hundred-kroner banknotes stuffed into his wooden chest. And now the checking of the herd was almost completed, and soon Per Oskal would be sharing them out.

Kristina had parted her own reindeer; several of the does had already calved, and the youngsters were trotting awkwardly behind their mothers. Separated from the main herd, her hundred and fifty-odd reindeer formed a tiny group, of which she was all too conscious, and she did her best to conceal how sad and bitter she felt. The animals that belonged to the Finn, inherited from Mikkel Mikkelsen

Sara, and those belonging to the Old Man, branded with the star, had been turned over to her. Away in the mountain, the Finn, who had been informed of Kristina's decision, had parted the stags belonging to them, leaving the main herd in charge of Mattis, Simon's nephew, who, together with Mikael Bongo, was now to look after the cita's reindeer and see to them being sold.

For the last time, Per Oskal called the members of the cita together, round the big fire that had been lighted out of doors. Simon Sokki had brought the big chest containing the money, and the Lappefogden divided it up. He began with the poorest, Thor Risak, Mikael, then Andis, Pier, Mattis, handing each of them a wad of banknotes, which they accepted with a bewildered expression, stuffing them into the large inside pockets of their kouftes. They had no idea of the value of the notes, except in terms of the number of bottles of spirits they represented. But it was certainly fabulous, they had never been so rich in all their lives.

'All this,' Per Oskal pointed out emphatically, 'is only a payment on account. When you get to the Tröndelag, you will all wake up to find yourselves better off than most of the Norwegians! Some of you even, will be very rich.'

He continued distributing the money, and said to Martha Risak:

'Here's your share, Martha.'

For a moment she hesitated. Then, looking at Per Oskal, she gravely rejected the proffered bundle of notes.

'I'm staying with Kristina! You hang on to the money, I'm going to part my reindeer.'

'Martha!' exclaimed Thor, shocked by his sister's attitude. 'Martha, why don't you come with us?'

'I've made up my mind, and that's that! Keep your banknotes.'

It was quite beyond their comprehension. She had always been the most frivolous and flighty of them all, and so greedy for money that, in order to get it, she would sometimes behave extremely badly, even according to Lapp standards. Yet here she was, refusing what amounted to a small fortune.

'You really understand what you're doing, Martha?' Per Oskal asked.

He could scarcely believe his eyes, and was trying to conceal his feelings beneath an impassive mask. He was still the judge, the Lappefogden, and mustn't take sides. Yet, in the depth of his heart, he felt as though a flame was burning, his whole being was flooded with a profound feeling of happiness.

'Did *you* really know what you were doing when you offered your resignation to the Minister?' Martha retorted.

'Oh Martha, Martha, my dear! You're a real Samisk! I'm sorry for all the times I've been so nasty to you,' cried Kristina, crazy with happiness and clasping her in her arms.

Now the chips were down. They all went off to their huts, and only Per Oskal and Martha remained standing beside the fire, which rose and fell in the breeze as though in answer to all the other fires blazing from the hills on every island in the fjord.

'We shall be leaving shortly, Martha,' said Per Oskal.

'What? You don't mean you're coming with us?'

'And where else do you suppose I can go now?'

'I don't really know. I thought you would be going back to Alta, to your parents' home and your fishing boat!'

'Is that why you stayed behind with me?'

She hung her head, blushing suddenly.

'Yes.'

'Well, Martha, that's why I'm going with you.'

'But you haven't got any reindeer!'

'I shall have, though.'

'How?'

'Mikael is in charge of selling the herd, isn't he? With what I've managed to save I shall be able to buy fifty reindeer, and Mikael has promised to pick them out for me— five geldings as draft animals, a dozen stags, and the rest does!'

He drew her towards him and took her in his arms.

'Don't you see, Martha, it's through loving you I have discovered reality. Isn't it love that gives Kristina such strength? Let's go and find them, for it's to them we owe our happiness.'

They loaded their sleighs with their personal belongings, and the food that Ellena, with tears in her eyes, had prepared for them. And then they drove off with their little herd, making for the mountain. Kristina had not seen Simon Sokki again. He had been drinking, and was hiding from her; and, as most of the other men were sleeping off their drink in their huts, their departure was almost like an escape.

Up in the mountain, at a spot where the melting glacier was transformed into a rushing stream, the Old Man and the Finn were waiting for them. They had assembled the small bunch of stags that belonged to them, and Mattis had already driven away the main herd to a grassy hillock at some distance from the glacier.

'Per Oskal? Martha? So there you are,' exclaimed the Finn. But the Old Man displayed not the slightest surprise at seeing them, nor did he ask any questions.

'When you have a moment to spare, Finn, will you give me a hand with ear-marking my reindeer?' asked Per Oskal. 'They used to belong to Mikael Bongo.'

'So you really mean to come with us?' said the Finn. 'Kristina, Kristina, God's on our side, there are going to be four of us! I'll be delighted to help you. Have you chosen what ear-mark you're going to have?'

'What's the point of having a new mark?' asked the Old Man. 'Mikael won't have a herd now, and in the Tröndelag all the animals will be owned communally. Take his mark. The Bongos have always been one of the great Lapp families, and now you'll be able to carry it on!'

Per Oskal bowed :

'I gratefully accept.'

And from that moment, he became a genuine Samisk.

'Now that everything has been settled, what are you proposing to do, Kristina?' demanded the Old Man.

From the form of his question, the others realized that Simon Sokki's daughter was to remain the undisputed leader of the new cita, for it had been decided by the Old Man in his wisdom. He was examining the reindeer, his own, Kristina's and the Finn's, Martha's and those belonging to Per Oskal.

'You know,' said he, 'it won't take long to turn this little herd into a really big one! Where do you want me to take you, Kristina?'

The young girl hesitated, conscious of the gravity of the occasion.

'The sensible thing would be to stay in the huts on the island, but I'm afraid they may come back and plague us. We've definitely made up our minds, but I'm not sure whether I should be able to stand up to a dozen emigration officials! Now that Per Oskal has become one of us, he won't be able to defend us any more. That's why I think it will be best for us to get the sleighs and reindeer away. The Old Man must surely know of some secret grazing ground in the mountains, where no one will think of coming to look for us.'

They all turned to the Old Man, who was considering his reply.

'With so few reindeer, that shouldn't be too difficult,' said he presently. 'I know a place the other side of the mountains, about four days' journey from here. It will mean crossing three passes and two glaciers, but it's a wild, inaccessible valley, with plenty of lichen and just right for rearing calves. We can build some huts there, but we shall have to get away again pretty soon, before the winter storms begin, if we are to reach the isthmus between the island and the mainland in time to reach the vidda. There's nothing to fear, the territory is vast and, from now on, the whole of it belongs to us.'

For the last time, they all turned to look back. The Arctic Ocean was gleaming like molten lead in the rays of the sun, which was at its zenith. Far away to the north a ship was making its way between the islands, heading into the waves and leaving behind it a long silvery wake. It was making for the island landing-stage.

From a huge gash in the side of the glacier oozed a stream of milky water, which, as it gathered force, hurtled wildly across the moraine, covered with mysterious little pale-coloured flowers that grow between the rocks. Elsewhere the snow had already disappeared, there were great patches of lichen and short grass, green as an English lawn, where the reindeer were content to linger.

The Old Man allowed the little herd plenty of time to graze, for later on, until eventually they reached the fertile valley, there would be nothing but glaciers and fantastic spurs of rock. Presently, when he decided that they had eaten their fill, he went ahead, calling to them :

'Come on, we must get going! We are lucky. Thanks be to God, it's not going to snow for several days, and by that time we shall be over all our difficulties.'

The little colony set out in orderly fashion, the Old Man leading the herd, while the Finn, Kristina, Martha and Per Oskal followed with the sleighs. Their job was not an easy one, for at this season of the year it meant choosing those places where the sleighs would run, and sometimes this meant making a long detour in order to take advantage of the permanent snow.

They proceeded gravely, listening to the loud murmur of the stream and the singing of the wind amongst the granite spurs, and they felt their souls to be in tune with this eternal song. They travelled in silence, their hearts overflowing with the happiness that stems from love and freedom. Soon they had reached the glacier, and, on this wonderful stretch of glittering snow, running gently uphill, progress was more rapid. Two hours later they had reached the first pass : beyond it another glacier flowed into a valley that was almost completely shut in, but the Old Man pointed out a narrow and apparently inaccessible cleft in the rocks, that looked as though someone had slashed them with a sword.

'Beyond that cleft lies the valley where we shall build our huts. There will be enough food there to last our little herd all summer.'

'Next year we'll use the other huts, near the coast,' Kristina declared fiercely. 'This is just a temporary expedient, in future we'll carry on as we always used to.'

Glancing at her, Per Oskal realized that this was no longer the wild little savage he had first got to know when she was running away from the Lapp school. Her whole bearing now displayed unmistakeable authority; she dominated the three of them with her will, already she was beginning to build the future.

'You're quite right, Kristina,' said he, 'it won't be long before we have a great herd once more!'

'We,' he had said, and it was as though he were hearing the sound of his own voice for the first time. They had reached a favourable spot, and the Old Man decided that they had travelled far enough for the first day and should put up the tents. He sat down on a huge block of stone overlooking the glacier, and relapsed into his usual state of meditation. The rest of them set to work and before long the two tents had been erected, but on this occasion they were content to sleep on nothing but reindeer skins, for there was no wood available as high as this.

'Come and give me a hand, Per!' called Kristina.

He hurried over to her, surprised that it should be he she appealed to.

'The Finn is with the herd,' Kristina explained, 'and this stone is too heavy for me.'

The two of them lifted the hearthstone and carried it into the main tent, Kristina's, which she shared with the Finn and the Old Man; and their preparations were complete.

'This evening we'll only light one fire, you and Martha can come and eat with us.'

She sat at the back of the tent, in the place always reserved for the head of the cita, within reach of the stew pot and her chest, and gravely began preparing the meal.

Later, when they had finished eating, they went outside. Stretching away below them, they could see the whole countryside through which they had been climbing. The white light from the sky, reflected from the glacier, drew their eyes towards the rounded, moss-covered hills, rising from the tundra that ran along the crest. Opposite them, beyond the fjord, the mountains of the sea were already beginning to rise again from the straw-coloured sea, climbing into the azure expanse of the sky.

Unconsciously they had drawn close together, and the two couples stood with their arms round one another, looking out over the ocean.

'Look, Kristina,' said Per Oskal, 'the mail boat is already on its way!'

The black steamer was gliding out to sea, and the stokers must have cleaned out the boilers, for a thick cloud of black smoke was coming from the funnel and gradually dispersing in the wind. Suddenly Per Oskal felt his heart contract, for this ship that was sailing away, carrying with it the members of the already disrupted cita of the Sokkis, was also bearing away his past life. His eyes rested for a moment on the radiant figure of Kristina and the Finn: these two were creating the future by continuing the past; through them, the indestructible chain of humanity would persist in this ever renewed land, and now he himself was about to become one of the links in that chain.

As though she had guessed what he was feeling, Martha squeezed his hand and cuddled up against him. He regretted nothing, for he had simultaneously discovered both love and freedom, the two most precious gifts of mankind, and what else mattered?

Behind them, still seated on his rock, the Old Man was idly stroking his aged reindeer, marked with the star. In his warm furs and faded cap he was scarcely distinguishable from the rock and the reindeer; he might have been a stallo carved from stone, guarding the mountain pass. He sat without moving, and the only sign of life was the little puffs of blue smoke that issued from his lips in time with his breathing.

In the snow, swept by the icy wind of a night without shadows, the reindeer lay and chewed the cud, heedless of their surroundings. Once more everything was as it had always been! For thirty thousand years nothing had changed, and for thousands of years to come nothing would change, for as long as there are cold and snow to make the lichen grow, reindeer to eat the lichen, and men to feed on the reindeer's flesh and clothe themselves with their skins, this country will be inhabited by Samisks. Elsewhere, men might go on killing one another in endless wars, or accepting the slavery of technology that reduces them to ants and insects in their monstrous artificial cities, but here life would go on and on and on . . .

There were four of them, the Finn and Kristina, the Scandinavian and Martha, and they would carry on the race; as for the Old Man, he had always been there and he always would be there. He was immortal, like the summer light that never disappears, like the midnight sun that turns endlessly above the ocean waves, lighting this strange country, where the whole year is divided into one night and one day, and where time keeps pace with the rhythm of eternity.

EPILOGUE

On the after deck of the mail boat, what was left of the cita of the Sokkis sheltered from the wind, and as they squatted there, the Lapps gossiped and dozed, apparently indifferent to their surroundings. Such an unbearable smell of grease and musk arose from this mass of badly tanned skins and fur garments that the other passengers had taken refuge in the forward part of the boat.

'Well, Simon Sokki, is everything going all right? There's nothing you need?'

The master of the cita looked up with red-rimmed eyes. Before him stood the Minister, Nylsen, with the captain of the boat and one or two Norwegian passengers. Simon was clutching a large bundle of banknotes, which he kept turning over and over in an effort to understand what all this paper represented.

'Kristina was right, you know, Minister,' said he, shaking his head. 'We never ought to have let the reindeer go. What's it left us with?'

'It's left you with all this money you have there, and all the rest that is waiting for you in the bank, in the Tröndelag!'

But Simon remained unconvinced.

'In the old days, when I had any money I used to buy reindeer to increase my herd, but you've taken my herd from me and given me this money in exchange, and now I don't know where I am. What can I do with it all?'

'Your children will soon realize, Simon, that money makes it possible for you to live decently. Wait till you get to the Tröndelag. Once you are there, you will find all your worries disappear.'

The visitors returned to the bridge: they did not want to miss the spectacle of the midnight sun, suspended above the horizon! Then, having satisfied their curiosity and finding that it was becoming bitterly cold, they all went off to their cabins, all that is to say, except the Samisks, who had to sleep where they were, despite the icy wind and the sharp pitching of the ship, which was now entering the Loppehavet. Now and then, a hand would emerge from a pile of furs and immediately disappear again; and the red caps and the coloured scarves of the women made bright patches of colour in the diaphanous light of the summer night.

Simon Sokki, his hand in the pocket of his koufte, could feel his bundle of banknotes and the accompanying bottle of aquavit. He was rich, very rich! But why did his thoughts remain out there beyond the ocean, beyond the mountains of the sea, whose sombre peaks cut off the country lying to the east, that country where life, eternally renewed, goes on and on without end? He closed his eyes, and now he was struggling through the snow at the head of five thousand, ten thousand, reindeer, and a string of sleighs loaded with women and children . . . And suddenly he realized that, for him, life was over.